VOODOO
HIDEAWAY

VOODOO HIDEAWAY

VANCE CARIAGA

atmosphere press

For Susan, who planted the story seed and championed me throughout the process. Much love.

He thought about making a run for it, testing his speed, seeing if he still had that quick first step. All he needed was that first step. Start in a crouch, down low, then sprint full-on, head down, leaning into it, leaning leaning leaning for maximum acceleration. Nobody here could catch him. Even at his age, in this condition, he'd outsprint them all. Just like way back when.

But the guns kept him frozen in place.

Man, there were a lot of guns. He found himself staring at them, even now, dazzled by the variety. Long barrels and short ones. Cylinders and clips. Most were silver or black, though one had a copper coating. A couple looked brand new. A couple looked like they'd been around the block a few times. He guessed they were all made of steel, but he couldn't be sure. He didn't know much about guns, didn't have any particular interest in them.

He knew what they were here for, though.

He counted six guns in all, attached to six different hands. Three guns pointed in one direction, three pointed in the exact opposite direction. He didn't have a gun himself, which was too bad, because he was stuck in the middle of all this firepower. If those guns went off, oh Lord.

Nobody spoke. Nobody appeared to be breathing. They looked like paintings of people rather than real people.

Time seemed to stop. Seconds passed like centuries. He wanted to kick time in the ass, tell it to get on with things. Make something happen one way or another. Good or bad, happy or ill. Just make something happen.

Maybe he'd make a run for it. Bend into a crouch and burst out, lightning quick. Just like way back when.

But it had to be the right moment. The right opportunity. So he waited. He breathed. He kept his eyes and ears open. He heard the shots, maybe before they were even fired.

Then he felt it.

Time, stopping.

Again.

Part One

Voodoo

Chapter 1

As walls go, there was nothing particularly special about it. Just a faded brick thing that stood on one side of a grimy alleyway in a part of town where the buildings were either boarded up or crumbling down. Elrod had seen his share of alleys during his years of bumming around the continent. He'd probably slept in a couple hundred from coast to coast. He could safely say this alley wall was no better or worse than any other. He didn't give it a second thought until, well, he wasn't sure exactly what happened.

The alley wall was there, and then it wasn't. Just like that. A doorway appeared in its place, right out of the blue. The door in the middle of it was blue, too, positioned below a single white ceiling lamp. On either side of the door were rectangular windows about five feet high and a foot wide. Three more windows were positioned above the door, forming a kind of semicircle. A soft pink light floated through from inside.

But inside of what?

It happened around dusk, maybe a little later. Daylight

had already faded into darkness. Elrod was lying on a bed of stretched-out newspapers, drifting off to an early sleep, unaware of and unconcerned about the time. A loud whooshing sound startled him out of his slumber, followed by a cold breeze. Elrod shot up with a start. He blinked his eyes open. He looked around. He saw a blue door that didn't belong here—that hadn't, in fact, been here a minute ago.

Elrod shook his head.

"The hell?"

He rose to his feet and took a couple steps forward to get a closer look. He spotted a paper bag on the ground and lifted it up. Inside the bag was a twenty-two-ounce bottle, and inside the bottle was the backwash of something called Voodoo Malt Liquor. Elrod had gotten the malt liquor earlier in the day from a corner grocery owned by a loud, grouchy Korean. Most of the liquid was gone, but Elrod tipped the bottle toward his mouth anyway. A little backwash drizzled out, but not much.

Elrod tossed the bag behind him. It landed with a crash. He looked around. Behind him was a concrete wall and a rusted metal trash can. Below was the cracked, weedy alley pavement and the bed of newspapers. To his right was the street, dark and barren. To his left was a metal fence that separated the alley from an empty lot. The lot was filled with busted bricks, rusting appliances, shattered glass, corroded metal, empty bottles, discarded trash, and God knows how many rats.

And in front of him?

Well, Elrod was pretty sure it was the same brick wall he'd first seen when he stumbled into this alley a couple weeks back. It just didn't look like a brick wall at the moment. It looked like a blue door surrounded by pink windows.

There was an obvious explanation. Elrod was seeing things again. Another hallucination brought on by decades of mind-benders.

"Eyes playing tricks on me," he said.

He closed his eyes. He peeked one back open. The door was still there.

He did it again. Same thing.

He did it again.

Same thing.

"Shit," Elrod said.

He took a step backward and nearly tripped over his feet.

"You're not there," he growled at the door. "You might think you are, but I know better."

Elrod considered moving along. Finding another alleyway. Maybe another town, another continent.

But he was tired. He wanted to lie down on that nice, comfortable bed of newspapers.

He studied the door. Did it look familiar, this pretty blue thing? Maybe, maybe. Elrod had been around, done his share of roaming. He'd seen more strange doors in more strange places than the desert has grains of sand. He'd wandered into his share of those strange doors. Maybe he'd wandered through a door like this one. Maybe that's why he was imagining it.

He wished he could turn the image off, though. It was keeping him awake. Who could sleep with that light banging against your face?

Elrod stepped closer. He stood there for a second and did some thinking out loud.

"You're a grown man living in an alley in the Year of our Lord 1999," he told himself. "You're seeing something that doesn't exist. Go back to sleep."

But Elrod didn't take his own advice. Instead, he inched closer to the door. It had a silver plate on the left-hand side that held a bolt lock. No doorknob. Just the lock. Elrod assumed the bolt was locked. He assumed if he reached out to push the door, it wouldn't open. He reached his hand forward to push it, prepared himself to feel the cold, sticky alley wall. But the door nudged open, slightly.

Sweet mother of God.

Elrod edged his hand forward a little more, pressing the door more firmly this time. It inched open wider. He pointed one foot back toward the alley in case he needed to haul away quickly. You never knew what mischief lurked behind doors that suddenly popped up out of nowhere.

He kept pushing, and the door kept opening. He craned his head inside to take a peek. He saw a narrow hallway. On the left was a pink neon light that said, "The Hideaway." Another pink neon light, in the form of a martini glass, was positioned to one side of the sign. On the other side, higher up, was a blue neon light in the form of a saxophone.

Elrod nudged himself inside and closed the door behind him, making sure it didn't shut all the way. He breathed in. He raised his left arm and wiped a small film of sweat from his forehead. The air inside was thick and humid. A fly buzzed up against Elrod's ear. He batted it away and made his way further inside.

On the right of the hallway was a wooden counter, maybe five feet long. It was positioned in front of a small room with red velvet drapes. A wooden sign above the counter said, "Coat Check." Elrod stepped past the counter and edged his way down the long, narrow hallway, an inch at a time, darting his eyes back and forth, not seeing much besides black walls bathed in soft neon. The hallway eventually crept around to the right. After about twenty feet, Elrod spotted a long, mahogany bar up ahead, lined with barstools. Behind the bar was a lighted mirror. Glass shelves held an assortment of liquor bottles.

The hallway opened into a large room with dining tables. The tables were outfitted with white tablecloths and glass vases that held fresh-cut flowers. Glass ashtrays in brass stands were scattered about the place—odd, considering the city had passed a law banning smoking in all public places. Maybe this was an after-hours joint that flew below the radar and under the rules, stuck beside the desolate alley, far away from probing eyes.

Just beyond the dining room was a bandstand that held a drum kit, an upright bass, a piano, and a single microphone stand. Chandeliers with soft lighting hung from the ceiling. The walls were lined with framed black-and-white photographs of various people and places. The Chrysler Building. Duke Ellington. The Brooklyn Bridge. Humphrey Bogart. Ella Fitzgerald. Count Basie. Ceiling fans moved the air around, cooling things down considerably.

Elrod leaned up against one of the barstools. He looked around again, once, twice, three times, side to side and floor to ceiling. He wiped more sweat from his forehead. *The Hideaway.* Was that what this place was called? The Hideaway? It was a pretty fancy joint, under any name.

He glanced at himself in the bar mirror. He hadn't

showered in a while, though he did make a point of scrubbing his face and torso daily in one of the public restrooms scattered in and around the city. His graying brown hair needed cutting and combing. A bushy salt-and-pepper beard covered most of his face, except for a little scar below his left eye that never seemed to take cover. He wore a plain black T-shirt, faded jeans, and a red-and-black coat similar to those worn by lumberjacks. Elrod had found the coat lying on a stoop a couple days ago, ripe for the taking. The whole ensemble hung loosely on Elrod's slight frame, which measured around seventy inches from head to toe and 150 pounds the last time he checked.

This wasn't the look you wanted to present in a high-dollar joint. Elrod tried to shrink into himself, but quickly snapped out of it. Why the hell did he care how he looked? There wasn't anyone around. He could be bareass naked with a bright purple bow wrapped around his prick and nobody would notice. It was all just a figment of Elrod's imagination, anyway. This place didn't exist. Soon enough Elrod would wake up on his bed of newspapers, back in the alley, back in 1999, the dawn of the new millennium. Back to real life, warts and all.

He eyed the liquor bottles lined up on the glass shelves and spotted all the premium brands: Crown Royal, Maker's Mark, Chivas Regal, Beefeater, Johnnie Walker Black, Dewar's, Glenlivet.

Elrod stared at the bottles. They looked real enough. Maybe what was inside tasted real enough, too. Elrod could use a snort, even in a dream. He peeked around to make sure nobody was looking. He walked over to the bar and stepped behind it.

"Good evening, sir. What's your pleasure?" Elrod

asked himself as he scanned the liquor shelves.

"Hmmmm," Elrod answered. "Hell, surprise me!"

"Might I suggest the Dewar's?"

"Brilliant suggestion!"

He chuckled and reached for the Dewar's.

"And how do you prefer it, sir?" Elrod asked himself.

"What do you suggest?" he answered.

"I'd go with a couple of ice cubes and a twist of lemon," a voice said.

"Well that sounds...huh?" Elrod said.

That last voice didn't come from Elrod. He knew his own voice, and that wasn't it.

Elrod jerked his head around. He saw a man standing on the other side of the bar gate. The man was tall and lean, with an angular face, high cheekbones, a long, thin nose, and narrow, penetrating eyes. He looked a few years older than Elrod, maybe late forties, or early fifties. His hair was black, slick with hair gel, and neatly trimmed. He wore a black tuxedo that fit so well it looked painted on. The man's smile looked painted on as well.

Elrod backed up a couple steps and set his feet in the fighting/fleeing position just in case he needed to flail his way out and sprint for the exit.

"Who the hell are you?" Elrod said.

"I could well ask you the same question," the man answered.

"I asked first," Elrod said. He bunched his hands into fists and lifted them belt high.

The man's smile grew wider. "Fair point," he said. "My name is Flynn. Douglas Flynn. I'm the maître d' here."

"Is that so?" Elrod said.

"And with whom do I have the pleasure of speaking?"

Douglas said.

"Huh?"

"Your name, sir. I don't believe we've formally met."

Elrod eyed him warily. Who was this dandy man invading Elrod's hallucination?

"None of your goddamn business what my name is," Elrod said.

Douglas stepped through the bar gate toward Elrod.

Elrod crouched into a boxing stance. "Back off."

Douglas ignored him. He grabbed a cocktail glass from the glass rack. He reached into an ice bin and dropped a couple of cubes into the glass, then poured three fingers of Dewar's into it.

"Water, sir?" he asked, looking at Elrod. "Or do you prefer it neat?"

Elrod studied the man. Why was he so friendly? Why didn't he hail a couple bouncers to toss Elrod out? That was the usual procedure in an upscale joint like this. Hell, it was the usual procedure in half the dives Elrod had been in.

"What's your angle, chief?" Elrod said. "Why the happy face and friendly service? I ain't exactly the normal clientele. And this joint doesn't even look open yet."

The maître d' looked at his watch. It was an expensive-looking watch.

"The club will be opening soon," he said. "And you appear in want of drink, if you don't mind my saying."

"In want of drink," Elrod said. "Yep, that's one way of putting it. In want of drink."

He squinted his eyes, looked back up at Douglas. Elrod reminded himself that this was all a dream, a hallucination, eye tricks. He was *projecting*, as they say.

Imagining himself in a high-end nightclub because real life didn't afford him that luxury.

"You always serve people like me here?" Elrod asked Douglas. "Folks who look like they just crawled out of a flophouse shitter? If so, you appear in want of a higher class of customer, you don't mind me saying."

"We do ask that you put on a proper dinner jacket," Douglas replied. "We keep extra jackets around for customers who need one. We'll be happy to take your coat and hang it in the cloakroom. You can pick it up when you leave. Other than that, we're not too rigid on the rules. We only ask that everyone have a good time and conduct themselves appropriately."

That smile again.

"Oh, you can bet I'll conduct myself appropriately," Elrod said.

He gazed back at the glass of Dewar's. He felt around in his pocket to see how much loose change and dollar bills he had hanging around. He'd had a pretty good day. He'd bummed a decent amount of money from passersby outside of the subway station. But his personal finances were still on the lean side, and probably wouldn't cover the cost of a single drink in this place.

"So, uh, how much does that particular cocktail run here?" Elrod said. "You know, currency wise."

"A Dewar's is ninety cents, sir," Douglas said.

"Ni...ninety cents?" Elrod said.

"Well, it is a premium brand, after all. If you'd prefer something less expensive, we have very acceptable well brands."

"Oh no," Elrod said. He laughed out loud. "Oh hell no. No no no. The price is fine. Juuust fine. By the way, my name's Elrod, and I'm the best customer you'll ever have."

He whipped out a few crumpled dollar bills and slammed them on the bar. "Keep 'em coming till the money disappears!"

Elrod grabbed for the drink but Douglas snatched it away before he could reach it.

"I'm sorry, sir," Douglas said. "We ask that customers sit on the other side of the bar. Rules, you know. And I'll be happy to take your coat and bring you another one. When you're properly attired, you're welcome to enjoy your drink."

Douglas pushed the drink out of Elrod's reach. He walked out from behind the bar to the other side. Elrod followed him out and sat on one of the barstools.

"Your coat, sir," Douglas said.

Elrod hesitated. He wasn't sure he wanted to part with his coat. It was a good coat, and good coats were hard to come by for people in Elrod's position.

"Hold up now," Elrod said. "I came across this coat fair and square. I'd rather keep it right here."

"I assure you we'll take good care of it," Douglas said. "In any event, if you want to stay here, you'll have to exchange that coat for a proper dinner jacket. The rules, sir. You understand."

Elrod looked back at the glass of Dewar's. Ninety cents. He could probably afford a dozen of them with his cash on hand. What the hell. It's only a coat. He took it off and handed it to Douglas.

"Make sure you don't lose it," he said.

"Not to worry," Douglas said, smiling. He checked his watch. "I'll be back shortly. The jazz orchestra should be arriving soon. Pay them no mind."

Douglas disappeared into the front hallway, leaving Elrod alone with his thoughts. *Hell of a dream I'm having*, he told himself, *hell of a dream*. Fancy nightclub. Lax entrance requirements. Cheap booze. Friendly maître d'. That's a combination you stumble across maybe once every never.

Elrod eyeballed the Dewar's. He thought about sneaking behind the bar for a swallow, but decided against it. No need to upset the apple cart. Follow the rules, son. You've landed in a fairy tale here. For once in your life, don't screw it up.

He caught sight of a newspaper lying on the bar, opened to the sports page. He snuck a peek at the lead headline:

Dodgers, Cubs Split Twinbill at Ebbets

Elrod looked at it again. *Ebbets*? He leaned in closer. Yep, Ebbets. Like most red-blooded American boys, Elrod knew baseball. He'd played it as a kid and followed it off and on ever since. He knew the Dodgers used to play in Brooklyn, and Ebbets Field was their home park. He also knew the Dodgers relocated to Los Angeles more than four decades ago.

Elrod reached for the newspaper and slid it closer. He read some other headlines.

Mize Drives Home Two as Yanks Down Feller, Indians
Musial Leads Cards Past Giants at Polo Grounds
Will Success of Robinson, Doby Pave the Way for More Negro Ballplayers?

Elrod let the words and names sink in. *Mize. Feller. Musial. Polo Grounds. Robinson. Doby. Negro.* All names from the distant past. He checked the date on the paper. Thursday, August 25, 1949.

"The hell?" he said.

He read the first line of the top story:

"Cubs moundsman Johnny Schmitz proved too much for the home-standing Dodgers as the lanky lefty tossed a six-hit shutout to lead his team to a 4-0 win in the second game of a twofer at Ebbets Field yesterday, though the boys in blue took the first affair to remain hot on the heels of the league-leading Cardinals."

If this was a dream, it had clearly planted Elrod fifty years in the past, before he was even born. He knew some of the names in the article, but not all of them. He'd never heard of anyone named Johnny Schmitz, baseball player or otherwise. Why would he dream up a name he'd never heard before? Dreams weren't supposed to work that way, were they? And all the game information further down— doubles through the gap, throwing errors, missed tags, a long fly ball that went just foul in the ninth inning. How could a dream have all this detail crammed into it?

Elrod didn't have long to mull it over. His attention suddenly shifted to a group of black men who appeared from behind the bandstand. There were five of them, all clad in elegant suits and shiny dress shoes. Four looked to be in their twenties or early thirties, slender and neatly groomed. Another was older and balding, with a slight paunch in the middle, maybe around Elrod's age. He was tall and well dressed, with a touch of gray around the temples.

This must be the jazz orchestra Douglas mentioned. A

couple of the younger guys picked up instruments and began fiddling around. A trumpet player honked out your standard scale. The piano player did a couple of runs up and down the keyboard.

The two other younger musicians looked over at Elrod, whispered to each other, and laughed. The whispers didn't work too well, though, because sound traveled pretty well in an empty nightclub. Elrod picked up the words "rag-ass" and "ofay" and "trash" somewhere along in there. He didn't have to guess what they were laughing at. He'd heard those kinds of whispers and laughs half his life.

Elrod glared at the two men. They glared back. One flipped Elrod the bird. Elrod returned the favor. The older musician stepped in front of the two younger ones and said something in a sharp voice. Whatever it was put a droopy look on their faces. They picked up their instruments and began tuning up.

The older musician walked over to Elrod and offered a handshake and a smile.

"My apologies for those two jackasses," he said. "I'd slap some sense into their brains if they had any brains to begin with."

Elrod shook his hand. "Not a problem."

"Anyway, welcome to the Hideaway," the man said. "My name's William, but my friends call me Red. The nickname harkens back to my younger days. I had more hair then, and it was indeed red."

"Pleased to meet you," Elrod said. He was about to give a fake name when Red leaned in close to speak into Elrod's ear.

"Your ass is in the shit right now, Doc, and you don't even know it," Red said in a low voice. "So listen up."

Elrod jerked his head back. "The hell..."

Red took hold of Elrod's shirt and eased him in close.

"I got no time for lengthy explanations," he said. "Douglas will be back any second, and he is one evil cat. You're from somewhere outside of this place. Something strange happened. One second you're in your own little world, the next second here you are."

Elrod opened his mouth to speak but Red cut him off.

"Don't talk, just listen," Red said. "You popped in here out of nowhere and you don't know if it's real or some kind of dream. One second an empty alley, the next second this pretty nightclub. It's real, believe that. Don't worry about the details right now. The important thing is you know I'm right."

Red pulled something from the inside pocket of his jacket. A piece of paper. He stuck it in Elrod's pants pocket.

"There's the name of a park on that piece of paper, as well as a map," Red said. "The map shows the location of a small café in the park. You need to go to that café when you get back to the other side. Go during daylight hours. Late morning, early afternoon. Keep an eye out for some big white mother following you. You probably won't see him, but if you do, run. Don't think, just run."

Elrod leaned back and tried to break away. "Buddy, I don't know what..."

"When you get to the café, sit down and wait," Red said. "Someone will approach you. You won't know this someone, but this someone will know you. Now when you..."

A tall, lean shadow suddenly engulfed the two men. Red glanced at it and slowly eased back from Elrod.

"Why hello, William," the shadow said.

It was the maître d', Douglas. He had a black dinner jacket draped around one arm and a humorless smile on his face. He looked at Red.

"I see you've met our friend Elrod," Douglas said. "He's a new customer of ours."

Douglas turned to Elrod. "Please stand up, sir," he said.

Elrod eyed him warily.

"Your dinner jacket," Douglas said. "I'll be happy to help you put it on."

"Oh, yeah," Elrod responded. "The jacket."

Elrod rose from his barstool and Douglas helped him slip the dinner jacket on. It fit just right, like it had been tailored for Elrod and Elrod alone.

"A perfect fit," Douglas said. He looked at Red. "Wouldn't you say that's a perfect fit, William?"

"Yeah," Red said. "Perfect."

Elrod sat back down on the barstool. Red pulled a cigarette from his jacket pocket and put it in his mouth. He was reaching for a lighter when Douglas produced one of his own. He sparked the flame and moved it perilously close to Red's face. It was one of those old-time lighters with the wheel and flint. Red lit up and moved his head back slowly.

Douglas put the lighter back in his pocket. He turned to Elrod.

"William, as you no doubt surmised, is a member of the jazz orchestra," Douglas said. "He's a marvelous bandleader and musician. We owe a great deal of our success to him. He keeps the customers coming in, the repertoire fresh, and the tempo lively. And unlike most jazz musicians, William steers clear of the usual vices that might threaten his cabaret license. Isn't that right,

William?"

Douglas winked at Red. Red stood stone-faced.

Elrod wondered why Douglas called him "William" instead of "Red." Red was the name friends used. Maybe they weren't friends.

"Another of William's many gifts is that he knows how—and when—to interact with the clientele," Douglas said. "He usually does so after a couple of sets when everyone is loosened up. It's a little puzzling to see William engaging with a customer so early in the evening when he normally keeps to himself. The curious cat inside me wonders what on earth he could be discussing with you."

Now Red smiled. "We were discussing the weather."

"Ah, the weather," Douglas said. "Fascinating subject. And what conclusions did you come to about the weather?"

"We both agree it's necessary," Red said.

Douglas laughed. Red laughed. It didn't sound much like laughter, though.

Elrod sat there and nice and quiet, content to watch the two men do their little dance, thinking he'd sure like to have that drink now.

Douglas seemed to sense as much. He walked behind the bar and fetched Elrod's Dewar's.

"But now's not the time for chitchat," Douglas said. "I have work to do, and so does William. And our new friend here is probably ready for his drink, now that he's suitably attired."

He slid the drink in front of Elrod.

"Cheers," he said.

Elrod raised his glass to Douglas, then took a long, slow drink. The scotch tasted like magic going down, smooth and smoky, like it was brewed in a faraway Neverland and pushed down the back of a rainbow straight into Elrod's throat.

"Just what the doctor ordered," Elrod said.

Douglas smiled. He patted Elrod on the arm. It felt like his arm had been scorched by a bolt of lightning. Elrod tried to slide his arm away, but Douglas kept it pinned there.

"The bartender should be in any moment," Douglas said, smiling. "He'll be happy to serve you."

Douglas slapped Elrod on the back and walked on to another part of the nightclub. Elrod watched him stroll away, thinking he'd never felt so threatened by generosity and good manners.

Pretty soon people started wandering in. Elrod looked at them with a mixture of fascination and dread. They were all dressed to the nines, in tailored suits and posh dresses, fedoras and berets, Italian loafers and leather pumps. It was a neatly groomed crowd, handsome and pretty, fair of skin and regal of nose. They blew smoke rings and traded laughs. They had the cool, confident look of folks who know their place in society—and know that place is a long, long way from the bottom.

Elrod stood out like a turd in a bowl of sugar. The nice dinner jacket he had on couldn't hide his shaggy hair or scruffy beard. He swiveled around on his barstool and stared straight ahead at his drink, figuring his back looked a lot more presentable than his front.

As promised, the bartender soon appeared behind the bar. He was a young guy, maybe twenty-five, with a handsome face and short blond hair slicked close to his head. He wore the standard bartender getup: white shirt, black slacks, black bowtie, black vest. He was busying himself with prep work, making sure the right bottles were in the right places and all the mixers were lined up properly. Elrod waited for him to make eye contact, grew impatient almost instantly, then tapped the bar.

"How about another one of these, chief?" he said. "Dewar's on ice, no water."

The bartender looked at Elrod and gave a friendly nod of the head. "Right you are, sir." He grabbed a cocktail glass, dropped a couple cubes in it and filled it to the rim with Dewar's.

Elrod reached into his coat to grab his cigarettes, then remembered his own coat was in the cloakroom.

"Well hell," he said. "I forgot my smokes are in my other coat. You think someone could fetch them for me over in the cloakroom?"

The bartender reached below the bar. He brought out a gold case with a paisley design engraved on it. He opened the case. It held a couple neat rows of cigarettes. He held it out toward Elrod.

"Compliments of the house, sir," he said.

Elrod grabbed a cigarette, thanked the bartender, then grabbed a few more before the bartender could pull the case away.

The bartender reached in his pocket and pulled out a lighter. He torched Elrod's cigarette and slid a glass ashtray his way. Then he reached under the bar and placed a book of matches on the bar in front of Elrod. The matchbook had "The Hideaway" printed on it.

Elrod thanked him again and slid the matches into his jeans pocket. He stared into the bar mirror to see the action going on behind him. The place was filling up fast with both people and smoke. The band had started into a couple of mid-tempo numbers.

Elrod wondered what kind of trip he was on here. Had someone spiked his malt liquor with a peyote button? He'd ingested plenty of drugs over the years, taken some mental journeys he wasn't sure he'd come back from. This experience didn't feel exactly the same. Elrod wasn't seeing people with seven eyes, for example, and the world wasn't exploding in shiny colors. But it still seemed surreal. Elrod closed his eyes and pinched himself on the arm. He slowly opened his eyes, thinking maybe he'd return to the dark, empty alley.

But no. Here he was, still in the nightclub.

Elrod thought about what Red had told him. *You're in the shit. You need to go meet someone at a café, during daylight hours. Keep your eyes out for a big white mother.* It sounded pretty ominous, and ordinarily Elrod would be spooked. But not just now. Just now, he actually felt pretty damn good. The music was first-rate, and the joint was hopping. The girls were pretty. The liquor was top shelf—and cheap. The smokes were free.

What the hell. Might as well enjoy it.

Elrod downed a couple more drinks, loosened up a little, grew less self-conscious. He decided nobody much cared how he looked, and even if they did, Elrod didn't much care anymore himself. He spun back around on his barstool and faced the band, which had kicked things into a higher gear with a swinging up-tempo number. He tapped his feet lightly, nodded his head to the beat, swayed his body back and forth.

"Go man!" he shouted as the trumpet player tap-tap-tapped the valves and bent the notes every which way—

upper register and lower register, short and long tones, minor keys, major keys, his head tilted skyward, his face moist with sweat, his back arched, the notes moving higher and higher up the scale until they eventually landed somewhere near Pluto as the rest of the band went into overdrive just trying to keep up.

Elrod slid off his barstool and jerked his body around. He did a little jig and shimmied his shoulders. He swung his hips back and forth, back and forth, then he swung his elbows, then his arms, then he knocked into a woman standing next to him at the bar and splashed her drink all over the place.

"Geez, mister!" the woman snapped.

Elrod twisted his head around. The woman had short, wavy brown hair, long brown eyelashes, and hazel eyes that were slightly Asiatic and instantly mesmerizing. She wore a black dress with thin straps that clung just loose enough to qualify as tasteful instead of provocative. She was an inch or so shorter than Elrod, which made her a little taller than average for a woman. She looked about thirty years old.

"Shit!" Elrod said. "So sorry, miss."

The woman frowned. She waved the bartender over.

"I could use a towel," she told him.

"Sure thing, doll," the bartender replied.

He reached under the bar, brought up a white linen towel, and handed it to the woman. She wiped her dress and arms and looked at Elrod.

"That's a swell way to meet a gal," she said. "Knock into her and spill her drink."

"Sorry again," Elrod said. "Guess I was grooving on the music a little too hard. Didn't realize you were there."

"'Grooving on the music'," she replied. "Never heard it put quite that way before. Just make sure you don't groove into someone else while you're at it, huh? Do you know how expensive that champagne was? And how expensive this dress is?"

"Let me buy you another drink," Elrod said. "Champagne, you said? Let's get you the best there is."

"I was already drinking the best there is," the woman said. She looked at her watch. "Anyway, I don't have time to wait on another drink. I'll just have some of yours."

She grabbed Elrod's Dewar's and knocked it down in a single gulp. She slammed the empty glass on the bar and winked at Elrod, then sauntered across the main floor toward the bandstand. Elrod took a deep breath, tried to shrink inside himself again. If there was a sure way to wear out your welcome in a pricey place like this, it was dancing around like a hillbilly and spilling expensive champagne on pretty women. He told himself to settle down, act civilized, be cool. He signaled the bartender for another drink, leaned back onto his barstool, and scanned the action, quietly.

Everyone was having a gay old time, laughing and dancing, drinking and smoking. It played out like ten million different scenes in ten million different saloons across space and time. If this was all in Elrod's head, more dream than reality, so be it. For once, his head was a pretty good place to be.

After one more upbeat tune, the band welcomed a singer to the bandstand. She entered from the rear and slowly sashayed her way to the front, planting herself in front of the microphone. It was the woman with the black dress, the one Elrod had banged into. So, she was a singer, was she? The night was just full of surprises.

The woman adjusted the microphone slightly so it rested in front of her mouth. She glanced around at the crowd.

"Hello cats and kittens," she purred. "Welcome to the Hideaway. I'm Jade, and I'm here to sizzle your little hearts."

The crowd applauded.

"Are we enjoying ourselves tonight?" Jade said.

The crowd clapped its approval.

"Are we being good tonight?"

The crowd clapped its approval.

Jade's face went into a pout. "Well that's no fun," she said. "I was hoping we were being naughty tonight."

The crowd roared and applauded.

"That's more like it," Jade said. "The band and I are in naughty moods ourselves. There's no telling where it might lead."

She turned toward the band and blew them a kiss.

"I'll be doing one set tonight, then I have to scoot along to go...entertain somebody."

Jade winked. The crowd applauded.

"It feels like a night for black magic," Jade went on. "Don't you feel it? A little magic in the air?"

She closed her eyes and grabbed the microphone. The band started into a slow, bluesy ballad. After waiting for the band to make a couple trips around the opening theme, Jade started singing. Her voice was low and sultry, a near rasp. She took her time, stretched the words out.

You do something to me
Something that simply mystifies me

Tell me, why should it be
You have the power to hypnotize me?
Let me live 'neath your spell
Do do that voodoo
That you do so well.

Elrod knew the song. It was an old standard, the kind his aunt back home used to favor. It was usually done upbeat, but this version was slow, torchy, with a blues feeling. The crowd grew quiet. Jade sang in a lower register, deep from the belly. She kept her eyes closed until she got to the final stanza. When she got there, she slowly opened her eyes.

For a brief moment, a few ticks of the clock, everyone else disappeared from Elrod's view. The band. The audience. The staff. The lights dimmed. The club turned black except for a single faint spotlight on Jade's eyes, which were lasered straight into Elrod's, a slight twinkle behind them.

Do do that voodoo
That you do so well

Elrod grew dizzy. He shook his head, tried to get his bearings. The Dewar's was beginning to work a number on him. He hadn't eaten in a while, so the liquor had taken the express train to his brain. He shifted his eyes around to gain more focus. When they came back into focus they landed on Douglas, the maître d', who was standing a few feet away.

Now the faint spotlight seemed to move toward Douglas. Now he was the only one in the nightclub, and it was his eyes that were lasered into Elrod's. Only his weren't twinkling.

It was mystifying.
It was hypnotizing.
It was terrifying.

Chapter 2

Elrod felt a sharp pain in the back of his head. He jerked himself up from the pavement and tried to get his bearings. He felt the pain again, sharper this time. He groaned, shook his head, blew air out of his lungs. He rubbed his eyes and coughed up a missile of phlegm. That pain. What was that pain? He must have banged his head against something. What had he banged it against? Where was he?

Right, of course.

He was in the alley, lying on his bed of newspapers. Well, partly on it. His lower body was on the paper, but his upper body was sort of dumped in a pile against the wall. His head throbbed. He felt around to see if there was a bump, or blood, or both. No blood. But a welt was beginning to form. Probably banged it against the wall or pavement. He looked across the alley, saw the same old wall, the same old dirt and grime, the same old graffiti.

No blue door. No windows or pink lights.

"Jesus," Elrod muttered to himself. "Helluva dream."

He pulled himself up and stretched his arms. He

yawned, coughed for thirty seconds or so, brushed the dust and dirt off his clothes. He stretched his back, which creaked and cracked. He looked up at the sky, or at least what he could see of it from the alleyway. Morning light had begun to filter in. A few clouds were floating about, mostly white and puffy. No smell of rain in the air. Shouldn't be too hot. Nothing to worry about weather-wise.

So, another weird dream. There'd been a lot of those lately. It was a bad sign, an omen, a signal that something strange was about to happen in Elrod's life. Once, many years ago, he'd had a series of dreams about cows. Cows that stampeded him, laughed at him, taunted him. Cows with red eyes and massive heads that would slowly circle while Elrod stood frozen in the middle, unable to move. A few days after the last cow dream Elrod was hit by a milk truck and had to spend a week in the hospital with bruised ribs and a big gash across his back. It could have been much worse. That's what the doctors told him: *You're lucky—it could have been much worse.* Of course, it could have been much better, too. Elrod could have not been hit by a goddamn milk truck in the first place.

This dream wasn't as weird as the cow dreams, but it was close. It didn't even seem like a dream. More like a hazy memory of something that had happened a long time ago. Elrod looked down at his hands and noticed them shaking. He figured he either needed another drink, or never to drink again.

Realizing the improbability of the latter happening, Elrod opted for the former. What he'd do, he'd head back to the store that sold him the Voodoo Malt Liquor. He'd gotten the bottle free of charge thanks to a promotional coupon he'd found in his new coat. Elrod had never heard of Voodoo Malt Liquor before yesterday, but it sure packed a wallop. He didn't have a coupon today, but he had more than enough cash thanks to yesterday's haul outside the subway station.

The store was located several long blocks away, which was fine with Elrod. A morning stroll would give him a chance to clear the cobwebs from his head and the dream from his memory. The dream had some good parts, Elrod remembered that much. Cheap booze. Good music. A pretty woman. But it also had some disturbing parts. An ominous warning. A wicked guy dressed up all dandy. Elrod's dreams usually evaporated from memory as soon as he slipped into consciousness, but this one lingered fresh in his brain.

Elrod exited the alley and made his way toward the store. He walked past the usual parade of vagrants, derelicts, psychos, drunks, junkies, hustlers, thieves, head cases, and hard cases you saw down here. One poor soul was barfing into a sewer grate. Another was screaming at a lamppost. A couple of mangy-looking dudes threatened each other with broken bottles.

The locals called the area LoDown, short for "Lower Downtown." The name fit, both geographically and otherwise. It was just south of the Lower East Side, and about as lowdown a place as you could find on this shiny island. Condemned tenements bound for the wrecking ball shared real estate with abandoned industrial buildings that now served as shooting galleries for the neighborhood's growing population of drug fiends. The sidewalks were falling apart and littered with overflowing trash cans and busted pay phones. The only legit businesses were either flophouses, pawnshops, or liquor stores with iron bars in their windows. Most of the residents didn't have two dimes to rub together. If they had any more than that, they'd either drink, smoke, snort, or gamble it away by sundown. The gentrification going on elsewhere in the city still hadn't dipped its toe into this part of town.

Many of the locals were still sound asleep this time of morning. You saw them lying on stoops, alleys, sidewalks, some covered with blankets or old coats, some covered with newspapers, some not covered at all. Elrod assumed they were sleeping, but you never could know for sure. Every so often a cop would cruise by, inspect an inert body, and then cover it with something until the corpse wagon showed up. Nobody seemed to pay the dead bodies much mind. They were just part of the scenery.

After four blocks Elrod hung a left and more or less exited LoDown. He walked down a long avenue that was higher class than the previous stretch of road, but only by a little. This avenue at least had businesses that were mostly legitimate, and sidewalks that were mostly free of trash and broken concrete. Elrod bought his beer, wine, or liquor around here when he had enough money saved up. When he was flush with cash he'd buy food at one of the fried chicken or Chinese takeout joints, or clothes at the Salvation Army store.

The closest public library was also located on this avenue. Elrod wandered into it from time to time to wash up, use the can, read, or fiddle around on the computer. The staff didn't mind him hanging around as long as he was reasonably clean and didn't cause a ruckus. He made a point of putting books and magazines back where they belonged when he was finished using them. When a computer was available, Elrod would make a beeline to it. He learned how to use computers at libraries, either by reading up on computer technology or sneaking glances at others. He got hooked on the World Wide Web, which most folks now called the internet. He could spend hours on the computer surfing the internet—a term he learned by surfing the internet.

The store was located a couple blocks past the library. It sat on a corner beside a twenty-four-hour laundromat. Elrod walked inside and made his way to the beer cooler. He scanned the malt liquor shelf in search of Voodoo. He saw the usual brands—Colt 45, Olde English 800, Mickey's, Cobra, Hurricane—but no Voodoo. Maybe they sold out.

Elrod approached the checkout counter, where the owner was sorting cigarette packs. He was a wiry fellow, medium height, mid-thirties, with a full head of black hair and a grim look on his face that Elrod imagined was stapled there permanently. People called him the Screamin' Korean.

"Looking for that Voodoo malt liquor, chief," Elrod said. "Don't see it in your cooler. Got any in the stockroom or whatnot? Doesn't need to be cold."

"Only malt riquor in cooler," the owner said, not looking up from his work.

"You sold out of Voodoo then?" Elrod said.

"What kind?" the owner said.

"Voodoo," Elrod said. He smiled. "Do do that voodoo that you do so well."

"Called Voodoo?" the owner said, still not making eye contact.

"That's the one," Elrod said.

"No Voodoo," the owner said. "Never sell Voodoo. Olde Engrish. Mickey's. Cobra. Colt forty- frive."

Elrod gave him a puzzled look.

"Whattaya mean, never sold Voodoo?" he said.

"No Voodoo malt riquor," the owner repeated, his voice rising. "Never sell it, never heard of it. Buy Olde Engrish."

"I got a bottle of Voodoo malt liquor in this very store yesterday," Elrod answered. "Free of charge. I had a special coupon."

"No Voodoo!" the owner screeched. "No such thing! No free of charge, either. How I make money, give malt riquor away free?"

Elrod stiffened his back.

"No offense, but that just ain't correct," he said. "I got a bottle of Voodoo right here, right at this counter, yesterday. Hell, you even accepted the coupon from me, free of charge! Now maybe you sold out of it, but..."

The owner whipped his head up and scowled at Elrod.

"You clazy man, hey?" he shouted. "That what you are? Clazy? Stupid? I tell you, no Voodoo malt riquor. No such thing! Never been. Brands come; brands go. No Voodoo. Never Voodoo. You clazy in the head. Buy something else. Buy or leave!"

Elrod snorted. To hell with this—he didn't need this kind of treatment. He'd take his business elsewhere. Go to another store, find the Voodoo there. Don't tell me *I'm* clazy, mister. *You're* the one who's clazy.

"Buy or leave!" the owner shouted. He turned his head, went back to sorting cigarette packs.

Elrod made for the exit, then stopped almost immediately and did a 180. Screw it. He was thirsty. He needed something to drink. He headed for the beer cooler and grabbed a bottle of Hurricane. He'd be goddamned if he'd buy the Olde English 800, not after the owner recommended it. He placed the bottle of Hurricane on the counter.

The owner rang it up and gave Elrod the total. Elrod reached into his coat pocket for the money he'd bummed yesterday at the subway station. He figured he had around twelve or thirteen bucks, some of it in change, some of it in dollar bills. He didn't feel any money, though. Odd.

The store owner tapped the counter with his right hand and repeated the price.

"Hold your horses, chief," Elrod said.

He felt around in his pants pockets. Nothing in the front pockets. Nothing in the rear left pocket. Nothing in the rear right, either, except for an old wallet that had photos and useless business cards but no cash. He reached back into his front pockets. This time, he felt something stuck way down low. Something made of paper. Didn't seem the right size for money, but he pulled it out anyway and unfolded it.

It was a piece of paper with a name written on it.

The name of a park.

And a map.

Sweet mother of God.

He dug down again and found a book of matches with "The Hideaway" printed on it.

Sweet mother of God.

Elrod remembered that piece of paper, and those matches. He dreamed about them last night. The musician gave the piece of paper to him. But if it was only a dream, then how in the world...

"You pay now!" the store owner barked. "Pay or leave!"

Elrod checked his pockets again for money but didn't find any. How was that possible? It was there last night when he went to sleep in the alley. It was there when he dreamed about the nightclub. It was there when he entered the club and sat down at the bar. It was there when he tossed it all on the bar.

It was there until the bartender swiped it away...

Sweet mother of God.

"You pay!" the owner snapped.

The words echoed in Elrod's ear and rattled around in his head, but he didn't really register them. He just stared at the piece of paper with the name of the park and the map on it.

Sweet mother of God.

Chapter 3

"So who's this homeless prick again?" Fat Sal said.

"He calls himself Elrod," Douglas said. "Another lost soul."

"He didn't suspect anything?" Fat Sal said.

"Please," Douglas replied, smiling. "He saw the premium liquor and cheap prices and from then on that's all he could or wanted to see. You could beam him back to the Resurrection of Christ and he wouldn't care if there was a cheap drink to be had."

"Everything went as planned?" Fat Sal said.

"Like clockwork," Douglas said. "He drank the bottle of malt liquor on the other side, saw the blue door, slipped through the magic portal..."

"This I know," Fat Sal said. "Why tell me what I already know? The other. Tell me the other."

"We got the package into his coat, if that's what you mean," Douglas said. "Elrod was so tight by the time he left here I doubt he even felt the coat on his body, let alone felt anything stitched inside. We spiked his last drink with the potion and sent him on his way."

"And the Jap sent word from the other side?" Fat Sal said.

Douglas nodded. "We found his note stitched inside Elrod's coat. Our last delivery got there with no problems."

Fat Sal drummed his fingers on the desk.

"What about this missing bottle?" he said. "That bugs me."

"We suspect it was one of the staff," Douglas said. "Inventory goes missing every now and then. Food, supplies, bottles of liquor. It's just part of running a nightclub."

"Except in this case it wasn't just a bottle of liquor, was it? It was something a little more important—and in limited supply."

Douglas waved his hand in the air. "Whoever stole it won't know that. He just thinks it was another bottle of vodka."

"All the same, I want this dealt with. Send a message."

"A busboy will be coming in later to meet with me. The message will be delivered."

Fat Sal drummed his fingers again. "So how much have we sent over so far? Four hundred grand, right?"

"Give or take. It depends on how much of the currency can be converted into 1999 dollars. But let's say four hundred thousand."

Fat Sal shook his head. He lit a fat cigar and stuck it in his fat mouth between his fat cheeks. He was sitting in a fat chair behind a fat desk in a skinny office located in the basement of the Hideaway nightclub. Fat stacks of cash were on the desk. A single floor lamp with a fat, round shade provided the light. A couple of skinny wooden chairs were situated in front of the desk. The tile floor was bare.

So were the walls.

Fat Sal leaned back in his chair. He jammed a couple of antacids into his mouth and gulped them down. His heartburn was getting worse. He loosened his belt. It was too tight. It constricted his belly, which hung too low and too wide. He needed to lose weight, or at least stop gaining it. He was tired of sagging out of the tailored clothes he wore. He was tired of watching the scale tip closer to 300 pounds. *You shouldn't weigh that much when you're six feet tall and forty-eight years old,* Fat Sal's doctor told him. You should be closer to 200 pounds.

Fat chance, Fat Sal remembered thinking.

"Four hundred thousand," he said. "We're not even a quarter of the way there yet. I've been here, what, eight months?"

He slammed his fist on the desk. He picked up a stack of cash and threw it across the room.

"That greedy Jap," he said. "I do all the work; he sits back and collects."

"Well, that's not entirely accurate, is it?" Douglas said. "The scientist did, after all, introduce you to the wonders of the magic hole. And he put you safely here, where the authorities from your era can't find you."

"The authorities from my era," Fat Sal said, nearly choking on the phrase. "Buncha mooks. Half of 'em are more corrupt than me."

He got up from his chair and tossed the cigar on the floor. He ground it out with his foot and kicked the butt against the wall. He picked up the money he'd thrown, then sat back down.

"Everything was fine until that cocksucker of a senator got involved," Fat Sal growled. "All of a sudden you can't walk ten feet without some federal jackoff breathing down your neck, waiting for you to get a parking ticket so they can haul you in. And now here I am, stuck until the scientist decides he's rich enough to send me back to where I can blow a hole into the back of Senator Miles McLaughlin's orange head. I should just kill the bastard now. Should be easy enough, considering he's what, two years old?"

Douglas smiled. "That would be time and effort wasted. Do you know how many McLaughlins there are in the whole of this city? The term 'wild goose chase' comes to mind."

Fat Sal sagged in his chair. He sighed. He belched. He lit another cigar, took a puff, and set it in an ashtray. He watched the smoke billow up. He looked at the cash on his desk. Sure, it looked like a nice pile. But it wasn't enough. It was never enough.

"You keeping those potion bottles locked up nice and tight now?" Fat Sal said.

"No need to worry. It's taken care of."

"All the same, I do worry. So how about doing me a favor and taking another look, huh? Make sure they're all there."

Douglas sighed. "I have to go to the men's room anyway. I'll check again when I'm up there."

Fat Sal watched Douglas walk out of the office and up the staircase. He wasn't sure he liked Douglas. He *was* sure he didn't trust him. But for now, Fat Sal was forced to work with him. It's just the way things were. Fat Sal didn't like it, but what can you do? He was stuck here until the money was paid off to that greedy scientist, Dr. Lionel Bunt.

And the money wasn't close to being paid off.

Fat Sal reached into his belt and pulled out a .38 Special. He rolled it around in his hands, aimed it at the wall, pretended to pull the trigger. It was a decent weapon: reliable, compact, accurate.

This particular gun had a lot of sentimental value. Fat Sal swiped it off the body of a rival family's enforcer during a turf war many years ago. It was one of the few possessions Sal still had from his former life—the life he should be in right now, the one he *would* be in right now if not for Miles McLaughlin. As it stood, Fat Sal was stuck here, in the basement of this nightclub, in this miserable time and place.

At least until Lionel got paid off.

Or Fat Sal got tired of paying him off.

Chapter 4

Dr. Lionel Bunt lifted the tea bag from his porcelain teacup and set it on a matching saucer. He gently stirred the tea with a small antique spoon he'd inherited from a great aunt, along with countless other knickknacks and doodads he had little use for but couldn't bear to part with. He was sentimental that way, Lionel. He kept things. Old postcards. Family photo albums of long-dead relatives. Letters from home. Old science texts. Souvenirs from childhood trips to amusement parks, ball games, county fairs, vacations.

One of his most cherished possessions was a polished conch shell he got during a childhood trip to Miami. Lionel was ten years old at the time. It was the first time he'd ever been east of Ohio or south of Missouri. It took his family two full days to drive from Chicago. He marveled at the white sand along the Florida beaches, the crashing waves of the ocean, the warmth of the saltwater as it massaged your feet. He looked in awe at the large and elegant homes that lined the beach. One day he would own one of those homes, he told himself.

Twenty-five years later, Lionel figured he was about halfway to that goal. The money from that Italian hippo, Salvatore Morino, was coming in on a regular basis, as promised. Lionel had no problem turning old money into 1999 currency. All it took was connections—and money. It's true what they said: It takes money to make money.

The plan was working to perfection.

Or had been, until today.

Today, Lionel's well-oiled machine had finally coughed and wheezed a little. Today was supposed to be payday—about fifty thousand dollars' worth of payday. Sometimes it was more, sometimes less. But always close. Always right in the ballpark of fifty thousand dollars. That was the arrangement Lionel made with Fat Sal and Douglas. Send around fifty thousand dollars every couple of weeks.

Lionel was supposed to have that payment today. He was supposed to get the coat and the money sewed neatly inside. But there was a problem. The courier—this fellow named Elrod—still had the coat. And the money.

Why had this happened?

Simple, really. Lionel's assistant had overslept and missed his appointment. He was supposed to arrive at the alley before Elrod slipped back through the portal, wait until Elrod left the alley, and then follow him somewhere he could grab the coat. But by the time Lionel's assistant got to the alley, Elrod was already in the wind.

There was always a chance Elrod had never made it back through the portal, but Lionel didn't think so. It had never happened to any of the previous couriers, and there was no reason to think it happened now.

No, the problem was Lionel's assistant, Bubba. He'd come up short. He'd failed. And now Lionel had to show him the penalty for failure.

The two men were sitting in Lionel's apartment. Lionel sat in an antique parlor chair on one side of a small wooden coffee table. Bubba sat on the other side in a cheap metal chair that folded up when it wasn't being used.

Lionel had never known an actual Bubba until he met this one. He assumed Bubba was from somewhere down South, but he was actually from Michigan. Where, Lionel didn't know, and didn't much care. All he knew was that Bubba looked big enough to handle himself around dark alleys in rough parts of town. He was well over six feet tall and somewhere in the neighborhood of 250 pounds. He was a nightclub bouncer by trade, one of those simians who spend a lot of time in the gym toning their muscles and softening their brains.

Lionel hired Bubba to do a simple job: stand near an alley in LoDown and keep an eye out for a homeless man wearing a red-and-black coat. The homeless man would emerge from the alley sometime in the morning. Bubba was to follow the homeless man until he got somewhere quiet and alone. Once there, he was to sneak up behind the homeless man, disable him, and take the coat. Then he was to bring the coat to Lionel.

It wasn't a difficult assignment. Most assistants were happy to get it, and none questioned why Lionel wanted it done. They heard how much he was willing to pay, and that's all they needed to know. None except for Bubba had failed to come through.

So here Bubba was, taking up Lionel's valuable time.

"So, you overslept," Lionel said.

Bubba nodded. "Yep," he said, yawning.

"I'm curious. How does someone oversleep when he

has such an important job to do? A job that pays a lot of money, I might add?"

Bubba shrugged. "Just one of those things. I said I was sorry. Want me to say it again? I'm sorry. Shit happens, what can I tell you? I'll find the dude and the coat. Relax."

Lionel sighed. He shook his head the way a disappointed teacher shakes her head at an underachieving student.

Lionel was, in fact, disappointed. He was disappointed that Bubba had overslept and blown his assignment. He was disappointed that Bubba decided to give up the search for Elrod so soon. He was disappointed that his payday didn't come in as scheduled. He was mostly disappointed in Bubba's smug, cavalier attitude.

Lionel had seen this attitude a lot in his life, especially from large men with meager minds. It was an attitude that said, *You're just a little egghead nerd. What are you going to do about it?*

Lionel was self-aware enough to know he didn't have the physical presence to command respect. He was a small man and an accomplished scientist—a combination that strikes fear in the hearts of exactly no one. He could hardly blame people for misjudging him—for not realizing how much damage Lionel could do, and would do, to those who crossed him.

But it pissed him off, nonetheless.

"You realize the problem here, don't you?" Lionel said. "It's not just that I don't have the coat. It's that this street bum, this Elrod, could be anywhere by now. You should have continued your search when he was still presumably close by."

Bubba shrugged again.

"Where were you when you were supposed to be keeping an eye on Elrod?" Lionel asked.

"I told you, I overslept. I...there was a woman I met last night. A guy has to have his fun, right? We had a drink after my shift, then went to my place, and had a couple more. I zonked out shortly after that and guess I slept through the alarm clock. Anyway, like I said, I'll find the coat. Hell, it's just a coat."

He looked at Lionel and grinned. "You worry too much there, professor."

Lionel sighed. He stirred his tea again. He lifted the cup and took a sip. He placed the cup back down and rose from his chair. He walked around the coffee table, stopped in front of Bubba for a moment, then walked behind Bubba toward a bookcase against the wall. Bubba didn't bother turning around.

A wooden baseball bat was leaning against the bookcase. Lionel's father had bought Lionel the bat when the two attended a White Sox game many years ago. It was a thirty-two-inch Louisville Slugger autographed by Dick Allen, the former Phillies and ChiSox star. Lionel loved baseball as a kid. He was a pretty fair player himself. Good glove, decent spray hitter, average arm. He would spend hours at the park tossing a rubber ball against a wall, practicing his fielding, pretending to be Luis Aparicio or Ozzie Smith. He had great range as an infielder and could scoop up anything that came his way. He got the ball out of his glove quickly and always made accurate throws. But he was usually the smallest player on the field, and coaches tended to look the other way whenever he tried out for the school teams.

Lionel's size was a constant thorn in his side growing

up. He never got picked for teams even though he was better than many of those who did. He always got stereotyped as a little half-Asian dork—meek, brainy, weak, a shrimp. He got picked on a lot. He got teased a lot. His parents told him to ignore it. They were no help. When you're a kid you can't just ignore it, not when it's something that confronts you daily.

Every so often Lionel would go into a blind rage and strike back at his tormenters. He surprised both them and himself by the intensity of his anger, and by the effective blows he would occasionally land with his fists, elbows, or knees. Lionel was not particularly skilled as a fighter, and almost always lost. But he caused enough discomfort to his opponents that they eventually stopped bullying him and moved on to someone else. Lionel fantasized about exacting his revenge on his tormenters. Instead, he went about his business, making straight A's and not getting picked for sports teams, saving up all his anger and resentment for a rainy day.

Like right now.

"It's not that I worry too much," Lionel said to the back of Bubba's head. "It's just that I want to ensure an efficient operation. You can't imagine how much I dislike inefficiency. I hate it worse than just about anything in the world."

He picked the bat up and crouched into his stance. Elbows cocked, bat horizontal over his right shoulder, feet spread shoulder length, knees slightly bent. He waved the bat slightly, the way hitters do in the batter's box. After a couple of practice swings he brought the bat around swiftly and cracked it against the side of Bubba's head. It was a pretty good swing. In a game it might have gone for extra bases.

Bubba flailed his arms and tipped over sideways onto the floor. He landed with a thud, taking his chair down with him. He lay there on his side, not moving except for a twitching right hand. Blood had already begun to form on his head. Lionel walked to the kitchen and grabbed a towel. He walked back to Bubba and placed the towel against the wound to stanch the bleeding. He didn't want blood getting on his floor or his rug. After a minute or so he returned to the kitchen and grabbed a spray bottle filled with water, the one he used to water his houseplants. He walked back to Bubba and sprayed his face with water.

Lionel was pretty sure he didn't kill Bubba. He swung just hard enough to knock Bubba silly and give him a terrific headache, but not so hard that it would fracture his skull or cause massive hemorrhaging. A few sprays of water and Bubba would probably stumble back into consciousness.

Lionel sat back down in the parlor chair. He picked up the tea and sipped it. It was green tea with brown rice. He drank it for its health benefits—it was rich in antioxidants known as polyphenols—but also because he enjoyed the nutty aroma and flavor. Lionel's mother used to drink this kind of tea. She was Japanese. His father was German and preferred beer to tea, and both to Lionel.

After a couple of minutes Bubba's body began to move on the floor. His eyelids flickered open, closed, then flickered back open. He moaned. Lionel rose from his chair and walked over. He sprayed some more water into Bubba's face. Bubba opened his eyes and tried to raise his head off the floor. He groaned and laid his head back down again.

Lionel leaned down and spoke to Bubba.

"You look pretty bad right now, Bubba," he said. "My guess is you suffered a concussion. The brain gets pushed against the inside of the skull, causing bruises in different points. You'll need medical attention, but you probably won't get it."

Lionel picked Bubba's chair up off the floor and sat in it.

"You won't remember anything I'm telling you right now, but I'll say it anyway," Lionel continued. "The reason you're lying there is because I bashed you against the side of your thick head with a baseball bat. If you want to know why, blame yourself. You had simple instructions, but you got sloppy and lazy and didn't carry them out. When I asked you to explain yourself, you reacted with sarcasm and more than a touch of animus. You can see how that might piss me off. The truth is, I want to keep bashing your head until it splits open and your useless brains spill out. But then I'd have a corpse on my hands I'd need to dispose of, and that would create logistical problems. As it stands, I'll put a bandage over your wound and a hat over your bandage. I'll help you walk outside to the street. I'll hail a cab and tell the cabbie you're a little woozy from a recent work injury. I'll give him a nice wad of cash to haul you across the river and drop you off where all types of sociopaths hang out. In short order you'll probably be surrounded by people who don't like you. After that, it's anybody's guess what happens."

That's what Lionel did. He put the bandage on Bubba's head and a hat over the bandage. He gathered Bubba up off the floor and led him downstairs. It wasn't easy. It took a lot of effort and a lot of strength, because Bubba was a big man with a groggy head. Bubba kept listing to the side. Lionel had to hold him up and lead him in the right direction. It took time, but eventually they made it to the ground floor and out onto the sidewalk.

Once outside, Lionel hailed a cab. He deposited Bubba into the back seat. He handed the cab driver a large wad of cash—triple the cost of the fare itself—and told him where to drop Bubba off. The cabbie didn't ask why he was supposed to drive this large man to such a rough part of town. He took the money and nodded his head. Lionel watched the cab depart, then turned his focus to other matters.

He'd have to hire another assistant. This was no problem. He switched assistants pretty regularly, and he'd make a call immediately.

The second task would be a little more complicated. He needed to find this homeless guy and deal with him.

Elrod.

Chapter 5

The Korean's voice trailed behind Elrod as he walked out of the store and onto the sidewalk, shouting *don't come back unless you have money, no Voodoo, you clazy man!* Elrod didn't pay any attention. He focused on the piece of paper that held the name of the park and the map.

The park was Colve Park, and Elrod knew it well. He'd slept there probably a dozen times or more. He'd done his business there more times than he could remember, either at one of the public bathrooms when they were open, or when they weren't, out among the trees. He used the bathrooms for other things, too, like washing up or brushing his teeth or taking refuge when the weather turned stormy. It was a big, lovely park with playgrounds and ball fields, a couple of ponds, and the occasional thick stand of trees where you might spot a deer or coyote that had roamed away from the outlying woodlands and into this hulking city. Elrod guessed the park spanned a hundred acres or so. The main pathways wound mostly north and west.

It was a nice day for a stroll in the park. Cool and

comfortable for late August. A slight breeze coming in off the waterways. You'd be hard-pressed to find a better day for a walk in the park. Even so, Elrod considered dropping the whole thing. Tossing the piece of paper in the trash and erasing it from his memory. There had to be a logical explanation for why this piece of paper was in Elrod's possession—an explanation that didn't involve nightclubs that popped up out of thin air in grungy alleys. Elrod had blacked out, that was all. He probably found the piece of paper somewhere else and simply forgot it was in his pocket. Same with the matches. He probably spent his money somewhere else and didn't remember that, either.

"Yeah, keep telling yourself that," Elrod muttered to himself.

He knew better. He really *had* been in that nightclub last night. He *had* talked to the musician, Red. And Red really *had* given him the piece of paper. Elrod didn't dream it up, and he hadn't been hallucinating. He needed to find the park café and learn what this was all about.

He suddenly remembered something else Red told him last night: Keep an eye out for a "big white mother" following him. In this case, the term "mother" meant a big boy with bad intent. Elrod looked up and down the streets, scanning the corners, alleyways and building entrances. He saw plenty of people, but nobody especially menacing or suspicious.

After a few blocks Elrod reached the southeastern corner of the park. He looked back at the map and saw that the café was located about halfway up the main path, heading north and west. Elrod had walked by the place a few times, though he wasn't sure if he'd ever been inside.

He was a little more isolated here in the park than out

in the streets, which meant he was more vulnerable to attack. He didn't have anything to defend himself with in case the big white mother made an appearance. He walked over to a small copse of trees and searched for broken limbs, something big enough to ward off an attacker. He found a fair-sized stick, about four feet long and a couple inches thick, and carried it with him back to the path.

The park had its usual crew this time of day. Mothers and nannies pushing strollers. Artists dabbing at their easels. A couple young guys tossing a frisbee back and forth. Street musicians plying their trade, their instrument cases open on the ground so passersby could drop in a buck or two. People smoking. People snacking. A few hustlers out hustling. A few vagrants staring into space.

Elrod walked at a brisk pace, keeping his eyes peeled for someone shadowing him. He wished he had a drink to steady his nerves, but he was out of luck on that score—stone-cold sober and stone-cold broke.

Sobriety did serve at least one useful purpose for Elrod—it gave him a chance to clear his head a little, recharge, refocus, take stock of his life, reflect on where all the time went, and why things turned out the way they did for him: broke, homeless, and on the wrong side of forty.

You didn't have to search too hard for the answers. There was the drinking, for one thing. And the narcotics and hallucinogenics. Elrod probably had an addictive personality. He might be an alcoholic, though there had been stretches when he went weeks or even months without anything more than a few beers. Every so often he'd hook up with a work crew somewhere and take a half-hearted stab at respectability before moving along again.

If Elrod was addicted to anything, it was roaming

around. He could scarcely remember a time in his adult life when he wasn't desperate for a change of scenery. He's not even sure why. You couldn't blame it on a rough childhood, because Elrod's childhood was about as ordinary as they came. He was a son of the heartland, born of solid Oklahoma stock. His parents put a nice roof over his head and made sure he did his schoolwork and stuck to the straight and narrow. His family wasn't rich, but things were comfortable. They were law-abiding, God-fearing, middle class, salt-of-the-earth people—and pretty well cemented in place. Elrod's folks lived in the same house together for fifty-three years. His older brother, Wally, never left his hometown. He married a girl he'd known since second grade and the two bought a house less than a mile from where Wally and Elrod grew up.

Elrod always reckoned he was cut from the same cloth. He was a good and obedient son who made decent grades, enjoyed camping and fishing, played baseball for the American Legion and high school teams, and didn't get into too much trouble. When he was eighteen he left for college, per his parents' wishes, figuring he'd do his four years there and then return to his hometown.

It was a small state school located about fifty miles up the road. Elrod's parents drove him up in the family sedan. They helped him get settled into his dorm room and chatted up his new roommate, a tall, freckled, sandy-haired, big-toothed farm boy named Rulon. The rest of their time was spent dispensing parental advice.

"Find a nice church near campus for Sunday worship," Elrod's mother told him.

Elrod's father gave the same speech he repeated maybe a half-dozen times on the drive up.

"You'll want to find a part-time job to help out with expenses," he said. "We won't be able to send money for things like pizza or soda pop or record albums or whatever you kids like to spend your money on. There's a few stores in town that might need stockroom help. Or find a job on campus. Go down to the student services office first thing Monday morning and put in an application. Study hard and don't get involved in a lot of nonsense."

Elrod's family wasn't much on long goodbyes. He and his dad shook hands. His mother kissed him on the cheek and said she loved him. Then they left.

Elrod chatted with Rulon for a few minutes over nothing much—where here they were from, who they thought might make the World Series that year, how the food might taste in the student cafeteria. Rulon said he'd like to take a walk around campus and invited Elrod along. Elrod thanked him, but said he'd probably just hang around the room for a while and put his things up. His roommate split, leaving Elrod alone.

Then, something happened. Elrod looked at the empty room. He looked outside at the wide, open sky. He realized that for the first time in his life, he was truly on his own—unbound, of legal age, able to set his own course without his parents or anyone else telling him what to do. He could do anything he wanted to do right now. He could go anywhere he wanted to go. He could be whatever he wanted to be. Nobody was around to stop him or talk sense into him. It was a strange, magical feeling. Elrod had never felt it before. He told himself to ignore it.

Elrod gave it the old college try in the beginning. He went to classes every day, on time, ready to learn. He took copious notes. He ignored the voices in his head every time he looked out one of the windows and wondered what lay beyond the vast open land, whether he was looking west toward the Pacific Ocean or east toward the Atlantic, and what it might be like to walk on out and disappear in either direction. He turned down offers to go into town and hang out at the taverns. He brushed off the city kids from Tulsa or Oklahoma City who asked him if he wanted to smoke a little weed.

After his fourth week in school, Elrod finally consented to go to a party with one of his hall mates. The party was held at a rundown house about five miles from campus, populated by students who'd grown sick of dorm life. The place was crowded with people and empty beer cans. Loud rock music blared on the stereo. Deep Purple. Grand Funk Railroad. The Allman Brothers. The Stones. The James Gang. Uriah Heep. Everybody singing along: *This is a thing I've never known before...it's called eeeeasy livin'!*

People passed bongs back and forth. They shoved beers at Elrod, and Elrod politely declined. He finally accepted a can of Falstaff so they'd stop pestering him about it. He took a sip. It tasted bitter and metallic, like something you'd kill insects with. He took another sip. Awful.

A girl came up to him and told him to chug the beer. Elrod didn't know who she was, or why she walked up to him. She was a plump girl with a friendly face, red hair, a gap between her front teeth, and huge breasts. She wore a yellow T-shirt with a smiley face on it. She appeared a little unsteady on her feet.

"I been watching you," the girl said. "You're cute. But you don't know how to drink a damn beer."

She grabbed the can out of Elrod's hand and chugged

it down in about four gulps. She belched, whooped, and pulled another can of Falstaff from a Styrofoam cooler. She yanked the tab off and shoved it at Elrod.

"Chug this, hot stuff," she said. "Show me what you got."

Elrod hesitated. The girl punched him on the arm.

"Chug it, sweetie," she said. "CHUG... it... CHUG... it... CHUG... it..."

Elrod shrugged his shoulders as if to say, what the hell, why not? He slowly tipped the can up and placed it against his lips. He let the liquid glide down into his mouth. He fought back the urge to spew it out. He swallowed it and swallowed it, slowly at first, then picking up speed. People gathered around and urged him on.

"CHUUUG...it, CHUUUG...it, CHUUUG...it!"

Elrod took small, precise gulps. He could feel the beer can getting lighter. He could feel his throat burning. He wasn't sure how many swallows it took to drain the thing. Maybe two dozen? At some point, the can was empty. The crowd gave him an ovation. He smiled. He'd never gotten an ovation before. His head tingled. His body loosened up. The girl in the smiley face T-shirt grabbed another Falstaff and shoved it in Elrod's chest. He took it and eyed it warily.

"CHUUUG... it, CHUUUG... it, CHUUUG... it!"

Elrod tipped the can up and let the liquid glide down in his mouth. He swallowed and swallowed and got it down in fifteen gulps or so.

The next one he got down in ten gulps.

The next one in eight gulps. The next one about the same amount.

Someone handed him a shot of tequila. He gulped it down.

In short order, Elrod grew wobbly. Smiley Face walked up and held him by his shoulders, steadied him a little. She put her arms around his neck and kissed him on the lips, wet and hard. She slipped her tongue through Elrod's teeth and worked it around until it made contact with his own tongue. Elrod stabbed his tongue every which way, madly, clumsily. A warm sensation bloomed in his crotch.

Elrod didn't know how long they kissed. Probably a couple of minutes. He just knew he felt good and loose, happy and free, horny and drunk, ready to conquer the goddamn world—all the way up until the moment his head began to twirl around like a tornado and his stomach erupted like Mt. Vesuvius. The beer made a mad dash north, up through Elrod's throat and out of his mouth. Vomit gushed in a dozen different directions—on the wall, the floor, the sofa, the cooler—on Smiley Face, on Elrod himself.

It was the last clear memory Elrod had of the party. The rest is a blur. He spent the next day lying in his dorm bed, semicomatose, interrupted only by the occasional trot to the bathroom to either throw up again or evacuate his bowels. Elrod swore he'd never take another drink for as long as he lived. He'd tried it once, and he'd never try it again.

Two days later, he was downing Miller High Life in a dorm room down the hall. A week after that he tried marijuana for the first time.

A week later Elrod was getting drunk and stoned pretty much daily, sleeping late in the morning, skipping classes, and having a genuinely great time. A month after that Elrod quit school, packed his backpack, wrote his parents an apologetic goodbye letter, and told them not to worry about him, he'd be fine. He walked a few miles to the state highway and hitchhiked west with another college chum, not stopping until they'd hit Portland, Oregon.

The college chum hooked up with a van full of longhairs heading south to California, but Elrod stuck around Portland. He found a room in a motel that rented by the week. He got a job pumping gas and changing oil at a filling station. He lived frugally. He survived on pork n' beans, bologna, and tap water. He stockpiled cash. When he'd saved up enough, he mailed his parents a money order paying them back every cent for the semester—room, tuition, meals, books, all of it. He enclosed a letter apologizing again for his abrupt departure from college, explaining why he did it, and letting them know he was never going back. He said he loved them and wished them well. He didn't see them again for five years.

Two days after mailing the letter, Elrod quit his job at the filling station and hit the road again. He'd been wandering ever since.

But he'd never wandered into anything as strange as what transpired over the last dozen hours or so: the alley, the nightclub, the note telling him to meet someone in the park café. He still wasn't convinced it had happened at all. But he had a feeling he'd know for sure, one way or the other, when he reached the café and made contact with this mysterious someone Red said would be there.

The café was located beside a maple tree, up a slight hill in a shady area off the main path. A few tables and benches were scattered outside, but none were occupied. Elrod inched his way past them to take a peek inside. He saw a handful of customers nibbling away at scones or sipping tea or coffee, but didn't recognize any of them.

He eyed the front door, which was propped open. He was hesitant to step inside. He knew from experience that the second he entered the café, someone who worked there would give him the *stare*. The kind of stare reserved for people who looked like they slept in alleys and bummed coins outside the subway station.

He decided to sit at one of the outside tables with his back turned to the café. If a café employee came up to tell Elrod to either buy something or split, Elrod would pretend he didn't understand English. That usually bought him a little time until he could figure out a way to buy more time. He hoped he wouldn't need much. He hoped whoever was supposed to meet him here would do so quickly and get this thing over with. He scanned the area for the big white mother, keeping a firm grip on his stick.

He thought about Red, the musician. Red seemed straight enough. He at least seemed a lot more trustworthy than Douglas, whose easy smile was about as comforting as a machete. But the truth was, Elrod didn't know Red any better than he knew Douglas. Maybe Red had lured Elrod into a trap.

While all this was rattling around in Elrod's head he felt a light tap on his shoulder. He jerked his shoulder back and whipped his head around, thinking he'd see one of the café employees glaring at him. Instead, he saw an attractive, stylish woman wearing dark blue slacks, a collared white blouse, a light blue blazer, and expensive-looking sunglasses. Elrod figured she was a customer getting ready to hassle him, so he took the initiative himself.

"What's the problem?" he said. "I ain't bothering

anyone, so..."

"Don't recognize me?" the woman asked.

"Huh?" Elrod said.

The woman took her sunglasses off to reveal a pair of hazel eyes that were almost crescent-shaped. Long eyelashes. Pretty face.

"Do do that voodoo that you do so well," the woman purred in a low, sultry voice.

Elrod jerked his head back.

"It's you," he said. "From last night. The singer from that nightclub. What the..."

"That's right. It's me, from last night," the woman said. "And you can thank me for saving your skinny rear end. But we'll get to that later."

She sat down in a chair and scooted it beside Elrod.

"I have a hotel room just a couple blocks from the park, the Northpark Village Hotel," she said. "We need to walk over there, you and me. I'll explain everything once we get there. For now, there's a little dwarf of a mad scientist on the hunt for you, and you don't want to cross paths with him right now."

Elrod gave the woman a sideways look. "Say that again?"

"Which part?" the woman said.

"The mad scientist might be a good place to start."

"Look, I'll explain later. You could be in danger. We both could. Just come with me to the hotel room. We need someplace private to talk, away from the crowds."

"Tell you what, how about if I just pretend I never saw you and we both go our separate ways," Elrod said. "You're either a crazy woman or trying to drag me into some kind of hustle, and I'm not in the mood for either. So if you'll just excuse me..."

He tried to rise from his chair but the woman gripped him by the arm. He tried to yank it away but she held it firmly in place.

"Not so fast, precious," she said.

Elrod tried to yank his arm away again but she kept it anchored in place.

"Hell, you are a crazy woman!" Elrod said. "Let go of my damn arm before I..."

"Before you what?" the woman said. "You're not going to break away from me, slick, I can promise you that. All I want to do is talk to you. That's all."

"So talk."

"Not here. Someplace more private."

Elrod knew he wasn't the biggest or most powerful guy on the planet, but he had a certain wiry strength when he needed it. That strength didn't do much good with this woman, though. The more he tried to pull away, the tighter her grip got.

"I grew up on a farm," the woman said. "I spent my childhood pitching hay and gelding horses and pounding fence posts and wrestling with my three older brothers. I don't mean or want to hurt you, but I'll break your goddamn wrist if you don't relax and come along with me."

She noticed Elrod's stick, grabbed it, and tossed it twenty yards into an open field. It was an impressive toss. She stood up and tried to pull Elrod up with her, but he refused to budge.

"Can we just do this the easy way?" the woman said. "I don't want to have to drag you all the way there."

"Forget it, lady."

The woman twisted Elrod's arm and yanked it up sharply behind his head, doing her best not to draw the attention of anyone else. Pain shot through Elrod's arm and on up to his shoulder before bouncing along to other body parts. He groaned. The woman yanked his arm a little higher. He groaned again.

"Jesus, ease up," Elrod whined.

"Only if you say you'll go with me. I just want to talk. That's it."

Elrod tried to break free but it was no use. This was one strong gal, and he was feeling a little weak and tired himself. One thing Elrod knew how to do was cut his losses when he was beaten. And right now, he was beaten.

"OK, I'll go along," he finally said. "Just ease up."

The woman leaned in and placed her mouth by Elrod's ear.

"You're not going to try and make a run for it, are you?" she said. "Because I'm also pretty fast, and I'll catch you."

Elrod wasn't so sure about that. Back in high school he was the fastest player on the baseball team, by a pretty good margin. The coach would put Elrod in whenever he needed just one run to either tie the score or win the game. Have Elrod bunt his way on, steal second, steal third, then score on a sac fly or a suicide squeeze. Elrod wondered whether he still had that quick first step, that instant acceleration. Then he quickly decided, no, probably not. That had been a long time and many hard miles ago.

"I won't run," Elrod said. "Just let go."

Jade slowly released Elrod's arm. He bent over and took a few deep breaths. He massaged his arm.

"Jesus," he said.

"Sorry. But you and I really need to talk," the woman said.

Elrod moved his arm around to see if that would help ease the pain. It did, but not by much.

"Let's say we do have this little talk," he said. "After that, I want you to leave me alone. You and all the others you're hooked up with on this thing. I don't want anything to do with it. Dragging me into that nightclub. Having that horn player put ideas into my head, conning me into coming out here to this café. Whatever it is you're up to, it has nothing to do with me."

"I'm afraid you're already up to your eyeballs in it," the woman said. "It's not your fault. You got pulled into it without knowing what was happening. You'll learn all about it later. For now, we need to get going."

Elrod sighed, shook his head, and sighed again.

"I forget what your name is," he said.

"Call me Jade," she said.

"Jade, right," Elrod said. "Wish I could say I'm happy to see you again, Jade, but that would be a pretty fair distance from the truth. I'm Elrod."

"I know who you are," Jade said.

She stood up, stuck her arm out and gestured for Elrod to walk. He did so, grudgingly.

Chapter 6

Fat Sal Morino put the .38 Special back in his belt and stared at the bare, ugly walls of the Hideaway office. He thought about how upside-down his world had become. The past was the future, and the future was the past. The life he was living two years ago wouldn't come around for another forty-eight years, at least in this world. Without Dr. Bunt's potion, Fat Sal might never see his old world again. He might have to live the rest of his life in a series of dead-ass, long-ago yesteryears. All he wanted to do was spring forward and murder a United States senator. Was that so much to ask? How many senators are there, anyway? A hundred, wasn't it? Would one dead senator really make that much difference?

Things had been going so well before the senator got involved. Fat Sal's gambling operation raked in millions a year. His side gigs earned tidy profits as well—extortion, money laundering, loan sharking, guns, stolen goods. He even bought a couple of legit businesses to make it all seem on the up and up. Local cops were no problem as long as you kept their palms greased. The feds were so focused on

Russian and Latin American drug cartels they had little time, energy, or desire to go after other rackets. Fat Sal was floating on a sea of cash, and all but untouchable. There was no reason to believe the gravy train would ever grind to a halt.

But grind to a halt it did when United States Senator Miles McLaughlin—a local boy no less, born on the west side—stepped into the mix. Fat Sal remembered that day well. He was on vacation in Miami, drinking a Cuba Libre out on the balcony, looking at the crashing blue waves. The phone rang. It was one of Fat Sal's lawyers, calling from back home.

"You get CNN down there?" the lawyer said.

"Yeah," Fat Sal said. "So what?"

"Go inside and turn it on."

Fat Sal did as instructed. He clicked on the TV and turned to CNN. He saw Sen. Miles McLaughlin standing in front of the Capitol Building on a clear, sunny afternoon. Miles was positioned in front of a row of microphones and a large gathering of media types. Cops in various uniforms flanked him on either side. He had a serious look on his pink Irish face.

"Organized crime is a cancer," Miles told the gathering, "and it's spreading to every corner of this great country, from our suburbs and small towns to farming villages and, yes, even our schools. It is time to declare war on this cancer. It is time to recognize it for what it is—an enemy—and battle it with every resource at our disposal. We must be relentless. To our enemies—those career criminals who profit from the misery of others—consider this a shot across the bow. We are coming for you. And we will find you!"

It made for great theater, and Miles was the perfect leading actor: tall, red-haired, imposing, a working-class kid who parlayed a basketball scholarship at the University of Virginia into a Yale law degree, a job as a prosecutor in the nation's biggest city and, eventually, a seat in the United States Senate.

Fat Sal clicked the TV off.

"You interrupt my vacation for this?" he said into the phone. "Some senator jerking off for the cameras so he can get a little airtime? Who gives a shit?"

"Not just any senator," Sal's lawyer said. "Miles McLaughlin."

"Right, Miles McLaughlin," Fat Sal said. "So what?"

"The name doesn't ring a bell?"

"Sure, he's the guy from back home. Used to be DA."

"That's right," the lawyer said. "He used to be DA, and before that he was an assistant DA. Remember McLaughlin's cousin? Loudmouthed kid named Slider?"

Fat Sal paused. He did remember. Miles McLaughlin's cousin was a petty criminal everyone called Slider. That's the way it was with the Irish in those days—half were cops, half were criminals. McLaughlin went the cop/DA route. His cousin Slider went the other way. Slider had a quick temper and a big mouth. He caught a bullet in the head following an argument in a westside bar called Callahan's. Fat Sal's crew was suspected of pulling the trigger, but nobody could prove anything, and no witnesses came forward. The case was closed with no arrests. It was reopened years later after Miles McLaughlin ascended to district attorney. Miles sent his team after one of Fat Sal's thugs. He never got anywhere as a DA.

But now he was a US Senator.

"He's on the Judiciary Committee," Fat Sal's lawyer said into the phone. "He has clout, and now he has this war on organized crime. Chances are he still has a hard-on for you."

Fat Sal waved his hand at the phone. "So, let him have his little war on crime. Who cares? What can he do, anyway? Don't call me on vacation."

Fat Sal slammed the phone down and went back to his Cuba Libre.

A few months later, Fat Sal found out what Senator Miles McLaughlin could do. He could schedule hearings and launch investigations. He could form a special commission on organized crime. He could sponsor a crime bill that flooded law enforcement agencies with money and people. He could go on TV, every five fucking minutes it seemed like, and lambast the suspected heads of major crime syndicates—including Salvatore "Fat Sal" Morino.

Miles McLaughlin's war on crime made things very difficult for crime syndicates in a very short amount of time. Fat Sal's business took a swift and sudden downturn. His connections got spooked and stopped doing business with him. His supply lines were shut down. His legitimate businesses were raided. His men were hauled in by the dozen. One of his men snitched in exchange for immunity and a new life under a new identity in Asswipe, Wyoming. Fat Sal's operation hit the skids—fast.

The feds pinned a couple of RICO charges on Fat Sal and froze his assets. The IRS audited him. Even the local authorities began hounding him. His second wife divorced him and went after the money his first wife didn't grab. His son knocked up a girl in college and Fat Sal had to slide money their way. For what, he didn't know or want to know. Everyone was circling like vultures, ready to drain Fat Sal's finances and implode his cozy little world.

Then somebody popped into his life and told him he could make all his troubles disappear.

That somebody was Lionel Bunt, PhD.

***

Lionel Bunt strolled into Fat Sal's life on a gray, chilly day in January 1999. It happened in a pizzeria across the river that laundered money for what was left of Fat Sal's empire. Fat Sal was sitting at a table in the back of the restaurant, eating a calzone, when a short, mousy-looking guy walked in. The guy was maybe five-and-a-half feet tall, with Chinese-looking eyes, thick black hair, thin lips, a babyface, and wire-rim glasses. He wore a neatly pressed blue dress shirt, tan sport coat, gray dress pants with sharp creases, and a pair of black dress shoes that looked newly shined.

The little man walked straight up to Fat Sal and introduced himself as Dr. Lionel Bunt—just like that, Dr. Lionel Bunt. Without being prompted, he provided a quick rundown of his bona fides. Bachelor of Arts in physics at the University of Chicago, minor in chemistry. Doctorate in biophysics from John Hopkins. Scientist at a non-profit research institute in the city. He spoke in a rich, baritone voice that sounded almost comical coming out of that little body and face.

Fat Sal looked Lionel up and down.

"Impressive," he said. "Why are you interrupting my lunch?"

"I'd like a meeting," Lionel said. "In private. It will only require a couple minutes of your time. I've read about your legal problems. I think I might have a solution."

Fat Sal stared at him.

"My legal problems, huh?" he said. "You're here to solve my legal problems. That's very kind of you. Now, shuffle on back to Chinatown before I twist your fucking head off."

Lionel smiled, as if he expected this kind of reaction. He reached into his coat pocket and pulled out ten crisp one-hundred-dollar bills. He laid them on the table in front of Fat Sal.

"A goodwill gesture," Lionel said. "It's yours, whether or not we end up doing business. That may not be a lot of money to you, Mr. Morino. But it's quite a lot to me. Oh, and I'm not Chinese. I'm half Japanese, half German."

Fat Sal looked at the guy. He looked at the money. He snatched the money off the table and slid it in his pocket. A couple years ago he might have balled it up and shoved it down little Lionel's throat. But things were different in January 1999. A thousand bucks might come in handy.

Fat Sal rose from the table. "Let's go in the back," he said.

They walked to a storage room in the rear of the pizzeria. Fat Sal pulled up a metal chair and sat down. He didn't offer one to Lionel.

"Take your clothes off," Fat Sal said.

"Excuse me?" Lionel said.

"Get undressed. Down to your tighty whities. Let's see if you're wired up."

"Wired up?"

"Wearing a listening device, *Doctor* Bunt, or whatever the hell your name is."

Lionel undressed. He took off his various layers of clothing and hung them on a hook against the wall. When he was down to his underwear—blue boxers, not tighty whities—Fat Sal stood up and looked him over. There was no wire.

"OK, get dressed again," Fat Sal said. He sat back down.

Lionel began the process of putting his clothes back on. He did so slowly and methodically, taking care that each item was properly aligned.

"So why are you here?" Fat Sal said.

"Like I said, I have a way to make your legal problems disappear."

"And how's that?"

"By making you disappear."

"By making me disappear."

Lionel nodded.

Fat Sal shook his head. "You come in here, walk up to me like we're cousins, toss me a grand, and tell me you're going to make me disappear. Like I couldn't think of that on my own. Waltz off to Brazil, set up shop in a nice Rio whorehouse. That's a great idea. The feds won't care, right? Got me under indictment, got a dozen eyeballs on me at a time—there's probably one outside right now—but they'll let me buy a plane ticket and go anywhere I want."

"I don't mean go to a different place," Lionel said.

"Then what do you mean?"

"I mean a different time. A different year."

Fat Sal breathed in and out, deeply. "You better come up with a reason you're interrupting my lunch, real quick, or I'm going to break you in half."

Lionel laid it all out. He could make Fat Sal disappear.

Not out of the city, or the country. But out of this entire time and place. Back to the past, where the present-day authorities couldn't find him.

Lionel had developed a biochemical solution, he told Fat Sal. A potion, if you will. One that did wondrous things. You drink it and it alters your molecular structure. It lets you pass through a tear in the time continuum, known as a portal. The portal acts like a door into the past. This particular portal is located in an alleyway in the part of town known as LoDown. Lionel discovered the portal through his personal research. He studied time warps, ancient myths, portals, biochemistry. It was sort of a hobby of his.

"The portal has been around for thousands of years," Lionel said. "The indigenous people discovered it, according to texts I've read. Back when this was all wild, untamed land. It falls under the category of ancient myths by the academic community, but they've obviously not done enough research. The portal will let you travel back fifty years in time. Exactly fifty years, to the day and minute. From today's calendar, that means January 16, 1949. You can go back to 1949, Mr. Morino. To a place where the federal authorities have no idea who you are."

Fat Sal smiled. He shook his head. He chuckled. He got up from his chair and walked over to Lionel. He patted Lionel on the shoulder. He patted Lionel on the face, affectionately, the way you do a favorite nephew. He raised his right hand, opened the palm, and brought it down hard against the side of Lionel's head with all the force his 280-pound body could muster. Lionel spun to the floor. When he was down, Fat Sal kicked him in the side. Twice. Lionel curled up and groaned.

"A funny guy, huh?" Fat Sal said. "That what you are? A funny guy? Who sent you here? Was it someone from that Irish asshole's office? Trying to get a few chuckles? Or are you fucking with me just for the fun of it?"

Fat Sal kicked Lionel in the side again. He was getting ready to do it one more time when Lionel rolled out of the way and struggled to his feet. He reached into his jacket and pulled out a small spray bottle. He pointed it at Fat Sal's face.

"This bottle contains Oleoresin Capsicum, otherwise known as capsaicin, or pepper spray," Lionel said, sucking in air. "It isn't the watered-down commercial variety, either. It has a higher concentration of the toxic chemical agent. Come at me one more time and I'll spray it in your face. You'll start coughing and won't be able to breathe. Your skin will burn and your nose will run. A fat-ass like you might keel over of a heart attack."

Fat Sal took a step forward, fists balled, ready to pounce.

Lionel moved the bottle closer to Fat Sal's face. He looked at Fat Sal and said two words:

"Stony Boy."

Fat Sal froze.

"What?" he said.

"Stony Boy," Lionel repeated.

Fat Sal dropped his fists.

"What the fuck is that supposed to mean?" Fat Sal said.

"It means I'm the answer to your problems."

Chapter 7

Senator Miles McLaughlin stared at the file folder on his desk. It held about forty documents, all official-looking. They were full of words, charts, and analyses, none of which told Miles what he wanted to hear. He pushed the folder away and glanced at a computer screen, which also held words and charts. These didn't help, either. He lifted a chicken pita wrap from a Styrofoam container and took a bite.

Miles was tired of having lunch at the office, and tired of looking at documents. He wanted to go out and have a proper lunch at one of New York's zillion great restaurants. When he was in Washington he hardly ever ate lunch at the office. Washington was a town where you needed to be out and about, networking, being seen, eating power lunches with powerful people. Back here in the district office, though, he seemed to have lunch at his desk a lot.

At the moment, he was having lunch with his deputy chief of staff, Brent, who sat on a small sofa across from the desk and gnawed on a slice of pizza.

Brent was fairly new at the job, and more than competent—young, energetic, bright, hard-working, dedicated. Nonetheless, he got on Miles' nerves in ways Miles couldn't explain or even understand. Maybe it was the way Brent always referred to Miles as "Senator," even when they were just having an informal takeout lunch in the office. Or maybe it was Brent's little tics—the clearing of his throat, the random eyelid twitches, the way his shoulders bounced around when he laughed, the way he twirled his fingers when he spoke, the constant scratching of his prematurely thinning red hair—the thinning red hair itself, which reminded Miles of his own thinning red hair.

Brent was a continual source of aggravation to Miles. Miles was ashamed of himself for feeling this way, which was another source of aggravation.

He looked at Brent, then at the file, then back at Brent.

"This is it?" Miles said grumpily. "Nothing else? No hidden surprise tucked in here to cheer me up?"

Brent shook his head.

"I take that as a no," Miles said. "The shaking of the head."

"Sorry, pizza in my mouth," Brent said. "Yes, it's a no. I mean, no, there's nothing else to report. No hidden surprise. Believe me, they tried. The FBI mobilized as many people as they could. But there's nothing there, Senator. Salvatore Morino is just gone. Technically, they're keeping the file and investigation open. But they want to cut all but the bare resources and move on to other things."

Miles brought the pita up to his mouth and then set it down again without taking a bite. He leaned back in his chair.

"Just gone," Miles said. "How can a guy like Fat Sal be 'just gone'? Jesus, he's so fat he couldn't hide behind a football stadium, yet he's gone. His face is almost as famous as De Niro's. Yet he's gone."

"It's a brain tickler alright," Brent said.

Miles took a document from the file. The document detailed Sal Morino's sudden disappearance several months earlier. An FBI agent had been assigned to keep an eye on Morino for the express purpose of making sure he didn't try to skip the country as the charges and indictments piled up. Morino was last seen getting out of a cab near the Lower East Side. It was an odd place for Morino to go, considering he was a high-ranking crime boss, and this part of town, known as LoDown, was a seedy magnet for drunks, drug fiends, and derelicts. After exiting the cab Morino walked into an alley located beside an abandoned warehouse and empty lot. That's the last anyone saw of him. He went in and never came back out.

A team of investigators was quickly assembled to turn the alley and surrounding area upside down and inside out, trying to find traces of Morino. But the team came up empty. They found traces of shoe prints in the alley, but those could have come from anyone. They looked for ways to access the adjacent buildings from the alley but came up empty there, too. Investigators spent the next few weeks surveilling the area to see if Morino might make an appearance, but he never did. Fat Sal Morino had simply disappeared into thin air.

"I don't see how the guy could just disappear from an alley," Miles muttered. "Did he slip into the empty lot? Nobody seems to know anything. How can they not know anything?"

"It's a real brain tickler," Brent said. He scratched his head. He twirled his fingers. He scratched his head again.

Miles looked at him. "Chrissakes Brent, would you just stop..."

Miles took a bite of his chicken pita so his mouth would have something to do besides rant at Brent. He washed it down with bottled water.

"The FBI still thinks he's alive?" Miles said.

"Yes, Senator."

"So why? Why do they continue to think that?"

"They keep insisting they would have heard chatter otherwise. Somebody would have said something if Morino had been killed, and then someone else would have repeated it, and then someone else and on down the line. I talked to the ASAC and he put it like this: It's Salvatore Morino we're talking about here, not some crack dealer on the corner. If someone killed him, the FBI would have gotten wind of it. It's a sure bet. And of course, no body has been found."

Miles rose from his chair and walked to the front of the desk. He leaned against it.

"But they're also convinced he didn't skip the country, make a new life for himself down in the ass-end of Bolivia or something?" he said.

"No, Senator," Brent said. "They believe he's hiding out somewhere here in the US. Maybe even here in New York. They just don't know where."

Miles returned to his chair and sat down. He leaned back and picked up the file folder. He held it in front of Brent's face.

"Do you know how much manpower, resources, and

money went into these reports?" Miles said. "The investigative hours, the subpoenas, the interviews and interrogations, the knocking on doors, analyzing data, scanning documents, compiling evidence, et cetera, et cetera, et cetera? And the only thing we know for sure is that a 300-pound goombah entered an alley and never came out."

Brent nodded his head in sympathy, like he understood and commiserated. Miles wished he wouldn't do that.

"LoDown, they call that area," Miles said. "When I was a young ADA I used to have to go down there every now and then on investigations, usually something that started out as petty street crime and escalated into something bigger. I'm pretty familiar with the area, and I doubt it's changed much. It was basically Shitsville then, and it's basically Shitsville now. No gentrification, no yuppies moving in and taking over. There's all kinds of empty buildings and hidden corners to hide in. You could probably hide an elephant there for years without anyone knowing about it. I'd like to see the bureau go back down there again and snoop around. See if they can turn up anything. Go back through that warehouse with a fine-tooth comb. Visit that alley again. Smash it all up with wrecking balls and jackhammers if need be."

"It'll be a tough sell, Senator. The budget folks seem pretty convinced that enough resources have already been put into finding Salvatore Morino, and that it's time to move on. Sending more agents back to snoop around might rankle some people. The current focus is on narcotics and gang-related crime. The war on organized crime has been a success—with the exception of not finding Salvatore Morino, of course. Most everyone just wants to move on from Morino. Plus, well..."

"Well what?" Miles said.

Brent cleared his throat. He scratched his hair.

"A lot of the folks on Capitol Hill think this is a...personal thing with you, Senator," Brent said. "The Salvatore Morino case. They just don't see him as that important anymore. I doubt you'll get much support."

Miles leaned back in his chair again. He put his hands behind his head and blew the air out of his mouth.

"Jesus, the crap you have to put up with in this job," he said. "When I was a DA I had more power and control than I do as a United States senator. At least back then I was the one in charge. I called the shots. But here? You have to get at least a dozen other people to nod their heads before you can even take the first step. Does that sound like fun to you?"

"No, Senator. Not at all."

Miles tapped his fingers on his desk. "A personal thing with me, huh? That's what they say?"

"Yes."

"If it were personal I'd just go after Morino myself. I wouldn't need to rally support from my esteemed colleagues in the United States goddamn senate. I'd just hunt down the fat bastard on my own watch."

Brent smiled the kind of smile that wasn't a smile at all.

"Relax, Brent," Miles said. "I'm just thinking out loud here. No need to worry that I'm going to go vigilante."

"Yes, Senator."

Miles leaned forward. He put his elbows on the desk and his face in his hands. He suddenly had a headache. He needed an aspirin. He needed a decent lunch. He needed a vacation. He needed to see Sal Morino behind bars so he could visit him in prison and tell him to fuck off. He needed Brent to once, just once, call him by his damn name.

"Brent?" Miles said.

"Yes, Senator?"

"Stop calling me 'Senator' all the time. My name is Miles. OK?"

"Yes, Sen....Yes."

***

After the lunch was over and Brent had gone on his way, Miles looked back over the files again. He was hoping maybe he'd read things wrong, that there was something he'd missed about the investigation. But no, he hadn't missed anything. Fat Sal Morino was still at large. The FBI was no closer to finding him now than they were when they let him slip away.

It was depressing and annoying—not least because Miles knew the FBI was probably right. There was no percentage in continuing to chase Fat Sal Morino around. So what if he got away? In the grand scheme of organized crime at the dawn of the new millennium, he wasn't really that big a deal anymore, anyway. Russian and Latino syndicates were much more dangerous. So were anti-government wackos and global jihadists.

Miles could understand, intellectually, why the FBI didn't want to expend any more energy on Salvatore Morino. But it pissed him off, nonetheless. Maybe it *was* personal with Miles, like everyone seemed to think. But it wasn't exactly what they thought. Did Miles still blame

Morino's crew for his cousin Slider's death all those years ago? Of course. But his cousin, God rest his soul, was a royal fuckup who probably had it coming.

No, what really bothered Miles was the way Morino always seemed to slither out of the long arm of the law whenever that arm seemed to have him trapped in a corner. It happened when Miles was an assistant district attorney. It happened when he was DA. It was happening now. Was Miles' ego bruised? Hell yes it was! Damn right it was! You'd better believe it was! Miles was tired of being outflanked by Salvatore Morino, and he was going to do something about it.

Miles' adrenaline kicked in just thinking about it. Oh, how he missed being a district attorney—the thrill of the hunt, the high that came from tracking down a bad guy and slamming down the trap. The US Senate, for all of its perks, was a pretty tedious place. You spent hours upon hours in long, drawn-out committee meetings that didn't seem to get anywhere, or poring over legislation that made your eyes glaze over, or glad-handing an endless parade of pricks and hucksters Miles wouldn't spend two minutes with in any other capacity. He's not even sure why he ran for the senate in the first place. Probably because people talked him into it and his ego decided he was right for the job. It was a fluke that he'd even won. He didn't expect to win. But he got caught up in a wave that carried a lot of people in his party to victory.

Well, screw it. He didn't have to be a senator all the time.

He reached for his personal cell phone and punched in a number. It belonged to Luis Baez, a former NYPD detective who used to be Miles' favorite investigator back when he was DA. On the second ring Luis' voice answered.

"*Como estas, muchacho?*" Miles said.

"Top o' the mornin', boyo," Luis replied. "How's life?"

"The usual misery," Miles replied. "You got plans this afternoon, around four-ish or so?"

"Is this Senator McLaughlin calling, or my old pal Miles?"

"Both."

"I guess I could juggle my schedule for Miles. What's on your mind?"

"Let's discuss it over beers, somewhere quiet and inconspicuous," Miles said. "You pick the place and get back to me."

"Oh Christ," Luis said. "I know that voice of yours. What are you getting me into?"

"Something that could pay off handsomely for you."

"Oh Christ," Luis said.

Chapter 8

Elrod's bowels sent him an urgent message as he and Jade made their way through the park and toward the Northpark Village Hotel. His bowels were telling him it was time for an evacuation, posthaste. This was standard operating procedure during the morning hours, or at least what constituted morning hours for homeless people who didn't keep regular time. Elrod found himself approaching red alert.

He stopped and took a look around. Colve Park had two public restrooms. One was up a small hill not far from where he and Jade were.

"Why are you stopping?" Jade asked.

"The call of nature," Elrod replied.

"What's that mean?"

"It means I have to use the bathroom."

"So go in those trees over there and let's move along."

"It's not that kind of bathroom visit."

"Can't it wait for the hotel? There's a bathroom in the lobby."

"No," Elrod said, moaning. "It can't. There's a

bathroom right up that path there. I'll use it."

"If you think you can slip away from me by..."

But Elrod had already moved on, walking at a pace brisk enough to get him to salvation quickly but not so fast that he'd start the process before he reached the can. You have to moderate your speed just right, trick the bowels into thinking that you're not rushing to an appointment you'll never reach, which would set off panic alarms. Elrod was an old hand at this kind of thing, an expert. In his circumstances, you either become an expert at it or you soil yourself daily. So he walked quickly but not too quickly toward the bathroom, Jade hot on his heels.

***

Not too far away, behind a big oak tree, Dmitri Zverev watched the homeless bum veer off course and make his way up a hill toward the bathroom. The bum looked like he was in a hurry. He walked at a quick pace, bent over. This was the look of a man in need of a toilet, in need of a shit. If so, it was a lucky break for Dmitri. The bum would walk into the bathroom, which was probably empty this time of day. Empty bathrooms provided cover. They made it easy for Dmitri to approach the homeless bum in the bathroom stall, bash him on the head with his iron pipe, and take his coat.

There was something special about that coat, and Dmitri was going to find out what it was. Dmitri had been hired a couple months ago to find the same type of coat on another homeless bum. A little Asian scientist had hired him. It was easy money, the scientist said. Just follow the homeless bum out of the alley, wait until the bum was alone somewhere, grab the coat, do whatever you want to the homeless bum, and take the coat back to the little scientist. Easy, easy money.

Dmitri was told it was a one-time job. Get the coat, get paid, thank you for your time. Dmitri began to wonder: What was so important about the coat? Why pay so much money to retrieve a coat from a homeless bum? He decided to return to LoDown, hang around, investigate further. One day he saw another homeless bum wearing the same type of coat. Dmitri followed the bum. He saw the bum step into an old, abandoned building. He saw another, bigger man follow the bum inside the building. He saw the bigger man come back out a few minutes later with the coat. The homeless bum never came back out again.

And now here was yet another homeless bum wearing the same type of coat. This bum had not been followed—except by Dmitri. Dmitri followed him from LoDown to the store, then up here to the park. Dmitri kept looking for places to grab the bum and the coat, but there were always too many people around, too many open spaces. But now it looked like the bum was heading for an isolated bathroom in a big park. A lucky break. Dmitri would wait for the bum to enter the bathroom stall and have his shit. Then he would wait for the homeless bum to come off of the seat. Then he would bash the homeless bum on the head with his metal pipe and grab the coat.

A woman followed the bum up the hilly path. Dmitri did not know who the woman was. She was very pretty, very well dressed. What business did she have with this homeless bum? Was she a government worker, there to help the downtrodden? Probably not. She was too well dressed for a government worker. Maybe this pretty woman was the homeless bum's sister, there to put him back on the path to respectability. Dmitri did not care who she was. If she tried to interfere, he would bash her on the head, too.

He watched the homeless bum creep his way to the bathroom, bent over, trying to keep the shit inside himself. Dmitri almost laughed. It was funny, seeing the look of desperation on the homeless bum's face. It was also funny watching him exchange angry words with the pretty woman. Americans are always arguing, always complaining. They live in the lap of luxury, Americans. The world at their fingertips. But still always complaining.

Dmitri waited for a couple of minutes, then staggered up to the bathroom himself, the way a homeless bum would. He approached the pretty woman and asked if she had spare change. He used his best American homeless bum voice. He wanted her to think he was just another bum looking for another handout. She would not suspect him of having other things in mind. She ignored him and turned away. He God blessed her and staggered into the bathroom, easing the iron pipe out of his pocket when he got inside.

Chapter 9

Fat Sal stared at Lionel Bunt for a moment and tried to digest what he just heard. Finally he said, "What do you mean you're the answer to my problems?"

"Stony Boy," Lionel said. "You remember the name, right?"

"What about it?"

"Aren't you curious how I know the name?"

"Not really."

Fat Sal sat back down on the metal chair in the rear of the pizzeria. He took a couple of deep breaths, tried to rake in air. Slapping Lionel around had taken the wind out of him.

"Cute dog, Stony Boy," Lionel said, still gripping the bottle of pepper spray. "A little odd-looking, with the two spots on his chest. One almost reddish, one kind of orange. Never saw that before. He loved to jump up in the air, that dog."

"How would you know that?"

"I saw him. I went there a couple weeks ago, through the time portal. Back to your old neighborhood. Back to

1949. I walked down to your old apartment building. Right next to the butcher shop where that nice man Mr. Rionelli sang opera while cutting meat. There's a stoop on the other side with *Geno Wuz Here* spray-painted on one of the steps."

Lionel slowly eased the spray bottle down.

"I learned about your childhood on the internet," he said. "There's quite a lot of news on you, as you well know, and a lot of information about your past: the apartment where you grew up, your old neighborhood. Some of the articles have pictures of you as a young boy, with your family. Grainy black-and-whites. One showed you holding a cute little dog with two spots on his chest."

Fat Sal shifted in his seat.

"You weren't even born yet in 1949, so of course I didn't see you," Lionel continued. "But I saw your mother. She was walking a dog around the neighborhood. She took him to a park. She called him Stony Boy. Quite an animal, full of energy and pep, could really spring up in the air. It was the same dog I saw in that photo on the internet."

Fat Sal rose from his chair and moved toward Lionel. Lionel stepped back quickly and whipped something out of his pants pocket. It was a digital camera, the kind that lets you view photos on the display. He shoved the display in Fat Sal's face. It showed a picture of a dog in a park. A mutt with two spots on his chest, one almost red and one kind of orange. Stony Boy. In living color.

"That photo was taken with 1990s technology," Lionel said. "Look how rich and vibrant the color is. There were no photos like that taken when Stony Boy was alive. I took it just a couple weeks ago, with a camera that wasn't even invented until decades after Stony Boy died."

Fat Sal thought it over. It had to be a trick, some kind of photoshop wizardry. Wasn't that what they called it? Photoshop? His son used to talk about that—photoshop. Let's you do all kinds of tricks.

He looked at the photo again. The image was crisp and clear. The only other photos of Stony Boy were grainy and dark.

Lionel also knew things about Fat Sal's old neighborhood that you could only know if you were there. Like Mr. Rionelli singing opera. Who could know that? The guy's been dead for thirty-five years, and he didn't leave any family behind. Never married. Never seen with a woman. Everyone assumed he was a fag. And the stoop with *Geno Wuz Here* spray-painted on it. Geno Cavella was a neighborhood kid who spray-painted that stoop before he left for World War II. He landed at Normandy, got off the boat, and immediately got blown in a dozen different pieces. Somewhere in France there's a grave with his name on it. Nobody had the heart to cover up the spray paint. It stayed there for fifteen years before the building was finally torn down. Who in 1999 could know about it?

"Stony Boy," Lionel said. "That's your dog."

Fat Sal stared at the photo on the digital display. Stony Boy. His dog.

***

Stony Boy was three years old when Fat Sal was born. He was the family dog, at least until Sal grew old enough to take care of him. After that, he became Sal's dog. They did everything together, Sal and Stony Boy. They ate together. They slept together. They went to the park and played ball together. Sal would pretend he was Yogi Berra banging fastballs into the bleachers. He'd toss the ball up in the air and give a mighty swing, connect, and knock it over a small fence that surrounded the ball field. Stony Boy would fetch the ball and bring it back. The process would repeat itself over and over, for hours.

They were inseparable, Sal and Stony Boy. Best friends, pals for life.

One morning Sal told Stony Boy it was time to wake up, but Stony Boy didn't move. Sal poked him, gave him a gentle push. He yanked Stony Boy's tail. He punched Stony Boy, gently. He punched Stony Boy again, not so gently. He commanded Stony Boy to wake up. But Stony Boy wouldn't wake up.

Wake up, Stony Boy. Wake up, kid. Wake up, wake up!

Sal picked Stony Boy up off the mattress and shook him from side to side. He slapped Stony Boy once, twice, three times. Stony Boy didn't move. His body was limp, his eyes dull and unfocused. Something was wrong, terribly wrong. Sal began to cry. He ordered Stony Boy to wake up. He kicked the walls. He fell to the floor and beat it with his fists. He cried and wailed and wailed some more. His mother came hustling in from the bathroom. She picked Sal up, asked him, "Whattsa matta, Salvatore, whattsa matta?" She saw Stony Boy lying limp on the floor. She bent down and looked at him.

She knew whattsa matta.

Sal cried the day away. He cried at breakfast, and then at lunch. He cried when the garbage man came to gather Stony Boy up and haul him away because there was no place to bury a dead animal on this block. He cried when his Pop got home from work, and he cried when his Pop beat the hell out of him for blubbering like a baby over a goddamn dog.

"Don't be such a *fascina!*" his Pop snapped. "No son of mine cries like a little girl."

Sal was eight years old at the time. He felt heartsick, then betrayed. How could Stony Boy die like that? He tried to erase it from his memory. He never talked about Stony Boy from that moment on, to anyone. He burned the drawings of Stony Boy he kept in his bedroom chest. He tossed the food bowl and water bowl into the trash. He tossed the dog collar out the window.

Sal never got another dog. He never wanted to be around another dog. He grew to hate dogs.

He found other ways to pass the time—and there was a lot of time to pass. Sal's parents both worked. His grandparents spent most of their time staring into space, mumbling in Italian. His siblings were all older and off doing their own thing. Young Sal hit the streets, learned things. How to fight. How to steal. How to hustle.

Sal was good at stealing, good at fighting, good at crime. One day after snatching a purse and bolting away he caught the attention of an older guy who ran one of the street gangs. The guy chased Sal down for a couple of blocks and then tackled him. Sal tried to fight him off but the guy had him pinned to the ground.

"Settle down, kid," the guy said. "You got balls; I give you that. But you gotta learn the rules. See, this is my territory. So half your profits go to me."

The guy grabbed the purse away from Sal and rummaged through it. He found a billfold with twenty-three dollars in it. He kept ten for himself and gave Fat Sal thirteen.

"Here, you take the bigger cut," the guy said. "Consider it a down payment on future work."

"Fuck you," Sal said.

The guy slapped Sal.

"Fuck you again," Sal said.

The guy laughed. "I love you already, kid."

Sal went to work for the street crews. They taught him tricks of the trade. How to break into stores and steal cars. How to crack a guy's neck or bash his nose to the back of his brain. He moved up the ranks. Crime became a full-time job, and school got in the way. He dropped out on his sixteenth birthday. His Pop kicked him out of the house, called him a cheap hoodlum. Sal didn't give a shit. His Pop slung crates sixty hours a week for barely enough money to scratch by on. Sal could make more money in a week hustling out on the streets than his Pop made in three months.

At seventeen-years-old Sal stole a delivery truck filled with booze while the delivery driver was inside the liquor store taking a piss. Sal spotted the keys in the ignition, cranked it up and went peeling down the street, muscling past other cars, cutting corners, and zipping through red lights until he made it to a warehouse in Brooklyn. He and two others unloaded everything in less than twenty minutes—cases and cases of booze, worth a nice piece of change on the black market. Sal was rewarded with a wad of cash and a promotion to collections, muscle work. Shaking down store owners, running down gamblers who were behind on their payments. He was good at it— young, strong, and mean.

Most of the men Sal called on paid up right away, but not all. One brave soul tried to test Sal; told him he was only going to pay the bookie directly, not some teenage errand boy. Sal grabbed the guy's neck with his left hand and slammed him against the wall. He popped a straight right into the guy's face, sending his nose in three different directions and his body to the floor. He picked the guy up with one hand and dragged him up the stairs. When they got to the top floor Sal opened the elevator doors with his hands. He picked the guy up by his collar and dangled him over the open elevator shaft. It was a steep drop, maybe ten or eleven floors.

"Long way down, right?" Sal said. "If you fell your head would splatter like a melon. Or, I could push the button and wait for the elevator to come up and maybe chop your head off."

The guy moaned.

"You gonna pay the money?" Sal said.

"Yeah, yeah," the guy said.

"You gonna pay?"

"Yes, hell yes!"

The guy paid—double the amount owed. Half for the bookie. Half for Sal.

Well, it was all a long time ago. Sal graduated to running his own crews and then heading up his own outfit. He didn't get the nickname "Fat Sal" until much later, when his appetite, aging body, and increasingly comfortable lifestyle turned his once steely muscle to flab. The tabloids came up with the name "Fat Sal" Morino, and it stuck. He didn't like it, but what are you gonna do? There were worse problems to have. He'd made a lot of money. He knew a lot of people—and a lot of people knew him.

But through all the years, and all the people, he'd never

told anyone about Stony Boy. Not a single person.

So how could this scientist know about him?

"That's your dog," Lionel said. "You can go back and see him if you like. Back fifty years, to 1949. You can set up your own operation there, use the skills that made you a rich man. I'm sure they'll translate well enough to 1949. You could make a good deal of money—something you're constrained from doing in 1999, if what I read is accurate."

Fat Sal didn't believe in time travel. But then, what did he really know about it? You could fill half the continent with the things Fat Sal didn't know. Algebra. Geography. Literature. How to use a socket wrench. How to surf the internet. For all he knew there was a team of spaz scientists up at Nerd U. right now, this very minute, building a dork ship that traveled through time.

"I could make a good deal of money, could I?" Fat Sal said. "You come in here and tell me you're the answer to my problems. Now all of a sudden the conversation turns to money. Tell me, why you so interested in sending me back in time to make a good deal of money?"

"Because part of that money will go to me," Lionel said. "In fact, most of it will go to me. In return, you're tucked safely away in the past."

Fat Sal reached into his shirt pocket. He pulled out a cigar and torched it. He blew the smoke into Lionel's face. Fat Sal had dealt with people like this most of his life. Everybody had an angle; everybody had a hustle.

"Let's say you can actually do this," Fat Sal said. "Why would I want to get stuck in 1949 just so you can get rich?"

"Once I'm paid off, you can travel out of 1949," Lionel said. "Into the future, to any year you want. When you enter the portal from this side you can only go back fifty years. But when you enter the portal from the other side, in 1949, you can move forward to the year of your choosing. Don't ask me why. It's just a quirk of the system. You can return to any year you want. You know, just in case there's something you'd like to do to alter history or whatnot."

This last part caught Fat Sal's attention—"to alter history or whatnot." There's something he'd like to do to alter history, alright. He'd like to jam Miles McLaughlin's head under the subway.

He snatched the camera out of Lionel's hand. He looked at the image again. Stony Boy, in living color. It was impossible. But there it was, plain as day.

"Time travel," Fat Sal said. "You expect me to believe in time travel."

Lionel shook his head.

"I expect you to believe in science. In evidence," he said.

"And the science tells you I can come back to any year I want, right?" Fat Sal said. "To 1989, or 1993, or 2525, or 1977."

Lionel nodded. "As long as I'm there to help you get to the right place."

Fat Sal's brain began clicking. If all this was real, he didn't have to return to 1999, where he was Public Enemy Number One. He could come back earlier, before everything went to hell. Before Miles McLaughlin was a senator, or even a district attorney. Fat Sal could come back to when Miles McLaughlin was nobody, nothing— when it would be easy enough to kill him without anyone important noticing. He could ensure Miles McLaughlin never became a thorn in Fat Sal's side. It would solve all his problems.

"So how much is this gonna cost me?" Fat Sal said. "What's your take?"

"Two million dollars," Lionel said. "I'd really like more, but I'm a reasonable man. I certainly can't expect you to make the same haul in 1949 that you could make in the 1990s."

"Two million," Fat Sal said.

Lionel nodded.

Fat Sal laughed.

"You're a crazy man. *Pazzo*," he said. He shook his head. "Two million."

"It might take less time than you imagine," Lionel said.

"And how is that?" Fat Sal said. "You're talking about 1949. That's probably a big piece of money for 1949. I don't even know anyone there. Nobody knows me. You can't just move in and take over."

Cigar smoke drifted into Lionel's face. He gently waved it away.

"We ran into some luck on that end," Lionel said. "As fate would have it, one of the leaders of a gambling operation in 1949 was recently found with a couple dozen holes in his chest. So there's a job opening, as it were. My understanding is that you have a certain flair for this kind of enterprise."

Fat Sal couldn't argue the point. He was the best there was at moving in on weak operations and consolidating them into his own personal kingdom. And gambling was one of his specialties.

"Yeah, I'm good at it," he boasted. "But I can't pull it off alone. I need some kind of connection there."

"Again, luck is on your side," Lionel said. "I've already

made a contact. The portal leads into a nightclub on the other side, in 1949. It's called the Hideaway. It must have been located beside the alley fifty years ago. It was a popular place in its day. Fancy, attracted all kinds of well-dressed people. My contact is the maître d' at the nightclub. His name is Douglas. He knows a lot of people in your line of work. He can put you in touch with the right connections and make it easy for you to move right in on the action. There's a lot of gambling business in 1949—and a lot of ways to make money. Douglas will vouch for you to the other organizations. Nobody will question you as long as Douglas does your bidding."

"This Douglas. You told him you were from the future? And he didn't get a little suspicious?"

"I gave him one thousand dollars just to speak with me. The same as I did with you. It's a lot of money in 1949. He didn't need much convincing after that."

Fat Sal thought it over. He had the location to work from. He had the connection. He had an opening into a gambling operation. He'd be far away from his current problems.

"OK, so how do we get the money back and forth?" Fat Sal asked. "Between 1949 and 1999?"

"I've given that a lot of thought," Lionel said. "We need couriers who aren't aware of what's going on. We don't want a lot of people in on this. Just you, me, and Douglas. Douglas can't carry the money back and forth because he's needed in 1949. You won't want to do it because you'll be a famous fugitive in 1999. I don't want to do it because if I somehow get stuck in 1949, then we're all stuck there."

"Who's gonna do it, then? Who are these couriers?"

Lionel loaded more photos onto the camera display. He

showed them to Fat Sal. They were pictures of ragged folks lying on sidewalks, leaning against street signs, or sleeping on park benches. Street people down on their luck—if they ever had any.

"These are homeless people," Lionel said. "Alcoholics, drug abusers, bums. Dozens of them live in LoDown, where the alley portal is located. They can be our couriers. We'll send them back and forth. They'll waltz right into the nightclub in 1949 and get the royal treatment. A seat at the bar, cheap drinks. They'll think they've died and gone to heaven. We'll send them there to get the money, then send them back here to deliver the money to me. It should be easy enough to get the potion into them on this side. I'll just add it to bottles of alcohol, malt liquor. Once they drink the malt liquor, they drink the potion along with it."

"We give a bunch of homeless drunks the money? And you believe they'll deliver it back to you?"

Lionel had worked this out, too. There was no reason the couriers should know about the money. It could be placed where they'd never find it, inside large, bulky coats with hidden pockets. Lionel would place the coats in strategic locations in 1999, near the alley portal. On stoop rails or in trash cans. Places where they're easy to spot, and where people will just assume they were discarded or simply forgotten. Secondhand coats, but in decent condition. Vagrants love coats, Lionel told Fat Sal. They also love alleys. Lionel would keep an eye out for the lucky bums who grabbed the lucky coats.

"We'll sew padded pockets beneath the interior lining," Lionel said. "When the couriers show up at the Hideaway, Douglas will check their coats. That's when he'll sew the money inside. They'll never even know the money is there."

Fat Sal took another puff of his cigar. "So why not just send bums from 1949 with the money and save the round-trip ticket?"

It was a good question, and something Lionel had considered. But he decided against it. He didn't want people from 1949 suddenly dropping into a world fifty years in the future—a strange, unknown, and entirely unfamiliar place they would never have conceived of on their own. They might start panicking, creating a scene. This would draw too much attention to the alley, he told Fat Sal. The alley needed to be kept as anonymous as possible.

"You can see why we prefer present-day couriers," Lionel said. "Going back in time is easier on the brain than moving forward."

"How much money do you think you can get into a hidden coat pocket?" Fat Sal asked. "I mean, two million bucks, you're talking a pretty big wad here. It'll take a lot of trips back and forth."

"Not necessarily," Lionel replied. "We'll use big bills, the kind they used to have back in 1949. Thousand-dollar bills, five-thousand-dollar bills. They even had ten-thousand-dollar bills."

"Those bills aren't even printed anymore," Fat Sal said. "How are you going to cash them in 1999?"

"Let me worry about that. Banks still offer credit for older currencies before taking them out of circulation. You just worry about making the money and sending it my way."

Fat Sal thought it over. Sending all that money back with homeless bums? Risky, risky.

"How you gonna make sure these couriers of yours get the money to the right place when they're back in 1999?" he said. "What makes you think they'll just hand the coats over?"

"We'll have someone waiting for the couriers when they return. Assistants of mine, good with their fists."

"And what, the assistant grabs the coat in the alley and waltzes off?" Fat Sal said.

"Not in the alley. Things might get rough. Again, we don't want to draw too much attention to that alley. I'll have my assistant follow the couriers when they leave the alley. Somewhere safer to recover the coat."

"Okay, so what's to prevent your assistant from running off with the money?"

"He won't know about the money. Just the coat."

"He won't get curious about why you're going to all this trouble for a coat?" Fat Sal asked.

"He won't care as long as I pay him well enough," Lionel answered. "We're not talking about the brightest minds here."

Fat Sal thought it over some more. There were still loose ends, gaps to fill.

"How you gonna get the potion into the malt liquor bottles?" he said. "And how you gonna make sure these couriers of yours even drink it?"

Lionel had that all worked out. He'd purchase a few cases of cheap malt liquor. He'd open the bottles, pour part of the malt liquor into new bottles, pour some of the potion in along with it, and seal it back up nice and tight. The new bottles would carry their own labels to distinguish them from the others. Lionel would call the brand something striking: Witchcraft, Black Magic, Voodoo. Names that draw attention. He'd place coupons for free malt liquor in the coats he left lying around. He'd pay off store owners to put the bottles on their shelves and honor the coupons. The kinds of store owners who didn't care as long as the money was good.

"Okay, but then these drunks have to make it down to the right alley," Fat Sal said. "There's lots of alleys down there. I don't like the odds of them just waltzing into the one alley where this, whatchacallit, this portal is."

"There are ways to get them to the right alley," Lionel said. "If they don't make it on their own, we'll pay someone to lead them down there when they're nice and drunk and don't care where they go. A prostitute, a vagrant, a drug addict in need of a fix. Someone promising them sexual favors, or just a nice place to sleep off the booze. It won't be a problem."

Fat Sal had to admit, it was a pretty good plan. Insane, yes. But thorough. Well thought out.

"What happens to these homeless guys after you grab the coats?" Fat Sal said. "They might be half out of their minds, but they'll know they've been traveling through time. They might freak out on the other side, or get back here and tell everyone about it."

"Again, let me worry about that. We'll keep them calm in 1949. When they return to 1999, and my assistants grab their coats, who knows what happens to the couriers? Maybe we'll fix it so they never tell anyone anything, ever again."

Fat Sal sat back down again. He looked at Lionel. He puffed on his cigar. He thought it over some more. It was crazy, yes. But brilliant in its own way.

And probably his only shot at escaping his current

problems.

"Okay," Fat Sal said. "When do we get moving on this?"

***

The memory of that first meeting with Lionel Bunt was a bittersweet one for Fat Sal. Yes, the scientist's plan worked. He gave Fat Sal the potion, Fat Sal drank it, and Fat Sal disappeared into 1949 months ago, well shed of his problems fifty years in the future. He got introduced to the right people in 1949 and quickly built a nice business. He started earning money and sending it via Bum Express to little Lionel in 1999. That part worked out fine.

The part he wasn't crazy about was being stuck in 1949, away from his world, away from the life he used to know. He picked up his cigar and puffed on it. He rubbed his eyes. He'd been in deep thought, recounting what had happened with Lionel. But now he snapped back into reality, back to the here and now, back to the basement office at the Hideaway nightclub. He watched Douglas return from upstairs and take a seat.

"Nineteen forty-nine," Fat Sal grumbled. "I ain't even been born yet. You ever think about that? I won't be born for two more years."

He looked at the bare walls and cheap furniture and shook his head.

"You know, people from my era actually look back on this period with nostalgia," he said. "Someplace they'd like to go back to, if only they could. I'd love to set them straight."

"It can't be that bad here," Douglas said.

"It can, and it is," Fat Sal said. "There's no air conditioning. The food is bland and overcooked. The TVs only get a couple of channels, and they keep blinking in and out. The rooms are too small. You know I have a 5,000-square-foot house in 1999? Sitting on two acres? With a 1,000-square-foot marble patio and an Olympic-sized swimming pool? Try finding a house like that here in 1949. You gotta be Rockefeller, right? I had five bathrooms in my house. You hear that? Five. Five! *Five, five five!* Now I live in a three-room apartment with one crapper and no A/C, all because I gotta send two million bucks back to Dr. Sushi in 1999."

Fat Sal got up from his chair. He circled the desk. He circled it again. Sweat formed on his forehead. He shoved an antacid into his mouth. He shoved himself back down into the chair. He looked at Douglas.

"Tell me about this horn player again. Red," Fat Sal said. "You say you found him talking to the homeless guy? Elrod?"

Douglas nodded. "Before the show. I don't know what they were talking about. I was returning from the cloakroom when I saw them chatting by the bar. When I stepped up, things suddenly got very hush-hush."

"I don't like the sound of that."

"It could be nothing."

"Or it could be something. I don't trust that guy. You keeping an eye on him?"

"We keep an eye on everyone," Douglas said. "Red is the most predictable of the lot. He leaves here after the show, goes to have a bite to eat, then goes home. No after-hours clubs, no catting around, no reefer or narcotics. He practices his saxophone for a couple hours, then the lights go out. He wakes up and practices some more. He's not like most jazz musicians, who spend most of their free time either whoring around or getting hopped up."

"That's why I don't trust him," Red said. "A musician who lives a clean, normal life? There's something wrong with that."

"We'll continue to monitor the situation."

"Yeah, do that. Continue to monitor the situation."

Fat Sal shook his head.

"I gotta be going," he said. "This place depresses me. My apartment depresses me, too, but at least I can lie down there. Call me if you need anything. Just don't need anything."

Fat Sal was already out the door before Douglas could reply.

***

After Fat Sal left, Douglas hung around a few more minutes to double-check everything. Most of the work had already been done by the staff the night before, and Douglas had checked each workstation before the employees clocked out. He knew everything was in good order. Still, he enjoyed these few quiet moments. He made sure the bar was properly stocked, the kitchen was clean, all of the dishes and pots were washed, the dining room tables were set, and the inventory was all accounted for.

Out of the corner of his eye, Douglas spotted a rodent scampering along the wall toward the kitchen. Another rodent. Maybe a large mouse or a small rat. He'd have to call the rodent control people again. There were so many rodents in this city.

Douglas thought about testing his skills on the animal, seeing if he still had the expertise he'd honed all those years ago on hunts with his uncle and the other tribal elders. Douglas became a skilled hunter as a child, second to none. He'd willed himself to become the best of all the boys in his village. He felt he had to be, given his circumstances. He developed the sharpest set of eyes, the quickest hands, the keenest ears and instincts.

Douglas tried not to think about those bygone days too often. But every now and then they came creeping back into his consciousness. Boyhood was no magical place for Douglas. He'd learned early on in life just how much he was worth to those he grew up around. The lesson was delivered when he was six years old, on a hike with his uncle in the deep woods. They were ostensibly there to check the traps set out by tribesmen to snare panthers, bears, and other predators that feasted on game animals. During a stop at the creek, Douglas reached down to fill his wooden jug with water when his uncle grabbed him by the back of the neck and plunged his face to within an inch of the water's surface.

"Look at that reflection in the water, boy," his uncle snarled. "It's not the face of your friends, is it? No, it's a pale, bloodless face, drained of all spirit and soul. You ever wonder why you look so different from the rest? Why your skin is pale, and your eyes are green? You ever wonder why no tribesman claims you as his own? It's because your blood flows with the stink of the white man. I can smell it from here. I can smell it from miles away. It fouls the air. You never knew your father, and you never will. Nobody knows your father's name. Nobody knows where he is, or where he came from. He arrived in the village one day, did what he came to do with the woman he wanted to do it with, and left. Your birth was no occasion for joy. Some of us wanted to toss you into the woods, let the wolves find you. Your mother pleaded for mercy. I could plunge your head into the water right now and drown you in the time it takes an eagle to snatch a rabbit. Don't think I don't want to, either. Don't think anyone would miss you—except your mother. This is the curse of mothers. They are blinded by love."

His uncle dunked Douglas' head into the cold water, kept it there for a few seconds, then yanked it back out. He twisted Douglas' face around and pulled his head up so they were eye to eye.

"The only value you will ever have here is what you can provide to the tribe," his uncle said. "You'll be trained as a hunter, like the other boys. If you bring dishonor through laziness or ineptitude, you and I will return to this creek. But only I will return to the village."

Douglas couldn't remember his initial reaction that day. He assumed it was some mixture of fear and confusion, anger and shame. Looking back on it now, though, Douglas felt he'd been given the greatest gift any boy could receive: the gift of clarity. It was the day he learned exactly where he stood in the world, and what he'd have to do to survive it. He would never fit in. He would never be accepted. He would have to be twice as good as the others to get half the reward. He would have to make do with himself, and himself only.

From that point forward Douglas dedicated himself to being a great hunter, the greatest hunter. He worked tirelessly, ceaselessly, obsessively. He followed the instructions of his elders with a blind intensity that surprised even them. He watched and studied, aping the way they scouted, stalked, and killed their prey. The other boys would tease Douglas, make fun of his green eyes and peach skin, call him names. He ignored them and focused on the job at hand. On hunting expeditions he kept to himself, on the flank, stalking prey and staying two steps ahead of the others. Douglas was never liked in his village. But he had never brought dishonor to himself or his mother.

At fourteen, Douglas carved his mother a wooden bowl. One night, very late, he left it on the tiny table in their tiny home. He walked over to his mother, who was asleep on her blanket. He bent down and kissed her gently on the cheek, then walked outside. He passed the other homes of his village, taking care to avoid notice, as if on a hunt. He tamped down the urge to visit his uncle's hut and slice his throat from ear to ear. Instead, Douglas walked on through the woods and toward the dirt road that would take him far away from his village. He would never return.

Douglas eventually landed in this fat, bright city, with its towers, tenements, and grime. He adopted a new name and identity, learned new skills, new ways of speaking, new customs. But deep down he still considered himself a hunter. A great hunter. The greatest hunter. The prey was different in this city than the prey in the woods. But it was still prey. The beasts looked different, but they were still beasts, primitive and cruel. Nobody was better at cornering prey than Douglas. And when he cornered the prey, it stayed cornered.

But what about now, in this nightclub, all these years later? Was Douglas still agile enough to corner the little rodent, or quick enough to grab it while it was making up its little mind up what to do next? Did Douglas still have it in him to squash the rodent's little neck with his bare hands? Or chomp its little head off with his bare teeth?

Probably not. Time has a way of softening you, taking the edge off. Time passed so quickly. Time was so hard to contain.

Douglas decided to let the animal go. He wanted to enjoy the peace and quiet of the Hideaway, not chase a rodent around.

These moments gave Douglas time for reflection, and he often reflected on the good fortune that had come his way when Dr. Lionel Bunt suddenly appeared from the future and laid out his plans to make them both a great deal of money.

Douglas didn't question the magical science behind Dr. Bunt's discovery, or the seeming impossibility of time travel. He took Dr. Bunt at his word the moment he shared his story. It wasn't even that surprising to Douglas. He understood, better than most, that the wonders of the universe were endless and incalculable. He had seen these wonders firsthand—had, in fact, experienced them in ways most humans could not even imagine. Time travel was no great revelation to Douglas. It was no more mysterious or interesting than the price of ham or the shape of a subway token.

Of greater interest was the profit that could be derived from time travel. That was the real magic behind it, the real revelation.

Douglas wondered why Fat Sal didn't feel the same way. Fat Sal was tucked safely away in 1949, far from the problems that plagued him in his former life. Why not sit back and enjoy it?

But Fat Sal couldn't enjoy it. Because of arrogance. And greed.

Dr. Bunt had told Douglas about how Fat Sal grew his old empire block by block, neighborhood by neighborhood, borough by borough, corpse by corpse. Douglas was fascinated by Fat Sal's insatiable appetite for more money and more power. It never ceased to amaze him how hard it was for people like Fat Sal to reach a sensible stopping point. You'd think a few million dollars would be enough. But it never was. When you had one million you wanted two million. When you had two, you wanted four. On and on it went.

Greed, greed.

Fat Sal's inflated opinion of himself was equally mystifying—this notion that he was too smart to ever get taken down. Deep down, Fat Sal must have thought he was indestructible. Why else would he ignore the fact that few career criminals ever make it through to a comfortable retirement in their golden years?

Arrogance, arrogance.

Well, arrogance wasn't much use to Fat Sal in 1949. He knew he couldn't afford to ruffle too many feathers. He needed to go along with the program and do as he was told if he ever expected to get out of here. He needed to keep a low profile to avoid making one of a million mistakes that could tell someone he wasn't from this time or place. He might arouse suspicion—and suspicion can get you hurt in Fat Sal's line of work.

To his credit, Fat Sal had stuck to the plan and done well. He'd only been in 1949 for a few months, but he'd already raked in large sums of money. He was a cunning criminal, good at his trade. He just wasn't as good as he liked to believe.

Fat Sal could not have achieved such success without help—specifically, Douglas' help. Douglas used his connections in the criminal underworld to iron out problems when they needed ironing out. He smoothed things over when Fat Sal ventured into enterprises where he didn't belong. He ignored Fat Sal's instructions when those instructions created too many headaches for the competition. He shared some of the profits with men outside of Fat Sal's organization to keep them happy. He took some of the profits for himself.

Most importantly, Douglas helped sustain the charade that Fat Sal was working toward a goal that would solve all his problems in the future. He nodded his head whenever Fat Sal talked about the damage he was going to do to Sen. Miles McLaughlin when he bolted back to 1977, or 1982, or some other year when it would be safe to dispose of the future senator. Douglas played along whenever Fat Sal waxed poetic about the good life he would return to once things were put right. Douglas didn't let on that none of those things were ever going to happen.

The truth was Fat Sal never was leaving 1949. He just didn't know it yet.

Chapter 10

Elrod hustled into the bathroom at Colve Park and hopped inside the first stall he found. He dropped his pants about halfway and planted himself down on the can. He'd made it just in time. If he'd waited around to argue with Jade a second longer, he might not have made it at all. She kept insisting that she come into the bathroom with him, make sure he wasn't going to make a run for it. Elrod told her preferred to do his business alone. And anyway, how did she expect him to run away from a bathroom that was built out of goddamn concrete and had no goddamn windows and only one goddamn way to get in and out?

Elrod didn't know what Jade's scheme was, or why she was dragging him into it, but he damn sure knew he was going to take a crap all by himself, without her standing right outside the stall, keeping watch.

Man, it was sweet relief. Sweet, sweet relief. If Elrod ever did get back on the straight and narrow, find a job, settle down and move into his own apartment, he'd make sure it had at least two bathrooms. He didn't care if the rest of the apartment was only a hallway and a futon—he was going to have two bathrooms. One to use, and one in reserve. That's what he missed the most about living in a real home—having his own bathroom, ready when he needed it.

He flushed once, sat there enjoying the moment, and flushed again. When the second flush began to quiet down, Elrod thought he heard footsteps. He bent his head down to look under the stall door and see if the feet were attached to women's shoes. If Jade were checking up on him, he'd just sit there for the next two hours until she disappeared. But it was hard to crane his head down low enough to get a decent look. Well, it *was* a public bathroom in a public park, so it's not like Elrod could expect to have it all to himself.

After another minute or so Elrod wiped up, stood up, pulled his underwear up, pulled his pants up, tightened his belt, buckled it, unlocked the stall door, opened it, and saw a guy standing there with a metal pipe in his hand.

Saw the guy raise the pipe.

Saw the pipe coming for his head.

***

Something was fishy about that hobo who approached Jade outside the bathroom and asked her for money. It wasn't the fact that he asked her for money, either, because hoboes ask for money all the time. Jade figured that much hadn't changed over fifty years. They did it in 1949, and they were doing it in 1999.

No, it was the way the hobo reacted when Jade told him she didn't have any money to spare. The hobo simply nodded and rushed on toward the bathroom. Most hoboes didn't give up that easily when they were trying to bum some spare change. They would either stare at you a moment, as if maybe you didn't understand their request for money, or they'd put on a sad face, as if you were the physical embodiment of all the problems plaguing this cold, uncaring world.

Jade also noticed how the hobo quickened his pace as he walked into the bathroom, and the way he turned his head slightly, like he was looking to see if anyone was behind him. It didn't sit right with Jade. Something was fishy.

She waited for the hobo to disappear inside, then reached into her purse, pulled out a handgun, and followed the hobo in.

***

Dmitri did not get off a clean blow. The homeless bum got his arm up just in time, blocking Dmitri's pipe so that it only glanced off the homeless bum's shoulder. The homeless bum screeched English gibberish and fell backward toward the toilet, twisting and spiraling, breaking the fall with his arms, and nearly plunging face-first into the toilet.

It was funny, watching the bum's face nearly splash into the toilet. Wouldn't that be a laugh if his face plunged into the toilet? Wouldn't that be a hoot, as Americans say? Dmitri didn't have time for laughter, though. There was still work to do. Since the first blow had not landed as Dmitri intended, he would have to land more blows. Dmitri needed to knock the homeless bum unconscious, or at least very groggy, so it would be easier to get the coat off of him. The problem was getting a clean shot. The homeless bum's head was too far from Dmitri's pipe, and it was a narrow toilet stall. Not much room to maneuver the pipe.

Well, Dmitri would have to pound the homeless man's back first, render him immobile, and then work his way up to the head. He raised the pipe for another blow, aiming for the lower back. He gripped the pipe tight with his right hand and steadied his left hand against the side of the stall. Just as he was going into his downswing he felt a crack on the back of his head, a painful one. He wobbled and felt the pipe slip from his hand. He felt his eyes fall out of focus. He spun around. He saw the pretty lady he had seen before, the one who had been walking beside the bum. She had a gun in her hand, and the gun was pointed at Dmitri. The pretty lady reached down and grabbed the pipe. She raised it up quickly and brought it toward Dmitri's nose.

Dmitri knew he wouldn't get his arm up in time to block the blow. He would try, yes. You must always try. His grandfather back in Russia had a saying: *It costs nothing to try.* But Dmitri knew he would be too late. The pipe came down too fast. His arm did not come up fast enough. His last thought before feeling the crack against his nose and blacking out: *I hate this country.*

Chapter 11

Dr. Lionel Bunt wasn't happy about having to return to 1949, and only did so when it was absolutely necessary. He knew what could go wrong when you traveled through time, and it had nothing to do with the usual fear, this idea that you could change the tide of history simply by showing up where you didn't belong. That risk was overstated, in Lionel's opinion. The average person simply wasn't that important. He or she stumbled through the world for decades and decades with no more real impact than a feather dropping into the ocean. You didn't start World War III or shift the tides just by showing up and breathing the air. About the most you could hope for was to convince some city alderman to widen a street or build a park, maybe attach your name to it if you were well-heeled enough. Most people didn't even accomplish that.

No, what worried Lionel was more personal in nature—that some unforeseen disaster might wipe out the small inventory of potion he kept in 1949, and that he'd get stuck there until he could make more. The odds of him developing more potion in 1949 were slim, given the available technology and materials.

So, Lionel tended to stay safely in 1999.

But there were times when he had to travel back fifty years, and this was one of those times. Lionel needed to see Douglas. He needed to find out if the last courier, Elrod, got sent through the portal with the money. Lionel was pretty sure he had. He was pretty sure Elrod was roaming around in 1999 with Lionel's coat and Lionel's money. But there was only one way to be one hundred percent sure. Talk to Douglas.

So Lionel guzzled the potion and prepared to enter the portal back to 1949.

The first time he'd traveled through the magic hole, he was drawn by nothing more than a nagging curiosity about whether all his research into molecular structures and ancient time continuums would bear fruit. It wasn't even curiosity about science, either. It was curiosity about money. Lionel figured there must be some way to benefit financially from time travel—to make a big pile of cash and retire from his life as a research scientist, with its long hours, stagnant wages, and endless minutiae.

There were a couple of obvious options for making money. You could bet on sporting events you already knew the outcomes to. Or you could invest in stocks you knew would skyrocket in value. But Lionel didn't like those options. Winning too many bets too quickly might put you on the radar of the wrong kinds of people. Similarly, pumping a lot of money into a stock just ahead of its breakout might land you in front of a regulatory panel.

One idea was to deposit money into a bank account in 1949 and simply let it earn interest over fifty years. But Lionel didn't like that idea much, either. For one thing, most of the banks in 1949 didn't even exist in 1999, what with buyouts, mergers, bankruptcies, and whatnot. Second, even if interest rates were on the historical high side in 1949—say, six percent or so—you'd still need a lot of money to earn a big payoff fifty years later. Lionel ran the numbers. If he deposited fifty thousand dollars in 1949 at a six percent interest rate, compounded monthly, he'd have about a million dollars in 1999. That was still only half of what he wanted—under the best of circumstances. More likely he'd get something closer to three percent. At that rate, he'd need to deposit four or five hundred thousand to reach his goal of two million. He didn't have five hundred thousand dollars, and even if he did, that kind of deposit draws all the wrong queries from all the wrong people.

No, Lionel wanted a bigger payoff that didn't require a lot of work or risk on his end. To make that happen, he needed a contact in the past, someone with the right connections, skills, and attitude to turn time travel into a commercial enterprise.

That someone turned out to be Douglas.

Lionel didn't believe in fate. But he did believe in luck. And he knew he was awfully lucky that Douglas was the first person he met when he made his maiden journey into the past.

Douglas was standing by the entrance to the Hideaway when Lionel arrived through the portal. He didn't seem to care that a strange man had suddenly appeared out of the mist. He simply smiled, said hello, introduced himself as Douglas, and said he was the maître d' at the nightclub Lionel had stumbled onto.

Lionel introduced himself as Lou Brock—a fake name

he settled on because it was easy to remember. In 1949, there was no way Douglas could know that Lou Brock would become a Hall-of-Fame baseball player in the 1960s and '70s. Lionel told Douglas he was in the area scouting investments, and wanted to talk with some of the local business owners.

"Well, you've come to the right place," Douglas said, smiling. "I'm pretty up to date on the commercial opportunities around here. Come on inside. We'll have coffee."

The two men walked inside the nightclub and sat down in the main dining area at a table draped with white linen. The place was closed, so they were the only ones there. Douglas made fresh coffee and poured it in white porcelain cups. They made small talk for a few minutes before Douglas steered the conversation to business.

"As you probably know, this neighborhood is teeming with enterprise," Douglas said. "Real estate is appreciating, and it shows no sign of slowing down. You couldn't have picked a better part of town to scout investments."

"Of course," Lionel replied. "Hence my interest. I represent a consortium of local investors. We're always on the lookout for profitable opportunities. And as you say, this neighborhood is rich with them."

Douglas smiled. He stirred his coffee. "Tell me about this consortium. What sort of business opportunities are they interested in?"

"The kind that make money," Lionel answered.

Both men laughed. They spent the next few minutes bantering back and forth about business, the neighborhood, its growth opportunities, its movers and shakers. Then Douglas leaned forward in his chair.

"May I be frank, Mr. Brock?" Douglas said.

"Of course," Lionel said.

"You're not really from around here, are you?"

Lionel raised his eyebrows.

"Your looks and mannerisms give you away," Douglas continued. "You appear to have Oriental blood. Your eyes slant. Your hair is as black as ink. You speak in odd cadences, and use expressions I've never heard before. I don't know if you're from the Jap tribe that killed so many of our boys in the Pacific, or if you're from the Chink tribe that wants to spread communism through the whole of that godless continent. To be honest, I can't tell your kind apart. What's clear is that you would know better than to enter a neighborhood like this, and talk to me the way you do, if you were from around here. We have a fair number of Orientals in New York. Many of them live and work not too far away from here, in Chinatown. But not too many venture into this neighborhood unless it involves opium or food deliveries. They know to stay in their part of town. And this is not their part of town."

Lionel tried to keep a poker face, not act offended. He was thinking of an appropriate response when Douglas cut him off before he could say anything.

"You don't seem to have done much research for this little consortium of yours, either," Douglas said, leaning in closer. "You didn't bother to question what I told you about the neighborhood— the teeming enterprise, the rising real estate values. In truth, this neighborhood is going to seed. Businesses are shuttering. Buildings sit empty. We don't mind so much, being a nightclub. The seedy neighborhood gives our place an air of decadent charm you can't find at the midtown clubs. It thrills our rich clientele no end. But no consortium with an ounce of business sense would invest a dime here."

Douglas leaned back in his chair.

"So why don't we lay our cards on the table?" he said. "Where are you from, what's your real name, and what do you want?"

Lionel looked at Douglas. He thought about making something up, but figured Douglas would see through that, too. So, he gave the straight story this time. He told Douglas his real name was Dr. Lionel Bunt. He was a scientist in the year 1999. He'd developed a method for traveling through time. He wanted to earn money in 1949 and send it back to 1999. He figured there must be some financial benefit to time travel.

Douglas sat and listened, stone-faced and expressionless. His eyes never changed, even as Lionel wound his way through this fanciful tale of time portals and molecular structures. Lionel kept waiting for Douglas to tell him to get lost. But Douglas just sat and listened.

When Lionel finally stopped talking, Douglas said, "Tell me what ideas you have to make money from your discovery."

Now it was Lionel's turn to be skeptical.

"That's it?" he asked. "No more questions? You just accept my story on the face of it? You're not skeptical of time travel? Or at least fascinated by it?"

Douglas waved his hand in front of his face.

"No more than I'm fascinated by the wonders of television images, or how a 400-ton machine can fly through the air," Douglas answered. "If I see that they can do the things they can do, there's no reason for me to know anything further. I saw you suddenly appear in front of my eyes. I knew you had some exotic story to tell. Let's focus on why you're here, shall we? How we can make your wonderful discovery beneficial to you. And me."

"You?" Lionel said.

"You'll need and want my help, Dr. Bunt, and I expect to be compensated for it. Managing a nightclub in this city has certain perks. One of them is getting to know people who've discovered the most ingenious ways to make money. Graft, prostitution, gambling, narcotics, extortion, similar enterprises. You can't believe how lucrative these things are—and how risky. It occurs to me that some of my criminal contacts might pay good money to hide assets in another year. Or contraband. Or themselves."

Lionel's ears lit up. He hadn't even considered organized crime as a way to benefit from his time travel discovery. It made sense, though. Mobsters were always looking for ways to hide from their enemies and the law.

"Do you have anyone in mind?" Lionel asked. "Someone willing to pay a lot of money to relocate fifty years in the future?"

"I know plenty of men who'd love to disappear," Douglas said. "Whether they have enough money to make it worth your while is another matter. That's up to you, of course, and how much money you'd expect. But if the normal rules of inflation apply, what is considered a lot of money now might not seem like much to you."

It was a good point. Lionel figured a couple million dollars might be a lot to ask in 1949. It would require someone with the right combination of connections, experience, and skill. Mobsters in 1999 could make a couple million in a couple of weeks. In 1949, it might take much more time and work. And mobsters from 1949 might not be too keen on traveling into the future, anyway, with all of its mystery and uncertainty.

Then something else suddenly occurred to Lionel: If someone from 1949 was willing to pay money to hide out in 1999, then it stands to reason that the opposite was also true—someone from 1999 might be willing to hide out in 1949. Someone with a proven track record of making money—and a lot of grief to escape from.

"Salvatore Morino," Lionel whispered to himself.

"Pardon me?" Douglas said.

"Fat Sal."

"I'm afraid I've never heard the name before."

Lionel laid out the story about Sal Morino, his problems, and how those problems were not going away in 1999.

"But they might go away if he took a little trip back in time," Lionel told Douglas.

They hatched a plan.

***

That was Lionel's first visit through the portal. He took a couple more trips to firm up the plans with Douglas and gather intel. Since then, Lionel and Douglas communicated via courier messages exclusively.

Now Lionel was back in 1949 to find out why the last courier, Elrod, was nowhere to be found. Maybe Douglas knew something about it.

Douglas looked surprised when Lionel showed up at the Hideaway with no prior notice.

"Dr. Bunt," he said. "I assume this is not a social call."

"You assume correctly."

"Trouble in 1999?"

"Let's talk in the club," Lionel said.

They walked to a table near the bar and sat down. The place was empty, this being the middle of the day.

"Something to drink?" Douglas asked.

"Not now," Lionel replied. "Let's make this as quick as possible."

"Then please proceed."

"My assistant wasn't able to find the courier this morning," Lionel said. "When he got to the alley, the courier was gone. I'm here to find out whether the courier made it back through the portal to 1999."

"This would be Elrod we're talking about."

Lionel nodded.

"I can assure you he made it back through the portal," Douglas said. "With the money sewn snugly in his coat."

"At the usual time?"

"On the dot."

Lionel shook his head and frowned.

"That's what I figured," he grumbled. "It was an error on our end. My assistant. That imbecile. He got involved with a woman and overslept. He was supposed to be at the alley early. He didn't get there until it was too late."

"Unfortunate," Douglas said. "I assume you spoke with your assistant about this?"

"I spoke with him, then I disciplined him, then I packed him in a taxi and shipped him to a part of town he's unlikely to return from."

"You'll have to find another assistant."

"That's not a problem," Lionel said. "The more pressing matter is finding Elrod."

"And the coat."

"Yes, and the coat. The missing money angers me. But I'm more bothered by the fact that Elrod is out there roaming around, sharing stories about nightclubs suddenly popping up in back alleys. We don't want that alley becoming a tourist spot for the wrong kinds of people."

"Then perhaps you should be there, tracking Elrod down," Douglas said. "You know what he looks like. He shouldn't be too hard to find."

"I don't have a lot of free time on my hands," Lionel responded, curtly. "I have other responsibilities, as you're well aware."

"Then you'll want to hire someone to find him for you. A shamus, perhaps."

Lionel gave him a puzzled look. "What's that?"

"A private investigator. Someone who's trained to find other people."

"Not a bad idea. I can probably find plenty online."

Now Douglas gave Lionel a puzzled look.

"Online means looking on a computer," Lionel said. "It's a machine that lets you find and analyze information in seconds. You can find anything you want on computers. It's fascinating—and lucrative. I should have used my science acumen to go into computer technology. I might be a billionaire by now."

"Well, you'll at least be a millionaire when this is all over," Douglas said. "That's nothing to sneeze at."

"A millionaire two times over, if everything goes to plan. And you'll make out pretty well yourself."

"The only one who won't do so well is Mr. Morino himself," Douglas said. "The irony would probably be lost on him."

"He still doesn't suspect anything?"

Douglas shook his head. "As far as he's concerned, he'll be free and clear to travel back once the two million is paid off. He can't decide which year he wants to return to. But if I had to guess, it would be sometime before 1980, when the senator he so dearly detests is nobody important. Salvatore is really looking forward to it."

Douglas smiled. Then Lionel smiled.

"Just keep an eye on Morino and make sure he doesn't get suspicious," Lionel said.

"Let me deal with Mr. Morino," Douglas said. "You find your missing courier."

Chapter 12

Elrod stood just outside the hotel room, trying to decide whether he should enter it. His head hurt. His arm hurt. His ego hurt, what with a woman having to save him from being mugged in a Colve Park bathroom. He didn't know what surprises this hotel room had in store for him, and wasn't sure he wanted to know. He regretted agreeing to come here with Jade, regretted agreeing to meet at the café, regretted hanging around that nightclub last night, regretted much of the past day and most of the last twenty years.

Whoever Jade was, she was not someone to be trifled with. Elrod didn't see much of the exchange between her and the bathroom mugger because it all happened so quickly. But he did glance back long enough to watch her bash the mugger in the face with the pipe. The mugger fell back in a heap, landing on Elrod's back. Elrod tossed him off, kicked him in the head, and scrammed out of there.

Jade caught up with Elrod after a few strides. She held him steady just before he hit the bathroom exit and told him to calm down.

"Calm down?" Elrod said. "I nearly got my brains bashed in and you tell me to calm down? Who is that guy? He somebody involved in all this business you dragged me into?"

"I don't know who he is," Jade said, looking back at the mugger, who was moaning on the bathroom floor. "Somebody trying to steal something. It happens a lot in this city."

"Steal what?" Elrod said. "Who's he think I am, Bill Gates? I'm a goddamn homeless person! "

"Who's Bill Gates? Anyway, never mind that. Let's just get out of here before he wakes up or somebody else shows up."

She took Elrod by the arm and led him outside. He stopped when they hit the path again.

"What are you getting me into?" he said. "I want answers."

"Let's talk in the hotel," Jade said. "I'll explain it there. I promise."

"Why can't you explain it here? There's nobody around."

"Because we need a place nice and quiet, with room to show you a few things."

"Show me what things?"

"You'll find out when we get there. Look, I'll make it worth your while. Give you some money. Certainly, you could use some money."

Elrod didn't like the sound of that, even though she was right—he could use some money. He shook his head and off they went.

When they reached the hotel lobby Jade hit the elevator button for the eleventh floor, where she led Elrod down a long hallway to room 1115. Jade opened the door and went inside, but Elrod hesitated. He took a peek inside. It was a nice room—bright, clean, nicely appointed, fresh smelling, tidied up so precisely you'd think nobody had ever stepped foot in it.

"Are you coming in?" Jade said.

"I'm not sure."

Jade stepped toward the doorway, pulled Elrod inside, and closed the door behind her.

The room was done up in a kind of muted beige and purple theme. There wasn't a lot of furniture. A queen bed and nightstand. A small dresser with a TV on top. A lounge chair in the corner beside a black floor lamp. Elrod's eyes wandered back to the bed, such a soft and cozy-looking thing. He tried to remember the last time he slept on a bed—a real bed, not the cots you find in the shelters. He shuffled over to the lounge chair and stood in front of it for a moment, like he'd forgotten what he was supposed to do next.

"Sit," Jade said.

Elrod sat.

Jade took a seat on the bed. Elrod thought it was both sad and a little comical that he was in a hotel room with a pretty woman on the bed, and he didn't give a single thought to romance. All he wanted was to lie down on it. Since that wasn't possible, he thought of the next best thing.

"Think we could have a little snort?" he asked. "Maybe call down to room service for a bottle of scotch? Or at least a couple beers? My nerves are shot, and my head is not great either."

"This isn't a social outing," Jade said. She pulled a

bottle of water out of her purse and handed it to Elrod.

"Drink that instead," she said. "We're here to talk about something important, and I need you sober to process it."

"You think me being sober is going to help me process things?" Elrod said, taking a couple gulps of the water. "You don't know much about me if that's what you believe."

"I know you're in danger right now."

"Thanks for the tip, but I kinda got the idea after what happened in the park. So how about we cut right to it and you tell me why we're here."

Jade looked at Elrod, then at the coat he was wearing.

"Take your coat off," she said.

"Excuse me?"

"Take your coat off."

Elrod grinned. "Mrs. Robinson, you're trying to seduce me. Can I at least shower first?"

"Don't be ridiculous, nobody's trying to seduce you. Take your coat off and hand it to me. The coat is an important part of what you need to know."

The grin fell from Elrod's face. "I found this coat fair and square, lying there for the taking. I intend to keep it."

"I'm not interested in taking your coat," Jade said. "I have plenty of coats, all nicer than that one. I just want to look it over. I'll give it back when I'm done. Now take it off and let me see it."

Elrod didn't move.

Jade shook her head. She reached into her purse and pulled out a wallet. She took out a twenty-dollar bill and pushed it toward to Elrod.

"Consider this a deposit on the coat," she said. "Just in

case you think I can't live without it."

Elrod eyeballed the twenty. It was a beautiful-looking thing. But he didn't grab it.

"Keep your damn money," he said.

He rose from the chair and shed his coat. He handed it to Jade and sat back down.

She opened the coat and ran her hand along the inner lining. When she reached a stopping point she stuck her hand inside her purse and pulled out a pair of scissors.

"Hold on there," Elrod said. "What's with the scissors? Don't go slicing up my coat."

"Relax, the coat will be fine. I'm just going to make a couple small snips to the inside. We can fix it later."

Jade made a few cuts to the interior of the coat and put the scissors down. She moved her hand inside the coat and pulled out an envelope. She used the scissors to slit through the top of the envelope, looked inside, felt around with her fingers. Her eyes widened.

"Here, have a peek at that," she said, tossing the envelope to Elrod.

It landed in his lap. He picked it up and looked inside. The envelope was filled with paper—green and white paper. All the same size, thickness, and weight. Cash money. Lots of bills, stacked tightly together.

"Feel free to take it out and have a closer look," Jade said.

Elrod pulled the bills out and whistled. There were a few $500 bills and a bunch of $1,000 bills. There were even a couple of $5,000 bills. He didn't even recognize all the faces. No Washingtons or Lincolns here. He did recognize Grover Cleveland on the $1,000 bill. He had to read the name of the guy on the $500 bill, McKinley. Madison was on the $5,000 bill. Elrod was no expert on money, especially these denominations. But they looked real enough.

"Sweet Jesus, I'm rich," he said. "Whoever lost this coat is probably having a good cry about now."

"Nobody lost that coat," Jade said, easing the envelope out of Elrod's hand and placing it on the bed.

"Somebody lost it. I found it lying on a stoop."

"That was by design," Jade said. "The coat was left there for you to find. It was no accident that you're the one who grabbed it. It was also no accident that you showed up at the Hideaway nightclub and checked your coat there. The money was sewn inside the coat after Douglas took it to the cloakroom."

Elrod leaned forward. "Uh huh."

"You were set up," Jade continued. "None of what happened to you is a coincidence. Not the coat, not the malt liquor you drank yesterday, not the alley or nightclub, not the coat check at the nightclub, not the nice way Douglas treated you. None of it."

Elrod looked outside. He looked at the ceiling, and then looked at Jade. He got up from the chair and immediately sat down again. He looked at the floor, then back at Jade.

"You care to expand on that?" Elrod said.

"The money is being sent from one person to another. You're just the courier."

"The courier."

Jade reached back into her purse. She pulled out the front page of a tabloid newspaper. The page had a picture of a man on it, a fat guy with a round face and a thick cigar sticking out of his mouth. Above the picture was a headline in large, bold type:

FAT CHANCE!
Mobster "Fat Sal" Morino On The Lam; Feds Clueless

Elrod looked at the headline and the man pictured below it. The paper was dated earlier in the year. He'd seen the man's photo on plenty of newspaper stands.

"He's the mobster who disappeared," Elrod said. "What about him?"

"He's the one sending the money from the nightclub to his connection on the other end," Jade said. "Douglas, the maître d', sews the money into the coat pockets. That's why he checked your coat. When the couriers get the coats back, they carry the money out of the nightclub without even knowing it. You're not the only courier. Just the latest one."

"I see. The most famous fugitive in the country has somehow made it his business to use me as a, what was it, as a courier. Little ol' me—Elrod Nobody from Jackoff, Nowhere."

"It's true," Jade said.

"Of course it is. And just where am I supposed to be taking the money?"

"Back into the alley you came out of," Jade replied. "Somebody was supposed to find you there this morning and follow you until it was safe to grab the coat and make you disappear."

Elrod looked at his legs. He raised his arms and looked at them. He looked at his hands.

"That's odd," he said. "I don't seem to have disappeared."

"That's only because I intervened before someone could grab you. The man who was supposed to follow you this morning was with me last night. I seduced him in a lounge and we went back to his apartment. When we got there he fixed us a couple of drinks. I slipped a narcotic into his drink when he wasn't looking. He was out thirty minutes later. He snoozed right through the time he was supposed to go meet you near the alley you slept in last night."

"And why did you do all this for me? Did you get a crush on me last night when I knocked champagne all over your dress?"

"You were in danger. That was part of it, but it's not the main reason, and there's no point in pretending it is. I wanted to keep Salvatore Morino's connection from getting the money. I don't like Salvatore Morino, or Douglas. I want to do everything in my power to disrupt them."

"That doesn't explain where I come in."

"Like I said, you're just the courier. The delivery boy."

"Why me?" Elrod said. "If this mobster wants to send money, he can just hire someone to do it. For that matter, he can do it himself."

Jade rose from the bed. She walked over to the dresser and picked up a pen that was sitting atop a pad of paper with the hotel's logo on it. She twirled the pen around in her fingers. She turned and looked at Elrod.

"Salvatore Morino doesn't live here," she said. "He's nowhere in this city right now."

"Well, *he* might not be in this city," Elrod said, "but that *nightclub* I stumbled into sure as hell is. I know, because I was there, and I haven't left this city in weeks. So if the nightclub's here, and Fat Sal's connection is here, then it still doesn't make sense that they need to plant the money on me."

Jade sat back down on the bed.

"You won't find that nightclub anywhere here, either," she said.

Elrod looked at Jade. He wondered, not for the first time, if she might be insane.

"I'm having a real hard time following you," he said. "If the nightclub isn't here, then where is it?"

Jade took a deep breath. Her eyes wandered around the room, then settled on Elrod again.

"It's in 1949," she said.

Elrod tilted his head the way a dog does when it hears a weird sound. He started to speak, but couldn't think of anything to say.

"I know it sounds crazy, but what I'm telling you is the truth," Jade said. "Just trust me on that. All I want you to do is listen. Don't say anything. Don't interrupt. Just listen."

She went into the details of what happened, or at least the details she was aware of. She spoke in a clear, matter-of-fact voice, as if she were explaining a recipe for pot roast instead of a trip through time that involved gangsters and large stacks of cash. No cranking up the drama to accentuate her points. She told Elrod about the scientist, the malt liquor and potion, the alley, the portal, time travel, the nightclub. She said Elrod had been picked as a courier to deliver a payment between Fat Sal and the scientist, and that his coat was the method of delivery. Once the money was in the coat, Elrod was slipped more of the potion and sent hurtling back to 1999. The whole scheme was designed to let Fat Sal hide from his problems in 1999 and make the scientist rich. She didn't know the scientist's name, just that he was a scientist.

What Fat Sal really wanted, Jade explained, was to return to another year and murder Miles McLaughlin before he became a senator. With McLaughlin out of the way, Fat Sal reasoned his problems would die along with him.

"You've heard of Senator McLaughlin?" Jade said.

Elrod nodded.

"So you can see why Salvatore would want him dead."

Elrod nodded.

"Anyway, that's the story," Jade said.

Elrod rubbed his forehead with his hand. He looked at Jade.

"A time portal," he said. "Lets you hop back and forth between decades. Just like in the comic books."

Jade nodded.

"This how you get your kicks, is it?" Elrod said. "Playing jokes on bums like me? Making up stories about time travel and scientists, magic potions, disappearing gangsters, US senators? You're a sick woman. I feel sorry for you."

"I'm not making it up, and you know it," Jade said. "Something happened in that alley last night. Something you can't explain. A nightclub appeared out of nowhere. You went inside and everything looked different. The prices weren't right. The music was what your grandparents probably listened to. The people weren't like the people you know in your life. They don't dress or talk the same. Nobody would go to all that trouble for a joke."

Elrod wanted a cigarette and a drink. A carton of cigarettes and a river of drinks. He told himself not to believe this story, that it was ludicrous, impossible. He leaned back in his chair and blew air out of his mouth. He sagged deeper into the cushions, like if he could sag deep enough maybe he'd disappear altogether. Jade was right. Something *did* happen in that alley. It was real. It wasn't an illusion, and it wasn't an elaborate setup.

"How do you know so much, anyway?" he finally said. "You say you don't even know who this scientist is, but you know how his little time machine works. You know what everyone's doing. The money, the couriers. How is that?"

"A friend of mine overheard Salvatore Morino and Douglas talking about it one night in the Hideaway," Jade said. "They talked about everything—the portal, the potion, time travel, money, the scientist, the schemes. About the only thing they never mentioned was the scientist's actual name. They didn't know my friend was listening in. They were in the downstairs office and thought the rest of the place was empty. He just happened to be within earshot."

"I don't suppose this friend you mention is that horn player who approached me last night?"

"Red, yes."

"And Red told you about it? The conversation? All the details? You two must be pretty tight."

"Red and I have a history, I guess you'd say," Jade said. "And anyway, he needed to tell *some*body. Who wouldn't? You hear all this talk about time travel and money, you need to tell someone. So, he told me. He doesn't confide in too many people. But he confides in me. Like I said, we have a history."

"You two just chat it over and decide it's got to be true? A time machine?"

"We didn't know what to believe. But the details Sal

and Douglas discussed were pretty specific. They even mentioned the man who was supposed to follow you from the alley and take your coat. His name is Bubba. Salvatore Morino knew him, or knew of him. Bubba worked as a bouncer at a nightclub called Ecstasy. That's where I found him, at the Ecstasy club. I hired a taxi and it took me right there. I sat at the bar and eyed Bubba. When his shift was over, I invited him to join me for a drink. The rest fell in place pretty easily."

Elrod leaned forward and narrowed his eyes. "And this guy today? The one who tried to mug me in the bathroom? How does he figure into all this?"

"Him, I don't know about," Jade said. "Maybe he knew the coat had money. That kind of money, word gets around."

Elrod rubbed his eyes. His head suddenly began to hurt worse than before.

"A time machine," he said. "I went and stumbled into a time machine."

He glanced at Jade.

"What year are you from anyway?" he said.

"I was born in 1920," Jade said. "My life is in 1949."

Elrod stared at her. "I know how the potion got into me—that bottle of malt liquor you mentioned. But how did you get it?"

"They keep bottles of it at the nightclub, where the liquor inventory is stored. Red found out about the bottles and paid off one of the kitchen staff to steal one. That's what I use to get back and forth."

"You weren't afraid of slipping through a portal and traveling fifty years in the future?" Elrod asked. "Most folks would probably take a pass."

"Yes, well. I'm not most folks. I'm not going to lie and say it hasn't been a little nerve-rattling. This is a confusing world, and there's a lot to figure out. On the other hand, a lot of things are the same. You can still get around in taxis or subways. Most of the streets and many of the buildings are the same, though there are a couple tall buildings near the harbor I don't recognize. People speak the same language. New York is a big, loud city in 1949, and it's still a big, loud city in 1999. Not that much has changed here."

"Guess not," Elrod said. "Anyway, you found me, you found the coat, you found the money. If that's all you need from me, you can slip a few thousand of those dollars my way for the trouble, and I'll be scooting along."

"Not just yet," Jade said. "The money's only part of it."

"What's the other part?"

"The other part is, I know of Sal's plans to kill Miles McLaughlin. And I want to prevent that from happening."

"Uh huh," Elrod said. "And why is that? You on a mission of mercy or something? No offense, but you just don't seem like the do-gooder type."

"Don't assume you know me."

"I don't know you at all. But I know a little about Miles McLaughlin from reading the papers, and I know he isn't that much older than I am. He might not even have been alive in 1949. So what's your interest?"

Jade folded her arms.

"I may know his mother," she said.

"His mother?"

"There's a woman who lives in my building, on the west side," Jade said. "Mary McLaughlin. She has a son named Miles. He's three or four years old in 1949, I can't remember exactly. I'm not sure it's the same Miles

McLaughlin. There may be plenty in New York for all I know. And there's probably hundreds of Mary McLaughlins. But on the off chance he's the same Miles McLaughlin, I want to protect him."

"You and his mom good buddies or something?"

"Just neighbors. We don't really socialize."

"Then why is she so important?"

Jade glanced away from Elrod and looked out the window. "She...saved my life one night."

"Saved your life?"

"It happened in our building," Jade said. "I was in the hallway, lying on the floor. I was shaking, breathing heavily, feverish, incoherent. It was the middle of the night. A couple neighbors opened their doors and peeked out into the hallway. They saw me and quickly shut their doors. They didn't want to get involved. In this city, you mind your own business. What's one lady lying in the hallway at three in the morning? But when Mary opened her door she immediately ran out to help me. She dragged me into her apartment. She put a blanket around me and a compress on my forehead. She called an ambulance. Her son Miles was in his bedroom, I guess. Nobody else was there. No husband, no other kids. I don't think she had a husband. Just Mary and Miles. The ambulance arrived a few minutes later. By then I was having seizures and my pulse was weak. They rushed me to the hospital. If Mary hadn't intervened, I would have died."

"So what, you had a stroke or something?"

"No. A heroin overdose."

Elrod's eyes popped a little wider. "Heroin overdose?"

"This was a couple of years ago," Jade said. "I don't use it anymore, but I'm still around it a lot. Heroin is pretty popular among singers and musicians where I come from. Maybe that's not the case anymore."

"Oh, it's still pretty popular among musicians," Elrod said.

He studied Jade, tried to get a read on how much of her story he should believe. Elrod had known a few junkies in his life, and Jade didn't look like any he'd ever seen. She was too healthy, too strong and youthful-looking. Heroin can age a person twenty years in six months. Elrod had seen it with his own eyes. Maybe being cured for a couple of years does wonders for your health and looks.

Or, maybe Jade was feeding Elrod a line of bull and had something else up her sleeve. There was a lot of money involved, and when there's a lot of money involved, you can bet somebody is lying about something. Maybe Jade figured Elrod was the kind of guy whose heart would get tugged in the right direction if she tried to convince him it wasn't about the money, but about saving somebody's life.

Elrod wasn't that kind of guy.

"You say you're not sure the Miles kid who lives in your building is the same one who grew up to be senator," he said.

"No. I'm not."

"We could probably find out more about it on a computer. There's this thing called the World Wide Web that can tell you all manner of things about people. You could even get a crash course in the last fifty years in case you want to take a little peek into the future."

"I'm not interested in knowing what's transpired over the last fifty years, and I don't want you to tell me anything, either. My only concern right now is repaying a debt I have to Mary McLaughlin. Even if I'm not sure the senator is her son, he could be. And on the off chance he is, I want to spare her the heartbreak of having her son murdered."

"She might not even be alive anymore."

"Or she might be fit and healthy. That's why I want to stop Salvatore Morino in his tracks."

"You're not going to do that by stealing more of his money," Elrod said. "That might work once, but it won't work again. No way they're going to let the next courier slip away."

"My idea is to locate the scientist," Jade said. "Find out where he lives, or works. Take him out of the picture somehow. Without him in the picture, the whole plan falls apart. He holds the key to letting Morino return to a year when he can kill Miles McLaughlin without getting caught. Without the scientist, Morino can't do anything."

"What do you mean take the scientist out of the picture? You mean kill him?"

"I never said kill him, though if it happened, I wouldn't waste a second's guilt on it. The scientist probably deserves it for what he's involved in. But there are other ways to take him out of the picture. Put him someplace he can't make any more potion or access the portal. Send him back to the past and leave him there."

"You might have a hard time finding that scientist in 1999," Elrod said. "Like you said, it's a big city."

"We'll find him."

"'We'? Who's 'we'?"

"We. As in you and me. Like I said, I need your help. The scientist will be looking for you and the coat. When he finds you, we find him."

Elrod laughed. "You're serious? You want me to hang

around somewhere this scientist might be looking for me and his money? No thank you, madam. Noooooo. Thank. You. My plan is to bounce out of here and head as far west as I can get. If that scientist wants to find me he'd better start somewhere around San Diego."

"You're not acting very grateful, considering I might have saved your life—twice," Jade snapped.

Elrod planted himself deeper into the chair. "Maybe I owe you for what happened in the park back there, so I'll buy you a drink sometime. The other thing, this mysterious thug you allegedly seduced last night, that's just your word I have to go on. And right now it doesn't carry a lot of weight, if I'm being honest."

"You're not the least bit suspicious you might have been used last night for something that could get you in trouble? Do you always get the VIP service when you step into nice clubs, looking the way you do? You don't wonder why Douglas was so hospitable instead of tossing you out on the street?"

"I wonder about a lot of damn things," Elrod said, his voice rising. "I wonder why you're interrupting my life right now. I wonder whether you and Douglas are in on this thing together, along with Red and everyone else in that club. I wonder why I'm not lying on the cool grass, looking up at the pretty sky, and drifting off to sleep."

Elrod fell back in the chair and yawned. He suddenly felt very tired. Well, it was no surprise. He hadn't slept much last night, and this whole ordeal was wearing him out. He eyed the bed. It sure looked comfortable.

Jade must have noticed his wandering eyes.

"You keep looking at the bed," she said.

Elrod yawned again.

"You're tired," Jade said. "Why don't you come lie down on the bed? It's very comfortable. The beds in 1999 are much more comfortable than those back where I'm from."

Elrod gave her a wary look. "This some kind of play you're making on me? Some kind of seduction move like with that Bubba character, trying to get me to do something I don't want to do? If so, save your energy. I'm not in the mood."

"Such a shame. I was really looking forward to making love with someone who probably hasn't changed clothes in six months."

Elrod yawned again.

"I was just seeing if you wanted to lie on a real bed for a change, that's all," Jade said. "Have a rest. I bet it's been a long time since you slept in a bed like this."

"Longer than I care to remember."

Jade rose from the bed. She walked over to Elrod and took his hands.

"Go lie down," she said. "I'll sit in the chair."

She pulled Elrod up from the chair. He looked at the bed. It sure looked inviting. He shuffled over to it and sat down on the edge. He massaged the bedspread with his hand. It was soft, and cool to the touch. He lied down. He spread his arms out. The mattress conformed to his back. It didn't sag, and it didn't sit there stiff and rigid. It went with the flow of his body. A perfect fit.

"If you don't want to help, fine," Jade said. "I'll figure out something. But I need to ask a small favor, which is actually to your benefit. I need to travel back to 1949, and I don't want to carry all this money with me. There's a safe in the closet with a combination. I can store the money there. I just need you to stay in this room for a day or two. Keep an eye on things, make sure nobody snoops around while I'm away. This room is paid up through the middle of next week. You can sleep in a real bed for a couple of days, take warm showers. I'll leave you some of the money so you can buy yourself a decent meal. You can at least do that much for me."

The words bounced around in Elrod's head. He heard them, but he didn't register them. He kind of knew the gist of them. Jade was working her voodoo on another guy, and Elrod was that guy.

But he didn't care right now. His thoughts were beginning to float away. He closed his eyes. A minute later he was fast asleep.

Chapter 13

The little man sitting across from Sidney Donovan's desk had a familiar look on his face. It was the look of disappointment. Sidney had seen it before—plenty. It annoyed her the first time she saw it, and it annoyed her now. She wanted to grab this little man by his little neck and shake that little look right out of him. She wanted to stand him on his little head and literally turn that frown upside down. But she couldn't. She had to be a professional. Make the pitch. See where it landed.

It was mid-afternoon. The little man's name was Dr. Lionel Bunt. He was here to talk business. He needed a private investigator. He had found Sidney's name on the internet and learned that her office was only a few blocks from his office. He introduced himself as Dr. Lionel Bunt. Not Lionel Bunt—Dr. Lionel Bunt.

Sidney knew what Lionel was thinking when he first saw Sidney. He was thinking, this woman doesn't look like a private investigator. She's not the right gender, or the right color. Most people get their ideas about private eyes from the movies or TV. Just about all those roles are played by white guys, even now, at the dawn of the new millennium.

If private detectives were all white guys, how could a black woman like Sidney possibly handle the job?

She'd tried to work around the problem. She changed the spelling of her first name to "Sidney" from "Sydney" (her real name) because "Sidney" is the masculine version. She kept her hair short to keep from looking too ladylike. She mastered the art of talking white, clipping the words off at the end, speaking through her nose, all in a low voice designed to mask her gender. She had a photographer lighten her skin color for her marketing materials and website. If anyone snuck a quick glance at her name and picture, they might decide she's a dude with a nice tan.

Sidney didn't like having to do all this, but business was business. It was the only way she could think of to lure potential clients to her office.

Those tricks were enough to get people through the door. But once they met Sidney in person, the mask was ripped off. They saw a black woman with short hair. Many were surprised. Some were disappointed. Like Lionel Bunt.

Sidney took a sip of her coffee. She offered Lionel a cup from the coffee maker she kept in a corner of her office. He declined. He didn't make eye contact with her. He didn't speak. He stared at his hands, which were on his lap. He glanced at his watch.

"What can I do for you today, Dr. Bunt?" Sidney said.

Lionel jerked his head up, as if he were surprised to find Sidney Donovan sitting across from him in her own office.

"Right," Lionel said. "Well, as I said on the phone, I'm

looking for someone to handle a job for me. A private investigation job. I'm currently fielding candidates."

"I see. What kind of job?"

"I'm trying to locate someone."

"Someone in New York?"

Lionel nodded. He looked around the office. His eyes rested on Sidney's framed private investigator's license on the wall.

"Can you talk a little bit about who this person is, and why you want to find him? Or her?" Sidney said.

Lionel didn't respond.

"Dr. Bunt?"

Lionel looked back at Sidney. "It's a man," he said. "I want to find him for personal reasons. I can't go much into it beyond that."

His eyes moved to another wall where Sidney kept framed copies of various awards and certifications. The U.S. Army Distinguished Service Medal. A certificate acknowledging that she successfully passed the detective's exam with the Baltimore Police Department. A membership certificate for the United States Association of Professional Investigators. An accreditation certificate from the Better Business Bureau. A degree in criminology & criminal justice from the University of Maryland.

"Dr. Bunt?" Sidney said. "Are you still with us?"

Lionel's eyes shifted again. They looked outside, then back down at his watch.

"I just...I'm actually not sure I want to go through with this," he said. "I'm probably overreacting to a situation. I've never had to talk with a private investigator before. I'm sorry to have wasted your time."

Sidney smiled. She leaned back in her chair.

"I see," she said. "So you're not sure this is the right service for you."

"Nothing against you personally, of course," Lionel said. "I'm just a little gun-shy about going through with it."

Sidney leaned forward.

"Understandable," she said. "But if you'll indulge me a minute, can I tell you a little about myself?"

Before Lionel could answer, Sidney went through a shorthand version of her life and career. Thirty-nine years old. A certified private investigator in New York for six years—four years with another firm before starting her own business two years ago.

"Right now it's just me, but I hope to hire another investigator during the coming months," Sidney explained. "Expansion is definitely on the agenda."

She leaned back in her chair. "Before becoming a private investigator, I spent seven years with the Baltimore Police Department. I started out as a patrol officer. After five years of that I sat for the detective's exam and passed it on my first try. I was immediately promoted to detective and worked mainly in surveillance."

Before entering the police force, Sidney told Lionel, she was an officer in the United States Army, specializing in analysis with the Criminal Investigation Command. She went to officer's candidate school after graduating from college and did a four-year hitch.

Sidney took a sip of coffee, cleared her throat.

"I went to the University of Maryland on a basketball scholarship," she said. "I was a power forward, back when power forwards could still be 5'11. I came off the bench and banged the boards and set picks and played defense and hardly ever scored."

She went over her family background. Her parents were from Barbados, she said. They came to the US shortly after they were married. Sidney was born here in the city about a year later.

"My father died when I was six," Sidney said. "My mother raised me alone. She worked as a domestic for a couple of families on the east side, but later trained to be a daycare worker. I've wanted to be a detective for as long as I can remember, Dr. Bunt, and I'm very good at my job."

Lionel smiled.

"You sound like you've given this speech before," Lionel said.

"I've had to," Sidney replied.

Lionel looked at his hands, then back at Sidney. "I'm curious about why you're doing private investigative work up here instead of advancing your career down in Baltimore. It seems like that would be the more secure career path."

"I left the Baltimore PD for personal reasons," Sidney said. "I wanted to be closer to my mother, who still lives in New York. She's getting older, and she doesn't have anyone else to look after her. No other kids, no family nearby. She didn't want to move to Baltimore, so I moved up this way. I went into private investigation on the recommendation of a professional acquaintance. I was hired by one of the better agencies. A couple years ago, I decided to branch out on my own. I was tired of doing most of the work while someone else took home most of the money."

Lionel grunted an "uh-huh." His eyes scanned Sidney's office again. She took a guess at what he was thinking.

This office is small. It had a single desk, a two-person sofa, a plastic fern in a pot, and a coffee maker. It had one window that looked out onto a brick wall. There was no reception area and therefore no receptionist. Sidney used an answering service when she didn't have her mobile phone turned on. The office was on the fifth floor of a tired old building in need of a facelift. The other offices were occupied by outfits that couldn't afford better digs. Ambulance-chasing lawyers. Bookkeeping services. Non-profits. A CPA who'd been in the same building for forty-two years. A publisher that specialized in erotic romance novels.

"So how's business?" Lionel asked.

"Business is good," Sidney replied.

She pulled a marketing brochure out of her drawer and slid it across the desk. It included a list of her specialties, testimonials from satisfied customers, a short professional bio, and a list of regular clients. The client list included bail bond companies that hired Sidney when they needed help tracking someone down, law firms that hired her to vet witnesses, and corporate clients that needed background checks on job candidates. Some of her work was with individual clients, usually spouses who suspected their better halves of catting around. She downplayed that end of the business.

"My client list is growing," Sidney said. "Certain prospects meet me the first time and are a little taken aback because I don't fit the usual profile of private investigators. But then we talk, and they realize I'm qualified. I charge competitive rates. I work long hours. I almost always complete the job to my clients' satisfaction. I keep this small, inexpensive office because I don't need or want a lot of overhead. My money is better spent elsewhere. When I expand, I'll move into a bigger office at a better address. In ten years, Donovan Investigations will be one of the most successful private investigation firms in the city."

She placed her elbows on her desk and leaned forward.

"Now tell me what you need, Dr. Bunt," she said. "Please."

He made eye contact this time.

"Like I said, I need to find someone," Lionel said. "A homeless man. He spends a lot of time in the LoDown area, from what I understand."

"Why are you looking for him?"

Lionel shuffled in his seat. His eyes darted to the window, then back to Sidney. He touched his face.

A lie was on its way.

"He's my brother," Lionel said. "He has problems. Mental problems. Emotional problems. He left the city many years ago, but it's my understanding that he's back in town. I'd like to find him. And help him."

"Your brother."

Lionel nodded.

"Older? Younger?" Sidney said.

"Older. Two years older."

"He was born in what year?"

"I hardly see how that's important. But he was born in nineteen...sixty-six."

"Do you have a photo of him?"

Lionel reached into his pocket, pulled out a photo, and handed it to Sidney. She studied it a minute. The man in the photo had graying brown hair and a bushy, salt-and-pepper beard. The only other distinguishing feature was a small scar beneath his left eye.

"He sends the family a photo once a year, no matter where he is," Lionel said.

"What's his name?" Sidney said.

"Elrod. E-L-R-O-D. Elrod Bunt."

Sidney studied the photo. "Your brother, huh?"

Lionel nodded.

"Doesn't look too much like you, does he?" Sidney said. "I mean, pardon me for noticing, but this man standing here is clearly white. And you appear to have Asian blood."

"I'm adopted. Elrod is not my biological brother. But he *is* my brother."

"I see," Sidney said. She looked back at the photo. "You say he's two years older than you, that he was born in 1966? That would make him thirty-three. I have to tell you, he looks older than that. But I guess we can chalk it up to hard living."

She laid the photo back down on the desk and leaned back in her chair.

"Dr. Bunt, can I be honest with you?" she said.

"Please do."

"I don't believe that's your brother. I believe it's someone else. I believe you're afraid to tell me the real story. That's fine, it happens a lot in my job. People are nervous to come in. They have something they need, but they don't really want to admit they need it. For example, a woman comes in and tells me she suspects that her sister is cheating on her husband. She's concerned because it's her sister. She wants me to catch her sister in the act, so she can counsel her about the risk she's taking. Only it's not her sister, of course. It's the woman who's screwing her husband. So let's start back at the beginning, shall we?

Tell me who this man is, and why you want to find him."

Lionel sat quietly for a few moments. He looked at the walls, then at Sidney, then back at the walls, then back at Sidney.

"Okay, he's not my brother," he finally said. "He's a homeless man named Elrod who spends most of his time in LoDown. I don't really know him that well. I met him once. On a park bench."

"Why do you want me to find him?"

"He has something of mine. A coat. A bulky coat, like you take on camping trips. He stole it from me. He grabbed it and dashed away. I want to find the man, and the coat."

Sidney doubted the homeless man stole it. He didn't look the type, judging from the photo. A middle-aged man who looked like he couldn't run ten yards without twisting his ankle? Not likely. But she let it pass. Little white lies came with the territory. Sidney had lied herself about the reason she left the Baltimore PD. It wasn't to be closer to her ailing mother, who wasn't ailing at all but was in good health and still worked three days a week at a fabric store. No, the reason Sidney left the Baltimore PD was because she beat the shit out of a perp who spit on her and called her a nigger dyke while she was handcuffing him. She shoved the perp to the ground and pistol-whipped him with her Glock, back and forth across his face, back and forth, back and forth, until she had broken his nose and loosened a couple of teeth. She'd never lost her temper like that before and still wasn't sure why she'd lost it then.

Sidney was suspended without pay, pending an internal review. The other officers covered for her, saying she acted in self-defense, even though she hadn't. She was cleared of any legal wrongdoing but was politely told she would be taken off the detective squad, effective immediately, and could look forward to a career writing parking tickets or booking drunks on the graveyard shift. She decided to resign instead, and that was the end of her police career. She doubted any other department would hire her. Word gets around. So, she became a private detective.

"When did this happen?" Sidney asked Lionel. "The stolen coat?"

"Yesterday afternoon," Lionel answered. "Around two or so."

"Where?"

"In Colve Park, downtown."

"What was in the coat?"

"Why is that important?"

"Because I doubt you'd go to all this trouble just to recover a coat. Hire a private investigator, spend money."

"Let's just say the coat has sentimental value."

Sidney turned in her seat to get more comfortable. She took a sip of coffee.

"Was there money in the coat?" she asked. "Jewelry? Valuables?"

Lionel folded his arms and sighed. "Money."

"How much?" Sidney said.

"Does it matter?"

"It could. Just give me a ballpark. A hundred? A thousand? More?"

"More," Lionel said.

"Did you call the police?"

Lionel shook his head.

"Why not?" Sidney said.

"The police in this city have other things to worry

about besides someone's coat being snatched, even if it has money in it. I doubt it would get very high priority."

"That's true," Sidney conceded, "but you could still file a report. In case the coat turns up, and the money, you'll have some claim to it."

She studied Lionel a moment. "How did you get the photo of this man? You said you don't know him that well, so you were obviously not telling the truth when you said he sends the family a photo once a year."

Lionel blinked his eyes and then shifted them slightly to the right. Another lie was on its way.

"It fell out of his pocket as he ran away," he said.

"Hmmm," Sidney said. "Lucky break for you, huh?"

Lionel shrugged.

"I'm just curious," Sidney continued. "You say it was a bulky coat, the kind you'd take on a camping trip. It's odd that you'd be wearing it in August."

"I wasn't wearing it," Lionel said. "I was carrying it."

"Carrying it. With more than a thousand dollars in it. Not too far from LoDown. Risky area to be carrying that kind of cash around."

Lionel rolled his eyes. "Ms. Donovan..."

"Call me Sidney, please."

"Sidney," Lionel said, "excuse me for being frank. But you're not a police officer, and this is not an interrogation. I'm here to inquire about your services. A man has my coat, and I want it back. I want someone to find the man and the coat. I will pay money for this service. Double your usual rate—if you give the job top priority. I'll pay you two hundred dollars upfront, right now, just so you know how serious I am about this. Call it goodwill. Do you want the job, or not?"

Sidney leaned back in her chair.

"I didn't mean to offend you," she said. "It's simple protocol. The more information I have, the better my chances of recovering your coat and your money. If I sometimes revert to my old police habits, my apologies. And yes, I want the job."

"Excellent," Lionel said. "Let's discuss rates."

Sidney pulled out her rate card. They haggled over a couple of particulars and finally came to an agreement. Sidney put her standard contract in front of Lionel. He signed on the dotted line and rose from his chair. He wrote Sidney a check for two hundred dollars and handed it to her before she had a chance to pretend she didn't need any money upfront. The two shook hands.

Lionel made a move to leave but stopped.

"Oh yeah," he said.

He reached in his pocket and pulled out another photo. "Here's a picture of the coat. It might be helpful in your investigation."

He handed it to Sidney and made for the door.

Chapter 14

Douglas pointed at the bottles and counted each one slowly, deliberately, out loud. He was in a narrow storage room at the Hideaway nightclub. The room was filled with unopened liquor bottles. Standing beside him was Alvin, a busboy. Alvin was a slight fellow in his early twenties, roughly five feet, eight inches tall, 130 pounds. He had greasy brown hair that was parted in the middle and slicked down against his head like a plastic helmet. His skin was pale and splotchy and held remnants of what used to be a forest of acne. He had dull brown eyes and a face that seemed wired in a permanent state of befuddlement. Alvin was hired a few months ago to pay off gambling debts. Half of his meager salary went into his pocket. The other half went to his bookie.

Douglas, much taller, turned away from the bottles and looked at Alvin.

"Do you know why I called you in early today, Alvin?" he said.

Alvin shrugged.

"I don't respond to body language," Douglas said. "Use

words, Alvin. Do you know why I called you in today?"

"Nope," Alvin said.

"The reason I called you in today is to talk about inventory."

"OK."

"I wear many hats here at the Hideaway," Douglas explained. "My official job title is maître d'. But in truth, I'm more like the general manager. I have a hand in pretty much everything— ordering, quality control, licenses, entertainment, payroll, accounts receivable and payable, receipts, disbursements. And inventory."

"Uh-huh."

"Inventory is an important part of this kind of enterprise. We need to keep a working inventory of everything to ensure an efficient operation. Food, supplies, utensils, linens, uniforms, dinnerware, glassware, spirits."

"OK."

"This storage closet is where we keep our inventory of unopened liquor. When we run out of something in the front of the house, we replace it with a bottle from this storage closet. It's very important that we keep sufficient inventory on hand to ensure we never run out of a particular brand. If a gentleman orders a Johnnie Walker Black, for example, we need to have Johnnie Walker Black available. If not, we will have disappointed our customer, and he may decide to take his trade elsewhere. We don't want that to happen."

"Righto," Alvin said. He looked at his feet and fidgeted around.

"Look at me," Douglas said. "Give me your full attention."

Alvin looked back up.

"Did you know that alcohol sales are where we earn most of our profits?" Douglas said. "It's not from food sales or door charges. It's from alcohol sales—specifically, sales of spirits. Liquor. Liquor is a very high-margin item. Unlike food, it requires very little investment in terms of staff and preparation. It's also much easier to mark up in price, and much easier to extend to multiple customers. You might sell a bottle of wine to a single table, or a bottle of beer to a single customer. But one bottle of liquor might provide drinks for as many as twenty customers. That's twenty separate orders, all high margin."

"OK."

"You can see why liquor is very important to our bottom line," Douglas continued. "One of my most important jobs, then, is to ensure the integrity of our liquor inventory. Do you know what that means? The integrity of our liquor inventory?"

Alvin shook his head.

"Alvin?" Douglas said. "Do you know what it means?"

"Nope."

"It means I must ensure that all bottles are accounted for, and none disappear before reaching customers. To put it in simpler terms, I must ensure that no bottles are lost or stolen."

"Yep."

"Unfortunately, that's not always possible. Inventory shrinkage is a common problem in our business. In some cases it's due to sloppy work. Accidentally throwing away a bottle, or knocking one to the floor and breaking it. But theft is also a problem. Employees steal things. Forks, ice cream, beef, wine glasses. Liquor."

"Hmmmmm," Alvin said.

"That's why we count our inventory—to figure out how much we should have vs. how much we do have. That way we can account for shrinkage. Some items, such as expensive bottles of liquor or wine, we count daily."

"OK."

"The other day I counted certain bottles of liquor that have a great deal of value. Do you know what I found? I found that a bottle was unaccounted for. Missing. Stolen, in fact."

"Uh-huh."

Douglas reached up and grabbed a bottle of bourbon off one of the shelves.

"It wasn't a bottle of this," he said. "This is cheap swill. I wouldn't have called you in today if a cheap brand had been stolen. No, the item that was stolen was much more valuable."

"OK."

"So I'm wondering: Would you know anything about that? How the expensive bottle suddenly disappeared?"

Alvin folded his arms. He thought about it.

"Nope, I wouldn't know anything about that, I surely wouldn't," he said. "You see, I..."

Douglas slammed the bourbon bottle against the side of Alvin's head. Alvin tipped to the side, spun ninety degrees, and began to tumble. Douglas grabbed him before he had a chance to go crashing into the shelves and knocking inventory all over the place. He held Alvin's body with one hand and yanked his face up with the other. Alvin's eyes were cloudy. Douglas slapped him twice, hard. Alvin's eyes came into clearer focus.

"I know you steal things," Douglas said. "You and the others. I've seen you snatch dinner rolls and shove them into your pockets. I watched you waltz off with a steak knife one night. I took it out of your pay, with interest, without you even knowing it. Whether you stole that bottle is immaterial to me. The important thing is, someone stole it."

Douglas grabbed Alvin by the collar and shoved him toward the kitchen. Alvin stumbled to the floor, so Douglas grabbed him by the shirt and slid him a few feet before kicking him the rest of the way. When they reached the kitchen Douglas grabbed a heavy meat cleaver from a rack and yanked Alvin up off the floor. He gave Alvin a hard push toward the counter where meat is sliced and tenderized. He slammed Alvin's right hand down on the counter and spread his fingers apart. He brought the meat cleaver down in a quick, efficient chop and sliced off Alvin's right pinkie. It was an expert blow, clean and tidy. Alvin's pinkie barely budged after it got disengaged from the rest of his hand.

Alvin shrieked and wailed. It was the first time Douglas had ever heard Alvin's voice rise above a barely lucid monotone. Alvin jerked back and forth, yelping to the rhythm of his body. Douglas grabbed a cast iron skillet and banged it against the back of Alvin's head. Not hard enough to knock him out, but hard enough to rewire his circuits a little so he'd quiet down. It worked. Alvin's wails turned into moans as he sagged against the counter. Douglas found a kitchen towel, wrapped it around Alvin's bloody hand and secured it with string used to tie up roasts. He picked up Alvin's severed pinkie and tossed it into a trash bin. He slapped Alvin's face a couple of times to get his attention.

"Go to a hospital and get that wound taken care of so

you can work your regular shift tonight," Douglas said. "Tell them you had a silly little accident at home. When you come back to work— and you will come back, or one of our Dago friends will go find you—I want you to spread the word that nobody is to steal liquor. Never. Ever. This time I went easy on you. There won't be a next time. Are we clear on that?"

Alvin nodded.

"Speak," Douglas said.

"Mmmmmm hmmmm," Alvin mumbled. "Clear onnat."

"I want you out of my sight now. Arrive on time tonight, ready to work."

Alvin staggered through the kitchen and out the rear door.

Douglas returned to the storage room and scanned the bottles one more time. Only one bottle of potion was missing, and he made sure there wouldn't be another. The others were now under lock and key in a different part of the nightclub.

Still, the damage had been done. One bottle of potion was plenty enough to get somebody back and forth through time on numerous occasions. A couple of gulps did the trick. Maybe whoever stole the bottle thought it was just regular liquor and had no idea about the magic hidden inside. But you never could know for sure, could you?

Douglas wondered, again, who the thief or thieves were, and whether they knew about the potion. And if they did know, what they planned to do with it.

Part Two

Time

Chapter 15

Elrod heard the music but couldn't see the stage. Two people were in front of him, a man and a woman. The man was tall and wore a ponytail. The woman was perched on top of the man's shoulders. Elrod stood behind them, straining to see around. He rose up on his tiptoes but that didn't work. He ducked his head under the man's elbow but that didn't work, either. He moved his head to the right, then to the left, but it was no use. There was no way to see the stage behind this human skyscraper. He couldn't carve out more territory to get a better view, either, because people were crammed too close together, one against the other. You'd think there'd be more room at an outdoor concert held on a big festival grounds, but the crowd was packed so thick you couldn't move a foot in any direction.

Well, at least the music sounded good, even if Elrod couldn't see the band. It was a psychedelic jazz-funk ensemble that featured a wild electric guitar player who ran up and down the fretboard at lightning speed, pulling dissonant chords out of the air. A similarly wild Hammond organ player filled in the gaps with a wall of sound, while the drummer pounded out a furious tempo that threatened to spin Elrod's head around. A sax player stayed ahead of the beat with a succession of staccato, guitar-like minor blues riffs. The electric bass player tied the whole thing together with massive, funk-infused licks that seemed to shake the very ground Elrod stood on.

The sky was clear and brilliant, as endless as the universe itself. Over in the distance you could see the faint outline of brown mountains. The ground was flat and barren, desert-like. Elrod wasn't sure where this music festival was being held, but wherever it was, it was a long way from where he last remembered being—that cramped city back east.

The people around him didn't look like any people he'd seen recently, either. Lots of long, flowing hair, bandanas wrapped around heads, skinny men with their shirts off, women in tie-dyed blouses or swirling dresses that went down to their ankles, a lot of folks in faded bellbottom jeans, either barefoot or wearing sandals or moccasins.

The air held the sweet, familiar aroma of cannabis. Plumes of smoke drifted everywhere. People were passing joints around right and left, left and right. One would find its way into Elrod's hand and he'd have a toke then send it on its way. A minute later another would find its way into Elrod's other hand, and the process would repeat itself. When he wasn't toking on a joint he was grooving to the music, hands raised, head jerking, body shimmying wherever the beat took him. Somebody handed him a bottle of wine and he took a long pull, sweet and fruity, before passing that along, too.

The music rose to an extended crescendo and then

came to a crashing, sudden halt. The crowd cheered and cheered. The ovation must have lasted two minutes. A voice came through the giant speakers.

"Thank you!" the voice said. "That's the first time we ever played that tune live. It's a new one by our sax player over there, Red the Head. He calls it 'Watergate Voodoo', in honor of our president."

The crowd went crazy. The band cranked it back up again, launching into a raucous, instrumental cover of "Superstition." The energy was so high you could power a city with it.

Elrod needed to take a mighty piss. He'd been holding it for a long time, and now the emergency light was flashing. But how to do it? Where to go? He didn't see any port-a-johns, and even if he did, he was trapped inside this massive crowd. He'd have to stiff-arm his way through like a fullback to get out. It would take him twenty minutes probably. He'd never last that long.

The other option was to just relieve himself right here and now, the way nature intended. It's not like anyone would notice. They were all focused on the music. Elrod unzipped his fly. He pulled it out. He let it flow. It felt good and unsatisfying all at the same time. The more he urinated, the more he needed to urinate. He aimed for clear ground, away from anyone else's feet or legs. But clear ground was in short supply, and he couldn't control it, anyway. His fine yellow river sprayed in every direction. Some of it found the tall, ponytailed man's leg. The ponytailed man jerked his leg up and lost his balance. He crashed into someone, who crashed into someone else, who did the same thing. People started crashing together like bowling pins.

The woman who'd been sitting on Ponytail's shoulders fell backward. She screamed. Elrod held out his arms to catch her. She landed hard in Elrod's arms but he managed to hold her in place before she hit the ground. She looked up at Elrod.

"That's a swell way to meet a gal," the woman said. "Tinkle on her boyfriend's leg and make her fall into your arms."

Elrod knew that voice. He knew that face. Hazel eyes, long eyelashes, wavy brown hair.

"Do do that voodoo that you do so well," the woman said, winking.

Elrod looked away from her toward the sky. He saw the tall man with the ponytail staring down at him. The man seemed to have grown ten feet higher. He had an angular face, thin nose, narrow eyes. Elrod knew this face, too.

"I'll be happy to check your coat, sir," the ponytailed man said.

The sky turned black. The music stopped. The crowd disappeared. The woman in Elrod's arms disappeared. The mountains disappeared. It was just Elrod and Ponytail, as far as the eye could see. Ponytail raised his right arm. He had a knife in his hand, a long one. He raised the silver blade high against the black sky and brought it down swiftly toward Elrod's neck.

Elrod screamed.

***

"You okay there, cowboy?"

Elrod jerked his head up and banged it against a

padded headboard. He groaned and kicked at the sheets, punched the air. He blinked his eyes open and saw something out the corner of his eye. A human form. A woman.

"Calm down before you hurt yourself," the woman said.

Elrod shook his head again. His hair was sweaty and matted against his head. His face was an atlas of sleep lines, punctuated by bloodshot eyes caked with rheum. He leaned back against the headboard, rubbed his face, yawned, stretched. His vision came into clearer focus.

The bed.

The hotel room.

Jade.

"I was beginning to think you'd sleep all afternoon," she said.

Elrod coughed. He'd had a crazy dream. Something to do with music. Happy, then horrible. He tried to snatch pieces of the dream out of his memory, but they were floating away, floating, floating, floating. It was like trying to grab bubbles in a windstorm.

"I was at this music, some music thing," he said. "The sky and the mountains, and there was a tall guy. A tall guy with a ponytail and..."

He rubbed his face.

"Hungry?" Jade said. She was sitting in the lounge chair.

"Wha?"

"I thought you might be hungry when you woke up, so I called room service," Jade said. "I got you a hamburger with fried potatoes. I didn't recognize half the stuff on the menu. Artichoke salad? Mushroom panini? I went with something I recognized."

Elrod grunted a thank you. He swallowed thick saliva. His mouth felt like a dust bin. His head throbbed. He had to take a raging piss.

"Be right back," he said, then dashed into the bathroom. Two minutes later he reappeared in the bedroom and took a seat on the bed.

"I think I just emptied three gallons," he said. "How long was I asleep?"

Jade looked at her watch. "About three hours, give or take."

"You been here the whole time?"

Jade shook her head. "I stepped out to run a few errands. I got back about an hour ago."

Elrod looked at the tray of food. "Got anything to drink there by chance?"

"They brought a pitcher of water," Jade said. "With ice in it."

"Water," Elrod said. "First you save my life, now you want to poison me."

"What—poison you?" Jade said. "Nobody's trying to poison..."

"It's a joke. What was it W.C. Fields said? 'I don't drink water. Fish fuck in it'. He's from your era, isn't he?"

"He died a few years ago."

"That's too bad," Elrod said. He yawned, wiped some sleep from his eyes. "Anyway, a cold beer always goes good with a burger."

He picked up the phone and dialed room service. "Yeah, I'd like you to deliver three, no four Budweisers," he said into the phone. "And, ummmm..."

He looked at Jade.

"A glass of red wine," she said.

"And a glass of red wine," Elrod said to the phone. "Make it a cabernet."

He hung up, looked at Jade.

"I could use some freshening up," he said. "I believe I'll take you up on that hot shower."

He rose from the bed and made his way toward the bathroom. Before stepping inside he started undressing. First his shirt, then his socks. He hung them in the closet opposite the bathroom. He looked at Jade.

"You might want to turn the other way," he said. "I'm kind of the modest type."

Jade smiled. "I've seen it all before. But I promise not to look."

Elrod peeled off the rest of his clothes and hung them in the closet. He stepped into the bathroom and closed the door.

Fifteen minutes later he emerged with a towel wrapped around his midsection. Thick steam followed him out. He heard a knock at the front door and opened it. The room service attendant held a tray with a bucket of beers, a small wine bottle, a beer glass and a wine glass. He was a short guy with jet black hair and brown skin. His eyes darted away from Elrod and found the floor.

"Room service," the attendant said. "I catch you at a bad time. I come back."

"No no, you're fine," Elrod said. "I just got outta the shower. Sorry for my appearance. Wait here. I'll be right back."

He walked over to Jade.

"Room service," Elrod said. "It's charged to the room number, right?"

Jade nodded. "That seems to be the way it works."

"Got a little something for the room service guy?" Elrod said. "You know, some tip money?"

Jade reached into her purse. She pulled out a one-dollar bill and handed it to Elrod.

"Tell him to keep the whole thing," Jade said.

"Wow, big spender," Elrod said.

He dropped the bill in Jade's lap and grabbed her purse. He looked inside and pulled out a twenty.

"We're rich now," he said. "No need to be cheap with the working man."

He held the twenty-dollar bill up to his face and inspected it. It was dated 1993.

"You got modern currency here," he said.

"I went to a business around the corner while you were sleeping," Jade said. "An electronics and souvenir shop. I asked the man there if he could provide change for a thousand-dollar bill— twenties, tens, fives, ones. He said he wasn't a bank, and even if he was, thousand-dollar bills weren't even circulated anymore. I said he could give me nine hundred for it and keep the difference, see if he could find a bank to cash the thousand. He tried to haggle with me, but eventually gave up when I wouldn't budge. We finally walked to a bank down the block and he exchanged the thousand for modern bills while I waited outside. He gave me nine hundred and pocketed the profit, so I had him do it a few more times at a few more banks."

"The guys who run those souvenir shops can turn anything into money," Elrod said.

Out in the hallway the room service attendant cleared his throat.

"Oh yeah, be right there!" Elrod said.

He walked to the door and grabbed the tray from the attendant. He handed him the twenty and told him to keep it. The attendant smiled.

"Thank you!" the attendant said. "Let us know if you need anything else!"

"Oh, that's a sure bet," Elrod said, winking.

He closed the door, then walked into the bedroom and set the tray on top of the dresser.

"Just gotta go put my clothes on," he said. "You mind pouring me one of those beers? Oh, and pour yourself a wine while you're at it."

A minute later Elrod walked back into the bedroom fully dressed. He grabbed the glass of beer off the dresser and raised it in a toast.

"To time travel and free money," he said.

The two clicked their glasses together. Jade took a small sip of wine. Elrod drained his whole beer in a single gulp. He belched and grabbed another bottle out of the bucket. He twisted the cap off, poured the beer into his glass and set the glass down on the dresser. He took the lid off the tray of food and saw a large hamburger, thick-cut french fries and a pickle spear. He carried the tray and the glass of beer to the lounge chair and sat down.

The burger had cooled down to about room temperature and the fries had grown a little limp. But Elrod didn't care. He tore into the food with a zeal that bordered on desperation. Half of the burger was gone in three bites. This was no ordinary burger, either. It probably had a half-pound of meat on it, along with lettuce, sliced onion, sliced tomato. Elrod plunged the fries in his mouth two at a time. He made the pickle spear disappear in a single swoop; the way a sword swallower makes a sword disappear. He grabbed a cloth napkin off the tray and wiped his face, then went back in for more. He took another gigantic bite of the burger, followed it with a long drink of beer, then stuffed the rest of the burger down in one mighty munch.

Jade watched the proceedings with a grin. Some people might be disgusted by the way Elrod attacked his meal, but Jade had seen it all before. She'd grown up on a farm with three older brothers. Mealtime at her house was a symphony of slurps, burps, chomps, gulps, crunches, snorts, and moans. Mountains of food would disappear in minutes. Heaping bowls of mashed potatoes and green beans, huge trays of pot roast and fried chicken, basketfuls of biscuits. Jade's mother would spend hours preparing and cooking the food, only to watch it get masticated down to bones and scraps in less time than it took to boil a small pot of water.

Elrod was not a very big guy—about average height, fairly lean and wiry except for the slightest hint of a belly beginning to form. He was nowhere near as big as Jade's brothers, who all stood well over six feet tall and probably weighed close to 800 pounds combined. Even so, Jade had a feeling Elrod could match them fork for fork.

She watched Elrod polish off the last fried potato and sag back into the chair. He opened his mouth and emitted a long, deep burp.

"You weren't hungry, were you?" Jade said.

Elrod shrugged. He took a swallow of beer.

"Do you want something else?" Jade said. "I could call down to room service again."

Elrod shook his head. "Did you eat?"

"I had an omelet at a café down the block."

"You weren't afraid I'd wake up and skip out on you?"

"You were pretty knocked out, so it didn't seem very likely you'd wake up," she said.

Elrod downed the glass of beer and got up to grab another. He twisted the cap off the bottle and made a move to pour it into the glass, but then pulled up short and drank it right out of the bottle.

He looked at Jade and chuckled.

"Something funny?" she said.

"Do do that voodoo that you do so well," Elrod said. "That's the song you sang last night, and I think it popped up in my dream. It was also the name of that malt liquor I drank yesterday: Voodoo Malt Liquor. Voodoo keeps popping up in my life, and somehow I don't think it's a coincidence."

"Nothing in life is a coincidence if you look at it a certain way."

"And what way is that?"

"The fact that you and I are in this room right now. Is that a coincidence? On the one hand, you could say it's a coincidence that you're the person they decided should drink the potion and visit the Hideaway. You just happened to show up in a time and place where you were convenient. On the other hand, every decision you ever made in your life led you to that time and place. The same can be said of me. Every decision I ever made in my life led me here."

"So fate led us here? That's what you're saying?"

"More like destiny. Fate is determined by something beyond your control. Destiny is determined by your actions. You set your course here a long time ago with your actions and decisions. So did I."

Elrod took a drink of beer.

"I'm not so sure about that," he said. "This just happened to be the city I landed in when I hitched a ride a few months back. If it had been another car that picked me up, I'd be somewhere else entirely. Seems pretty random to me."

"But it wasn't another car that picked you up," Jade said. "That's the point. It was that specific car, with that specific driver, at that specific time. It was that car because of every action and decision you made up until that point, every minute of every day of your life. If you ate a doughnut twenty-three years earlier, that impacted everything that came after, including the car that brought you to this city."

Elrod narrowed his eyes. "I guess there's a certain logic to what you're saying, if you twist it around in your head enough to make all the parts fit just right. On the other hand, maybe it's all a load of crap. What I can say, it sounds an awful lot like you're trying to convince me of something here."

"What do you think I'm trying to convince you of?" Jade said.

"Why don't you just tell me yourself and save us the suspense?"

"I'm not trying to convince you of anything. We're just having a conversation. Make of it what you will."

She looked at her watch.

"Anyway, I need to get back to 1949," she said. "I have another show tonight at the Hideaway. It's Friday night, so we'll work into the wee hours."

"And then what?"

"Then I'll make my way back here at some point. See

if I can track down this scientist."

"What time do you expect to get back here?"

"As soon as I can after the show. Early in the morning, before the rooster crows."

"What time would that be in 1999?" Elrod said.

"The same time as 1949," Jade said. "We operate on the same clock. Just fifty years apart. That's how it seems to work."

"Kind of a dangerous time to go scooting through a portal into 1999. I don't know what that part of town is like in 1949, but here in 1999 it's no place you want to be alone during the wee hours."

"It's the best time to come back here, trust me."

"I'd advise against it. For what it's worth."

Jade stood up. She reached into her purse and unzipped one of the pockets. She pulled out a handgun. It was a small, nasty-looking thing with a black barrel and brown grip.

"This city isn't any safer in 1949," she said. "That's why I carry this around."

Elrod's eyes widened. "You know how to use that thing?"

"I told you, I grew up on a farm," Jade said. "I probably spent half my youth taking target practice with my Daddy's Colt revolver. I even shot small game with it. Rabbits, mostly. Something we could eat. There wasn't much else to do besides help my mother with the chores, and I hated that."

"I don't know much about guns," Elrod said, "but that doesn't look like a revolver."

Jade twirled it around her finger.

"This is a Luger, made by the Krauts," she said. "My

father brought a few back from the Great War. He gave me one on my fifteenth birthday and taught me how to use it. Pretty thoughtful of him, don't you think?"

She reached it toward Elrod.

"Have a look," she said. "See what it feels like."

Elrod put his hands up, palms forward.

"I'll pass," he said.

"Suit yourself."

Jade twirled the Luger around her finger again and put it back in her purse. She closed the purse and looked at her watch.

"I have to get going," she said.

She stood up, looked at Elrod.

"You're welcome to stay here if you like," she said. "Enjoy a little comfort. There's an extra key on the dresser. Or what they call a key, anyway. It's square and plastic. I had to ask one of the maids how it works."

"You're being awfully accommodating to someone you don't even know," Elrod said.

"Maybe I'm trying to soften you up. Set you up here in all this luxury, maybe you'll change your tune about helping me."

"Not likely."

"Then call it my good deed of the year. Most people in your position would jump at the chance."

Elrod couldn't disagree with that. It was a nice room, and he was long overdue for some comfort. He'd been sleeping on newspapers, park benches or stoops for weeks and months and years. There were worse things in the world than a couple days of R&R in a nice hotel room, with room service he could bill to someone else.

"I'll give it some thought," he said. "I'm not saying I

will. I'm not saying I won't, either."

"Good to see you come to your senses."

She reached in her purse and pulled out a thousand-dollar bill and a couple of twenties.

"For spending money," she said. "That souvenir shop is two blocks west of the hotel. You can't miss it. Tell the man you need to exchange the thousand-dollar bill for something smaller."

She grabbed her purse and headed for the door without saying goodbye. Elrod watched the door close behind her and wondered if he'd ever see her again. He wondered if she'd find the scientist, and what would happen if she did find him. He wondered if he wouldn't just take that thousand bucks and skip on out of town.

He walked over to the phone and dialed room service. He ordered a bottle of Dewar's and six bottles of Budweiser for immediate delivery. He also ordered two T-bone steaks, medium rare, and two baked potatoes to be delivered later.

That should get him through the night.

***

Downstairs, Jade walked out of the hotel lobby and onto the sidewalk. She headed east toward Colve Park, LoDown and the time portal. She grabbed a flask out of her purse, unscrewed the cap and downed some of the potion inside.

After a block Jade saw a tall, middle-aged black man standing beside a parking meter. He had on a red baseball cap, navy blue polo shirt about a size too small, a pair of tan slacks that sagged below his midsection, and a pair of light brown dockside shoes. Ill-fitting sunglasses drooped down on his nose.

Jade walked up to the man.

"You look ridiculous," she said.

"I'm aware of that," the man said. "You said I needed to look like I'm from around here, so I went to that store over there. The Gap. Happened to be where we agreed to meet. Bought the clothes and changed in a public restroom. This is the kind of shit they sell. I spent more than a hundred dollars for this getup. You believe that?"

"High prices, cheap clothes," Jade said. "Welcome to the 1990s."

The man looked down the street toward the hotel.

"He up there in the room?" he said.

"Yeah, I finally convinced him to hang around, enjoy the comfort. You'd think a hobo like that would jump at the chance, but I actually had to talk him into it."

"He didn't suspect anything?"

"He suspected everything, but I was able to finesse my way around it. He thought I was trying to seduce him in exchange for some favors."

"Weren't you?"

Jade grinned. "Of course I was."

"How long do you expect him to be there?"

"Hard to say. If I have him pegged right he's probably ordering booze as we speak, so he might be there awhile. But I'm pretty sure he's got his mind set on leaving town soon. This whole scientist thing has him spooked."

"I can believe it," the man said. "And now I have to hang around to keep an eye on him."

Jade leaned into him and put her hands on his shoulders. "It's the price we pay for wealth and riches, darling. But I'll be back in the morning. Early."

She pulled a room key from her pocket.

"Here's the key," she said. "The room number is 1116. The eleventh floor. Elrod is in 1115, right across the hall."

The man stared at the key. It was square and plastic.

"It's how keys look in this decade," Jade said. "You just slip it into the narrow slot and wait for the green light, then pull it back out again. The door unlocks automatically."

She demonstrated how to do it.

"You should be able to hear Elrod's door open and close," Jade said. "If you hear it open and see him leave, make sure you follow him."

"We covered that already."

"Just make sure you don't lose him."

"Yeah, we covered that, too. Remember, when you get back..."

"Tell Douglas you've come down with the flu and can't play tonight."

"Let them know I'm really sick," the man said. "I don't want them thinking I'm playing hooky or something. The weekends are big business. They expect the bandleader to be there."

"I'll handle it," Jade said. "If our plan works out—when our plan works out—we'll have plenty of money. You can open your own club and tell the Hideaway to get lost."

"We already have about fifty thousand up in that hotel room. That's plenty of bread."

"Not nearly as much as we'll have in a few months."

She kissed the man on the cheek.

"Patience, Red, patience," Jade said. "Our meal ticket is up in that room right now. Just don't let him slip away."

Chapter 16

Fat Sal stared at his plate and wondered how anyone with a nickel's worth of knowledge about food or cooking could create something like this. The eggs were a runny mess. The sausages were dry and chewy. The home fries were limp and bland. The toast was OK, though Fat Sal would have preferred a loaf of warm Italian bread. It was lunchtime, but Fat Sal had ordered breakfast on the theory that it's hard to fuck up breakfast. But this place had somehow pulled it off. He swallowed a couple of antacids and washed them down with a gulp of weak coffee. He glanced across the table at Douglas, who'd ordered a grilled ham sandwich on white bread with a side of sliced tomatoes. His meal was probably better, but not by much.

The two men were in a booth in the corner of an eastside diner. The two tables closest to them were empty. The rest of the diner was nearly full. The manager knew not to sit anyone near Fat Sal when he was here. He needed privacy to talk. In return, the manager didn't have to pay Fat Sal money for whatever Fat Sal decided he needed money for.

Fat Sal turned away from his plate and looked at Douglas.

"Tell me you're kidding," he said.

"Unfortunately, no," Douglas said.

"Fifty grand. That's how much we sent through the magic hole, right? Fifty grand? And it never made it back there?"

"A little bit more than that. But for rounding purposes, call it fifty thousand. And no, the scientist never got the payment."

"Why? Where was his so-called assistant? Bubba?"

"Apparently Bubba got mixed up with a woman and overslept," Douglas said.

Fat Sal took a bite of toast. He forked a piece of sausage and shoved it into his mouth. He chewed. He swallowed. He went through the motions of eating because he was hungry.

"Bubba. That dumb hick," Fat Sal said. "I knew it was a mistake hiring him. This is on the Jap, you want my opinion. Let him eat the losses."

"Unfortunately, the scientist seems to hold all the cards, given the complexities of time travel."

Fat Sal ignored that. He pushed his eggs around the plate.

"Bubba tried to hook on with one of my crews, you know," he said. "Thought he was a real swinging dick. We gave him some work, tested him out. We'd send him around to do odd jobs. Small collections, that kind of thing. Minor shit. He couldn't even get that right. He'd go to the wrong place, brace the wrong guy. He's an idiot. Now there's fifty thousand floating around in a coat because Bubba was trying to get laid."

"The scientist intends to find Elrod," Douglas said. "I think I talked him into hiring a private investigator. It's a pretty sure bet Elrod still has the coat, because coats are prized possessions to vagrants like him. I also doubt he's discovered the money. He's probably a little spooked by the experience, so the scientist wants to locate him before he starts sharing his story with others."

Fat Sal shook his head. He plunged another bite of sausage into his mouth.

"'The scientist,'" he said. "We can only refer to him as the 'scientist,' as if the feds are wired into 1949. Meantime, I'm that much further away from getting out of here. It's not that easy hustling up fifty grand every couple of weeks. You got expenses. Overhead. People skimming off the top maybe."

He eyeballed Douglas. Douglas eyed him back.

"What I'm saying, it adds up," Fat Sal continued. "And that dwarf goes and hires a hillbilly to try and collect it."

"Procedures are being put into place to prevent this from happening again," Douglas said. "The scientist will do a better job of vetting and monitoring the people he hires from now on."

"That's great for all the money I'm supposed to send in the future," Fat Sal said. "But it does nothing to find this Elrod and get the fifty grand back. You said the scientist is going to hire a private eye?"

Douglas nodded.

"Some ex-cop who couldn't make it on the force probably," Fat Sal said. "He'll ask a few questions, get nowhere, and still charge a fee. What the private eye won't do, and should do, is crack heads until somebody spills. We should send one of our own through the portal to find him.

Hell, I'll go. I know that area of town. I put the squeeze on a couple of those homeless assholes, they'll give up their own mothers."

"I'm pretty certain you don't want to go back to 1999. You may recall that you're pretty famous there. For all the wrong reasons."

Fat Sal wasn't so certain about it. He looked at his plate of tasteless food, done up 1949 style. He looked at the diner. He belched, shoved another antacid into his mouth. He took a sip of coffee. It was maybe the worst coffee he'd ever tasted. He thought about what he used to eat, and where. The more he thought about it, the angrier he got. He wanted his money back. He wanted control back. He wanted his life back. He was tired of having to lay low, play nice.

He wanted blood, and he was going to get it.

Chapter 17

The pub was nearly empty when Senator Miles McLaughlin walked in, making it easy to spot Luis Baez at the far end of the bar. Miles strolled past a bored-looking bartender who was staring at a TV perched on a shelf above a row of liquor bottles. The TV was tuned to a game show with the sound off. The only other soul in the joint was a rumpled-looking guy at a table who eyeballed his drink like he thought it might jump up and make a run for it. A fuzzy rock song played on a stereo whose speakers had long ago been blown beyond repair.

Luis was sitting in front of two glasses of beer. Miles walked over and patted him on the back.

"*Muchacho*," Miles said. "You're looking good."

"You too, boyo," Luis replied.

"Bullshit."

"Yeah, you're right. You look terrible."

Miles sat down and pulled one of the beers his way. He took a sip and glanced around. The place was dark, narrow and dusty, weary-looking, as if it didn't want to be a pub anymore. Barstools were placed haphazardly in front of the bar, pointed every which way. Against the far wall were six or seven plain wooden tables that looked like they came half-price at a flea market. A few of the tables had chairs, but none of the chairs matched. The only light came from a handful of neon beer signs, so you couldn't see much, which was probably an advantage. It had the musty smell of old beer and stale cigarettes. Miles guessed people still lit up here from time to time, even though you weren't supposed to.

"You know all the classy joints," Miles told Luis.

"You wanted to meet someplace quiet and inconspicuous, so here we are. Nice outfit, by the way."

Miles checked himself in a mirror behind the bar. He had on a Knicks cap tilted low on his forehead, a pair of brown horn-rimmed reading glasses, a New York Jets retro jersey, and baggy blue jeans. Black workboots completed the look. He looked like your average middle-aged slob, only taller. But it at least kept people from recognizing him—he hoped. It wasn't easy going incognito when you're a United States senator who stands a shade under six-foot-six.

Miles was here because he was chasing a hunch that he knew, deep down, should not be chased. The hunch was that Fat Sal Morino was still floating around this city somewhere, and if the FBI and local cops weren't going to find him, then Miles damn well would. And he wanted Luis' help.

Luis was a former detective who served with the NYPD just long enough to earn his pension, quit, and start his own security consulting company. He and Miles worked on numerous cases together when Miles was with the DA's office. Luis was the best investigator Miles had ever known. A little unorthodox, with a tendency to go rogue and massage the rules if need be. But the best investigator out there, hands down. If anyone could find clues to Morino's whereabouts, it was Luis. About the only thing Miles held against Luis was his looks—lean, fit, and handsome, with all of his hair still in place and not a gray stray to be found. Luis was only a few years younger than Miles but looked like he was born two decades later.

"So," Luis said. "I know you didn't call us together like this to reminisce about old times. You were a little dodgy on the phone, which worries me."

"Let's grab a seat at one of those tables," Miles said.

They ambled over to a table in the back corner of the pub, out of earshot of the others. Luis took a seat by the wall. Miles took the seat directly across and leaned in close to Luis so he wouldn't have to talk too loudly.

"So," Miles began, "you may or may not have heard that the FBI is putting the brakes on its active pursuit of a certain well-known Italian fugitive. They'll keep a token agent in place to pretend he's working on the case, but the rest of the bureau is interested in moving on to bigger game."

"Salvatore Morino?" Luis said.

Miles nodded.

"I hadn't heard that," Luis said. "But I guess I'm not surprised."

"I'm not surprised, either," Miles said. "But that doesn't mean I have to like it. It's my considered opinion that they're giving up the chase too early."

Luis took a drink of beer.

"The bureau always knows when to cut its losses," he said. "Maybe they lost interest, what with so much other mayhem to worry about."

"Yeah, well, like I said, I don't have to like it," Miles said. "The man is out there somewhere. He's not dead, and he didn't skip the country. He's right here in the good old US of A, according to all the intelligence. They need to find him, send a message that you can't get away with what he got away with."

"They'll catch up to him eventually," Luis said. "You know how it works. Bad boys always make mistakes. Morino will screw up at some point and that will be that. Anyway, what's it to you? My guess is you have more important things to worry about."

"Yeah, you'd think so, wouldn't you?" Miles said. "I should be giving some defense contractor a blowjob right now, bringing home a little bacon to our fair state. Or cutting ribbons at Trump's latest pimped-out, shitty-looking building. But the thing is, it pisses me off that Morino is out there roaming around like any other upright citizen, and nobody can seem to find him. Maybe they don't have the right people looking."

"They had a full team of agents on it. These things happen."

"Well, maybe they need new blood on the case. Somebody willing to take a fresh approach."

Luis tilted his head and gave Miles a weary look. "What's that supposed to mean? 'Somebody willing to take a fresh approach'?"

"It means what it says. Maybe somebody else needs to look for him. Somebody not bogged down by so many rules."

Luis rolled his eyes. "Oh, Jesus. You're not really thinking about..."

"Just hear me out..."

"You called me away from my office to talk about this?" Luis interrupted. "Hiring me to find Sal Morino?"

"I called you out to discuss consulting work."

Luis shook his head and took a sip of beer. "Let it go, brother. You've been chasing him so long he's making you soft in the head. Time to move on. *Es hora de moverse.*"

Miles leaned in closer. "That evil tub of lard is still out there, free as the wind. My gut tells me he's in New York. Call it intuition, a professional hunch. He disappeared in LoDown and may still be hanging around there. You think about it, it's a good place to hide out. Nobody important goes near that part of town. It's so rundown the cops don't even give a shit about it anymore. He's here, *muchacho.* Mark my words."

"So what if he is?" Luis replied. "From what I've read and heard he was running low on money and juice even before he disappeared. His bank accounts were frozen, a lot of his property was seized. Most of his crew is either dead, in jail, headed to jail or in witness protection. None of the other outfits will have anything to do with him. Let sleeping dogs lie."

"Duly noted," Miles said. "Still and all, I'm gonna go down there and sniff around. Check the alley he disappeared from and the surrounding area."

Luis rolled his eyes again. "The feds and the local cops have already turned that area upside down. What are you gonna find that they didn't?"

"The initial investigation was months ago," Miles said. "Since then, they've only sent a couple token agents around every couple of weeks to do a quick walk-around. You know how it is. Sometimes a different set of eyes can see things others didn't. Sometimes evidence gets moved or changed over the course of a few months. Call it an itch I need to scratch."

Luis leaned forward in his chair.

"You're a United States goddamn senator now," he said. "You're not some cheap gumshoe charging by the hour. Think about what you're getting yourself into. One, you might get recognized by some crackhead who'd love to sneak up behind a Washington bigshot and bang him on the skull with a forty-ounce. From a security standpoint, I'd advise against it. Two, what do you really expect to find down there? Fat Sal roaming around for all the world to see? Some hidden passage the FBI couldn't find even after a full and thorough investigation? Some magic hole he disappeared into? Come on, man. You're supposed to be the rational one here, not me. It's a dead end. Go back to Washington and forget about this."

Miles swatted a fly from his face and leaned back in his chair.

"I'm going down there, friend—tomorrow, while I'm still in town," he said. "Telling my staff I'm taking some personal time. I'd like to have a good right-hand man tagging along. I'll pay triple your usual fee, out of my own pocket. If we *do* see something that eventually leads to Morino's capture, you get the FBI reward all to yourself."

"What makes you think I'd have any interest at all in doing that?" Luis asked.

Miles grinned. "Because you're like me. You miss the action. You love hunting down the bad guys. You go on your consulting calls and teach some Ivy League douchebag how to protect his company from embezzlement, when you'd much rather be on the streets chasing down psychos."

"Save it. I like my work, being my own boss."

"Not only that," Miles went on, "you're a loyal *camarada* who still owes me a ton of favors for saving your job—and your pension—every time one of your commanding officers wanted to fire you."

"That again?"

"Swing by and pick me up early tomorrow," Miles said. "You drive."

Chapter 18

Jade watched Douglas stir his tea and marveled at how he managed to make the most mundane activity seem threatening. He stirred it slowly, deliberately, menacingly, in small precise circles, taking his time, as if when he finally finished, the steam would rise from his teacup and slowly strangle Jade. He stared at her the whole while, a crooked smile on his face, and listened to her spin a yarn he probably knew was fiction.

They were sitting at a table in the Hideaway nightclub, before opening time. Nobody else was around. Soon the staff would show up, and then the band—short one member. Red wouldn't be sitting in tonight, Jade had informed Douglas. Red was feeling a little under the weather. Red sends his apologies.

That's when Douglas' smile made its first appearance.

"A pity that he came down sick like that," Douglas said. "And on the weekend, no less. The weekends, as you know, are very important to this enterprise. Our customers expect only the best. And the jazz orchestra is only at its best when William—or shall I call him 'Red'—is present."

"Well, you can't really choose when you come down with the flu, can you?" Jade replied.

Douglas pulled the teaspoon from the cup and laid it on a napkin. He took a sip.

"True enough," he said. "Illness is rarely convenient. Even so, I've never known Red to call in sick. It's one of the reasons I value him. He is a dedicated and wholly professional musician. That's a rare trait in the jazz community, which is so heavily populated with Negro hopheads and layabouts. It's also odd that Red didn't actually call in sick, but instead sent his lovely singer to deliver the news. I hope it's not more than the flu he's come down with. Perhaps we should give him a call to check up."

"There's only the one hall phone in his building. He wouldn't be able to answer it unless he was up and about, which he isn't. As I told you, he took some medicine and went straight to bed. He wants to be well-rested so he can make tomorrow night's show. For now, there's a replacement saxophonist lined up who is more than competent."

"Still, I do worry about Red. He hasn't been himself lately. For example, last night I saw him socializing with one of our new customers at the bar, before the show. Maybe you remember that customer. He was a rundown fellow who called himself Elrod. It's odd that Red would chat with Elrod before the show. He doesn't usually do that. Would you know anything about it?"

Jade waved a strand of hair from her eyes. She picked up a glass of water from the table and took a drink.

"Well, there's a first time for everything," she said.

Douglas chuckled. "Right you are, as always. One of

your many charms, Jade, is your downhome candor. In this city you grow tired of people putting on airs. It's nice to hear plain-speak from a farm girl who has maintained her blunt edge, even after she so obviously outgrew the farm."

"Now you flatter me."

"Not flattery, my dear. Simple truth."

Jade leaned forward and put her elbows on the table. "It's nice to know you hold me in such high regard, Douglas. I would blush if I were the blushing type. And I have to say, I'm a little surprised. You're not usually so generous with the praise, at least to the hired hands."

"I'm not sure what you mean. I've always been very supportive of you and the band."

"Not always. Some of my ideas you've shot down pretty quickly. In fact, we discussed one a month or so ago, and you haven't bothered to bring it up since."

"And what idea is that?"

"About the cocktail hour," Jade said. "Remember? I told you maybe we should open a couple hours earlier, serve drinks and hors d'oeuvres, have a piano player provide a little atmosphere. Make a little extra money. I'd oversee it, serve as manager and hostess. You wouldn't have to worry about a thing. Just give me a cut of the profits."

Douglas took another sip of tea. He leaned forward in his seat and reached his hand out to Jade. He patted her on the arm.

"And what do you know of profits, young Jade from the farm?" he said.

"More than you might suspect."

Douglas put the teaspoon back in the cup and stirred

it again, slowly and methodically, around and around.

"Right, the cocktail hour," he finally said. "I did give that some thought. And what I thought was this: You're a lovely girl and a fine singer. Those two things were enough to lift you out of that cow patch back in Iowa, or wherever it is you're from. Iowa? Kansas? Nebraska? One of those flat, miserable states. You should spend every waking moment thanking the good Lord that you don't look like the cows you used to milk. A lot of farm girls do, you know. They look like cows and sows and mules. You, on the other hand, were gifted with beauty. That's your meal ticket, kiddo. Your insurance policy. Those pretty eyes and perky tits. Hold on to your looks for dear life, because once they disappear, your value to the rest of us will be disappear faster than shit down a toilet, just like the whores in Times Square. What you won't do now, or ever, is discuss the Hideaway's business. That's not a place for little prairie girls. It's a place for men. I shared your idea with Mr. Morino, by the way. And since you appreciate honesty, let me just say that he and I both thought it was a pretty good idea. And if we ever decide to do it, we'll pay you the usual wage and keep the profits to ourselves."

He rose from his chair and walked over to the other side of the table, planting himself directly in front of Jade. "Don't ever bring this up with me again. Just sing, look pretty, and shut up. Do we understand each other?"

Jade felt her body tighten up. She resisted the urge to slug Douglas in the crotch, double him over and watch that smug smile burst into agony. Instead, she breathed deeply and collected herself.

"The cocktail hour was my idea," she said in a flat tone. "And neither you nor that fat..."

Before she could finish Douglas grabbed her by the collar and yanked her closer.

"And tell that coon boyfriend of yours that if he's ever too sick to play, he needs to call me directly," he said. "Also, tell him to never, under any circumstances, speak with the clientele unless he clears it with me first."

Jade jerked his hand away.

"Don't you ever touch me like that again," she said.

Douglas froze, just for a second. Just long enough for Jade to remember he was only made of flesh and blood, and his flesh and blood could be ripped apart just like anyone else's.

Chapter 19

Red held the plastic device in his hand and pointed it at the large box sitting on top of the dresser, just like the instructions said. He pressed a button on the device but nothing happened. He pressed another button. Nothing happened. He pressed all the buttons until something blinked on the large box and it started screaming at full volume.

"WELCOME TO THE NORTHPARK VILLAGE HOTEL WE SINCERELY HOPE YOU'LL ENJOY YOUR STAY PLEASE VIEW THIS SHORT VIDEO TO LEARN MORE ABOUT OUR AMENITIES AND ENTERTAINMENT OPTIONS AND HELP ENSURE YOU HAVE THE MOST PLEASANT AND REWARDING VISIT POSSIBLE BLAH BLAH BLAH"

Red jumped back and tripped over his feet. He stumbled and spun around, waved his arms in the air, dropped the device, and landed on the bed hands first. He popped up quickly and grabbed the device off the floor. He pointed it at the large box, which was still screaming at him at full volume about the COZY LOUNGE and

GOURMET DINING and MORE THAN ONE HUNDRED CHANNELS INCLUDING FREE HBO.

He jabbed the buttons on the device in a half panic, over and over again, all of them, every one, trying to find the one that would either turn the volume down or cut the box off altogether. After about twenty jabs the picture on the screen switched to a handsome, gray-haired man shouting about ERECTILE DYSFUNCTION. Red jabbed the buttons again and the picture shifted to a bunch of white folks sitting in a café. One of them was named Joey and he shouted something stupid and you could hear the sound of LAUGHTER in the background, and then this blonde girl shouted something stupid and you could hear more LAUGHTER, and then this boy named Chandler shouted something stupid and there was more LAUGHTER. Red jabbed the buttons again and now there was a big fat Negro on the screen with a ball cap sitting sideways on his head and about ten gold chains around his neck, and he was wearing some kind of purple sunglasses and holding a microphone, and he was shouting "HITTIN' DAT ASS FROM BEHIND FROM BEHIND, YO! HITTIN' DAT ASS FROM BEHIND!" and so Red jabbed the buttons again and again and again until the screen went blank and the noise stopped and the room fell silent.

Red fell back on the bed and took a few deep breaths. He tossed the device toward the corner of the bed, where it skidded across the bedcover and tumbled to the carpet. He left it there. No more devices. No more boxes screaming at him.

He rose up on his elbows, gathering himself, scolding himself. Why the hell was he here in this hotel room? Why had he gone along with this madness? What kind of fool does this—tumble through a time tunnel, chase money across the decades, hole up in a hotel room with gadgets and boxes he didn't know how to use, all so he could keep an eye on a white hobo on the off chance the hobo might help make Red and Jade rich?

What kind of fool does this?

"The kind of fool who knows not what he does, yet believes himself wise enough to do so anyway," is what Red's father down in Charlotte would say. *"The kind of fool who seeks dust to quench his thirst, and air to soothe his hunger."*

Red's father had a hundred of these sayings, and every one of them rang in Red's ears as he lay on the hotel bed. He got up and walked over to the door, opened it just enough to peek across the hallway to Elrod's room. He heard the faint din of something, maybe the room's television set, so he assumed Elrod was still in there.

Red went back to the bed and laid down. He rubbed his eyes, took a few deep breaths. He looked at the time on the digital clock. It was 10 p.m. on a Friday night. He should be at the Hideaway, blowing his horn. Instead, he was in this hotel room—all because he let Jade talk him into being greedy.

Okay, that wasn't entirely fair. Red himself got the ball rolling on all this misery when he hung around the Hideaway later than usual one night. He'd spent most of his time in the bathroom, dealing with an evil case of the trots. When he walked out he overheard the conversation between Douglas and that Dago gangster, Fat Sal.

Douglas and Fat Sal had been talking crazy talk about time portals, time travel, payoffs that went from 1949 to half a century in the future, a magic potion they kept stored in liquor bottles. There was a courier named Elrod, and a man named Bubba who was supposed to grab Elrod when he got back to the alley in 1999. A senator who needed to be "whacked," a scientist who got rich while Fat Sal did all the hard work.

Crazy talk. *Loco*, as the Cubans say.

Crazy as it was, it drew Red in.

The time travel part might have been the least interesting part of the conversation. Red wasn't sure he believed in time travel, but he didn't not believe in it, either. It might be bullshit, or it might be the word of God. Who knew? The world was a mystery. What quickened Red's pulse was the money. Douglas and Fat Sal were talking about some serious bread. All Red could think about was what he'd do with that kind of money.

Red's mistake was when he told Jade about it. She heard about the scheme, and the amount of money involved, and that girl's eyes lit up like Times Square. You could almost hear the ideas churning around in her head—and when Jade got an idea in her head, forget it, a tornado couldn't shake it out.

Jade and Red went back a few years. He caught her act at an amateur show one night and decided she had the right sound, and look, to bring in decent crowds. He invited her to sit in with his band from time to time, and every now and then they'd just bump into each other at nightclubs or after-hours joints. You spend that much time together in the wee hours, things are bound to happen—and things had surely happened between Red and Jade.

Well, those days were mostly over. Red and Jade still performed together regularly, and they remained close. But the steam between them had been dialed way, way down. They were more or less just friends now. They enjoyed each other's company. They confided in each other. They shared stories when a story was good enough to share, and this thing involving Douglas and Fat Sal was good enough to share.

Red told Jade about it one night following a show. They were in Red's uptown flat, the wee hours, closing in on sunrise. Red sat at the kitchen table eating a bowl of oatmeal. Jade was on the sofa sipping a glass of wine. A radio played Chopin in the background. It was hot in Red's apartment, and the fan didn't do much besides stir the hot air around. Red had on a white sleeveless shirt and a pair of underwear, but he was still sweating from the heat. Jade had on a burgundy cocktail dress and looked cool and comfortable.

She listened to Red describe the conversation between Douglas and Fat Sal. She didn't raise an eyebrow when the story veered into time travel. But when Red got to the part about the money, her face sprang to life.

"Fifty thousand dollars?" she said.

"Cash," Red said.

"What's the money for again?"

"To pay off some scientist there in the future, the cat who came up with the magic formula and found the magic hole. Fat Sal's here in 1949, hiding out from the law. Has to pay the scientist a couple million before the scientist will let him go to the year he wants to go to."

"What year is that?"

Red shrugged. "Not sure. I just know he wants to go back early enough so he can kill this senator who caused him so much woe."

He tapped his fingers on the table.

"What I wouldn't do with fifty grand," he said. "Open up my own club, be my own damn boss for a change. Just play my music, run my club, make my money, and go home. Nobody to answer to."

Jade put her wine glass down and gave Red one of those looks that always spelled trouble.

"Maybe you can have all that," she said.

"All what?"

"The fifty thousand, for starters. Maybe we can grab it."

"And how do you propose we do that?"

"We know all the details: when the courier should show up at the Hideaway, how the money gets planted on him, who's supposed to meet him back in 1999, where the potion is hidden. We can have someone steal a bottle so we can drink it and travel ahead fifty years. We'll figure out a way to keep this Bubba from meeting the courier in 1999. Then we'll figure out a way to meet the courier ourselves. From there, it's easy. He'll still have the coat—and the money."

"You're really considering this," Red said.

"Why not?"

Red laughed. "Why not? You really asking me that, why not? I'll give you a few why nots. One, if we get caught, that Dago and his Dago friends will chop our heads off and dump them in the harbor. Two, I'm not exactly anxious to hop in some time machine and see where I might land. I could end up going backward to some cotton plantation. And three, I don't steal."

Now Jade laughed.

"Steal?" she said. "Do you know how that money is made in the first place? Gambling, prostitution, extortion, probably murder. And from what you tell me, once Fat Sal gets this scientist paid off, the first thing he's going to do is zap himself to someplace where he can kill a senator. I don't think I'd be too worried about the ethical angle."

"Okay," Red said. "But what about the rest of it?"

He walked to a small refrigerator and pulled out a can of tomato juice. He reached in a drawer for a can opener and punched a hole in the can. He grabbed a glass off a counter and poured the juice in.

"How are we going to steal the potion?" he said. "How are we going to meet up with the courier?"

Within five seconds Jade was laying out a plan, off the cuff, improvised, the gears in her brain chugging furiously. She would talk one of the Hideaway's employees into stealing some of the potion. Red had overhead Douglas and Sal mention which bottles the potion was in. Once she had the potion, she could slip through the portal on her own. Have a look around the world of 1999, get the lay of the land, figure out where things are located and how the world works fifty years in the future. Book a hotel as a base of operations, paid for with money she could easily squeeze out of a hopelessly romantic loan shark who was hopelessly infatuated with her.

The second part of the plan was to establish contact with the courier, Elrod. He'd be easy enough to spot. Some street hobo waltzing into a swanky nightclub like the Hideaway? You could spot him from a mile away. Once they had Elrod clocked, Red could approach him and give him a note to meet someone back to 1999. Meantime, Jade would slip out of the Hideaway that same night, early, ahead of the courier. She'd go through the portal, make her way to 1999, and find Bubba. They knew he worked at a nightclub called the Ecstasy. She'd find the club, and she'd find Bubba. After that, it was just a matter of making sure Bubba wasn't around when Elrod slipped back through the portal and out of the alley.

"How are you gonna make sure Bubba's not around?" Red said.

Jade leaned back, spread her arms, crossed her legs, and showed Red the full package.

"You seriously have to ask that question?" she said.

Red nodded. "Right. You have your ways."

He took a drink of tomato juice.

"So then what?" he continued. "What happens when you do meet up with the courier?"

"Then I get the coat from him myself," Jade said. "And we're fifty thousand richer than we were the day before."

"He might not want to hand that coat over, you know."

"I'll come up with something," Jade said, winking. "We'll be rich, Red."

***

That was the original plan, anyway.

But when Jade actually arrived in 1999 she got another idea, right there on her way to meet Elrod. When she and Elrod got to the hotel room she slipped a sedative into Elrod's water so he'd take a long nap, then she hightailed it back to 1949, to Red's apartment, and filled him in on the details.

She told Red she wanted to take over the whole operation, collect every delivery from Fat Sal—all of them, not just the one that got them fifty thousand. The key was to find this scientist and eliminate him from the equation.

"We'd be the ones on the other side getting the coats and the money, not the scientist," Jade said. "Fat Sal and Douglas wouldn't even know about it because they're here in 1949, and the scientist is way up there in 1999. We could make a whole lot more than the fifty thousand back in that hotel room."

Red stared at Jade, waiting for the punch line. Waiting, waiting, waiting. Waiting for her to say she wasn't serious. Waiting for her to laugh and punch Red in the arm, good-naturedly, tell him it was all just a joke. But it never happened.

"You're serious?" he finally said.

"You're damn right I am."

"You're just gonna muscle in on the whole operation, just like that. Take the whole thing over. Shove Fat Sal out of the way, and the mad scientist, and Douglas. You—little Jade from the prairie."

Jade shook her head. "That's the problem with you, Red."

"What's that?"

"You always think small."

"Wrong. I think logically. I think things through."

"You think too goddamn much."

"You wanna know what I think?" Red said. He pushed his oatmeal away and looked at Jade. "I think you don't want to go messing around with that gangster's money. That's first of all. But let's ignore that for the moment. How about this: You don't even know who this scientist is. You don't even know his name. They won't even *say* his name. There's probably thousands of scientists in this city up there in 1999. So how you even gonna find him?"

"That's where Elrod comes in," Jade said. "He's the key

to finding the scientist, because the scientist is out fifty thousand, and he's going to try and track that money down. The way he does that is to find Elrod. I'd bet you anything he's looking for Elrod right now, looking for the coat. When the scientist finds Elrod, we find the scientist. Then we take over his operation and start sending bums through the magic hole ourselves. We just have to make sure we never let Elrod out of our sight."

"What are you planning on doing to the scientist?" Red said. "I don't want any murder hanging on my conscience."

"Nobody's murdering anyone," Jade said. "Let me figure that part out. Work my own voodoo on him."

"Okay, but how we gonna keep an eye on Elrod up there in 1999 when our lives are here in 1949? Hell, we perform together some nights. And while we're here, he's there with nobody to keep an eye on him."

"We'll just have to figure out a way around it. Work in shifts. Keep Elrod happy in the hotel so he doesn't disappear on us. Come up with a plan to lead him near the portal, where the scientist will be looking for him."

Red took a deep breath, had another drink of tomato juice. He gave Jade a good, long look.

"You know, I'm not exactly thrilled with all this time traveling business," he said. "Back and forth, back and forth, trying to figure out 1999 all over again whenever I step foot in it. It's not my world, Jade. People are bound to be different. They might speak the same language, eat the same things, still piss in a bathroom, the way you tell me. But they're still not my people. They know things I'll never know, but there's nothing I know that they don't know because it's all written down in the history books. It's just not our world, and never will be. What's more, it's not natural, traveling through time. Things can go wrong."

"Like I said, you think too much," Jade responded. "They're no smarter in 1999 than we are in 1949. They just have more information. All we have to do is find the information, and it will tell us everything we need to know and do. It's like reading an instruction manual. Do you know a woman came up to me in 1999 and said she was conducting an informal poll? Asked me who I supported for president in the 2000 election. So I said Smith just to get rid of her, because there's always a Smith, isn't there? And there *was* a Smith, because the woman said, 'You mean Bob Smith, the senator from New Hampshire?' And I nodded yes: him, Bob Smith of New Hampshire. Then she said she was from out of town, and asked me whether I could recommend a good New York-style deli, so I told her Katz's. Because Katz's is still open—I actually passed it while walking around. That's how much the world has changed, Red. There were Smiths running for president in our world, and there are Smiths running for president in 1999. Katz's was open then, and it's open now. The difference is, we can get rich in 1999. But we'll never be rich in 1949."

Red shook his head again. His instinct was to settle for the money they've already made, split it right down the middle. Leave 1999 behind. Go back to being a saxophone player, at least twenty-five grand richer. But Jade, she just had a way with people.

And that's why Red was sitting in a hotel room in 1999, dressed in ugly clothes, keeping an eye on Elrod.

Chapter 20

Elrod stretched his arms and legs across the bed and let out a mighty yawn. He looked at the clock on the nightstand. 10 a.m. He yawned again, stretched some more. He'd been asleep a long time, more than ten hours. It was the best night of sleep he'd had in a long, long time.

Empty dishes and bottles were scattered around the hotel room. He'd eaten both steaks the night before, and one of the potatoes. He knocked down most of the Dewar's and all of the Buds. He watched part of an old Henry Fonda western on TV before falling asleep with the lights on, the TV on, and his clothes on. He'd dozed clear through to right now.

Elrod wasn't exactly thrilled to be mixed up in all this time travel mayhem, but he had to admit it had its perks. He was in a nice hotel room with a comfortable bed and air conditioning. He was dining on steak and Dewar's instead of whatever grub and swill he could afford with the money he scrounged. He could take a hot shower, and he had plenty of spending money. Life could be a whole lot worse. It had, in fact, been a whole lot worse as recently as yesterday. And the day before that. And the ten thousand days before that.

It's funny how a full stomach and a good night's rest can change your perspective. Maybe Elrod had been too hard on Jade. She was just looking for a little help, and Elrod knew what it was like to need help. He depended on the kindness of strangers to get through the day. Jade had put her trust in Elrod by letting him stay in this nice hotel room, order room service. She clearly felt her mission here was important. Maybe her motives were purer than Elrod gave her credit for. Maybe he should give her the benefit of the doubt.

Or, maybe not. Life was a conundrum.

He didn't see signs of Jade anywhere, but that didn't mean she hadn't been here. She told Elrod she'd be back in 1999 early in the morning, before the rooster crows. Maybe she slipped in while Elrod was zonked out, checked that he was still there, and moved along to some other felony.

Elrod looked at the phone and considered calling room service for a big breakfast, but then thought better of it. He had a few things he wanted to do first, and a big meal might slow him down. He planned to take another hot shower and then go get a shave and haircut. After that he'd buy some new clothes.

Thirty minutes later Elrod was showered and dressed. He took a nip of Dewar's, took another for good measure, then headed out the door and strolled to the elevator. As he punched the down button another guy walked up. He was a black guy, a couple inches taller than Elrod and around the same age. He had on a red baseball cap, blue T-shirt, and sunglasses. They rode in silence as the elevator delivered them down to the lobby.

Elrod took a right out of the hotel and made his way to the souvenir shop Jade mentioned. He needed to break the thousand-dollar bill into smaller currency. It was another sunny and mild day outside. Elrod spotted the store after a couple blocks and stepped inside. He was greeted by a dark-haired man with a thick mustache and a smile on his face that looked like it had been welded on twenty years ago and was now frozen permanently in place.

"My friend, my friend," the man said. "How I can help you? Half-price electronics today. Walkman, headphone, boom box, cellular phone. All half price!"

The man had a thick accent that Elrod couldn't quite place. Maybe Eastern European, maybe Middle Eastern. He patted Elrod on the back like they were old Army buddies or something.

"What you need today?" the man continued. "Souvenir? Two for five dollars, four for forty. Ha ha ha! I am joking! What you need?"

"Well here's the thing," Elrod said. "I'd love to buy something, but all's I got is this thousand-dollar bill. See, I cashed a paycheck at the bank down the block and they went and gave me this. You believe that? So, if you accept thousand-dollar bills, then we can conduct business."

The man smiled. Smiled and smiled and smiled.

"Crazy world!" he said. "The bank gives you a thousand-dollar bill when these are not even circulated anymore. Silly bank, yes? Somebody need to fire that teller! Just yesterday a woman comes in with the same kind of bill. Such a pretty lady. What could be the odds? Two people come in, two days in a row, both with thousand-dollar bills. Crazy world!"

Elrod leaned in closer to the man. He lowered his voice and said, "Well to be honest, I happen to know that pretty lady. And she told me, you know, that you might be willing to take this bill off my hands for a little profit in your direction."

The man frowned. Away went the smile, gone in a flash.

"Let me see this bill," the man said.

Elrod pulled it out of his coat pocket and handed it over. The man held it in his hands and rubbed his fingers against it. He yanked both ends. He held it up to the light and inspected it.

"Very risky for me," the man said. "Very risky! I have to go in back, speak with my partner. You wait here."

The man shoved the bill in his pocket and disappeared into the back of the store. Elrod suddenly regretted giving him the bill. What if the guy just pocketed it? It would be his word against Elrod's—and no cop in the world would take a homeless guy's word over a business owner's. Elrod was about to storm to the back of the store himself when the man returned, along with his smile.

"Good news, my friend!" the man exclaimed. "My partner has agreed to accept this bill, even though it might be fake, we don't know. Very risky! But you look like a nice man. We must trust, yes? Where are we without trust?"

"OK," Elrod said. "How much do you..."

"We give you seven hundred dollars," the man interrupted. "Very risky for us!"

"Seven hun...that's a thousand-dollar bill there," Elrod said. "I know for a fact you gave the other woman nine hundred bucks. I want the same or I'll walk out of here and make a deal with someone else."

He snatched the bill from the man's hand and started for the exit. The man grabbed Elrod by the arm.

"Please, please," the man said. "Wow, you drive a hard bargain. You are very slick. So slick! But this is business, yes? Eight hundred! Very risky."

"Nine hundred," Elrod said. "Take it or leave it."

"Yes, but such a big risk," the man said. "I give you eight-fifty. What you want? Twenties, fifties, tens?"

"Nine hundred," Elrod said. "That's the deal. You get a hundred dollars profit for doing nothing but trading currency."

The man's smile weakened.

"I be right back," he said. "You wait here."

The man walked out of the store. Again, Elrod regretted giving him the money. He perused the souvenirs, saw about three dozen little Statues of Liberty, a similar number of Empire State Buildings. Five minutes later the man was back, holding a bank envelope in his hand. He handed it to Elrod.

"You count," the man said. "Nine hundred dollars."

Elrod opened the envelope and pulled out a wad of cash. He looked around the store, checked to see who might be a threat. The only others were an elderly couple done up in I Heart NY shirts. Elrod doubted they were a threat to swipe his cash. He counted the bills. Five fifties, twenty twenties, twenty tens, ten fives. Nine hundred dollars.

"Nice doing business with you," Elrod said. He turned and headed for the exit.

"What you like to buy now?" the man said. "Walkman, brand new! Souvenirs, half price! All T-shirts discounted!"

The man's voice followed Elrod halfway down the

block, but he didn't pay it any mind. He kept walking until he reached the edge of the park, where a halal food cart was parked. Elrod passed these kinds of carts a lot in the city. He wasn't sure what spices they used to cook the chicken and lamb, but whatever they were immediately set his stomach to growling. He rarely had enough money to buy anything, even though you only needed six bucks to get a Styrofoam container packed with chicken, rice, and salad. Now Elrod had plenty of money, and he was hungry. He got in line and pulled out enough cash for two orders, one lamb and one chicken. He planned to eat both right then and there, in the park.

***

Half a block away, Red watched Elrod stroll up to some kind of food cart and wait in line. The cart was located in a round, open plaza surrounded by benches.

Red looked at his watch. It was eleven in the morning. Jade was up in the hotel sleeping. She'd gotten back from 1949 early, about 7 a.m. She woke Red up and told him to go keep a watch out for Elrod. Red hadn't woken up at seven in the morning since he was a kid. In his line of work you were more likely to fall asleep at seven in the morning than wake up. Red had only been asleep a few hours when Jade came barreling in. She didn't seem happy that he was sleeping at all. She told him Elrod could have slipped away without Red noticing.

"He wasn't going anywhere," Red said. "They delivered a bunch of food and liquor to his room last night so it's a pretty sure bet he drank and ate himself into a long slumber. I figured a few hours of sleep was my just desserts for sitting in this hotel room doing a whole lot of nothing."

Jade didn't argue. She told Red she was going to catch a few hours of sleep herself, said he should keep an eye and ear out for Elrod. After Jade crawled into bed, Red sat near the door, listening for stirrings across the hallway. It took a few hours, but he finally heard the door open across the hall. He glanced over at Jade, who was still asleep. He hurried over and roused her awake.

"It's our boy," Red said. "I think he's heading out."

Jade's face sprang to life.

"Follow him!" she said. "Don't let him get out of your sight! Put your hat and dark glasses on so he doesn't recognize you."

"What are you gonna do?" Red said.

"Bathe, eat, go across the hall and wait for him," Jade said. "Scram before you lose him!"

Red tossed on his hat and glasses and rushed out the door. He noticed Elrod waiting for the elevator and strolled up beside him. When the elevator delivered them to the lobby, Red walked slowly behind Elrod and followed him outside, keeping far enough behind to avoid notice. After a couple blocks Elrod stepped into a store advertising electronics and souvenirs. Red waited outside until Elrod came back out, then followed him to the food cart. Red tried to blend in with the crowd. He was pretty sure Elrod had no idea he was being followed.

Whatever they were cooking in that cart smelled awfully good. Red wasn't the only who thought so, either. The line was about twelve people deep when Elrod showed up. It would probably take a while for Elrod to get the food, so Red found a park bench nearby and sat down. He grabbed a discarded newspaper off the bench and pretended to read it. He hid his face behind the paper and kept an eye on Elrod.

A musical trio performed nearby. Trumpet, drums, and upright bass. Street musicians, playing for tips. The drummer didn't have a whole kit—just a snare, bass, and hi-hat. They were playing a medium tempo number in 4/4 time. The horn player had skill but little imagination, staying in the mid-range and on the beat. The bass player was a little more adventurous, plucking a few melodic notes every now and then. The drummer was the best of the three. He could shift the tempo on a dime, quickening the beat and then breaking it in half, working his sticks in a way that made it sound like he had a full kit.

A crowd of about fifteen people gathered around and watched. An open trumpet case lay on the ground in front of them, filled with bills of different denominations. You could find street musicians back in Red's world, too, but they rarely got this much attention, and never got that much bread. Red wondered how much he could make blowing his sax for a couple hours in this park.

Red hadn't been in 1999 very long, but the experience was eye-opening. People chatting into little wireless telephones—outside, inside, all over. Folks with earplugs listening to loud music as they strolled down the street. Young men with half their asses hanging out of their trousers, exposing underwear and cracks. Women barely clothed at all. People typing into metal boxes with no typing paper, getting money out of machines, walking through doors that opened on their own.

Some things Red couldn't imagine seeing back in his world. Men walking hand in hand with each other right there in plain sight. Negro men with their arms draped around white women, strolling little brown babies around, not the least bit concerned that they'd get hassled by cops or crackers. And the cops themselves came in all types—brown, black, white, Oriental, female.

The newspaper held even more fascination. The former mayor of this city was a Negro—or as the paper put it, an "African American." One of the highest-ranking police officials was an African American. Some of the biggest movie stars and musical performers were, too. Black and brown athletes dominated the sports headlines. Women, Orientals, and Spanish people had been elected senators, congressmen, and governors. Even homosexuals.

Red opened to the entertainment section of the newspaper. Dozens of clubs advertised live music, but only a few seemed to specialize in jazz. A couple featured blues, or country & western. Most mentioned idioms Red hadn't heard of: hip hop, rock, techno, reggae, funk, punk.

Red wondered if any of these venues could use a good sax player. He wondered if it was any easier earning a living as a musician in 1999 than it was fifty years ago, when nightclub owners nickel and dimed you over every little thing, and you were in constant fear of losing your cabaret card if you got on somebody's wrong side.

Red didn't have much time to mull it over. He was just getting ready to curse the sons-of-bitches who run the business when a voice clattered in his ear.

"Hey brother man, how you livin'?" the voice said.

Red popped his head up from the newspaper. He saw a tall, skinny, straggly brown man standing in front of him, smiling the fakest smile you've ever seen. The man had Negro features but light skin. His hair was nappy and unkempt and his face was dirty. He smelled of alcohol and body odor. His blue and orange shirt had Mets written across the front, and his black trousers were sliding off his waist, revealing yellowed underwear.

The man looked at the trio and nodded his head to the music.

"Them boys is tight," the man said. "That brother on the sticks got the most game, but them white boys got skills, too. Personally speaking, I ain't really about all that old-time shit. But respect: they can play."

The man looked back at Red.

"Got a couple dollars, help a brother get a bite to eat?" the man said. "I'm starvin' like Marvin. Matter of fact, my name is Marvin, so you *know* I'm starvin'."

Red looked at the man. Some things never changed. You had street beggars back in his day, you have them now. You had them 1,000 years ago and you'll have them 1,000 years in the future. *God bless the child that's got his own.* He reached into his pocket and pulled out a quarter, handed it to the man. The man looked at it and frowned.

"This it?" Marvin said. "A quarter? Can't even buy a bag of chips with no quarter. How about something a little higher up the currency chain, maybe folds up."

Red shook his head. A quarter could buy you a hot meal back in 1949, but it obviously didn't go very far in 1999. The only paper money Red had was a few hundred-dollar bills Jade gave him, and he wasn't about to part with those.

"Sorry, friend," he said. "That's as good as I can do."

"Well ain't that some shit," Marvin said. He pointed across the way to where Elrod sat with his food on another park bench. "See that raggedy-ass white boy over there, shoving his face full of that dee-licious Ay-rab food? He broke as I am, so how he got the money for all that food? I'll tell you how: some generous, kind-hearted, God-fearin' motherfucker gave it to him, that's how. Now you over here trying to tell me you can't give a brother no more than a quarter."

Red shrugged his shoulders. "Wish I could do more."

"Wish you could too, Fred Sanford. Take your money and buy some new clothes."

Marvin waved his hand and moved along. He walked past Elrod, stopped, spun around, and got up into Elrod's face. The two exchanged words before a police officer intervened and separated them. Marvin headed one way and Elrod headed the other, dropping the empty cartons in a garbage can.

Red hated to leave the relative calm of the park bench, but duty called. He followed Elrod, making sure to stay about fifteen or so yards behind. Elrod was headed back in the direction of the Northpark Village Hotel, which was fine by Red. He wanted to hand all this back off to Jade and return to his own world.

But Elrod didn't go to the hotel. Instead, he stopped into a hair salon. Red wondered why. Did men get their hair cut at hair salons in 1999? He sighed and walked across the street to keep an eye out. He propped himself up against a utility pole, grumbled, waited, grumbled some more.

Thirty minutes later Elrod emerged from the salon, looking like an old Chevy that had just been overhauled and spit-shined. His hair was cut short and styled up slick and neat. His beard was gone, making him look ten years younger. Red might not have recognized Elrod at all if he didn't have the same outfit on—the coat, the black shirt, the blue denim pants. Red's first thought was that this could throw a wrench into the works. If Red couldn't recognize Elrod, chances are the scientist wouldn't, either—and Jade's whole plan depended on using Elrod as bait to trap the scientist.

Well, so be it. Maybe it was for the best. Maybe this time Jade would drop the whole thing and they could just enjoy the financial haul they'd already made. Fifty thousand dollars, all in 1949 currency. Twenty-five grand each. That was a whole lot of bread back in 1949, and probably a pretty good piece of change here in 1999. It might be enough to buy Red a little club uptown where he could set up a trio and not have to answer to anyone else. That's all he wanted.

But Jade, she always wanted more. Red didn't understand it, but there it was.

After exiting the salon Elrod took off in another direction, away from the hotel. Red shook his head and followed. Four blocks later Elrod stepped into a public library. Red waited a couple of minutes before walking into the library himself. It wasn't very big, and Red had no problem spotting Elrod. He was sitting at a row of desks with machines on them. The machines had keyboards that looked like typewriter keyboards. The machines also had screens and some kind of oval-shaped doodads you moved around with your hand. Red wasn't sure what these machines did, but whatever it was, Elrod looked pretty well locked in.

Red found a seat in the periodicals section. He picked up a magazine, flipped through a couple of pages, got bored, put it back down. His brain was tired. He wanted to turn it off for a spell, soak up the quiet of the library. He had to stop himself from closing his eyes and dozing off.

After about twenty minutes or so Elrod got up from the machine and made his way toward the exit. Red followed him outside and into the street. At the next block Elrod strolled into a large department store. Red trailed him inside.

The place was pretty crowded. Red quickened his step to make sure he didn't lose sight of Elrod. He followed him up an escalator and then to the men's clothing department. Elrod walked over to the shirts section. Red held back in an area that sold sport coats, and pretended to shop. He checked the fabrics and styles and decided they were medium quality at best, way overpriced, and poorly designed.

Elrod was not so discerning. He grabbed a handful of collared shirts off the first rack he saw and went into a dressing room. A minute later he walked back out, tossed a few of the shirts back on top of the rack and kept a couple for himself. He strolled to the cashier, dumped the shirts on the counter and paid in cash. The cashier delicately folded the shirts and placed them in a plastic bag. Elrod snatched the bag off the counter and moved along.

His next stop was the pants department. He grabbed several pairs of tan khaki trousers and denim jeans, walked into a dressing room, came back out a couple minutes later, threw a few pairs back on top of the rack, and kept a couple for himself. He walked to the cashier and dumped the pants on the counter. Again, he paid in cash and snatched the plastic bag off the counter.

Elrod moved on to footwear. He grabbed two packages of socks and then headed for the shoe section. Red planted himself within earshot and watched in mild amusement as Elrod told the salesman exactly what he wanted: casual dark brown loafers you can slip on real easy, size nine medium, that will hold up under tough conditions and are comfortable to walk in. The salesman disappeared into the stockroom and came back five minutes later with a couple boxes of shoes. Elrod tried on the first pair and walked around in them.

"These'll do," he said.

Back to the cashier station, where cash was paid, boxes and packages were placed into a plastic bag, and the bag was snatched off the counter. Elrod combined all the bags together into a single bag and moved along.

Red figured that was it, but Elrod had one more stop to make: luggage. He took a little more time here, picking up suitcases and bags and inspecting each one carefully. He lifted them over his head to check their weight. He rubbed his hands against them. He adjusted the straps and threw them on his shoulder to see how they felt. He punched one bag with his fist to test its toughness and durability. Red guessed that when you lived on the street, you needed a bag that was roomy but not too bulky, and could withstand the elements.

Eventually Elrod found a bag to his liking. It was one you could strap over your shoulder or on your back, probably big enough to hold all of Elrod's worldly possessions. He carried it to the cashier station, along with his other purchases. The cashier rang him up. Elrod pulled more cash out of his pocket and handed it over. Red wondered how much money Elrod had spent in the space of the last thirty minutes. Probably more than he'd spent in one place in twenty years, if ever.

After finishing the transaction Elrod took his plastic bags and stuffed them into his new travel bag. He rode the escalator down and headed for the exit, Red following about ten paces behind. When Elrod got to the exit he was stopped by some guy in a security uniform. The two exchanged words. Elrod reached into his pocket and pulled out a handful of receipts. He shoved them at the security guard. A couple fell to the ground. The security guard picked them up and looked them over. He said something to Elrod and Elrod handed over his travel bag. The security guard looked inside and checked the merchandise against the receipts.

"I oughta go talk to your manager, tell him you're harassing paying customers," Elrod said in a voice loud enough for others to hear.

The security guard handed the travel bag and receipts back to Elrod.

"Thanks," the guard said.

"Hell of a thing," Elrod snapped. "Treating paying customers like they're common thieves. You'll be hearing from my attorney, that's a promise!"

The security guy nodded and wished Elrod a good day.

Elrod stomped out of the store and took a left. He walked at a brisk pace for a couple blocks, took a right, and walked another two blocks. Red kept his usual distance, ten yards to the rear. Elrod didn't seem to notice him. In short order they were back at the Northpark Village Hotel.

Elrod headed straight for the elevator. It was a welcome sight for Red, who was hungry and tired of following this cat around. He waited for Elrod to take a car up and reach the eleventh floor, then Red did the same thing. As he was about to enter his own room he heard a couple of voices from the room across the hallway. Jade and Elrod.

That was a welcome sound to Red. Let Jade babysit Elrod for a while. Red just wanted to use the can and hustle on back to 1949, where he could get a plate of ribs and have a quick snooze before tonight's show. He used the can, left a note for Jade, then bolted.

Chapter 21

Sidney Donovan crawled out of the taxi and felt her foot slip as soon as it hit the sidewalk. She looked down and saw a puddle of puke just below her nice pair of black loafers. She cursed and pulled a pack of antibacterial wet wipes from her purse. She reached down to wipe her shoe and used another wipe on her hands. *Welcome to LoDown. Hope you enjoy your stay.*

Sidney was here because Dr. Bunt said this is where she might find Elrod, the notorious coat thief. Sidney had her doubts. Homeless folks don't tend to hang around areas where the only other people are homeless folks, at least during working hours. They needed to hit the richer parts of town, where they had a better chance of scrounging up some cash. But Dr. Bunt insisted she start in LoDown, so here she was.

Her first order of business was to chat up a few of the locals, show them Elrod's photo, ask if they'd seen him around. This would require money. Money for information. That's how it worked in this part of town. It's how it worked just about everywhere.

Sidney knew it wouldn't take long for some street hustler to approach her. That's also how it worked in this part of town—especially when someone like Sidney showed up, dressed professionally in a gray pants suit, black blouse, black loafers, Ralph Lauren bag. Sure enough, a tall, bearded man with brown skin and a bald head walked right up to Sidney as soon as her cab disappeared from view.

The man wore a T-shirt with *Muy Loco* printed on it, a pair of gray sweatpants cut off at the knees, red high-top sneakers, and an eyepatch over his left eye. He stopped just in front of Sidney and gave her the *crazy stare*. He was a couple inches taller than Sidney, but not much heavier. Sidney sized him up immediately. Hard eyes, curled lip, chest bowed out, full psycho badass mode. She had seen plenty of these types during her days as a cop. They were the wolves who kept their eyes open for the easy prey.

"Spare a few dollars?" the man growled. "I'm hungry, need to eat. *Unos pocos dolares para poder comer?*"

Sidney kept her feet firmly planted on the ground and returned the man's stare.

"Nope," she said. "No *dolares*."

The man edged a little closer.

"Why you come here, then, you got no *dolares*?" he said. "You from the probation office? Tryin' to run down a dope fiend? You from the church, here to save souls? I know you ain't no five-o because cops don't take cabs. Maybe you an investor looking to open a Starbuck. This a good place for a Starbuck. We all rich yuppies down here, love our Starbuck. Me, I'm a crazy man. *Muy loco*. Gimme some money, *hermana*. I need money."

This time Sidney moved closer.

"What you need, *hermano*, is to step off," she said. "I'm here on a job, and you're not part of it. I want to talk to people, and you're not one of them. You slide one inch closer and you and I will have a problem."

The man squinted his eye, frowned. He held his stare a couple more seconds. Then he laughed.

"Shiiiiiiiit," he said. "You a stone-cold gangsta, is what you are! A thug. *Un gamberro*. You scare me, you talk crazy like that. Crazy woman! *Muy loco*! What's the matter, you don't like me? *No me quieres?* I treat you nice. I treat all the pretty ladies nice."

He laughed again, then turned around and strolled on.

With that out of the way, Sidney went back to scouting the area. She kept her eye out for either Elrod or the right kind of person to talk to about Elrod. It had to be someone who appeared reasonably sane, a little worn down but not too worn down, and just desperate enough to talk to a stranger in exchange for a few bucks.

Sidney didn't see a lot of winning candidates as she made her way down one block and to another. She spotted about a dozen people. Some were passed out on stoops or sidewalks. One stared at a stop sign. Another screamed at the back of a transvestite's head while the transvestite admired herself in a pocket mirror. One happy, horny dude was dry humping the air.

Finally, Sidney spotted a white guy, medium height, skinny, sitting on a stoop, leaning forward, and staring at the sidewalk. He had short hair and looked pretty young, maybe in his early twenties, but he was the only one in this group who looked anything remotely like Elrod. She pulled the photo of Elrod out of her pocket and checked it against the man sitting there. She knew he wasn't Elrod, but she walked over anyway.

"Hiya," she said. "Got a second?"

The man stared at the sidewalk without responding.

Sidney sat down beside him.

"My name's Sidney Donovan," she said. "I'm a private investigator."

She pulled a PI license from her coat pocket and showed it to the man. He glanced at it briefly then stared at the sidewalk again.

"I've been hired to find someone," Sidney said. "He's a white male, probably in his forties. Medium height. Thin build. Beard, shaggy hair, goes by the name of Elrod."

She showed the man Elrod's photo.

"This is him," Sidney said. "Does he look familiar? Anyone you might know?"

She pulled out the photo of the coat and showed it to the man. "He's probably wearing this coat now."

The man studied the photos. He turned his eyes back to the sidewalk without saying anything.

"Do you have a name?" Sidney said. "I guess we haven't been properly introduced."

The man didn't say anything.

"OK, I understand," Sidney said. "Strange woman comes up to you out of the blue, shows you a PI card, starts asking questions. What's in it for you, right?"

She reached into her coat pocket and pulled out a ten-dollar bill.

"This is yours for whatever help you can give me," Sidney said, holding the bill in front of her. "It's part of my expense account. You know, to get information I can't get for free. I don't mind giving these bills away because they're not really mine anyway. My client foots the bill. I could give it to you or give it to somebody else. I'm pretty sure you could use it."

The man leaned back on the stoop.

"Dude might look familiar," he said. "Lots of folks 'round here. Hard to keep track. The coat looks familiar. Mighta seen a few of those around. Probably somebody stole a crate of 'em and traded 'em for crank or something."

Sidney nodded but didn't say anything.

"Might've seen that dude down at the Screamin' Korean's a couple times," the man went on. "I go down there when I got money. Buy Doritos, smokes, bumpers. So there's your helpful information, and that's my money."

He reached for the ten-dollar bill. Sidney snatched it back.

"Not so fast," she said. "Who's the Screamin' Korean?"

"Korean guy, owns a store, yells a shit-ton," the man answered. "Everybody calls him the Screamin' Korean. He charges too damn much. You can get it cheaper just about anywhere in town. But it's convenient to *this* side of town, so it ain't like you got a real choice. Location, location, location."

"Where's the store?" Sidney asked.

The man pointed to his right. "Couple blocks down that way, hang a left. It's on the corner. Right beside a laundromat. Can't miss it."

"Thanks for the help," Sidney said. She released the bill and it slid into the man's hand.

"No problem," he said. "Got a smoke?"

Sidney shook her head and walked on. A couple minutes later she spotted the store and stepped inside. A man was sitting on a stool behind the counter. He had a slight frame, black hair, and wire-rim glasses. She figured he was mid-thirties or so. He was reading a newspaper with Asian language characters. He didn't look up when Sidney entered.

"Excuse me," Sidney said. "Are you the proprietor?"

"I own store," the man said without looking up. "Owner, manager, proprietor, owner."

"Good," Sidney said. "I was hoping to ask you a couple of questions..."

"You need something, find yourself," the man interrupted. "Food, battery, wine, malt riquor, candy, soda, newspaper, canned good. Chef-Boy-R-Dee. Pringles. Cash only. Lotto and cigarette you buy at counter. Cash only. No check. No credit card. Cash only."

"I'm not a customer," Sidney said. "I'm here in an official capacity. I'm a private investigator. I'd like to ask you a couple of questions."

The man jerked his face up and glared at Sidney.

"You from health department, hey?" he grumbled. "We fix problem already. Everything back up to code now, all fixed! Wiring fixed. Refrigeration fixed. Nice and cold now, nothing spoil. Why you here? Something else to cost me money? New rules now? Every week new rules! New rules, new regulation! Cost lots money!"

"No no no, nothing like that," Sidney said, smiling. "I'm not a health inspector. I'm a private investigator, working for a private client. My client is trying to find someone, a man who spends time down in this area. A homeless man. I'm talking to people in the neighborhood, see whether they've seen him around, where I might be able to find him. He might have been in your store recently."

She pulled the photo of Elrod out and placed it on the counter. She put a photo of the coat beside it.

"Here's a photo of the man I'm trying to find," Sidney said. "It was taken a few weeks ago. He's probably wearing that coat now. His name is Elrod. I just need to know if you've seen him. We're offering a reward for anyone who can help us find him. Cash."

The man set the newspaper on the counter and got down from the stool. He looked at the photo.

"Yeah, this guy," he said. "A real laugh a minute. Comes around from time to time, tosses a few coins on the counter, expects me to give him the royal treatment. He was in the other day, in fact. Looking for malt liquor. Only he didn't have any money."

Sidney gave the Korean a sideways look. The voice he just spoke in wasn't the voice he'd used earlier. It was a crisp American accent now, with the slightest hint of North Jersey.

"Say that last part again?" Sidney said.

"He didn't have any money," the man replied. "Not a huge surprise around this neighborhood. This ain't exactly the Hamptons."

"Your accent sure did change in a hurry," Sidney said.

The man smiled. "Yeah, well. I only use my loud crazy Korean voice when I need to. It's pretty effective when I need to keep the clientele in line or stonewall the inspectors. When you bark at them in broken English they figure you're a hopeless case, crazier than they are. Since you're not a customer trying to con me or an inspector trying to squeeze me, I can talk normal. I don't get to do that much here."

"Are you really the owner?"

The man nodded. "This business is the family legacy, quote unquote. My father retired a few years ago and left the empire to me. I plan on keeping it until I finally get my real estate license, then I'm selling it to the first sucker who can come up with the down payment. I was born and raised in Newark. My name's John."

Sidney chuckled. "It's very good, John. Your fake accent."

John shrugged.

"You saw this man the other day, was it?" Sidney said.

"Yep, mid-morning, something like that."

"You say he didn't have any money?"

"No money. So I shooed him away."

"Do you have any idea where he went?"

"Out the door is all I know. But he probably didn't roam too far. This neighborhood is a magnet for homeless people. Lots of empty buildings to hole up in, not a lot of cops to hassle you. Chances are your guy is somewhere between here and Colve Park, just like all the others. They go around in circles, around and around, every day, like hawks. And people like you are the prey, so don't be surprised if you get a lot of requests for money. You know where the park is?"

Sidney said she did. She thanked John and handed him a business card.

"If you see him, would you mind giving me a call? Don't tell him anyone is looking for him. Maybe find out if there's any special place he likes to hang out or sleep."

"So how much is this reward you mentioned?" John said.

"Call it a hundred bucks," Sidney said. "Maybe more,

depending on the information."

"You interested in buying a store?"

Sidney chuckled. "Not me."

"Oh well, I had to ask," John said. "I'll let you know if I hear anything. Good luck finding him. He clazy man! Clazy! Too much malt riquor!"

They both laughed.

Chapter 22

Douglas wondered how the same human race that could create a mind as transcendent as da Vinci's could also create the drooling lump standing in front of him now.

The lump's name was Sammy Berg. He and Douglas were in front of the Hideaway entrance, talking about magic. Douglas told Sammy that people liked to practice magic out here. They might suddenly appear, Douglas explained, or suddenly disappear. It was all magic. Nothing more. Douglas wanted Sammy to stand guard beside the portal in case anyone appeared from 1999 or tried to disappear to 1999. Douglas didn't mention the time travel part, of course. He just explained, as simply as he could, that it was all illusion, eye tricks. The same way you'd explain it to a child. But Douglas was beginning to wonder whether Sammy was the right man for the job.

Sammy stared at the space around him. "Magic, huh?" he said.

"That's right," Douglas said. "You know, disappearing acts. Illusion."

He pointed toward the invisible time portal. "They do it right there, where I'm pointing. It looks like people can appear and disappear at the snap of the finger. But it's just illusion. Magic."

"Geez," Sammy said.

"What I want you to do is keep watch here to see if anybody practices their magic acts. Don't let them do it. If anyone walks to that spot, detain him, and come get me. If anyone suddenly appears out of nowhere, detain him, too."

Sammy nodded in a way that reminded Douglas of those nodding dog toys you saw in some of the stores, just nodding brainlessly and thoughtlessly, nodding and nodding and nodding some more.

Sammy was a hulking beast of a man with a square jaw, wide shoulders, thick chest, and dim eyes. He was the biggest, dumbest Jew that Douglas had ever known. He was, in fact, the only dumb Jew Douglas had ever known. Douglas would have preferred putting someone else in charge of this duty, but nobody else was stupid enough to believe in magic acts. As far as Douglas could tell, Sammy had only one discernable skill: cracking heads. He was very good at cracking heads.

"You know how it is," Douglas said. "Everyone wants to get into show business. They'd like to do an act here at the Hideaway. We just don't want them practicing their acts in front of the club though, do we?"

Douglas wanted the portal guarded for one reason—to keep Fat Sal from slipping through. This had become a recent worry. Douglas got the sense, after chatting with Fat Sal at the diner, that he was now seriously considering going back to 1999 to find Elrod and the money. Fat Sal was angry about the missing fifty thousand. He was angry about being holed up in 1949 and having to take orders from Dr. Bunt. His pride was wounded. So was his ego. He thought he was the only one sharp enough to find Elrod and get the money back.

Sammy glanced in the direction of the portal.

"Disappearing acts?" he said.

"Yes," Douglas said. "Like what you might see at vaudeville shows or the circus."

"Never been to a circus," Sammy said. "Been to a zoo once. Saw a buffalo bison and an ostrich. And a gorilla that played with its dick."

He took a closer look at the portal. "So what happens, somebody disappears here?"

Douglas nodded.

"Why?" Sammy said. "Where do they go?"

Douglas sighed. Why can't people take straight orders anymore? Why do they have to confuse the issue, and themselves, with pointless questions?

"They don't go anywhere," Douglas said. "They just *appear* to. Anyway, it's not important, is it? The point is, we don't want anyone practicing magic out here. I want you to stand here until further notice and block this area off. Don't let anyone enter. I don't care who it is. Nobody gets to practice magic here."

"What if they ignore me and do it anyway?" Sammy asked.

"Then stop them. Break their necks if need be."

Sammy thought it over.

"Yeah, OK," he said. "That ain't a problem."

"Fabulous," Douglas said.

"Disappearing acts," Sammy said. "Geez."

Chapter 23

Jade heard the click of the door and put down the magazine she was reading. She was back in room 1115, sitting in the corner chair. The door opened and a beardless, clean-cut, not unhandsome man walked in. At first she thought he was with the hotel staff. This annoyed Jade because she gave strict orders that no one should enter the room unless she personally requested it.

Then she noticed the clothes on the man. Plain black T-shirt. Faded blue jeans. Red-and-black coat. She knew those clothes, and that coat. They belonged to Elrod. Except Elrod didn't look like Elrod anymore.

Dammit.

What had Elrod done? Where were his beard and shaggy hair? Nobody would recognize him now. The whole key to Jade's plan was for the scientist to recognize Elrod and make his move. But if the scientist couldn't recognize Elrod...

Dammit.

And what's this now? Elrod had some kind of travel bag. He opened the bag up over the bed and dumped a bunch of clothes out. New clothes, with the price tags still on them. More bad news. Now he won't even be dressed like Elrod anymore.

If the scientist doesn't spot Elrod, then Jade won't spot the scientist. And if Jade doesn't spot the scientist...

Dammit.

Elrod noticed Jade sitting in the chair.

"You're here," he said.

"You went to the *barber*?" Jade said.

"Shave and a haircut, two bits," Elrod answered, winking.

He grabbed the bottle of Dewar's off the dresser. He took a drink, wiped his mouth, and took another drink.

"So how was 1949?" he said. "Is Truman still president, or did some time travel voodoo put Mickey Rooney in the White House? Could happen, you know. Ronald Reagan was president in the '80s. You believe that?"

"You went to the *barber*?" Jade repeated.

"Well, technically they call it a hair salon. Sounds fancier, so they can charge more. But hell, we're rich now."

"You look really different," Jade said. "Just really, really different."

"New look, new beginnings."

Elrod pulled his coat off and tossed it into a corner of the room. "And goodbye to you, too. You were a fine coat. Until you weren't."

Jade watched the coat dance in the air and float toward the floor. Her eyes widened, as if they'd just seen a wolf lash its teeth into a young calf.

"What do you mean 'goodbye'?" she said. "You're not getting rid of the *coat*, are you? What if the weather turns cold?"

Elrod chuckled. "Where I'm headed the weather won't turn cold."

Jade took a couple of deep breaths, tried to calm herself. Her plans to get rich and stick it to Douglas and his fat Italian friend were vanishing in front of her eyes. Nobody was playing along. Elrod kept threatening to leave town. Red offered resistance at every turn. His heart just wasn't in it. He wanted to take what they already had and leave it at that. Jade wanted more. Of course, she wanted more. Why wouldn't she?

Men were such dopes. You had to hold their hands every step of the way. They didn't see the big picture. They were like pets, content to lie around and lick themselves as long as there was plenty of food in the bowl.

Jade knew a lot about men—too much. She grew up surrounded by them, then kept surrounding herself with them well into adulthood. Men had no imagination. They got stuck in their ruts, welded to their routines. They grew comfortable, content, boring, lazy, stupid.

Jade's three brothers were prime examples. She loved them, sure she did. But Jesus, what had they ever accomplished, or even tried to accomplish? The oldest, Clint, could have gone to the state university on a football scholarship. He could have studied science or engineering and accomplished something. But he chose to forego college and help with the farm. Jade's two other brothers went off to fight the Nazis—helped liberate Paris, for God's sakes—then scrambled right back to the farm as soon as the war ended. All her brothers were back in the same Kansas town, married now, with a bunch of runty kids running wild.

It was just assumed that Jade would follow the same path, marry one of the local boys and raise a bunch of runts of her own. But that idea never set up shop in her mind. Jade wanted more—always, as long as she could remember. She wanted to see the world, make a name for herself, earn a big pile of money. Her parents didn't understand it. They didn't even see the point of Jade sticking around high school long enough to graduate when a life of matronly duty followed.

"You have all the education a girl in these parts will ever need," her mother said.

"Maybe I don't want to be a girl in these parts," Jade answered. "You ever consider that?"

Jade liked school. She liked learning. She was smart—smarter than any of the other kids at her school (admittedly, no great feat). She had a talent for math, for numbers. She thought she might be good at business. She watched her father and brothers work sunup to sundown trying to turn crops and livestock into profits, only to barely squeak by most years. Jade figured there had to be an easier way to earn a buck. She studied hard and graduated at the top of her class (again, no great feat). But no college was interested in offering scholarships to women, and Jade's parents couldn't afford to send her even if they wanted to, which they didn't.

Jade's only other option for escape was to pursue her other talent: singing. She sang in the church choir. She sang in the school choir. She won competitions at county fairs. She spent hours listening to the radio, mesmerized by Billie Holliday, Ella Fitzgerald, Peggy Lee, Kay Thompson.

In high school Jade all but begged her father to let her

tag along on one of his occasional trips to Kansas City to drum up business. She wanted to hit the nightclubs, see the swing bands. He finally relented just so she'd shut up. She got hooked then and there, watching the jazz singers in the Kansas City clubs while her father sat beside her staring at his watch.

If Jade couldn't be a businesswoman, she'd be a singer. She worked part-time jobs throughout high school, against her mother's wishes, saving money. Two weeks after graduating she sat down with her parents and laid out her plans: She was heading east to New York City, the entertainment capital of the world. She was going to be a professional singer.

Her mother's response was quick and to the point.

"You're not going to that filthy, crime-ridden cesspool," she said. "I won't allow it."

"I'm not asking permission," Jade said. "I'm eighteen years old, a legal adult. I can do as I please. I have enough money saved for the train fare and a few weeks rent until I find a job."

Her mother insisted that Jade drop her plans, but her father stepped in and surprised everyone.

"Let the girl go," he said. "Like she says, she's a legal adult now. She's free to make her own mistakes on her own dime. She's gonna do what she wants anyway, always has. She's got a talent for the singing trade. Might as well let her chase after it."

He handed her a twenty-dollar bill and told her to use it for train fare and save her own money for when she really needed it. It was a lot of money for her father, and she tried to give it back. But he insisted that she keep it.

"Send a wire when you get there, let us know where

you're living," he told Jade. "Don't trust anybody. Work hard, spend your money wisely. Use your common sense, the way you were raised. Knee a man in his sack if he tries to get fresh, just like I showed you."

He wrote down the phone number and address of a couple he knew back east, an old Army buddy and his wife.

"I'll let them know you're moving into the area," Jade's father said. "Go visit them, you'll probably get a good meal out of it."

Two days later Jade hugged her family goodbye and hopped on an eastbound train. Once she hit New York she found a room at a boarding house and worked a series of menial jobs to pay the rent and buy clothes. In her spare time she hunted singing gigs. She failed one audition after another, and got propositioned more times than she cared to remember. Her break, if you can call it that, came during an amateur night contest at a midtown cabaret. Red happened to be in the audience. He approached her after the show and asked if she might like to sit in with his group sometime.

"Depends on the pay," Jade said.

Red laughed.

"You've never even had a real gig and you're already negotiating?" he said. "You're gonna go far in this business, sister."

They reached an agreement over drinks and Jade took the gig. She'd been singing with his group ever since. She'd realized her dream of becoming a professional singer in the entertainment capital of the world.

It was nice, but it still wasn't enough. Jade wanted more. More money. More control. She saw how much the musicians got paid versus how much the nightclub owners raked in. She was nothing more than the hired help—long hours for little pay. The musicians pulled in the crowds, but the club owners called the shots and pocketed the winnings.

Jade wanted to be the one calling the shots. She sat down and laid out ideas on how to bring more business to the Hideaway. Special promotions, special events, a cocktail hour, a Sunday brunch with live music. She bounced all of these ideas off of Douglas—and Fat Sal if he happened to be around. Jade told them she'd handle all the organizing and heavy lifting. All they had to do was cut her in on the profits. But they swatted her ideas down at every turn. Not only that, they did so in a way designed to put her right back in her place.

Now Jade had a chance to make her own money, call her own shots—and exact a little revenge on Douglas and Fat Sal in the process. All this cash was changing hands between Fat Sal in 1949 and the scientist in 1999. She wanted that cash, and she didn't feel bad about taking it. But she kept running into roadblocks. Elrod with his plans to scram out of town. Red with his lack of ambition, his fear of the future and all it represented.

Jade could understand that fear, up to a point. Sure, 1999 was a weird place to land. It's not like Jade was exactly *comfortable* here. People looked different, they spoke differently, they dressed differently, they drove around in these tiny automobiles with loud colors and silly designs. You had to push buttons to make a telephone call, and the telephone numbers had too many digits. Doors opened and closed on their own. Toilets flushed on their own. Everybody was loud; every*thing* was loud. The kids with those large headphone contraptions, the way they thump thump thumped up and down the street. Everything was expensive. Eight dollars for a hamburger. Three dollars for a cup of coffee in some places. It was all mind-boggling, and Jade had to put on her best act to shuffle through without looking lost.

Even so...

There was an energy to the future. A magic. Jade saw women wearing suits and carrying briefcases, looking important, sitting at tables with businessmen and controlling the conversation. This very hotel seemed to be run by a woman. Jade noticed her down in the lobby, giving instructions to other workers. People seemed to have a lot of money. They even gave out money at machines, right there on the sidewalk. You put some kind of plastic card in, jabbed a few buttons, then out came the money. The air was full of capitalism, and Jade wanted to breathe it all in, suck it through her mouth and fill her lungs with it.

But she was surrounded by dead weight. Elrod. Red. *Hoo-boy.*

It was enough to make a girl scream.

Jade looked at Elrod, who was arranging his new clothes on the hotel bed.

"What are your plans?" she asked.

"First I'll take a shower to wash out all this perfumy gel they put in my hair," Elrod answered. "Then I'll iron my nice new clothes. After that, we'll see. My gut tells me to head to the nearest transit station and catch the first bus heading west."

"I wish you'd stick around, just for a bit. I need your help. Just walk to that LoDown area with me and see if we can spot the scientist. I have plenty of money. You can have more of it."

Elrod gave her a sharp look. "You know, technically that's not even your money. You'll recall that it was in my coat when I left that nightclub."

"And you'll recall that I saved you from this Bubba goon. If it weren't for me, you might not even be here. And you wouldn't have known about the money anyway."

"Look, I'm not in the mood to argue. I'm a reasonable guy, and you seem pretty hell-bent on carrying through with your plan. You keep most of the money. I'll just grab a few thousand to keep me flush until I settle down somewhere else."

"Nix. The money is in the safe, and I'm the one with the combination. It stays there until we see my plan through to the end."

"Right," Elrod said. "Your plan."

"That's right."

"The one that includes saving the senator? That the plan you're talking about?"

"That's part of it, yes."

"The senator whose mama maybe saved your life that fateful night?"

"That's right."

"Funny thing about that," Elrod said. "I did some research on this senator down at the library today. You remember I told you about computers, the World Wide Web? It's amazing what you can learn with just a few clicks—especially about senators. I learned the most interesting things. Like, Senator Miles McLaughlin didn't even grow up on the west side. He was born there in 1947 but a few months later his family moved to Queens after his dad got promoted by the fire department. His dad, his mom, Miles, his brother, and sister, who was still in the womb. His mom's name is Annette, by the way, not Mary. She's still alive."

Jade kept silent. Elrod pressed on.

"You said your apartment is on the west side, and that this Mrs. McLaughlin lives right down the hallway, and that she has no husband and no other kids," he said. "So either you know a different Mrs. McLaughlin, or you're lying."

"So maybe this World Wide Web of yours is wrong," Jade said.

"Oh, I doubt that. I got about a dozen different sources giving pretty much the same biography of Miles McLaughlin. Which means the Miles McLaughlin you told me about, if he really exists at all, is not the same Miles McLaughlin who's now a US senator."

Jade leaned back in the chair. She looked up at the ceiling, then back at Elrod. She almost went for the lie again but decided it was no use.

"OK, I lied about the mother. And the overdose," she said. "None of that happened. I thought maybe if you heard a story like that you'd be willing to help. I was wrong to lie about it. But even if I was lying, we still know that Fat Sal wants to come back and kill the senator. Don't you think we should at least do something about it?"

"I don't know what to think, to be honest. All I really know for sure is that I seem to be in the middle of something I don't want to be in the middle of."

"You don't have to be in the middle of it. I just need you to be the decoy, the bait. Just lure the scientist in, then I'll handle it. After that you can go on your merry way. He'll be looking for you. That's a sure bet."

Elrod studied Jade a moment.

"Why are you so hell-bent on doing all this, anyway?" he said. "You have a nice stash there in the safe. I bet in 1949 it can carry you through the next few years. My advice is take what you got and leave it at that."

"There's a lot more money where that came from, and I intend to get it," Jade said. "But that's only part of it, if you want to know the truth."

"And the other part?"

"The other part is, I don't like Douglas. He's arrogant and vicious. I want to look him in the eye one day and let him know I outsmarted him. I don't like Salvatore Morino either, for that matter. And I probably wouldn't like this scientist if I knew him. They're bad men, and I want their money."

"What did they do to get you so riled up?"

"Things only a woman would understand."

Elrod sat down on the bed and took his shirt off. He tossed it on the floor.

"So you got your feelings hurt and now you want to square things," he said. "The only problem is, it almost never works out that way."

"You're an expert, are you?" Jade said.

"Not hardly. But I know one thing: revenge clouds a person's judgment. You end up doing things you'd never do with a clear head. You got a lot going for you. Looks, talent, a brain that seems to work okay. Be a shame to jeopardize all that on revenge."

"Thanks for the advice. I'll be sure to remember it when I'm rich on Morino's money."

"Hey, it's your life, you can do what you want," Elrod said. "Just like me. And what I want right now is take a shower, iron my clothes, and figure out my next move. As far as I'm concerned, you're on your own."

He took his pants off and tossed them on the floor, then did the same with his socks. He was down to his underwear when he looked up and saw Jade holding something in her hand. It was shiny, made of steel.

A Luger, she'd called it.

Pointed right at Elrod.

Chapter 24

Maybe the rats ate Salvatore Morino. Maybe they saw his round, fleshy body and envisioned a buffet of well-marbled meat that would sustain them for weeks or even months. That's what Luis Baez was thinking as he canvassed the abandoned warehouse beside the notorious alleyway in LoDown, where Fat Sal Morino was last seen. There had to be hundreds of rats in this foul place. You could hear them skittering inside the walls, on the floors, above the ceiling tiles. Every now and then you'd spot one dart around a corner or into a hole in the wall. They say that for every rat you see, a dozen more are lurking nearby. Luis considered himself a pretty brave man. But rats creeped him out.

He could hardly blame the rats for setting up shop here. The floor was strewn with empty food wrappers and containers, empty liquor bottles, soda cans, beer cans, milk cartons, crack pipes, syringes, toothbrushes, newspapers, comic books, porno magazines. Moldy, half-eaten food Luis couldn't identify contributed to a brutal stench that also included notes of urine, feces, vomit, and

God knows what else. The two main entryways had been chained shut, but there were plenty of busted windows available for would-be trespassers. Why any human would want to enter this shithole was another matter. Maybe people came here because it kept the snow and rain out and didn't charge rent. One man's shithole is another's Ritz Carlton.

Luis looked at his watch. Nearly noon. He and Miles McLaughlin had been here more than three hours. They'd swept through the building a couple times already, checking for clues to Morino's disappearance, anything that might provide an escape route: hidden shafts, loose floor tiles, soft spots in the ceiling or walls. But they came up empty. It's possible Morino went into the back lot behind the alley to get away, but not likely. That lot was surrounded by a tall fence with barbed wire. A middle-aged, out-of-shape blob like Salvatore Morino could barely rise out of a low-seated chair, much less scale a fence and navigate barbed wire.

It was all folly, a fool's errand. There were no clues to be found here. The FBI had already done a full investigation of the alley and surrounding area. They didn't find anything, and neither would Luis and Miles. Luis knew this. So did Miles, in all likelihood. But it was probably therapeutic for Miles to go through the motions of an investigation, especially since the FBI had put the brakes on its own manhunt.

Sal Morino was Miles' white whale, both literally and figuratively. Miles had been chasing the mobster for roughly half his professional life. Luis didn't necessarily agree with it, but he understood it. Miles was like most cops and prosecutors. He obsessed over the ones who got away—and Fat Sal had gotten away more than once. Luis knew the feeling, having felt it himself. The least he could do was provide a little moral support as Miles snooped around the warehouse, checking for clues that didn't exist. Luis figured he owed Miles that much for all the times Miles helped save his job whenever some NYPD bureaucrat threatened to take his badge and foul up his pension. Luis loved detective work, but hated the bureaucracy. He spent the last years of his police career counting the days until he could get his full pension, quit, and start his own consulting business.

Luis wondered if Miles even knew what he was looking for. Miles had been an excellent district attorney, a master at putting together cases and winning them in the courtroom. But he wasn't a field investigator. He kept staring at the same corners, the same ducts, the same walls, as if a key piece of information he'd missed before would suddenly hop through his zipper and give him a hummer.

"I don't know, boyo," Luis told Miles. "The only thing I see here is a building that needs to be condemned. The FBI should have been looking for new strains of bacteria instead of Morino."

Miles glanced at Luis with a tired, frustrated face.

"That fat wop," he said. "I bet you anything he paid off one of those FBI..."

"Miles," Luis said.

Miles started to say something, but stopped short. He checked his watch.

"Let's walk up the block a little way, poke around," he said. "Maybe chat up a couple locals. Show them photos of Fat Sal, see if they've spotted him out and about."

"You don't want to break for lunch or something?" Luis said.

"Now there's an idea. Whattya suggest? The steakhouse around the corner? The sushi place next door?"

Luis shrugged. "Right, not a lot of choices down here."

"It's not even noon yet," Miles said. "Let's give it an hour or so and then head back uptown, grab a decent meal. I'll buy."

"Okay. Just do me a favor and let *me* talk to the locals, OK? That's more my territory than yours. You hang back and listen in."

The two men walked out of the warehouse and into the comparatively fresh air outside. They headed north, toward Colve Park, figuring that's the only direction anybody civilized would go.

Luis didn't hold out much hope they'd get any useful information from the derelicts who hovered in these parts. They'd probably find someone *claiming* to have seen Fat Sal, just for a shot at the FBI's reward money. There had been numerous Fat Sal sightings over the months. He had been spotted eating at an Olive Garden in Cleveland, getting out of a Cadillac in Oakland, shooting pool in Corpus Christi, lying on a beach in Clearwater, playing the cheapo slots near the Nevada line, selling holistic candles in Asheville.

It was all bullshit. Luis figured Fat Sal was either dead or tucked away in some foreign backwater where the local authorities looked the other way as long as you stuffed their pockets full of cash. He doubted Fat Sal was anywhere near LoDown. But Miles wanted to talk to the locals, so that's what Luis did.

The first man he approached was sitting on a stoop and drinking from a paper bag. The man had sunken cheeks and bloodshot eyes, and smelled like the inside of a sour mash factory. He told Luis he *might had seen* someone who looked like Fat Sal.

"When was this?" Luis said.

"Oh man, musta been a couple weeks ago," the guy said. "Saw him from up in my suite."

"Your suite?"

"Yeah. What happened was, I was up in my executive suite on the fortieth floor, reviewin' the portfolio. You know, stocks, bonds, mutual funds. Buy low, sell high, get paid. I look out the window and seen this fat Guido motherfucker eatin' one of them big cal-zoneys waaaaaay down on the street. I say to myself, 'Hmmmmm, now where I seen that face before? Was it at the country club? The alumni association?' Then it hit me: it was that eye-talian gangster been in all the papers. Down on the street, eating a cal-zoney, right in broad daylight!"

The guy cracked up. Luis thanked him for his time and moved along.

"Got a couple dollars?" the guy called after him.

Things didn't get much better after that. Most of the people Luis approached either talked to their shoes, spoke nonsense, or didn't speak at all.

The one exception was a tall, African American woman, late thirties maybe, with short hair, a sharp jacket and blouse ensemble, fit and trim. She looked as out of place down here as Luis and Miles. Luis figured she must be a social worker or something. He approached her at the same time she approached him.

"Pardon me, miss," Luis greeted her. "Mind if I ask you

a couple quick questions?"

"Not if you have a second to answer a couple of mine," the woman replied.

"Deal," Luis said. He pulled the photo of Fat Sal out of his pocket and showed it to the woman. Miles hung back a few feet away, still within earshot. The woman glanced at Miles suspiciously before turning her attention back to Luis.

"We're trying to locate the man in this photograph," Luis said. "Our information suggests he may have been in this neighborhood within the last several months. I'm checking with people in the area, see if they've seen him around. And if so, when and where."

The woman took the picture in her hand.

"Sal Morino," she said. "Public Enemy Number One."

The woman handed the photo back to Luis.

"You're either with the bureau or you're trying to score some reward money," she said.

Luis put the photo back in his pocket and looked at the woman. She was nice to look at.

"Actually, I'm a security consultant. That's my partner over there," Luis said, nodding toward Miles. "And yes, we're looking to earn some reward money, give our business a shot in the arm. And you are?"

"I'm a private investigator," the woman said. "My name's Sidney Donovan. I'm trying to track down somebody, too."

"A private eye, huh?" Luis said. "That means you used to be a cop?"

Sidney nodded. "Baltimore PD. Left as a detective,"

"I was a detective with the NYPD," Luis said. "Small world, right? Mind if I ask who you're looking for?"

"Not Fat Sal, if that's what you're thinking. I'm looking for a coat thief, if my client is to be believed, which he probably isn't. Anyway, I can't be much help to you. If I'd seen Salvatore Morino I'd be phoning the FBI to collect the reward myself. I haven't seen my guy, either. But I've had some interesting conversations with the locals."

"You and me both," Luis laughed. "My name's Luis, by the way. Luis Baez."

The two shook hands.

Sidney pulled out a couple of photos and a business card and handed them to Luis.

"Here's my guy, and that's the coat he may be wearing," she said. "I don't suppose you've seen anyone like that around here?"

Luis studied the photos a moment, then handed them back to Sidney.

"Sorry, can't help you there," he said.

"That's what I figured," Sidney said. "I doubt this guy is in this neighborhood, but my client insisted I look. If you do happen to see him, could you give me a call? His name is Elrod. That's my mobile number on the card. I keep my phone on me. There could be a reward in it for you. Let's say, a hundred bucks?"

Luis took Sidney's business card and pocketed it. He handed her his own card.

"And if you happen to see Sal Morino, can you give me a call?" he said. "I promise to share the reward money."

"Deal."

"Or you could just call me anyway and we could have dinner."

Sidney wagged her finger.

"Back to work, Detective Baez," she said.

Luis winked. Sidney winked back and went on her way. Miles sidled up beside Luis. They both watched Sidney stroll down the street.

"Nice," Miles said.

"Quite," Luis said.

"I bet even your ex-wife would approve."

Luis chuckled.

"Let's try a couple more blocks then get the hell out of here," Miles said.

"Yes, let's."

Chapter 25

Red walked at a brisk pace as he snaked his way out of Colve Park and toward the alley and time portal. It was more like a half-jog than a walk. Red usually strolled at a leisurely pace wherever he went, but not now. Now, all he wanted to do was get back to his own world, ASAP.

He told himself he was done with this scheme. Just done with it. Let Jade go it alone. As far as Red was concerned, fifty thousand dollars was plenty, even if you had to split it in half. He was going to tell Jade that, straight up, the next time he saw her.

He was so deep in thought he didn't notice the woman coming straight toward him. He nearly walked right smack into her before shifting at the last minute and brushing lightly into her side. He looked up to find a good-looking Negro woman, taller than average, with short hair and a strong-looking body. She was wearing a black blouse, gray jacket, and gray pants. Dressed like a man, like a lot of women in 1999.

"My apologies, miss," Red said. "Guess I was lost in my thoughts. Didn't see you there."

"No problem," the woman said. "They must have been some deep thoughts."

"Yeah, well...," Red said, but then got stuck there. "My apologies once again. Enjoy your day."

"Wait a minute," the woman said. "Maybe you can help me. Are you from around here?"

Red hesitated. Technically, he lived uptown. But the uptown he lived in was fifty years in the past. He decided to split the difference and tell a half-lie, which was also a half-truth.

"No ma'am," he said. "I'm from North Carolina."

"Ah, too bad."

The woman reached into her jacket pocket and pulled out a couple of photos.

"My name's Sidney Donovan," she said. "I'm a private investigator, trying to find someone who hangs around this part of town. I've been interviewing some of the folks in the area. Would you mind looking at these, seeing if he looks familiar? He would have been wearing that coat."

She handed the photos to Red. He glanced at them and felt his throat plunge into his stomach. One photo was of that hobo, Elrod. The other was of his coat. Jade was right—someone was looking for Elrod. Not just anyone, either—a private investigator. Probably hired by the scientist.

Red stared at the photos.

"Sir?" the woman said.

Red kept staring at the photos. He told himself to snap out of it, put on his game face.

"Does this man look familiar?" the woman asked.

"Oh, no," Red finally replied. "No ma'am. Can't say I've seen this cat."

He handed the photos back to her. "Sorry."

The woman studied Red for a second.

"Are you *sure* you haven't seen him?" she said.

"Pretty sure. I mean, for a second there I thought he looked a little like this ofay from down-home. But that's not him."

"Well, I appreciate your taking the time to speak with me," the woman said.

She pulled a card out of her jacket pocket and handed it to Red.

"My business card," she said. "If you see someone who looks like this, or is wearing this kind of coat, would you mind giving me a call? I keep my mobile phone with me at all times."

Red took the card and looked it over. *Sidney Donovan, Donovan Investigations. Licensed Private Investigator. Competitive Rates. Guaranteed Results.*

He put the card in his pocket and thought about what he should do. The business card could be a big help in finding the scientist. But getting the card to Jade would require Red walking all the way back up to the hotel, then turning around and coming all the way back down here.

"Sir?" Sidney repeated.

Red looked at her.

"You appear to be lost in thought again," she said.

Red shrugged.

"So, you'll give me a call if you happen to see this man?" Sidney asked.

"You bet," Red answered, then turned to walk away.

"Sir?" Sidney said before Red could take a step.

He turned around to look at her.

"Just wanted to let you know, you're in a rough part of

town," she said. "It might not be the safest place for tourists to roam around in."

"Thanks, I'll keep an eye out."

Red quick-stepped away before the woman could get another word in. He put his hand in his pocket and palmed the business card. It would still be there tomorrow if he decided to slip back here and give it to Jade.

For now, he just wanted to go home.

***

Sidney watched the man walk away and thought to herself, *That dude was lying.*

The moment the man saw Elrod's photo he looked like he'd swallowed a frog. He told Sidney he'd never seen Elrod, but his body language told a different story. He'd not only seen Elrod. He might even know Elrod.

Sidney hung back and kept an eye on the man as he made his way further south. She thought about tailing him but decided against it. The man probably already had his radar up for her. If he saw her following him, he might start zigzagging every which way just to throw her off course. She decided to keep walking north. Chances are they'd cross paths again. She was an expert at remembering faces, and she had a feeling the man would work his way back north eventually.

There was something strange about that man. Something that didn't fit right. You don't see too many black folk walking around in those preppy clothes, especially middle-aged men. He used expressions you don't hear too much these days. "My apologies" instead of "sorry." He called Elrod a "cat" and an "ofay." Nobody talked like that anymore.

Sidney decided to check out Colve Park. Maybe she'd find Elrod lounging on a bench or hitting people up for money. There was no shortage of street people in search of handouts around here. Sidney had already been approached by a half-dozen of them. Instead of giving them money, she showed them the photo of Elrod. None wanted to talk—until Sidney mentioned that there might be some cash in it. Suddenly they sprang to life, said they'd seen Elrod here or there, behind that building, around that corner, on top of that lamppost. Sidney forked over a few dollars and followed their tips, but they were all dead ends. She was done paying money for tips that didn't pan out.

That didn't stop homeless people from approaching her, though. As soon as she reached the park she was approached by a man with nappy hair, a dirty face, a stained Mets jersey and black pants that sagged halfway down his ass.

"How you doing, sister?" the man said. "I wonder through the grace of God if you could spare some money? I'm starvin' like Marvin. In fact, my name is Marvin, so you *know* I'm starvin'!"

Sidney kept walking. Maybe if she ignored Starvin' Marvin he'd get the hint and move along.

He didn't. He kept walking alongside Sidney, matching her stride for stride.

"I ain't no welfare case, understand," Marvin said. "I'm more or less between careers at this particular juncture in my life."

Sidney stopped. She sighed and gave Marvin a weary look. She smelled the funk rolling off his body and tried to ignore it. She reached into her jacket pocket and pulled out the photo of Elrod. She shoved it in front of Marvin's face.

"You know this guy?" she said. "Or seen him around?"

The man studied the photo a moment.

"Could be, could be," he said.

"Could be?" Sidney said. "You either do or you don't."

"Information costs money," Marvin said.

Sidney shoved the photo back in her pocket and walked on.

"Wait a minute, wait a minute," Marvin called behind her. "Boy's name is Elrod. Just seen him chompin' on two plates of Ay-rab food from one of them halal carts. Didn't even offer me none, and me always givin' him smokes."

Sidney's eyes and ears perked up. She turned around and looked at Marvin.

"When was this?" she said.

"I don't know, an hour ago, maybe less," Marvin said. "He might still be hanging around after a big meal like that. Napping on the grass or something."

"Where's the halal cart?" Sidney said.

Marvin grinned. "Information costs money."

Sidney rolled her eyes. She reached into her pants pocket and pulled out a five-dollar bill. She dangled it in the air.

"Where?" she said.

"You off to a good start," Marvin said. "But not quite there yet."

Sidney pulled another five out of her pocket.

Marvin put his chin in his hand and acted like he was deep in thought. "Hmmmm. Still close, but..."

"Forget it," Sidney said. She shoved the bills back in her pocket.

"Nah, we good, we good," Marvin said. "Ten bills is

fine. Let me just hold on to 'em, make sure they ain't no Monopoly money."

Sidney pulled the bills back out of her pocket and stiff-armed them toward Marvin.

"Just keep walking up this path," Marvin said. "There's an open area with food carts, benches, lots of people and pigeons. You got your vagrant types and your yuppies and your *artistes* and your street performers and whatnot."

"That's where you last saw him?" Sidney said.

"It's where I see him and all God's lost children. Trying to hit up nice ladies like yourself for a little spare change. If you don't see him somewhere between here and there, then my name ain't Starvin' Marvin."

"Your name's probably not Starvin' Marvin anyway," Sidney said.

"It is today, sister. It is today."

The man laughed.

Sidney turned and followed the path north.

***

Red pulled a metal flask out of his pocket and took a drink of the potion. He returned it to his pocket and walked on, picking up his pace. The portal was only a couple blocks away, and Red was more than ready to hop through it to 1949.

He must have been approached by a dozen different people since arriving in this sad part of town, all looking for a handout. Money. Cigarettes. Something to eat. Something to drink.

It reminded Red of the Great Depression, which was still a recent memory in his world. The main difference this go-round was that the folks asking for help in 1999 were more aggressive and less apt to take no for an answer. During the Depression they kept their heads and eyes down when they asked for a few coins, like they were ashamed and embarrassed. Here in 1999 they waltzed right up on you, looked you in the eye. People had some pretty high expectations in this decade.

Red kept looking behind for the private investigator, Sidney. He had a feeling she didn't buy his story about not seeing Elrod. Red was not a good liar, and he knew it. He didn't need Sidney making a return appearance, asking more questions. When he got near the alley he craned his head around one more time to see if Sidney was lingering behind. She wasn't, but someone else was: a brown-skinned man dressed in a collared shirt, blue slacks, and black loafers. He was with a tall white man wearing an ugly ball cap, ugly eyeglasses, ugly sports jersey, and ugly denim pants.

The brown-skinned man walked up to Red and introduced himself as Luis. He said he wanted to ask a couple of questions. The white man hung back a few feet, close enough to hear.

Red sighed. The alley with the portal was only half a block away. He wondered if he'd ever get there.

"I'm kind of in a hurry," Red told Luis.

"It'll only take a second, I promise," Luis replied.

Before Red could tell him to get lost, Luis pulled a photo out and showed it to Red. Another photo, another familiar face. This time it was the Italian mobster, Sal Morino. Red could feel his face and body tighten up.

"I'm looking for this man," Luis said. "I understand he was seen in this area a few months back. I'm asking some of the people here if they've seen him recently."

Red didn't bother pretending he didn't know the guy in the photo. Fat Sal was a famous fugitive in this decade. Lots of people probably recognized him.

"He's that missing mobster, right?" Red said.

"Fat Sal Morino," Luis said. "One and the same."

"What about him?"

"Seen anybody who looks like this?"

"Who's asking?"

"My associate over there and I work for a private security consultancy," Luis said, nodding toward Miles. "We're contracting with the local law enforcement authorities to try and find clues to Salvatore Morino's whereabouts. Somebody seems to believe he might still be in the area, so I'm asking around."

"Hmmmmm," Red said. "Can't say I've seen him. No sir. Can't say I have."

"You sure? I mean, anything you tell me is just between us. Be some reward money in it for you, too."

"Nope. Haven't seen him. Wish I could be more help, but I gotta run along."

"Well, thanks anyway. You know, you don't look like you're from around here, Mr...."

"You can call me Red. And no, I'm not from around here. Just visiting from North Carolina."

"Well, watch your step, Red. This is a rough part of town. Not a lot of tourists come down this way."

"Thanks for the tip."

Red hoped that would end the conversation, but Luis just stood there.

Red decided to go on into the alley anyway. He didn't care anymore. He didn't even care if Luis saw him disappear into the thin air. He just wanted to get back to his world, grab a bite to eat, and go home. Lie down a bit, then head to the gig.

"You don't mind, I gotta answer nature's call," Red said. "Thought I'd slip into that alley over there, someplace private."

Luis smiled. "Have at it. When you gotta go, you gotta go."

Red excused himself and walked into the alley. He turned around to make sure Luis wasn't peeking in, then stepped into the portal. He heard a loud whoosh and felt a cold breeze. A couple moments later he was standing beside the entrance to the Hideaway nightclub, back in good old 1949.

He saw the familiar blue door.

He saw the familiar windows.

He saw Douglas standing beside a big white guy.

He saw Douglas pull a pistol out of his jacket and point it at Red.

"Why hello, William," Douglas said. "Now where on earth could you have been?"

"Geez," the big guy said. "It's like you told me. A magic act."

"That's right, Sammy," Douglas said. "A magic act."

Chapter 26

Elrod tried to look at the bright side of having a gun pointed his way. At least Jade had it pointed at his belly instead of his face. If she happened to squeeze the trigger by accident, he might have a fighting chance with a belly shot. He didn't like his odds if the bullet tore into his face.

God, he was getting tired of this shit. A couple days ago he was plain old Elrod, your average random harmless homeless bum. Now he was the center of all kinds of attention he didn't ask for and didn't need, from people he didn't know and didn't much like.

He wasn't even that mad at Jade for pulling a gun on him. More like disappointed. She was just blinded by money, that's all. Like so many other folks. Just blinded by money.

"Now why'd you go and do a thing like that for?" Elrod said.

"You've given me no choice," Jade said. "I've tried being reasonable. I've given you money, a nice place to sleep, free room service. I even saved you from harm. Yet you battle me at every turn. All I asked was that you help me find someone. That's all you had to do. If it didn't work out for me, fine, you could go on your way. But no. You had to be stubborn. *You* forced me to do this. Now, you and I are walking down toward that time portal. We're going to wait for this scientist to make his move. When he does, you're free to go. For now, do as I say."

"And what if I refuse?" Elrod said

He sat down on the bed and watched the gun barrel follow him.

"Then I'll shoot you," Jade said.

"Oh, I doubt you'll do that."

Jade pointed the barrel a little closer. She raised the gun slightly higher, so the barrel was centered on the middle of Elrod's forehead. She brought it to within inches of him.

"Easy there," Elrod said. "We don't want that thing going off accidentally."

Jade yanked the trigger back with a sudden snap of her finger. The Luger clicked. Elrod jumped up with a start.

"Jesus!" he yelped.

"That's odd," Jade said. "I could have sworn I put a loaded magazine in there, but I guess not. Good thing for you, huh?"

She reached into her handbag and pulled out a pistol magazine. She shoved it into an opening at the bottom of the gun handle and pushed it higher until it clicked into place. She pointed the gun back at Elrod.

"This magazine is very full," Jade said, "and this gun is very accurate. I can fire a bullet anywhere I want with pinpoint precision. I could easily send one into your kneecap—something that will hurt like hell and leave you limping the rest of your miserable life. I'll never get caught, either. I'll just grab the money out of the safe and scram on back to 1949 where nobody will find me. Meanwhile, you'll be in here wishing you'd done the smart thing and played along."

"Now look...," Elrod said.

"Put your clothes back on—the old ones, not the ones you just bought. Then put that coat on. We're taking a walk, you and me. Downtown. Through the park, toward the portal. Don't waste any more time."

Elrod saw no percentage in testing just how far this woman might go for money. He still didn't think she'd do it, but he knew enough about humans and greed that it wasn't worth risking his health, or his life, on the off-chance that his hunch was incorrect. He put on his dirty old clothes and looked forlornly at the crisp new shirts, pants, shoes, and travel bag he'd just purchased. They were the first new things he'd bought in years. He really liked them. He hoped to see them again.

He walked to the door and opened it. Jade followed behind with the gun just inside her jacket. The two headed for the elevator and made their way down to the lobby and the street.

***

Miles McLaughlin checked his watch again, waiting for the man who called himself Red to come back out of the alley. Red had been in there a few minutes already. It didn't take that long to take a piss, no matter how badly you needed to go. Miles had kept out of Red's sight, not wanting to deprive him of his privacy, but now Miles was growing impatient. He had a few questions for Red—like why he reacted the way he did when Luis showed him the photo of Fat Sal. Miles noticed right away. Red seemed to stiffen at the sight of the mobster. Luis didn't seem to care. He was on his mobile phone, talking to a client.

Miles finally decided to check the alley for himself. If Red was in there taking a piss, or smoking crack, or jacking off, so be it. Miles was going to ask Red more questions.

But when Miles got to the alley, it was empty. No Red. No signs of urine or any other bodily function. Miles didn't see any way out of the alley other than the rusty fence at the rear, and it had barbed wire on top. Red couldn't have cleared that fence so quickly, if at all.

"Luis!" Miles barked. "Need you to come here, quick."

Luis hustled into the alley, the phone at his ear.

"What's up?" Luis said.

"The guy's not here," Miles said.

Luis spoke briefly into the phone and then clicked it off. He turned to Miles and said, "So where is he?"

"Good question," Miles said. "You didn't see him leave the alley, did you? Because I sure as hell didn't. He seems to have disappeared."

"I never saw him leave," Luis said. "What do you mean, disappeared?"

"Disappeared, as in gone."

Miles checked the walls beside the alley to see if there were any loose blocks or bricks leading to a passageway. Nope. Just the usual blocks and bricks and concrete.

"He can't access either building from the alley," Luis said. "We already checked it out twice today. You think he climbed the fence?"

"Do you? Look at that fence."

"Nah, probably not."

Miles kicked at the pavement. "Then where the hell did he go?"

Chapter 27

Douglas looked at the sweat collecting on Red's forehead and almost felt a twinge of pity for the poor Negro. Red must know he's losing the battle, but he's game enough to press forward anyway, like a doomed fawn trying to escape a mountain lion's jaw. He was a poor liar, Red. Maybe not the worst Douglas had ever known. But very bad at it. Red made the same mistakes all the amateurs make, shifting his eyes, scratching his face, blinking too much, sweating. So many people were poor liars.

The two men were in the basement office of the Hideaway nightclub. Fat Sal was also there, sitting behind his desk. Douglas had called him as soon as Red showed up through the magic hole. Sammy kept guard upstairs.

Red was spinning a yarn about how he'd blacked out and didn't know how or why he suddenly disappeared and reappeared into the portal.

"All I know is I woke up, and there I was," Red said. "Back at the entrance to the club. No idea what happened in between. I looked up and saw you and that big guy.

That's all I know."

"How disconcerting that must be," Douglas said, smiling. "Do you have some kind of medical condition that causes you to pass out in front of nightclubs? High blood pressure? An old brain injury? Aftereffects from the flu you apparently had last night?"

"None that I know of," Red said.

"Perhaps you should have it checked out."

"Maybe I'll do that."

Douglas crossed his legs and leaned back.

"Do you know what I've always admired about the Negro, William?" he said.

"What's that?"

"His wiliness. You are a very wily people. You can move in and out of different situations, different crowds, and adapt immediately. You can put on a brand new face for every circumstance. Most white people are lousy at it. They stay the same no matter what. This probably comes from being the dominant race for so long. It never occurs to them that they would need to adapt to anything. No, they're arrogant enough to believe that circumstances should adapt to them, rather than the other way around. But the Negro knows better. The Negro has been beaten down enough, for long enough, to learn the value of playing to the crowd. So, they see somebody like me and put on a big grin, letting me know how happy they are to be in my company. Or they shuffle their feet and look at their toes and let me know they got no quarrel with nobody, don't know much o' nothin'. But the second they're back among their own tribe, they slap skin and boast about how they conned that silly old white motherfucker again."

"Uh huh," Red said.

"That's what you're doing right now, William," Douglas said. "You're putting on the humble coon act, don't know nothin' 'bout nothin'. Only it's not working. I can see right through it. You're not very good at it, for one thing. And even if you were, I'd still see right through it. So why don't we just speak plainly and honestly, like grown men? We know where you went. You went through the time portal, to 1999. We just don't know why you went there."

Fat Sal got up from his chair.

"Oh, I got a pretty good idea why he went there," he said. "To steal fifty grand of my money. He's in on the whole thing."

Fat Sal walked over to Red. He leaned down so they were face-to-face.

"They saw you talking to that street bum Elrod at the bar the other night before the show," Fat Sal said. "What'd you two chat about, huh? Basketball? Jungle music? White pussy? Here's a guess: You told Elrod about our operation so you could cut yourself in."

He raised his hand and slapped Red across the face. Red slapped Fat Sal back. Fat Sal put his hands around Red's throat and shoved him back into the chair. Red grabbed ahold of Fat Sal's arms and tried to pry them away.

Douglas let this go on for a few seconds before stepping forward and easing himself between the two men.

"Gentlemen, please," he said. "This gets us nowhere."

Fat Sal ripped an elbow into Douglas's chest and sent him halfway across the room.

"Stay out of this," Fat Sal growled.

He pressed his hands harder onto Red's throat. Red tried to get up from the chair and gain some leverage, but Fat Sal had too much strength and mass. Red tried to loosen Fat Sal's grip, but Fat Sal dug his hands in even further. Red struggled to breathe.

"You better start talking," Fat Sal said.

Douglas raised his gun in the air. He pointed it at Fat Sal's head, adjusted the barrel a notch, and fired off a shot. The bullet whizzed just past Fat Sal's ear and ricocheted off the wall.

Fat Sal released his grip on Red and jumped back. Red fell forward and gulped in air. Douglas kept the gun on Fat Sal.

"Enough," Douglas said. "I suspect our friend William is an important piece of the puzzle. Trying to choke the life out of him would be counterproductive."

"The fuck you think you are?" Fat Sal said.

"A voice of reason," Douglas said. "And the one holding the gun. Now, let's calm down and act like intelligent men."

"Wrong," Fat Sal said. "If I want to choke this lying piece of shit, your job is to stand there and watch me do it. I'm in charge, not you."

"On the contrary," Douglas said. "You're in charge of nothing at the moment. You've lost control of your emotions, and the situation. You'll agree with me later when you've had time to think it through. For now, back away from him."

Fat Sal kept his eyes on Douglas and slowly moved his hand toward his belt. Douglas raised his gun and fired another shot just past Fat Sal's ear.

"Keep reaching for that gun and the next shot will find your ear," Douglas said. "The one after that will land between your ears."

Fat Sal froze. "You really don't know who you're fucking with, do you?"

"A man who's letting emotion cloud his judgment, that's who," Douglas answered. "Your anger is understandable, but in time you'll see the benefit of letting cooler heads prevail. So please, lift your hands in the air and keep them that way until I say otherwise."

Fat Sal raised his hands about halfway up. Douglas kept the gun on Fat Sal and turned his eyes toward Red, who was still bent over and breathing heavily.

"You and I are taking a little trip together, William," Douglas said. "To 1999. Oh, don't bother acting like you don't know what I'm talking about. You and some mysterious cohort have discovered the magic of time travel. My guess is Jade, but never mind that. You're going to lead me to the money and to Elrod."

"What if I refuse?" Red said, still struggling to catch his breath.

"Then things will turn out rough for you—and for Jade. She has no idea you've been caught. When she shows up back here in 1949, I'll have one of my Dago friends gather her up and bring her down here to the office. A couple of others will also be on hand. These gentlemen have a particular genius for inflicting pain."

"You leave her out of it," Red said. "She's got nothing to do with this."

Douglas walked up to Red. He raised his gun and brought it down swiftly against the side of Red's face. Red's head snapped to the side.

Red groaned, wiped blood from his face. He moved his eyes back to Douglas and planted them there. "I'm gonna remember this. You bear that in mind."

"By all means," Douglas said.

He turned back to Fat Sal. "As for you, Salvatore, my advice is to go back to business as usual. Forget this little episode. Go back to making money. That's why you're here. To make money."

Fat Sal kept silent and watched Douglas walk to the office door and open it. Douglas pressed a button on the stairway wall. A buzzer buzzed up in the nightclub. A few moments later the sound of heavy footsteps echoed down the stairs. Sammy Berg appeared in the doorway.

"You need something?" Sammy said.

Douglas nodded toward Fat Sal.

"Keep an eye on him," Douglas said. "Take the gun from his belt. Make sure he doesn't go anywhere. If he attempts to do so, harm him."

Sammy looked at Fat Sal. "Yeah sure. He ain't no problem."

Sammy walked over to Fat Sal and lifted up his shirt, exposing a belly and a .38 Special. He grabbed the gun with one hand and pushed Fat Sal back with the other.

"Go siddown," Sammy said.

Fat Sal gave him a hard look, then walked behind the desk and sat.

"My friend William and I have errands to run," Douglas said. "We may be a while. Your job, Sammy, is to keep your eye on Salvatore until I return."

"He ain't no problem," Sammy said.

"Excellent," Douglas said. "Come along, William."

Douglas and Red stepped through the office door and

climbed the stairs to the nightclub. Sammy and Fat Sal watched them leave. Then they watched each other.

Chapter 28

The halal food cart immediately grabbed Sidney's attention with its piquant aroma of chicken, lamb, and onions sizzling on the grill, and its head-spinning array of spices. Sidney checked the time, saw that it was after 2 p.m. She'd completely skipped lunch, unless you counted a granola bar as lunch, which she didn't.

A carton of chicken and rice was awfully tempting. But there were a lot of people standing in line, even at this hour. Sidney didn't want to waste any time waiting. A lonely hot dog stand just across the way had no line, but Sidney wasn't in the mood for a pink meat tube swimming around in lukewarm water.

She stood in a stand of trees, away from the plaza crowd. She scanned the faces and looked for someone who resembled Elrod. There were some ragged folks milling about, but none looked like Elrod, and none had on a red-and-black coat.

A tatted-up white guy with a shaved head, rebel flag T-shirt, and several missing teeth stumbled up beside Sidney and stood there, a foot away, staring at her. He didn't say anything, just stood and stared. You could smell the funk on him, a goulash of sweat, booze, and cigarettes. Here we go again, Sidney thought. Another hard case. She ignored the guy, thinking maybe he'd go away and let her focus on the job at hand. He didn't.

Sidney turned and looked at him, keeping one eye peeled for Elrod. "Something I can help you with?"

The man didn't answer.

Sidney put both eyes on the man now.

"Listen, I'm not in the mood," she said. "If you're looking for money, sorry, I don't have any to give you. I'm kind of busy, so why don't you hurry on along?"

"Free country," the man slurred. "Can stand anywheres I like. You don't like it, too damn bad. I got a black cat bone, I got a mojo too, I got John the Conqueror, I'm gonna mess with you."

He moved closer to Sidney, got right up in her face. She took a deep breath and glanced around to see if anyone else was looking her way. Nobody was. She moved her right hand forward, grabbed the man's crotch, and squeezed hard. He howled and fell to the ground.

"Oh my goodness, you okay, mister?" Sidney said, bending down toward the guy. When she got close enough she whispered in a low voice, "Be careful who you fuck with, Gomer."

She twisted the man's ear as he squirmed on the ground, then rose back up to her feet. She pulled out a wet wipe and wiped her hands down good. She was so busy wiping that she nearly missed the red-and-black coat moving past.

***

Grumble, grumble, grumble, bitch, bitch, bitch. That's all Elrod had done since he and Jade left the hotel. Grumble grumble grumble. Bitch bitch bitch. Jade tried to tune it out, focus on the walk, focus on keeping her hand near the gun in her jacket. But it was impossible. Her ears got filled up with Elrod's constant moaning. It was nonstop, stereophonic. *You people, dragging me into this. Pulling guns, feeding me all kinds of nonsense. Time travel, magic potions, senators, scientists. I don't give a shit about the scientist. Hell, I don't even know him. Don't even give a shit about the money, you wanna know the truth. Here I was, minding my own business, all of a sudden I'm caught up in all this misery. Horseshit, nothing but horseshit. Horseshit horseshit horsey horsey shit shit.*

It was riding on Jade's nerves as they slogged toward the park. Okay: Elrod was an innocent pawn in a wicked scheme. A tough break for him. But what good did grumbling do? What did it solve? The fact is Elrod *was* involved. He was, in fact, a key piece of the equation right now. It wasn't Elrod's fault, but what could you do? Reality was reality. Jade had to keep reminding herself that there were other considerations. Preventing a potential murder. Getting rich. Putting Fat Sal and the scientist out of business—and putting Douglas in his rightful place beneath the dung heap.

Getting filthy, filthy rich.

"What makes you think you'll even find this scientist, or he'll find us?" Elrod whined as they entered the park. "What makes you think he's even looking for us?"

"You stole fifty thousand of his dollars," Jade answered. "Trust me, he's looking for you."

"I didn't steal a damn thing. *You* stole it. You're the one they should be looking for."

"What difference does it make who stole it? It's been stolen, and you're the only one they know about. As soon as they see you with the coat on they'll make the connection and make their move. Once they make their move, I'll know who they are, and you can go on your way."

Elrod stopped walking and turned toward Jade. "Or I could just go on my way, anyway. What are you gonna do about it? Shoot me here in this park, with everyone watching?"

Jade rolled her eyes.

"No, I'm not going to shoot you," she said. "I'm just going to remind you, again, that I might have saved your life. If that's not enough to get you to do something simple like walk around with me, maybe something else will. Just tell me what you want. Do you want me to get down on my knees and beg? Just give me the signal, and down I'll go. I'll beg you right here in front of all these people."

Elrod muttered something to himself and looked at the halal cart.

"I'll tell you what I want," he said. "A plate of that halal food. The smell is working on my belly. All this excitement has stirred my appetite again."

"Look at that line," Jade protested. "Can't you just get a hot dog?"

"Those hot dogs might kill me quicker than your gun. I'll grab a quick lamb pita. Then, if I'm feeling well enough, I'll decide whether to help you out with your little heist."

Jade shook her head as Elrod got in line. It was always something with this guy. Always something.

***

Sidney Donovan's eyes followed the coat as it moved into the halal food line. That coat, hmmmmm....She pulled the photos from her bag. The photo of Elrod didn't look much like the man wearing the coat. He was just a normal-looking, middle-aged white dude with a trim haircut and no beard, standing in line beside a woman with short, wavy brown hair done up in some kind of retro forties 'do. Sidney wouldn't have noticed them at all if not for the red-and-black coat.

Next, she compared the photo of the coat with the one the man was wearing. A perfect match. The same colors, style, size.

Sidney stepped closer to get a better view. She studied the man's face. The area around his jaws and chin were lighter than the rest of his face, which is usually the sign of a freshly shaved beard. She looked at his eyes. The left one had a little scar beneath it. She glanced at the photo of Elrod. The left eye in the photo also had a little scar below it.

The woman standing beside Elrod began looking Sidney's way. They briefly locked eyes before the woman shifted hers away. Sidney didn't know who the woman was, but she was pretty sure who the man was.

Elrod.

She strolled over to an empty space near a tree at the edge of the plaza. She pulled her mobile phone out of her purse and punched in a number. After a couple of rings a voice said, "Dr. Bunt speaking."

"Dr. Bunt?" Sidney said.

"Yes, this is Dr. Bunt."

"This is Sidney Donovan. I think I might have found your boy."

***

The tall black woman across the plaza kept eyeballing Elrod, squinting at him, studying him, like she was a zookeeper and Elrod was a rare orangutan. The woman pulled something out of her coat pocket, scanned it, looked back at Elrod, then scanned it again.

"Hmmmm," Jade thought to herself. "Now why did she do that?"

Jade watched her. They briefly made eye contact before Jade looked away. She pretended to look at something else, but kept the woman in her peripheral vision. The woman strolled toward a less crowded part of the plaza. She reached an arm into a purse and pulled something out. Jade shifted her eyes just long enough to see that it was a wireless telephone.

"Hmmmmm," Jade thought to herself. "Now who could this woman be calling?"

It was only a hunch, but Jade decided to play it. She and Elrod needed to leave the area, see if the woman followed. If so, she might be someone trying to track Elrod down for the scientist.

Jade gently elbowed Elrod in the stomach.

"Let's go back to the hotel," she said. "You're right, this is silly walking around, trying to see if the scientist will just pop up out of the bushes. Let's relax, have a drink in the lounge. You can order food there if you want. On me."

"But there's only a couple ahead of me now," Elrod

said. "I'm hungry for a lamb pita."

"Maybe the hotel has lamb chops or something," Jade said. "Anyway, a quick drink might be good for you. After that you can go back up to the room, pack your stuff and go wherever it is you want to go. I don't even care anymore. Just do me this one favor. I feel like a drink, and I don't want to drink alone. My nerves are getting the better of me. I never should have gotten involved in all this. It's worn me out."

Elrod cocked his head. "Why the sudden mood swing? A few minutes ago you were ready to blow a hole in my kneecap. Now you want a drink?"

"Can't a gal have a change of heart? Anyway, it's what you wanted, right? To be done with all this? Here's your chance. Just have a drink with me. God, I can't believe you of all people aren't jumping at the chance to have a drink."

"You're about the confoundingest woman I've ever met," Elrod said, "and I've met more than a few, let me tell you."

He stepped out of the halal cart line. He looked at the meat sizzling on the grill, frowned, then started walking toward the hotel.

Jade followed behind, turning her head every now and then to make sure the tall woman was hot on their heels.

Chapter 29

Further south, Douglas and Red made their way toward Colve Park. Red was tired, hungry, and on edge. He found himself envious of the street bums they passed. Those bums might be in a world of want and woe, but at least they didn't have to deal with Douglas and his gun right now.

Red weighed his options. He could try to make a run for it, but the prospect of Douglas blowing a hole square in the back of his head—something he didn't doubt for a second Douglas would do—nixed that idea. He could yell for help. But who around here, in this desolate neighborhood, would be willing to step in and save him? They'd be more likely to circle like buzzards, wait for him to bleed out, and then check his pockets for cash.

Red kept his eyes peeled for a police station or cop car, thinking he could get help that way. But he wasn't sure that was a good option, either. Red didn't know what things were like in 1999, but back in 1949, the cops in this city didn't exactly go out of their way to save Negros from white men.

Maybe Red could just wander around aimlessly, wear Douglas down, make a move when Douglas tired out a little. Red was much heavier than Douglas and could probably overpower him physically if it came down to it. The problem was Douglas would get wise to Red long before he got tired of walking. He was smart, Douglas. Sneaky smart, like a viper. Red had to give him that.

So, there were no good options for wiggling out of this situation. Red decided the best course of action was to keep walking to the hotel, where the money was. The only leverage Red had was the money. Red knew where the money was, and Douglas didn't. Red knew the combination to the safe, and Douglas didn't. He figured his best hope was to negotiate with Douglas when the time came. Work a deal where Red was free to go on his way in exchange for access to the cash.

Red cursed himself, again, for going along with this scheme of Jade's. It was the middle of the afternoon on a Saturday. He should be home, resting up before tonight's show. Instead, he was walking through 1999 with a gun pointed at his back.

For his part, Douglas seemed pretty chipper. He whistled as they walked, pausing only to comment on how lovely the day was, how fascinating 1999 was, how different the cars looked, how very *futuristic* it all was.

"Time travel truly is a marvel, isn't it, William?" Douglas said. "Here we are, a half-century in the future, walking around as if this is our natural habitat. And no one's the wiser. We hold a secret the others can only fantasize about. It's so tempting to walk up to one of these hoboes and tell them we're visiting from 1949. But they'd probably vomit on my shoes."

Douglas laughed. Red kept silent.

"Not in the mood for humor, eh?" Douglas said. "More's the pity. Laughter is the best tonic for someone in your position, my friend. It must be difficult to swallow this predicament you've found yourself in. You didn't reckon on matters turning out this way. Well, *c'est la vie*, eh? Such is life. It rarely works out the way we plan it. Just make sure you don't try anything stupid because you'd come out on the losing end."

Red didn't respond to this, either. He kept walking toward the park and hotel.

A couple blocks behind them, a fat man in a hurry huffed and puffed to keep pace.

Chapter 30

"Perhaps you could take an alternate route," Dr. Lionel Bunt said from the back of the cab. "There's a lot of congestion here."

The cab was on the westside highway, cemented in place. Traffic was thick and gooey. The cab driver didn't seem to mind, but Lionel was growing impatient. He needed to get downtown in a hurry. Sidney Donovan said she might have spotted Elrod. Her first call came from Colve Park. She called back a few minutes later from a hotel located a few blocks northwest. Elrod and an unidentified woman were having drinks in the hotel lounge—probably paid for with Lionel's money.

Lionel leaned forward in the cab.

"I'm in a bit of a hurry," he said.

"Bad traffic today," the cabdriver said in a thick accent. "Probably accident. Bad traffic, man. What you gonna do?"

"What you could do," Lionel said, "is take a left at one of the cross streets and then head south on one of the avenues. Maybe there's less traffic there."

"Yes, and everyone else think the same thing. Get off,

take alternate route. Then they get stucks again. Everybody in a hurry. They want be there yesterday. But traffic is traffic, man. You cannot control traffic. What you gonna do?"

"Just...take the next left and drive five blocks east," Lionel said. "I'll catch the subway from there."

The cab driver did as instructed. He hung a left, crawled five blocks east, and dumped Lionel off near the subway station. Lionel stepped out and paid the fare. He tipped the driver a quarter, just to be spiteful. He sprinted to the station and caught a train that stopped a couple blocks from the hotel where Sidney was positioned.

Lionel saw a few empty seats on the subway but decided to stand. It was the best way to properly conceal the gun tucked snugly in his belt. The gun was a Beretta Pico—compact, reliable, easy to hide. Lionel didn't know if he'd need it, but it was handy to have around.

The train arrived at its stop in a matter of minutes. Lionel hurried off and walked quickly along the platform, up the stairs, out onto the sidewalk, and down to the hotel. He found Sidney standing beside a lamppost outside the hotel entrance.

"Are they still inside the lounge?" Lionel said by way of greeting.

Sidney nodded.

"Why are you out here, then?" Lionel asked. "Shouldn't you be inside keeping an eye on them?"

"I don't want to spook them," Sidney said. "I get the feeling the woman with Elrod is on to me. Anyway, you can see the entrance to the lounge from out here. They can't come out without me spotting them."

"Do you at least know where they're sitting in the

lounge?"

Sidney looked at Lionel. "They're in a hotel lounge, not a football stadium. They should be easy enough to spot when and if we go in there. You're welcome, by the way, for finding him so quickly."

"If it's indeed him. You mentioned that the man has no beard."

"I also mentioned that he looked like he might've just gotten a shave and a haircut. These things aren't that hard to spot. He has the same coat on. That's the important thing."

Lionel craned his head to see inside the lobby and to the lounge beyond.

"Wait here," he said. "I'll go have a look."

He stepped through the hotel lobby and into the lounge. He grabbed a seat at the bar and ordered a mint julep. It was the first thing that popped into his head, a mint julep. The bartender gave Lionel a wry smile, as if she didn't get a lot of requests for mint juleps from grown men. Lionel didn't smile back. He shoved a twenty-dollar bill on the bar and told her to keep the change.

Lionel kept his back to the crowd for a couple of minutes and sipped his mint julep. It tasted minty, sweet, syrupy, and horrible. It tasted just as bad as every other alcoholic beverage Lionel had ever consumed in his life, which you could probably count on two hands. He pushed the cocktail away and slowly swiveled around to scout the crowd.

It didn't take long to find the right couple. They were sitting at a round table in the far corner of the lounge, beneath a black-and-white photo of Central Park. The table had three chairs. One was occupied by a pretty woman with short, wavy brown hair. Another was occupied by a man wearing a black T-shirt and hair slick with gel.

The third chair had a coat draped over it. It was a red-and-black coat similar to those worn by outdoorsmen. Lionel knew that coat. He'd purchased a few dozen of them. The guy sitting there didn't have the beard or unkempt hair anymore, but he had the same clothes on, and he was the right size. It was Elrod. Lionel had no doubt.

Lionel had to give Sidney Donovan credit for finding Elrod so quickly. He also had to get rid of her—fast. Lionel didn't want her hanging around to see what Lionel had in store for Elrod and the woman, whoever she was. He got up from the barstool and made his way back outside. Sidney was still standing beside the lamppost.

"It looks like the right guy, or at least the right coat," he told her. "Thanks for your help. Bill me the remaining balance, as well as any expenses you've accrued. I'll remit payment immediately. You've done good work. I'll be happy to write you a letter of recommendation."

"That's it?" Sidney said. "You don't need me to do anything else?"

"You've completed your assignment," Lionel said. "That's Elrod inside, and the coat. So, no. I don't need you to do anything else."

"You sure about that? If you confront him about the coat, he might get frisky. Things could turn real ugly real fast. My training would be an asset in that type of situation."

Lionel gave her a cold look. It irked him that Sidney felt he couldn't handle the situation. Lionel could handle

Elrod. He could handle five Elrods at one time without breaking a sweat.

"I'm going to walk in there and tell the man the coat is mine," Lionel said. "I'm going to tell him he stole it from me, and I want it back. I doubt he'll try to kick up a fuss about it, especially in a hotel lounge with other people around. But if he does, I'll handle it. I hired you to find the man and the coat. You've done so. Thank you, but that's all I need."

Sidney shrugged. "Well, your call. Let me know if I can be of any further assistance in the future."

Lionel nodded and hustled back inside to the lounge. He didn't go back to his barstool, though. Instead, he walked over to the table where Elrod and the woman were sitting. He lifted the coat up from the unoccupied chair, tossed it on top of Elrod, and sat down without speaking. Elrod and the woman stared at him. Lionel eased the gun from his belt and kept it low, out of sight. He moved the gun beneath the table and poked the end of the barrel into Elrod's crotch.

"Hello, Elrod," Lionel said. "That's the barrel of a Beretta you're feeling. If I pull the trigger, it will mangle your penis beyond recognition. Neither of us wants that."

Elrod gave him a quizzical look.

"The coat on your lap is my coat," Lionel said. "I assume you've found the money, or you wouldn't be in this nice hotel lounge spending it. I want the money back."

Lionel turned to the woman sitting in the other chair.

"You're the scientist," she said.

"Correct," he said. "You must be the brains behind this little operation. My name is Dr. Lionel Bunt. Tell me where my goddamn money is."

Chapter 31

Sweat pooled in the valley of Fat Sal's lower back, broke off into tributaries, drizzled down into his ample derriere, and then wandered south to his thighs. This made it very difficult to jog, all this sweat rubbing against his thighs—and Fat Sal needed to jog if he expected to keep pace with Red and Douglas, who were a few blocks ahead.

The two men were headed north and west, away from the alley with the time portal. Fat Sal didn't know where they were going, but he hoped it wouldn't be too far. He couldn't keep up this pace too long. The red toupee on his head kept sliding down, obstructing his view. The toupee lay beneath a New York Yankees baseball cap that didn't want to stay in place, either. A fake beard and pair of large, cheap sunglasses covered his face. His clothes were the kind he'd never get caught dead in if he weren't trying to hide his identity. Blue Hawaiian shirt. Loose-fitting jeans. Cheap, off-brand casual shoes made out of some kind of synthetic material. Not exactly the kind of getup you wanted to jog in.

Fat Sal couldn't remember the last time he'd jogged,

and his body wasn't happy about it. His lungs wheezed. His heart seemed to be doing somersaults. Sweat drenched his face and torso. His feet, knees, back, and hips sent jolts of discomfort to various parts of his brain.

Fat Sal had been moving in high gear since he'd taken care of Sammy back at the Hideaway. That was the easy part, taking care of Sammy. As soon as Red and Douglas strolled out of the Hideaway office and left Sammy in charge, Sal hatched his escape plan. He sat behind his desk and started wiggling in his seat. He reached his right hand down toward his pants.

"Keep your hands where I can see 'em," Sammy said.

"I gotta adjust my balls," Fat Sal answered. "They're all jammed up down there. What, you wanna come adjust them for me?"

"Don't be a wise guy," Sammy said. "Just keep your hands where I can see 'em."

A moment later Fat Sal reached for a .357 Magnum revolver he kept taped below the desk. He grabbed the weapon and brought it up in one swift, fluid motion. He blasted a shot into Sammy's chest. Sammy grabbed at the wound, then gathered himself and moved forward. Fat Sal raised the weapon again and fired a bullet into Sammy's neck. Sammy stumbled sideways, did a little pirouette, and spun to the floor.

Fat Sal walked over to Sammy and kicked him in the head. Sammy grunted. Fat Sal kicked him again, harder. He raised the weapon with the intention of putting a bullet into Sammy's skull, but stopped short of pulling the trigger. He didn't want to waste rounds. He'd need as many as possible back in 1999, and he didn't have time to buy more. Sammy wasn't going to make it, anyway.

Fat Sal grabbed a key out of his desk and scrambled over to a small metal footlocker located in a corner of the office. He quickly unlocked the trunk. Inside was a small flask of time travel potion—Fat Sal's personal stash—and the getup Fat Sal kept on hand just in case he'd need it: the toupee, Yankees cap, fake beard, Hawaiian shirt, jeans, shoes. He guzzled some potion and stripped to his underwear and socks. He threw the other clothes on, stuck the toupee and beard on, shoved the flask in his pocket, and bolted through the office door and up the stairs. He scrambled out of the nightclub and through the front door, then slipped through the portal to 1999.

Fat Sal figured Douglas and Red had a fifteen-minute head start on him, no more than that. He ran out of the alley and bolted in the direction of Colve Park, figuring that's the only logical place to go in this part of town.

Fat Sal's idea was to follow Douglas and Red to where the money was and then take the money for himself. After that, he'd take care of Red and Douglas. If Elrod happened to be there, Fat Sal would take care of him, too. Then he'd find *Dr. Lionel Bunt* and force *Dr. Lionel Bunt* to send Fat Sal to a time and place he could rid the world of Sen. Miles McLaughlin once and for all.

Fat Sal jogged to make up lost ground. He passed a few street people who tried to approach him for money. He stiff-armed them out of the way and hustled on.

About three blocks from Colve Park he spotted a tall, beefy black man walking in front of a tall, slender white man. The black man had on a blue T-shirt, tan pants, and red baseball cap. The white man had on a tailored suit.

Red and Douglas.

Fat Sal slowed his pace and kept a safe distance behind

as the two men walked into the park and headed north.

***

The fat guy in the Yankees cap seemed to be in a hurry. He was in a half-trot, struggling to catch his breath. Miles McLaughlin watched him pass by from the other side of the street. He wondered who the fat guy was, and why he was in such a hurry. Where had he suddenly appeared from? Had he come out of the alley, too?

There was something hinky about that alley. Fat Sal had disappeared from it months earlier. Then the black guy named Red, the alleged tourist from North Carolina, disappeared from it. About thirty minutes later, Red reappeared from it just as suddenly. Only this time he wasn't alone. A tall, slender white man in a nice suit was with him. Red's face had a bloody bruise on it that hadn't been there before.

Miles was alone when he spotted the two men. He'd told Luis to head on back uptown, thanked him for helping out, apologized for dragging him down here, and told him he owed him lunch. Miles didn't want Luis hanging around, trying to talk sense into him. Miles had a hunch about Red, and he was determined to follow that hunch through, no matter what Luis said. Luis protested, said a United States goddamn senator shouldn't be hanging around this part of town by himself. But Miles managed to shoo him away.

Miles followed Red and the tall, slender man as they made their way north. He let them get a little ahead, then shadowed them from the other side of the street. A little while later Miles spotted the fat guy, hustling at a brisk pace. Alarms went off in Miles' head. He told himself to stay calm. It could be nothing. A false alarm. Don't make a move too early. The odds of the fat guy being Sal Morino were slim, next to nothing. Play it cool. Don't get ahead of yourself here.

But still.

The guy certainly *looked* like he could be Fat Sal. He was the right height and girth. He was obviously wearing a fake beard and toupee. His Yankees cap was angled low over his forehead. Dark shades covered his eyes. It was your typical sloppy attempt at hiding your real identity.

And Red—he'd had a weird reaction earlier when he saw the photo of Fat Sal. Now a fat guy seemed to be hustling down the street, hot on Red's heels.

Stay calm, Miles told himself. Don't let your imagination run wild. Could be nothing.

Or it could be something.

Miles thought about calling Luis, getting backup. But no, not yet.

Better to go solo for now. Stay cool, Senator. Follow the men. See where it led.

Chapter 32

Sidney Donovan knew a gun bulge when she saw one, and that bulge in Dr. Lionel Bunt's midsection looked an awful lot like a gun bulge. Not a big gun by any means. Probably a compact model, poorly concealed.

She suddenly regretted taking this job. She wished she could turn the clock back, travel back through time, and tell Dr. Lionel Bunt that her plate was full and she couldn't take on any new assignments. Lionel's lies should have been a red flag. He began lying to Sidney from the second he sat down in her office. An even bigger red flag was when Lionel offered to pay double Sidney's usual rate. Nobody does that.

Red flags, red flags.

Sidney made a mental note to never again let dollar signs cloud her judgement.

For now, she decided to linger around the hotel and keep an eye on things. She was in this up to her ear lobes. If Lionel did something stupid with that gun and anyone got hurt—or, God forbid, killed—Sidney would get dragged into it. She was the one who led Lionel to Elrod and the woman. She might have her PI license revoked or suspended, or even face jail time as an accessory.

Sidney wasn't going to let that happen. She wandered into the hotel lobby and grabbed a free magazine from a rack by the entrance. She took a seat in one of the cushioned chairs located beside a wall opposite the service desk. The chair gave her a good vantage point of the lounge, where Lionel, Elrod, and the woman were still seated at a table. Sidney hid her face behind the magazine and pretended to read.

She didn't notice the two men who entered the hotel lobby and made their way to the elevators. One of the men was black and balding, with a paunch in the middle. The other was white and slender, with a narrow, angular face.

The white man was smiling.

The black man wasn't.

***

Red pressed the "up" button when they reached the elevator in the hotel lobby, feeling Douglas's breath on the back of his neck as he did so. The two men waited silently for one of the cars to make its way down.

Red told himself it wasn't a mistake bringing Douglas to the hotel. It was the smart play, the only way he'd wiggle his way out of this jam. Only two people knew the combination to the safe: Red and Jade. Douglas wouldn't do anything with the gun as long as Red had the power of money over him.

That's what Red told himself, anyway.

But he wasn't sure he really believed it. Douglas, he just wasn't the kind of cat you made normal assumptions about. There was nothing to stop Douglas from shooting Red the second that safe came open.

Red thought over his options, again. He could pretend he forgot the hotel room key. He could pretend he forgot the room number. He could make a dash for it, right here and now. They were in a hotel lobby, surrounded by people. Surely Douglas wasn't foolish enough to try anything here.

But again, you never could tell about Douglas.

As if on cue, Douglas said, "You're thinking again, William. I can tell by the look on your face. You think way too much, about all the wrong things. Just keep reminding yourself that once the money has been returned to its rightful owners, this will all be over. Now is not the time for errors in judgment."

The elevators were slow coming down. One appeared to be stuck in place. The other stopped on every floor. That was just fine by Red. Time was his friend right now.

"You'd shoot me right here, in front of all these people?" Red said in a half-whisper. "Doesn't sound like the smart play, you don't mind me saying."

"The question is not what I would or wouldn't do," Douglas said. "The question is how willing you are to roll the dice. Maybe I'd let you go. Or maybe I'd shoot you in the back of the head. It's all about risk vs. reward. You might get away, or you might die. Or, you could simply hand over money that's not yours to begin with and walk free and clear."

"Not exactly," Red said. "The risk is you still shoot me after you get the money, with nobody around to witness it. From that angle, the smart play is to make my move now, in front of everyone. I think you're wicked enough to shoot me right here. But not dumb enough."

"That's your call, of course," Douglas said. "But you keep forgetting the other card I'm holding. Jade. She still doesn't know what's going on. She'll waltz right back into 1949 thinking her little scheme is still in play. Run away, and we'll just use her to get the money. And you can believe this, my friend: She'll be begging to take us to the money after what we put her through."

It was a pretty effective card to hold, Red had to admit. Red was no hero, but he doubted he had it in him to put Jade through unspeakable misery on the off chance that he escaped from all this. As much as he resented Jade for dragging him into all this, he didn't want her harmed.

The ding of the elevator shook Red out of his trance. The door opened and eight or nine grumpy people poured out. Douglas opened his hand in a gesture for Red to enter first. A few people filtered in behind them. An elderly couple. A harried mother and her cranky daughter.

And a fat man with a red toupee, fake beard, sunglasses, and Yankees cap.

Chapter 33

Jade's father had always told her: A gun is no good if you couldn't get to it quickly. When you're out hunting, keep the rifle positioned so you could fire the moment you spotted the prey. If you're in a jam, keep the pistol where you can whip it out and send a round into the other bastard's forehead before he has a chance to blink. It was good advice. Too bad Jade hadn't followed it this time.

Her Luger was in her purse now, useless. She'd slipped it in there when she and Elrod first sat down in the hotel lounge. She'd like to have it somewhere closer at hand, ready to use if need be. As things stood, Dr. Lionel Bunt had the only gun that mattered right now, and it was under the table, pointed at Elrod's dick. Jade wasn't sure she cared about Elrod's dick. But she was pissed off at being outgunned. Lionel was a pocket-sized runt of a fella, and Jade figured she could take him in a fair fight. But it wasn't a fair fight right now.

Jade did have a hole card, though. She knew where the money was, and Lionel didn't. She just needed to figure out a way to use that information to her advantage. The first move was to get someplace more private, away from the lounge. Like the hotel room.

Jade had booked two rooms when she cooked her scheme up. Both were on the eleventh floor, way down at the end of the hallway, near the stairwell. The money was in room 1115, beside a utility room that could block out a lot of noise. She kept her clothes and personal items in the other room, 1116. Jade would take Lionel to 1116. If Lionel got too frisky with his gun and demanded that Jade open the safe, he'd see nothing but empty space inside. That would buy Jade enough time to figure out her next move: how to disarm Lionel, conk him on the head, and take over his little moneymaking operation.

It was a pretty good plan until Elrod, being Elrod, turned to Lionel and said, "The money's on the eleventh floor. Room 1115. Go get it and wrap this thing up."

The words ricocheted around in Jade's head for a moment, journeyed to the part of the brain where anger resided, and prompted her to reach across and whack Elrod in the head with her open palm.

Elrod whipped his head back. "What the f…"

"Swell idea, genius!" Jade snapped. "Give him the room number! Why not just go grab the money and stuff it into his pockets yourself?"

Elrod leaned back, out of Jade's reach.

"I don't give a shit about the money," he snapped. "I just want to be done with this once and for all. If this fella says the money's his, fine, he can have it. Good riddance, far as I'm concerned."

Jade raised her hand up to smack Elrod again, but this time he stopped the blow mid-flight with his hand.

"I'm done with this, you hear me?" Elrod said. "Done!

Done with the money, done with you people, the whole deal."

Lionel cleared his throat.

"As tempting as it is to watch you two lovebirds tear each other to pieces, we have business to attend to," he said. "Let's settle our tab here and go up to 1115, huh? Elrod's right. The sooner I get my money back, the sooner we can all go about our lives."

"To hell with you," Jade said. "Try getting into the room without a key."

Elrod reached into his pocket and slid his key across the table to Lionel. "There's your key. Now go on up and make yourself at home. The money's in the safe."

Jade sent another angry look Elrod's way, then turned to Lionel.

"Yes, it's in the safe—a safe that can only be opened with a combination, which you don't have," she said. "Not even Elrod knows it, so don't try working on him this time."

Elrod stood up.

"That's right," he said. "The money's in the safe, the safe has a combination, the combination is in her head, and I'm outta here. Been nice knowing you folks. Check that. It hasn't been nice at all."

Lionel eased the gun back into his belt and stood up. He raised a hand in front of Elrod.

"Sorry, but you'll be coming up to the room with us," Lionel said. "I can't have you out there in the wide world, telling others about our little situation here."

"I could do that right now," Elrod replied. "I could yell that a crazy man with a gun is trying to hold us hostage."

"And I could let them know you stole my coat and my

money, and I'm only trying to get them back," Lionel said. "Which is all true, by the way. Who do you think a court of law will believe? You, a homeless degenerate? Or me, a respected scientist with a valid gun permit?"

"I didn't steal a damn thing," Elrod said. "You planted that money on me without my knowledge. And anyway, I told you I don't care about the money. Go on up and get it, nobody's stopping you. You don't need me tagging along."

"When I get the money, you're free to go wherever you want," Lionel said. "Until then, I'm just going to have to insist that you come along with us."

"And what are you gonna do if I don't come along?" Elrod asked. "Shoot me? Go ahead, have at it. Right here in the lounge. See how well that'll play out in a court of law."

"You seem to forget who I am," Lionel said. "I'm the one who discovered the magic of time travel. I could fire a bullet right through your head—or better yet, through your pretty friend's head—and pop right out of here into the past. The only thing left would be you and her dead body."

"He's bluffing," Jade interjected. "You need a special portal to travel through time. He can't just pick any spot to do it."

"Maybe that's what you heard, and believe," Lionel told her. "But you don't really know for sure, do you?"

He looked at Elrod.

"Forget yourself," Lionel said. "Think about your friend here. Are you willing to put her at risk, just so you can try and make a run for it? Do you want that cloud of guilt hanging over your head the rest of your days?"

"Don't believe him," Jade said.

Lionel moved his hand toward the gun. He kept it close to his stomach, hidden behind his jacket. He turned his back to the lounge crowd and pointed it at Jade.

"Don't mess around with that gun," Elrod whispered.

Lionel extended the barrel. "Your call, Elrod."

He tightened his finger on the trigger.

"He's bluffing," Jade said.

Elrod looked at Lionel. He looked at the gun. He looked at Jade.

"Well hell," Elrod said. "Let's go up there and get this over with."

He stood up, threw his coat on, and began walking toward the hotel lobby. Jade tried to stop him, but he kept on walking. She shook her head and followed close behind. Lionel brought up the rear.

Neither Elrod nor Lionel noticed Jade's hand slipping into her purse to ease out the Luger.

Chapter 34

Fat Sal tucked himself into a corner of the elevator so neither Red nor Douglas could get a good look at him. He tried to collect himself, slow down his breathing after the long and tiring slog up to the hotel. Red and Douglas got off on the eleventh floor and turned right. Fat Sal eased out behind them and headed left. After a few yards he peeked around, saw that nobody was looking, and reversed direction. He pulled his gun from his pocket and tucked it behind his arm, trailing behind Red and Douglas at a leisurely pace, stepping quietly. When the two men stopped in front of door number 1115, Fat Sal quickened his pace.

Red pulled a plastic key from his pocket and slid it into the lock. He turned the handle, pushed the door open and disappeared inside. Douglas was set to follow him in when Fat Sal snuck up from behind. Douglas whipped his head around and saw a fat man in a beard and New York Yankees cap pointing a gun at his nose.

"How's kicks, Dougie boy?" Fat Sal said.

He snatched Douglas' gun out of his hand.

"Go in the room," Fat Sal said. "Let's chat."

***

Sidney watched Lionel, Elrod, and the woman disappear inside the elevator. After the doors closed behind them she rose from her chair and strolled to the elevator herself. She eyed the light to see which floor they were headed to. She gave herself a little pep talk, tried to convince herself she was doing the right thing by getting mixed up in all this. The businesswoman inside Sidney told her to head back to her office, move on to other jobs, and hope Lionel didn't do something stupid. But the ex-cop told her she had a duty to make sure nobody got hurt. And truth be told, she was getting an adrenaline rush from it all, just like the old days.

The elevator light lingered on the eleventh floor. Sidney decided that's where Lionel & Co. got off. She was jabbing the "up" button with her finger when a voice addressed her by name.

"Ms. Donovan, right?" the voice said, "The private eye?"

Sidney turned around. The voice belonged to a tall white man with glasses. He was wearing a Knicks cap, a Jets jersey, and brown horn-rimmed glasses. He looked familiar, but Sidney couldn't place him.

"Do I know you?" she said.

"You know my partner, Luis," the man said. "You all met each other earlier, in LoDown. I was with him, but he did all the talking. You said you were looking for someone, and so were we. Luis had other business uptown and left me in charge."

"Right, Luis. The security consultant," Sidney answered. She checked the elevator light to see where the cars were. Still heading up.

"Are you following me around or something?" she said.

"I've been following someone, but not you," the man said. "Three other people. A black man, a white man, and a fat man."

"A fat man. Sal Morino?" Sidney asked. She watched the elevators move to the upper floors, stop, then begin their descent.

"Probably not, but it's worth a shot," the man said. "I shouldn't tell you this, but hey, you're an ex-cop, right? The fat guy is wearing a fake beard and fake hair. It's pretty obvious he's trying to hide his identity. The white guy looks like he stepped out of a Buick ad from fifty years ago. The black guy told Luis he was a tourist from North Carolina, but he must have gotten a bad travel tip because he was doing his tourist thing in LoDown."

This last part got Sidney's attention.

"The black man," she said. "Describe him."

"Forty-something, a little thick in the middle," the man said. "Red baseball cap, blue T-shirt, tan slacks. Calls himself Red. We talked to him a while ago. He went into an alley to relieve himself, disappeared for a while, then came back out about thirty minutes later with a fresh bruise on his face. The tall white guy was with him."

"I think I talked to the same black man, in LoDown," Sidney said. "I showed him a photo of the guy I'm trying to track down. His face changed when he first saw it, then changed again. He said he didn't know the guy."

The elevator made its way to the fifth floor, stopped

there, then moved down to the third.

"He had the same sort of reaction when we showed him the photo of Sal Morino," the man said.

"You say you saw him get on the elevator?" Sidney said. "The black guy?"

"Yep."

"Did you notice what floor it stopped on?"

"Eleven is my guess."

The elevator finally made it to the lobby. The doors opened and a crowd of people squeezed out.

Sidney moved out of the way to let them exit. She inched closer to the man.

"I think you and I need to go to the eleventh floor," she said.

They stepped inside the elevator just as another man hurried up and stepped inside with them.

"Good to see you again, boyo," the man said to Miles. "And you as well, Ms. Donovan."

Sidney looked at the man. So did the tall guy with the Jets jersey.

"Jesus, Luis," the tall man said. "What are you doing here?"

"You didn't think I was really going to let you go through with this alone, did you?" Luis said. "I've been tailing you the whole time. And the fat guy with the disguise."

He opened his jacket to reveal a holstered .44 Magnum.

"I assume you're not strapped," Luis said to Miles. "If that's really your boy up there, then you're going to need someone who is."

He looked at Sidney and winked. "Nice to see you

again."

The elevator made its way up.

Chapter 35

Douglas sat in a corner chair with his legs stretched out, one crossed in front of the other. It was the best way to conceal the small handgun he had holstered to his right ankle. He always kept the gun there in case it was needed. The sudden appearance of Fat Sal holding a gun of his own—and taking Douglas' other weapon—meant it might be needed soon.

They were in room 1115. Red sat on a queen-sized bed just a few feet away. The bed had a travel bag on it and a pile of new clothes. Fat Sal stood beside a small dresser with one gun in his hand and another in his pocket, his fake beard drooping, his face dewy with sweat. The gun in his hand was a .357 Magnum. The one in his pocket he'd taken off Douglas.

"Glad we could all get together," Fat Sal said. "Not a bad room, eh? A little smaller than I normally like. But not bad, not bad."

"Why are you here?" Douglas said.

"Better question: Why are you and Satchmo here?" Fat Sal replied. "Wait—I'll answer for you. You're here for my money."

Douglas leaned back in the chair and smiled. "The scientist's money, to be precise."

"My money," Fat Sal said.

Douglas waved his hand in front of his face.

"Semantics," he said. "The point is, here we are, and here you are. I assume young Sammy either cut a deal with you or suffered some unfortunate fate."

"You left a retard in charge, so take a guess what happened," Fat Sal said. "But he's fine, he's fine. He has a lot less blood now than he did an hour ago. Other than that, he's great."

Douglas shook his head. "Sammy is a continual source of disappointment."

"I ain't interested in talking about him," Fat Sal said.

"What are you interested in talking about?"

"Now's not a good time to try my patience."

"We all realize you're interested in the money our friend Red here ran off with," Douglas said. "I'm sure he'll show it to us presently. But you're not seeing the big picture, Salvatore. The scientist is the only one who can deliver what you want—a chance to change your fate for the better. This kind of erratic behavior, popping back into the one year you should avoid, might make him question the sanity of continuing to work with you."

"You know what? What he thinks, what you think, means nothing right now. What matters is what I think. And what I think is that my money is in here somewhere, and I want it."

Douglas considered how best to retrieve his pistol. He just needed to lean down a little to grab it. But he had to pick the right time.

"Where's the money?" Fat Sal said.

Douglas nodded toward Red. "Ask him."

Fat Sal walked over and placed the barrel of the gun against Red's forehead.

"Speak," Fat Sal said.

Red sighed. He looked at Fat Sal.

"The money is in a safe," he said. "You can't open it without a combination. I have the combination, and you're not getting it until we go someplace safe, where there's a lot of people around."

"You're not going anywhere," Fat Sal said. He glanced around the room. "Usually I take a luxury suite when I stay at hotels. This ain't no luxury suite, but I'm pretty sure the safe is in the closet. Now you just shuffle your black ass over there and open it before I get angry."

Red didn't move. Fat Sal placed the barrel of the gun against Red's throat. The two men locked eyes.

A moment later they heard a click at the door. Three people walked in.

Chapter 36

Lionel followed Elrod and Jade into the hotel room. The first thing Lionel saw was a black man sitting on the bed. The second thing he saw was a fat guy with a red beard and Yankees cap holding a gun against the black man's throat.

The fat man looked up and pointed the gun at Lionel. Lionel pointed his gun back.

The fat man grinned. "Well, well, if it's not Dr. Toyota himself," he said. "Just the guy I'm looking for."

Lionel recognized that voice. The face was vaguely familiar, too.

"Don't recognize me?" the fat man said. "Here, let's give you a better look."

He took off his hat. He took off his toupee. He took off his beard and sunglasses. He put his hat back on and tossed the rest on the floor.

Sal Morino, in a cheap disguise. Here in this hotel room. Back in 1999, with a gun in his hand.

Lionel felt his blood begin to boil. Why was Fat Sal here? What kind of stupid, ill-considered stunt was he up to? Why couldn't people follow simple instructions? Why did they insist on improvising, wandering off course? Lionel had devised a brilliant plan to make money. It was simple to execute—if everyone stuck to it.

But you couldn't really depend on people. They were undisciplined. Unreliable. Stupid.

Lionel raised his weapon higher and pointed it at Fat Sal's fat face. Fat Sal pointed his gun at Lionel's face. The two men stood there, pointing their guns at each other's faces. The others in the room were quiet and still.

Lionel noticed that one of them was Douglas, sitting in a lounge chair across the room. Lionel looked at him.

"And you, too," Lionel said. "Of course."

"Dr. Bunt," Douglas responded. "Fancy seeing you here. And the lovely Jade as well. I had a sneaking suspicion she was in on this. And our old friend Elrod, newly groomed. What a happy reunion for all."

Jade saw Red sitting on the bed and gasped. "Why are you here?" she said. "What happened to your face?"

Red was about to answer when Lionel interrupted them. "You two shut up," he said. He turned his attention back to Fat Sal.

"What I really want to know is why you're here," Lionel said. "I gave you specific orders..."

"You gave *me* orders?" Fat Sal said. "No no no no no. You don't give orders. You take orders. You screwed up and got my money stolen. I'm here to get that money back. Then you and I are going to take a little trip together—let's say to 1977, so I can drop in on an old pal. So, put your gun down, *Doctor* Bunt."

Lionel held his gun steady. "Not until you put yours down."

Fat Sal chuckled. "That's cute. That's very cute."

He looked over at Red. "Don't you think that's cute? The Nutty Professor here thinks he knows something about guns."

Fat Sal turned back to Lionel. "See my gun?" he said. "It's a lot bigger than yours. Maybe your gun will nick my flesh, sting a little. Who knows? But it's a sure bet my gun will send pieces of your head flying in a thousand different directions. Some maid fresh off the boat will still be finding parts of you in the carpet twenty years from now. Put the toy pistol down and let's talk business."

"You mean the business you're determined to ruin by showing up here?" Lionel said.

"I mean the business of doing what I'm paying you to do, which is to take me where I want to go."

"Where is that again?"

"I told you. 1977, 1978, 1981. One of those years."

Now Lionel chuckled. "You really are dense, aren't you?"

"How's that?" Fat Sal said.

"Dense. Unintelligent. Stupid. A big, fat, dumb Italian guinea ape."

Fat Sal started to say something, but Lionel cut him off.

"So you want to go back to 1977, do you?" Lionel said. "Or some other year of your choosing?"

"That's right."

"You really think time travel works like a taxicab, don't you? That it will just drop you off at any time and place you want. I depended on you believing that. It was a key part of my plan."

Douglas snickered in the corner. Fat Sal whipped his

head around to look at him, then whipped it back toward Lionel.

"The fuck you talking about?" he said.

"Time travel doesn't work like that. Picking your own destination. It only drops you off from point A to point B, then back again. That's it."

"The fuck you talking about?" Fat Sal repeated.

"I can't take you back to 1977, or 1978, or anywhere else but fifty years back and forth, back and forth, back and forth," Lionel said. "Don't ask me why. Just a quirk of the system. Your idea to go to any year you wanted was only a pipe dream. The money you've been paying me won't do what you want it to do. It's simply your contribution to my personal fund. I conned you, *Fat* Sal."

Douglas laughed.

Fat Sal took a step closer to Lionel. "You little..."

Lionel raised his gun higher.

Red sat frozen on the bed. Elrod and Jade stood frozen by the wall.

Douglas laughed again.

A knock came at the door.

Chapter 37

Sidney, Luis, and Miles were pretty sure this was the right room. They'd canvassed the entire eleventh floor, listening for sounds behind doors. They heard kids' voices behind one door. Behind another door a guy was screaming about the lousy goddamn concierge service, he didn't pay good money for this shit. A third door carried the unmistakable sound of two lovebirds grinding and grunting away.

This door, to room 1115, was the best prospect. The voices behind it carried an edge. One of them sounded like Lionel's.

Luis tried to talk Sidney and Miles into letting him go in by himself. He'd had plenty of experience dealing with this kind of drama, he said. He'd know what to do when things got rough. Sidney reminded him that she used to be a police detective, too.

"I think my client's in there," she whispered. "He might be up to something that could turn out bad for him, and for me. This is my business, too."

Luis looked at Miles. "You really need to disappear."

"No way," Miles said. "If that's Morino in there, I want to look him in the eyes when the hammer drops."

Luis didn't see any point in arguing.

"OK, you knock on the door," he told Sidney. "I'll follow behind. Miles, you keep behind me. Be on your toes."

Sidney gave him the thumbs up and knocked.

***

Lionel jerked his head around at the knock on the door. Fat Sal tightened his trigger finger. Red, Jade, and Elrod eyed the door. Douglas eased his hand toward his ankle holster. Nobody said a word.

There was another knock, then another. Finally, a voice behind the door said, "Dr. Bunt, are you in there? It's Sidney. Sidney Donovan. If you're in there, let me know. I want to see if everything's OK."

Lionel looked around the room. His eyes scanned everyone until they rested on Elrod. He leaned over and whispered in Elrod's ear.

"Go open the door, slowly," he said. "Tell her she has the wrong room. Keep the chain on the door and your face hidden."

Elrod walked to the door and unlocked the chain. He swung the door open wide and saw a black woman, a Hispanic-looking guy, and a tall white dude in glasses and a Jets jersey.

"Come on in," Elrod said. "Plenty of room for everyone."

He looked back at Lionel and winked.

Sidney walked through the door. Luis walked in

behind her, then Miles. The door closed behind them.
Then the guns came out.

Chapter 38

Fat Sal's gun was out. Lionel's gun was out. Sidney saw their guns and pulled hers out. Douglas stood up with his gun out, which prompted Luis to pull his out.

Miles stared at all this weaponry for a couple seconds before his eyes locked on something else—the portly man he'd been shadowing. The man still had the Yankees cap on, but he'd lost the beard, toupee, and dark glasses. Miles knew that face. For a moment, he forgot about the guns.

"Jesus, Mary, and Joseph," he said. "It *is* you."

Fat Sal looked back, confused. Miles took his cap and glasses off. Fat Sal's eyes lit up.

"What the...this some kind of setup?" Fat Sal said.

"Nice to see you again, Sal," Miles said.

Fat Sal raised his gun higher and pointed it at Miles' face. "Don't bet on it."

Luis stepped in front of Fat Sal's gun and pulled out a wallet. He flipped it open and dangled a private security badge in the air, then whipped it back into his pocket before anyone could get a closer look.

"My name is Special Agent Luis Baez of the FBI," he

lied. "I'm ordering everyone here to lower your weapons. You first, Morino."

Fat Sal held his gun steady.

Sidney and Lionel eyeballed each other.

"What are you doing here?" Lionel asked.

"Put the gun down, Dr. Bunt," Sidney said.

Lionel kept his gun where it was.

Douglas took a step forward with his pistol raised. "I'm afraid the two of you are outgunned. If it comes to a shooting match, the odds are not in your favor."

Jade whipped her Luger in the air and pointed it at Douglas.

"Now the odds are even," she said. "The first shot lands right in your neck."

Miles stepped closer to Fat Sal. "Lower your weapon, Morino. Everybody else do the same. He's a wanted man, and this is a federal matter. Nobody needs to get hurt."

Nobody lowered any weapons.

Luis told Fat Sal to lower his gun.

"Fuck you," Fat Sal answered.

Outside on the street you could hear horns honking and machines rattling. Inside, the air had that fresh hotel room smell, with the faint aroma of human sweat mixed in.

Chapter 39

Red sat quiet and still on the bed, looking at the guns, looking at the people holding them. He thought about the jams he'd been in. Dealing with rednecks down South. Having a knife pulled on him by a hophead in Detroit. Being robbed at gunpoint in a Kansas City flophouse.

One thing Red learned over the years is that if you sit back and wait for bad things to happen, bad things will happen. And this hotel room was just full of bad things ready to happen.

Red assessed the situation, laid the odds of making a move vs. sitting tight. Fat Sal was the most clear and present danger. He was cornered, and didn't give much indication of wanting to go quietly. Fat Sal reminded Red of those feral dogs he'd see every now and then near his grandfather's house in the country. You get one of those dogs cornered and it would gnaw its own heart out to keep from being trapped.

Douglas was dangerous, too, but in a different way. You got the feeling Douglas had motorcycle grease running through his veins instead of blood. Red had never seen the man angry. Not once. He never showed emotion. What kind of human doesn't get angry?

A human who's not really human, that's what kind.

But Douglas was way over there in the corner of the hotel room, out of Red's range. Fat Sal was right in front of Red. Red could leap out at him, knock the gun from his hand and disrupt things long enough for the others to grab control of the situation.

He weighed the odds again.

Do something?

Or sit tight.

***

Elrod didn't know which side of the room to focus on. Neither brought much joy. On one side he saw three guns pointed his way. On the other, he saw three more guns pointed his way. He was standing in the middle. If those guns started going off, forget it. *Adios, muchacho.*

It was a hell of a spot to be in. Elrod blew air out of his mouth and tried to keep himself from tipping over. His eyes darted back and forth, back and forth, searching for an option that didn't involve him being shredded into confetti. Could he make a run for it? Could he read the situation correctly, the way he used to read pitchers when he was on the basepaths? Could he get that quick first step and then bolt out the door at full speed? Was he willing to bet his life on it?

No, he wasn't.

He recognized a couple of the faces. One belonged to the mobster, Sal Morino. The other belonged to that politician, Miles McLaughlin. What a world Elrod had landed in. What a damn world.

Miles and Luis kept telling everyone to lower their weapons, and everyone kept not lowering their weapons. Elrod hoped at least one would lower a weapon just to get the ball rolling. But that hope was fast circling the drain.

What to do, then?

Elrod wasn't an especially brave guy, but he was practical. He'd been in some hairy situations where being brave was the only rational course of action. Once down in New Orleans he got backed into an alley by a skinny, grungy dope fiend brandishing a knife and seeing monsters everywhere. The dope fiend wasn't going to be satisfied until he carved up all those monsters, Elrod included. Elrod sprang at the dope fiend with everything at his disposal—fists and knees, feet and elbows, shoulders and hips, his head, his teeth. He slammed the fiend to the ground and jackrabbited out of there.

This situation wasn't exactly the same. But it was close.

"There's no way you're getting out of here, Sal," Miles said. "Just lower the weapon. We don't want anyone getting hurt."

"Fuck you," Fat Sal said.

"You need to listen to him, Morino," Luis told Fat Sal. "Come in quietly, we'll..."

"Fuck you."

Elrod was within arm's reach of Lionel's gun hand. That close. He could chop at Lionel's hand in no time and knock the gun loose. Create a little havoc. Stir things up.

But something else beat him to the punch—a body bolting off the bed toward Fat Sal. It happened quickly. First the blur of movement, then the sight of Fat Sal being knocked against the dresser by Red, the sax player.

Elrod raised his right hand and snapped it down on Lionel's wrist, karate style, just above the pistol. The pistol didn't come loose, but the barrel got moved in a different direction.

Then came the gunfire.

Chapter 40

Loud, cracking sounds filled the room, followed by the ricochet of shrapnel bouncing every which way. Blood sprayed the carpet and bed. Bodies tumbled and danced. Smoke and cordite fouled the air. Somebody moaned. Somebody else shrieked. A couple of somebodies cursed, loudly. Something crashed against the wall and then fell with a thud, knocking over a lamp. The TV on the dresser exploded. More shots rang out.

Elrod tumbled to the floor and tried to get his bearings. He saw blood splatter against the dresser. He took in deep breaths to lap up air, but mostly inhaled smoke. He felt a biting pain in his abdomen. Parts of his body were being crushed by other bodies. He got elbowed in the eye and kneed in the neck. A bullet screamed past his ear. His face got shoved into the carpet. He heard loud voices.

"Stay down!"

"Don't move!"

"Stay down!"

Elrod tried to wrest himself free of the chaos, but the bodies kept him planted in place. The pain in his abdomen grew sharper. The world spun around in circles, blurry, misty, fuzzy. Elrod caught a glimpse of Fat Sal's face, bright crimson now, with a protruding tongue that wagged desperately in search of someplace to go. Two brown arms formed a vise around Fat Sal's neck. Fat Sal strained to free himself. He gasped for air. His eyeballs rolled up and down like fruit in a slot machine.

"Drop your weapons!" a voice shouted.

Another shot rang out, then another.

Elrod eased his head up, tried to focus on something that could help him navigate the situation and find an escape hatch. But all he saw was a gun barrel from across the room, pointed right at his face.

He heard another loud cracking sound, then another. He gasped and tried to breathe.

Someone slumped to the floor. Someone else fell with a thud.

***

Douglas aimed his gun accurately; you can bet on that. But the bullet didn't go where he had aimed it. He fired it at Luis Baez, the spic who introduced himself as an FBI agent.

A faulty weapon—that was the only explanation. Douglas had heard such good things about it, too. It was a Colt M1911 45-caliber pistol—semi-automatic, magazine-fed, favored by American soldiers in both wars, prized for its accuracy and dependability. That's what Douglas had been told, anyway, when he purchased the gun from a little Dago greaseball a few months ago. But this model had let Douglas down. It didn't hit its target. Douglas blamed the gun rather than himself. His aim had been precise, he was sure of it. No, he'd been sold a defective model.

It was all so disappointing. Douglas cursed the gun. He cursed the greaseball who sold it to him. He cursed the stinging sensation in his throat. He felt dizzy, weak, unable to gulp in enough air. He felt he might topple over any second. There was a lot of smoke in the room, a lot of frenzied activity. Douglas' gun felt heavy in his hand as he raised it back up to take another shot. It felt like it weighed two tons. This time he tried to point it at Elrod, who was twisting around on the floor.

But something caught Douglas' attention. It was the barrel of another gun, pointed right at his head. The eyes behind the other gun were hazel, crescent-shaped, very pretty. Maybe the prettiest eyes Douglas had ever seen. They belonged to Jade. Pretty little Jade. Pretty little rube from the prairie. What was Jade doing with that gun? Why was it pointed at Douglas? Oh Jade. Dear, lovely Jade. Why are you pointing that gun at me? What mischief are you up to now?

A loud, deafening pop rang in Douglas' ears.

Everything went white, then everything went black.

***

Elrod crawled toward the dresser and gulped in air. The room had gone quiet except for the sounds of moaning and heavy breathing. He watched Luis scan the room, pistol at the ready. Fat Sal was piled on the floor, blood trickling from his thigh, white foam circling his mouth.

"Keep an eye on everyone," Luis told Sidney Donovan.

Luis holstered his gun and leaned down toward Fat Sal. He touched Fat Sal's neck. He bent over and put his ear against Fat Sal's mouth, then his chest. He got on his knees and began to perform CPR, first one set of compressions, then another set. Fat Sal's head bobbed slightly.

"Heart attack," Luis said. "Go figure."

Red was lying on the floor near the bed, breathing erratically, his face drenched with sweat. Miles bent down to look at him. He saw a large red circle near Red's chest.

Another bolt of pain shot into Elrod's abdomen. He scanned the room. Sidney stood behind Lionel Bunt, her left arm wrapped around his neck, holding him in place. Lionel had a red spot on his jacket near his right hip. The jacket had a hole in it. It wasn't a big hole, but it was a bloody one. Lionel looked at it. He touched it with his finger. He brought the finger up to his face and studied the blood on it.

"I've been shot," Lionel said, sounding both surprised and disappointed.

Elrod looked at the lounge chair in the corner. A long, well-dressed leg was draped over it. The leg was attached to a long, well-dressed body that spilled onto the floor in different directions— one arm pointed this way, the other pointed that way, its torso bent and twisted, the other leg lying beneath a black table lamp that had crashed to the floor. The body belonged to Douglas, the maître d' from the nightclub. A pool of blood had formed on the carpet, just above Douglas' head. A large red hole was in the middle of his forehead. There was another hole in his neck. Douglas' eyes were open. They looked bewildered, glassy, long gone.

Jade stood above Douglas and stared down, the Luger dangling by her side. Her hands were shaking.

Luis walked over and inspected Douglas' body. He turned to Jade.

"You're a good shot, I'll give you that," he said. "You okay?"

"Why wouldn't I be?" Jade said.

"It's just. That guy on the floor, you know."

"Don't assume it bothers me killing him."

"Roger that," Luis said. "Who is he, anyway?"

"A bad guy," Jade replied.

"He's mixed up with Sal Morino?"

Jade nodded.

"And what about you?"

"What about me?" Jade said, glancing at Luis briefly before turning her eyes back to Douglas.

"Never mind," Luis said.

He gently removed Jade's gun from her hand.

"Better let me take this," he said. "Gonna be a lot of questions to answer when the police arrive. I'm going to take a leap of faith and assume you're on the side of God here. You probably saved lives, mowing this guy down."

Jade didn't answer. She just stared at Douglas

Elrod watched her standing there, staring down, trembling, her face a mixture of rage and shame, as if she didn't know what she was supposed to feel.

Later on, when he had time to digest it all, that's what stuck with Elrod: Jade's face. Not the red spot below his abdomen, where the pain was. Not the bodies of the dead or dying. Not the blood or smoke.

Only Jade's face.

Chapter 41

Miles hustled into the bathroom and sprinted back out a moment later, holding a towel. He pressed it against Red's stomach wound, trying to stanch the bleeding. It didn't look promising. The blood was spreading quickly. Red's breathing had grown more erratic. His eyes floated open and shut.

Jade noticed him lying there. She rushed over and kneeled down beside him.

"Red, no," she said, her voice cracking. "God, no..."

Luis reached down and tapped her on the shoulder.

"Miss, I'm sorry, but you need to leave," he said. He turned to the others in the room. "All of you need to clear out of here, like right now. I'll stay here and sort things out with the cops. They'll listen to me. But the rest of you need to scatter."

"I'm not going anywhere," Jade said.

"Lady, please," Luis said. "We got no time for..."

Red reached his hand up slowly and patted Jade on the arm. He opened his mouth, tried to say something, stopped, then gave it another shot.

"Go on, Jade," he said in a bare whisper. "Do as the man says."

"Red..."

"Go on, now," Red repeated.

Jade hugged him around the neck, her eyes red and moist. Red patted her on the head.

"No need to be all blue," he said. "Everything's cool here."

He coughed out blood.

"Red..." Jade said.

"We had us some times, Jade," Red said. "Some real good times. We'll meet up again. Just next time, let me run the show, huh?"

He smiled, then tilted his head to the side and fell silent again.

Chapter 42

Sidney pushed Lionel up against the wall and stuck her face an inch from his.

"Start talking," she said. "What did you drag me into?"

Lionel didn't answer.

"*Talk*," Sidney repeated.

Luis walked up and touched her on the arm.

"There's no time for this," he said. "You need to go."

Sidney yanked her arm away from Luis and kept her eyes on Lionel. "Talk. *Now*."

A voice from behind pierced the silence.

"He's hooked up with Sal Morino," the voice said.

Sidney spun her head around. It was Elrod. He had pulled himself up from the floor and was leaning against the dresser, his hand over his abdomen.

"What do you mean, hooked up with Sal Morino?" Sidney asked.

"He was helping hide Morino from the law," Elrod said. "Morino was paying him off. That tall fella lying on the floor over there was in on it, too."

"Who's the guy on the floor?" Sidney asked.

"Works at a nightclub, is all I know," Elrod replied. "Name's Douglas. He was part of a scheme where Morino would send money to that scientist fella there. For helping hide him out."

Sidney jammed her gun barrel into Lionel's right eye. "You got me mixed up in something with *Sal Morino*?"

Luis stepped between Sidney and Lionel.

"Look, you can iron this out later," he said. "For now, you need to leave and take the others with you before the police arrive."

Sidney raised her gun and smashed it against the side of Lionel's head. Lionel made a move to strike back but Luis separated them.

"That's enough!" he told Sidney. "You used to be a cop; you know better. I'll keep this guy here and let the police deal with him. You and the others clear out before you get caught up in something you don't want to get caught up in."

"Wait a minute," Miles said. He looked at Elrod. "What's your story? How are you and these two involved?" He pointed toward Jade and Red.

Elrod hesitated.

"Quickly," Miles said.

"You're that senator," Elrod said. "I seen your picture..."

"Never mind who I am," Miles interrupted. "Talk about yourself."

Elrod looked at Jade, then back at Miles.

"Red and Jade played music at the nightclub where Douglas worked," he finally said. "They found out about the money scheme and figured out a way to take some for themselves. They hid it here in this hotel room, in the safe.

I was dragged into it without even knowing what I was dragged into."

Jade snapped her face toward Elrod.

"There's no point chasing this thing any longer," Elrod told her. "They'd find the safe, anyway. It's over."

Miles kept his eyes on Elrod. "Who booked this room?" he said. "Whose name is it under?"

"Ask her," Elrod said, nodding toward Jade.

Miles looked at Jade. "Miss? What name?"

Jade didn't answer.

Red lifted his head, waved Miles over. Miles kneeled down.

"We booked two rooms, two different names," Red whispered. "Other's across the hall, 1116. Key's in my pocket."

"Whose names are the rooms booked under?" Miles said.

"Fake names," Red said. "Ben Webster. Dinah Washington. We..."

Red's voice trailed off and then disappeared altogether. He let out a deep, throaty wheeze. He tilted his head to the side and stared blankly into nothing much at all. Jade went down to the floor and held him.

Miles patted Red on the cheek and then checked his pockets. He found the key to 1116 and looked up at Luis. "The others should hide out across the hall while we work this thing out with the cops."

"You can't hang around here," Luis said. "That'll only create a shitstorm we'll never be able to explain away."

"Look, I have connections..." Miles said.

"No," Luis interrupted. "Take the stairs and scoot. I'll handle the police when they get here, leave you out of it.

Help me get her up."

Miles shrugged. He and Luis lifted Jade to her feet, struggling to keep her steady as she tried to hold onto Red. Elrod stepped in and draped Jade's arm around his shoulder.

"They're right, we gotta go," Elrod said. "He'll get help for Red. There's nothing else we can do."

Miles put his cap and glasses back on. He walked to the door and opened it, peeked out into the hallway, saw it was clear. He waved the others over, gestured for them to hurry. Elrod gathered his new clothes and backpack off the bed, then he and Jade followed Miles out into the hallway. Miles crossed the hall and unlocked the door to room 1116. Jade tried to turn back toward room 1115, but Sidney stopped her and shoved her the other way. Miles headed for the staircase while Jade, Elrod, and Sidney disappeared inside 1116. Police sirens screamed in the distance.

Chapter 43

Sidney closed the door behind her and locked the chain. She looked at Jade and Elrod.

"I'll stand by the door and keep an ear out," she said. "You two take a seat. Try to keep quiet."

Elrod dumped his backpack and new clothes in the closet and turned to make his way inside the room, but Jade stood still. She looked at Sidney.

"Who are you to be giving orders?" she said.

Sidney sighed. She pulled out her PI license and flashed it in front of them.

"I'm a private investigator and former police detective," Sidney said. "Dr. Bunt hired me to find Elrod. He wanted his money back, and he figured Elrod had it. I had no idea the money was mixed up with Salvatore Morino, otherwise I would have called the feds and collected a reward. If the police come knocking on this door, it's better that an ex-cop talks to them."

"That doesn't put you in charge," Jade said. "You're mixed up with that scientist over there. Why should we take orders from you, or even trust you? Who knows if you're not in on the whole thing?"

Sidney glared at her. "And you're mixed up in a felony theft that involves a mafia boss, so why should I trust you? Nobody's trying to order anyone around. I have experience in these kinds of situations, so maybe I know the best way to proceed. Calm down and play nice until this thing blows over, OK?"

Jade gave her a hard look, but Sidney ignored it. She walked toward Elrod and lifted his shirt up. She bent over and studied his wound.

"This probably came from a small-caliber pistol," Sidney said. "It looks nasty, but it's not as bad as it looks. The bullet didn't go in very far or you wouldn't be upright. You got lucky. Go in the bathroom and wash it with soap and warm water. Keep a washcloth over the wound. When we're clear to leave you need to have it checked out. I'd suggest the free clinic near LoDown. They don't ask a lot of questions there."

Elrod went into the bathroom and did as instructed. Sidney was right—it looked nasty, but the pain was manageable. He also had a nasty shiner on his left eye, and God knows how many other scrapes and bruises on other body parts. He tucked his shirt in to keep the washcloth in place and returned to the room, taking a seat on the bed. Jade sat in a cushioned chair in the corner.

They waited quietly while the scene played out across the hall. First came the sound of running footsteps down the hallway, then the sound of voices, then the sound of a pounding on the door across the hall. A police officer identified himself in a very official-sounding voice. He said he was responding to a disturbance, and that other officers were present.

"Open the door slowly and come out with your hands above your heads," the officer said.

The next voice was Luis', from room 1115. He identified himself as Luis Baez, private security consultant, ex-NYPD homicide detective. He said he was inside with a known fugitive, two other suspects, and a wounded bystander. The fugitive and one of the suspects were incapacitated. The other suspect was injured. The bystander was in need of immediate medical attention.

"Shots were fired, but the situation is now contained," Luis shouted through the door. "I'm going to open this door slowly and reach my left hand out. It will be holding my security badge and identification. After that, I am going to open the door wider so you can confirm that it's me."

"Make sure you open the door slowly," a cop responded. "Don't make any sudden movements. When we tell you to exit, do so with your hands in plain sight."

Elrod couldn't hear much after that except for the faint stir of movement and voices. No shots were fired, and nobody screamed, so Elrod guessed things played out pretty much the way everyone wanted. Luis opened the door slowly and presented his badge and ID. He peeked his head out, hands raised, so the cops could match his face to the ID. The cops confirmed that Luis was who he said he was.

After that, it was anybody's guess what happened. Elrod suspected Luis gave the cops a truncated version of the events. Just some bad boys involved in a shooting match with a good guy, that's all. I'm an ex-detective on the force. Maybe y'all know my name and face. Oh, and that fat guy on the floor there? He's Salvatore Morino. You believe that? Score one for the home team. Anyway, since

Morino is involved, this case is a federal matter. I expect I'll get a little reward money out of it...

Time passed slowly in room 1116. Nobody said much of anything. Sidney hung by the door. Jade sat in her chair, looking lost. Elrod lay on the bed, trying not to think about his wound or his pain. You could hear activity across the hall, probably investigators investigating and medical personnel attending to the deceased and wounded.

After an hour or so Sidney's mobile phone rang. Sidney held her hand up, letting everyone know to be quiet. She clicked the phone and said hello. That was followed by a series of "uh huhs" and "mmm hmmmms" and "yeahs" and "okays." She hung up after a couple of minutes.

"That was Luis Baez," Sidney said. "He's still sorting things out with the police but he was able to slip out long enough to call on his mobile phone. He suggests we leave soon. There's a crime scene across the hall and the cops might want to ask some questions when we step outside. I'll go first, make up a story about how we didn't hear anything because we were otherwise occupied. Something plausible, like a lover's spat or three-way. If any officers want to speak with you, just play dumb. Take all your personal belongings. Don't leave anything behind that can identify you. Leave the hotel immediately and don't come back."

Elrod nodded, but Jade just sat there. She looked better than she did before, or at least calmer. Elrod felt sorry for her. She'd shot somebody, and that somebody was pretty damn dead. It couldn't be an easy thing to deal with. Even worse was Red, who looked like he'd be joining the dead man sooner rather than later.

Elrod felt like he should say something. He stood up

and walked over to Jade. He put his hand on her shoulder.

"Look, I just wanted to say I agree with that Luis guy," he said. "You had no choice but to shoot Douglas. God knows what might have happened otherwise. Like Luis said, you probably saved lives. Probably saved my life. Far as I'm concerned, you deserve a medal or something. All I can do is thank you. Tell you how much I appreciate..."

Jade shoved him with both arms and sent him stumbling back toward the bed. He tripped and went spinning to the floor. The pain from his wound flared up.

"The hell?" he said.

"You told them about the *money*?" Jade barked. "Are you simpleminded?"

She made a beeline for Elrod, fists raised. Sidney sprang forward and grabbed Jade by the arm. She yanked her backward like she was made of string and held her in check.

"Easy, now," Sidney said. "You need to relax."

"That's my money over there!" Jade said.

She struggled to get away, but Sidney's grip was too tight.

"Keep your voice down," Sidney snapped. "First off, it's the US government's money now. It's a pretty sure bet they called in the FBI since Morino is involved. They'll seize the cash and use it to buy new computers or something. Second, do you seriously think investigators wouldn't have found it anyway? You think they wouldn't have noticed a safe in a hotel room where a famous fugitive was involved in a shootout?"

"Take your goddamn hands off me," Jade said.

"Not until you pull yourself together and stop making a scene."

"Just take 'em off."

Sidney loosened her grip, slightly. Jade relaxed for a moment, waited for Sidney to loosen her grip some more, then broke free and sent a blistering right hand against Sidney's jaw, knocking her backward. She followed that up with a kick to Sidney's left knee that caused her to buckle and drop to the floor.

Sidney grabbed her knee, grimaced, then looked up at Jade. "Damn. You didn't tell me you were a badass."

Jade hovered over Sidney and stared down. "Who the hell do you think you are, ordering people around?"

"You're taking this way too personally, sister," Sidney said. "But if you insist..."

She bolted up from the floor and wrapped her arms around Jade's waist, lifting her off her feet. Jade pounded her fists into Sidney's back and tried to wiggle free, but Sidney was too strong. She slammed Jade down on the bed and laid on top of her, pressing the full weight of her body into Jade's slighter frame. Jade grabbed at Sidney's hair and struggled to get away. The two wrestled around for a few moments before Sidney tightened her hold on Jade's body and pressed her harder into the bed. She grabbed Jade's arms and pinned them back, then put her face up against Jade's.

"You better cease this shit," Sidney said in a low, angry growl. "We'll stay in this position for three weeks if you want to, but there's no way you're breaking free. Don't go mistaking me for somebody else. I'll crack your neck right here on this bed."

Elrod stood bedside, paralyzed, unsure of what to do. Sidney had moved her right forearm onto Jade's throat and was applying more and more pressure. Jade slipped one of her arms free and sent a weak punch to the side of Sidney's head, causing Sidney to grind her forearm in even further. Elrod finally decided he needed to act. He leaped onto the bed and tried to separate the two women with his hands, but Sidney sent a forearm into his chest so hard he went tumbling off the bed and onto the floor, sending sharp pain to his abdomen.

"Are y'all stone crazy?" he said, groaning. "You want to create a ruckus, have the cops come pounding on the door asking a bunch of questions? Break it up! My nerves are shot, I gotta tell you."

"Tell your friend here to relax and I'll let her up," Sidney said.

Elrod crawled back up on the bed, trying to keep out of Sidney's reach. He moved his head just close enough to get a look at Jade's face.

"Jade, this ain't the time to go getting all riled up," he said. "This woman's on our side. Let's just do as she says and get the hell out of here."

Jade kept her focus on Sidney. "Your scientist might have gotten Red killed. He..."

"He's not *my* scientist," Sidney said. "I told you, he hired me to help him track down the money. I saw him talking to you two in the hotel lounge and knew something was wrong. That's why I followed you all up here, to stop him from doing something stupid. I didn't know he was involved with Sal Morino. I'm sorry about Red, but you're blaming the wrong person."

Jade thrashed around trying to break free, but Sidney held her in place. Elrod could see the muscles and veins bulging in Sidney's arms. As tough as Jade was, she was no physical match for this woman. Jade struggled a bit longer, her face getting moist with sweat, before she ran out of breath and gave up the fight.

"You want more of this, or are we finished here?" Sidney said.

"Get off me," Jade replied.

"You're not gonna try anything?"

"Just get off."

Sidney slowly lifted her body up off of Jade and loosened her grip. She kept her arms in front just in case Jade tried something. But all Jade did was roll over on her side and lap up air.

Sidney rolled onto the other side of the bed and lay on her back, breathing heavily.

"You're a tough bitch, I'll give you that," Sidney finally said. "You ever want to be a private eye, you can come work with me."

Elrod slid to the center of the bed and sat between the two women, thinking he'd better form a barrier in case they got violent again. A few minutes passed as Jade and Sidney caught their breath and rubbed their various aches and pains. Finally, Sidney pulled herself up and got off the bed.

"I'm walking out of here now," she said. "If the cops stop me I'll give them a story that'll throw them off your tracks. After that, I'm going to leave this hotel and hope to never see it or you two ever again."

Sidney caught her reflection in the mirror. She straightened her hair and patted her face dry with a tissue. She took a few breaths, composed herself. Finally, she glanced over at Elrod and gave him a goodbye salute, then grabbed her things and made for the door. She opened it and walked outside without turning around.

When the door was closed Elrod tiptoed over to see if he could hear anything out in the hallway. He didn't hear much. He thought he heard Sidney say she didn't notice any noises across the hall. He thought he heard her say something about catching a slut with her fiancé—now her ex-fiancé—and having a little scene about it. He thought he heard someone snicker, maybe a cop. He thought he heard someone else ask Sidney if she wanted to grab a drink sometime.

After that, he gave up listening.

Chapter 44

Jade sat on the edge of the bed, bent over, holding her face in her hands. Elrod thought about doing something to comfort her, but the prospect of Jade launching into another violent tantrum cured him of that urge. He kept his distance and suggested they think about getting out of here.

"That private eye lady is right," he said. "We should move along soon."

Jade didn't answer. She stayed glued in the same position with her face in her hands, her fingers slowly massaging her forehead. Elrod walked to the desk chair. He picked it up, set it in front of Jade and sat down. He started to say something but came up empty.

After a minute or so Jade broke the silence.

"Nothing ever works," she said. "Nothing. Ever. It always falls flat. No matter what I do, it always falls flat."

She lifted her face from her hands. Her eyes were wet, her makeup smeared in a way that made her look like one of those sad clowns. Elrod leaned back and reached into his pants pocket. He pulled out a napkin he'd gotten at the halal food cart and handed it to Jade. She took it and dabbed her eyes.

"Fifty thousand bucks," Jade said. "You know how much that buys in 1949? It buys the world, that's what. Nice clothes. A nice apartment. Nice restaurants."

She glanced up at Elrod.

"I never ate a restaurant until I was fifteen years old," she said. "Never. Not once. We ate all our meals at home. Daddy insisted. Mother didn't argue. I had one store-bought dress when I was a kid. The rest of our clothes, my mother and I sewed ourselves. I hated those clothes. Hated that life."

Elrod shifted in his seat. The bullet wound stung. His head ached. His body ached.

"I had big ideas," Jade continued. "I was going to the big city, the entertainment capital of the world. Be the biggest singer in the biggest clubs. Make records. Ride the Super Chief out to Hollywood with the movie stars. Eat at the best restaurants and stay at the best hotels. Get filthy rich. Wear expensive clothes and jewelry, live in a mansion. And look at me. Sitting in a hotel room with a few hundred bucks, while nearly fifty thousand sits across the hallway. It might as well be on the other side of the world. My one shot to get rich, me and Red. Red..."

She looked like she was going to start crying but pulled up just short.

Elrod leaned forward. He tried to think of something to say, something wise or comforting. But all he managed was, "You wear nice clothes now."

Jade laughed.

"Nice clothes. Sure," she said. "These are secondhand. I buy them at charity sales for less money than it takes to buy a steak dinner. Rich ladies get bored with them after two weeks and donate them so hicks like me can buy them and pretend we're socialites. My apartment is smaller than this hotel room. I have to cook my meals on a hot plate. You don't make much money singing in nightclubs, don't kid yourself. They're all run by cheap hoods like Douglas who wear tuxedos and use big words and smile real nice and screw you eleven ways from Sunday."

She laughed again, almost choking on it.

"I sure did a swell job of setting my life up," she said. "Big nightclub singer, big plans, big star, big shot. Gonna take the world by storm."

Jade put her face back in her hands. Elrod leaned a little closer. He slowly moved his hand toward her knee. He patted it, lightly, then let his hand rest there. He waited for Jade to smack it away, but she didn't.

"You're a good singer," Elrod said. "Not that I know that much about singing. But what I heard, you know. I think it was very good."

He leaned in closer and rubbed Jade's knee with his hand.

"I gotta say, too, you got a real head for money," Elrod said. "That plan you had for taking over the operation? I mean, you put a lot of thought into that one. It was pretty damn brilliant. Not too many people could pull it off. You damn near did."

Jade looked up.

"That supposed to cheer me up?" she said.

"Well, maybe something else will cheer you up," Elrod said.

He reached into his pants pocket and pulled out a tattered wallet. He opened it and produced a handful of thousand-dollar bills. He placed them in Jade's lap.

"I snatched those out of the envelope when you weren't looking," Elrod said. "I figured they'd look pretty good in my wallet. I didn't figure you'd miss them. It's not much, but it's all yours. You can probably sell them to that souvenir store again."

Jade picked the bills up from her lap and held them in her hands. She rubbed them with her fingers, flipped them over, rubbed them again. She looked at Elrod, then slapped him across the face.

"You stole my money, you son-of-a-bitch?" she said

"*Your* money! You know I really oughta..."

"I trusted you!" Jade snapped.

Elrod laughed. "*You* trusted *me*? Hell, that's a real knee slapper. Trusted me. All you ever did was hustle and use me. You and the rest of 'em. And now I'm part of some crime scene, some goddamn..."

Jade lifted her hand again. Elrod went into defense mode, covered his face with his arms. But this time Jade brought her hand down. She took a couple of deep breaths.

"Okay, okay," she said. "Okay, you're right. My temper, I can't control it. Never could. I'm sorry. I just..."

She looked at the bills, rubbed them again. She stayed that way for several minutes, staring at the bills, rubbing them, wiping her eyes, staring at the bills, rubbing them, not saying a word, her hands shaking every now and then, but her grip tight on the money. Finally, she looked back up at Elrod.

"Why are you giving this to me?" she asked.

Elrod rubbed his face. "Well hell, it seems pretty obvious you need it more than me."

Jade slipped four of the bills into her jacket pocket. She

rolled the other one up so it looked like a cigarette. She leaned toward Elrod and placed it on top of his left ear. She leaned in closer and gave Elrod a peck on the cheek. He sat rigid, not knowing how to react. Jade pulled his face closer and kissed him on the lips. They stayed that way for a few seconds before Jade pulled away.

"You haven't kissed a girl in a while, have you?" Jade said.

"Is it that easy to tell?" Elrod said.

Jade leaned back.

"You really think my plan was good?" she said.

"Sure it was," Elrod said. "A little devious and underhanded. But pretty goddamn brilliant."

"I have a thousand ideas for making money," Jade said. "If I were some big shot in a fancy office people would line up for miles to hear me out. But when you're a gal from the sticks, they just snicker and pat you on the head like you're a puppy dog."

"Not anymore," Elrod said. "Maybe back where you're from it's like that, but things are different in this world. Women have a lot more power. They can run things, head up businesses, call the shots. Not as much as men do. But a lot more than it used to be."

"Who'd listen to me? A farm girl from 1949 who sings in a nightclub. I don't know anything about this world."

"I'd listen to you," Elrod said. "You could bounce your ideas off me. Then I'll get in touch with a few of my billionaire pals and we could set up financing."

Jade laughed the world's smallest laugh. "If I met one of your billionaire friends I'd probably sleep with him and steal his money."

"Either way, you're rich," Elrod said. "Seriously,

though. I know I'm just a homeless guy, but I can teach you a few things. Take you down to the library and show you the World Wide Web on the computer. You can learn amazing things on the World Wide Web."

"Why would you do that? I've been a real bitch to you."

"Yeah, well. You probably did save my life across the hall there, so let's call it square. And you're not all that bad. A little hot-tempered. Crazy. Unpredictable. A little too smart for your own good. A little selfish. A little..."

"I get the idea," Jade said.

"Anyway, we still got a few thousand bucks left between the two of us," Elrod said. "We could make do until we figured out something for the longer haul. The world's changing awful fast—so fast most people can't even keep up. This World Wide Web? I mean, I sit there at the computer for hours sometimes reading about all the ways you can make money off it. All the ways people are *already* making money off it. Selling things. Creating these websites where they charge people just to take a look. There's young folks, barely out of college, dress worse than me, getting millions just for creating a website that'll let you buy cheap dog food or whatnot. I ask myself, 'Now why can't I do that?' There's nothing magical about it. It's just dog food. The World Wide Web is the great equalizer, believe me. The old rules don't even apply. You don't need a college education and a nice suit to get rich. You just need a computer and the right ideas. Like, I had this one idea..."

Jade leaned forward and put her arms around Elrod's neck, pulled him toward her. She kissed him on the lips again, long and slow. When it was over she moved her head back and looked Elrod in the eyes.

"OK, Rockefeller," she said. "You show me the

wonders of the World Wide Web."

Jade hugged Elrod around the neck, tightly. She pressed her face into his shoulder and kept it there for a long time, as if it were pulled down by gravity, cemented in place, as if his shoulder might keep her from falling any further, and Elrod didn't mind, not a bit. He didn't care if she kept it there forever, until the end of time, until time didn't exist anymore, didn't exist at all.

Epilogue

"Run that by me again, Brent," Miles McLaughlin said. "I could have sworn you said he was born in 1900."

"That's what his ID says, Senator," Brent said. He pulled a document from a manila file and looked it over. "Douglas Flynn, born November 5, 1900. That's the birthdate on the ID they found. He didn't have a driver's license. Just a municipal identification card issued to a Douglas Flynn in 1944. They suspect it's a fake name and ID."

"That would make him ninety-nine years old," Miles said.

"Almost ninety-nine. Just a couple months shy."

"Clearly, the man was not almost ninety-nine years old."

"No, Senator. The coroner's office put his age at probably late forties. What we know for sure is he seemed to have a fascination with the 1940s. His clothes dated to the forties, which I can only assume were purchased at a vintage clothing store. They found a book of matches in his pocket from a nightclub called the Hideaway. It was popular a long time ago but closed in 1959. And of course you probably heard he had 1940s currency in his wallet."

Miles nodded. "Just like the money they found in the safe. All issued in the 1940s or earlier."

He took a bite of his chicken pita. Another chicken pita, another office lunch with Brent. Miles had to check himself every time the subject of the hotel shooting came up. He didn't want Brent catching on that Miles was actually there when the shots were fired. It was all so exhausting.

"Let's move on to other business," Miles said. "The arrangements have been made to honor Luis Baez?"

"Yes, Senator. He'll be feted at a ceremony at the Justice Department. You'll be the one giving him the medal."

"Good," Miles said. "That man is a goddamn hero for catching Morino. He deserves a medal and the reward money. I knew him when I was DA and he was a detective. Helluva guy."

He took another bite of chicken pita and pushed it away.

"How is our boy Morino, anyway?" he said. "Any change in the prognosis?"

Brent shook his head. "Still in serious condition, though they expect him to pull through. He's under heavy security at the hospital. In addition to a coronary, he suffered a bullet wound to the thigh. When he's well enough, they'll transport him to the federal penitentiary pending a court date. No chance of bail this go-round."

"Good. I want to look that prick in the eyes when they stroll him into prison."

Brent nodded.

"How about the other man, Red?" Miles asked. "What's his condition?"

"He's still on life support and shows no brain function," Brent answered. "It's doubtful he'll pull through, but they can't find any family to consent to pull the plug. He had no ID on him, just a photo of himself and a pretty lady, so all they know is his name is Red, based on Luis Baez's statements. One elderly woman from North Carolina saw his photo in the paper and insisted she was Red's niece. But she's probably twenty years older than Red, so it's mathematically unlikely. She may have dementia. A couple of very old jazz musicians say they also knew him. A real brain tickler."

"And what about this scientist, Bunt? Any word on his whereabouts?"

"None, Senator. He's still missing. All we know is he was under house arrest and fitted with an ankle monitor while he was out on bail. He was last traced to that alley in LoDown, the one where Morino had disappeared. That's where Lionel Bunt's monitor suddenly stopped working. They don't where the monitor is, or Bunt."

Miles shook his head. "There's something really screwy about that alley."

He looked at the chicken pita but stopped short of grabbing it.

"To hell with this," he said. "I'm hungry. Call Perrone's and get us a table. I feel like a thick steak and three or four martinis."

He tossed the pita in the trash and rose from his chair. He picked up a photo of Lionel Bunt and studied it again.

"The guy looks like he should be building computers in his parents' garage, and now he's a fugitive from justice," Miles said. "How does that happen? How did he just disappear? Where did he go?"

He placed the photo back on the desk and put on his coat.

"And what's he's up to now?"

Acknowledgements

Thanks to Nick, Bryce, and the team at Atmosphere Press; Patrick for reading an early draft and providing valuable feedback; Miss Tyson for encouraging my writing way back in junior high; Lena and Lauren for giving my heart a tug every time I see them; Mom, Dad & Joyce for the love and support; and all my family and friends, too numerous to name.

About Atmosphere Press

Atmosphere Press is an independent, full-service publisher for excellent books in all genres and for all audiences. Learn more about what we do at atmospherepress.com.

We encourage you to check out some of Atmosphere's latest releases, which are available at Amazon.com and via order from your local bookstore:

House of Clocks, a novel by Fred Caron
Comfrey, Wyoming, a novel by Daphne Birkmeyer
The Size of the Moon, a novel by EJ Michaels
Nate's New Age, a novel by Michael Hanson
Relatively Painless, short stories by Dylan Brody
The Tattered Black Book, a novel by Lexi Duck
All Things In Time, a novel by Sue Byers
American Genes, a novel by Kirby Nelson
Newer Testaments, a novel by Philip Brunetti
Hobson's Mischief, a novel by Caitlin Decatur
The Red Castle, a novel by Noah Verhoeff
The Farthing Quest, a novel by Casey Bruce
The Black Marketer's Daughter, a novel by Suman Mallick
This Side of Babylon, a novel by James Stoia
Within the Gray, a novel by Jennifer Ash
Where No Man Pursueth, a novel by Michael E. Jimerson

About the Author

Vance Cariaga is a writer, editor, and journalist whose short story collection *Money, Love and Blood* was published in 2017. His work is also featured in the anthologies *With One Eye on the Cows* and *Return to Factory Settings*, both published by Ad Hoc Fiction. His story, "Saint Christopher," placed second in the 2019 *Writer's Digest* Short Short Story Competition. Vance is a native of North Carolina who currently lives in London with his wife and two daughters. Visit his website at vancecariaga.com.

CPSIA information can be obtained
at www.ICGtesting.com
Printed in the USA
BVHW070716180621
609823BV00005B/930

9 781637 529171